Cat-Eyed Trouble

Cat-Eyed Trouble

Robert Skinner

KENSINGTON BOOKS

http://www.kensingtonbooks.com

KENSINGTON BOOKS are published by

Kensington Publishing Corp.
850 Third Avenue
New York, NY 10022

Library of Congress Card Catalog Number: 96-073754
ISBN 1-57566-250-7

First Kensington Hardcover Printing: February, 1998
10 9 8 7 6 5 4 3 2 1

Printed in the United States of America

For Thomas Bonner, Jr., scholar, gentleman,
and a friend when you need one

"It's been a long time since I've seen a real cat-eyed woman," Coffin Ed remarked.

"I wouldn't have one for my own for all the tea in China," Grave Digger declared.

"You just ain't sayin' it."

—Chester Himes, *The Heat's On,* 1966

The way up and the way down are one and the same.

—Heraclitus

Prologue

New Orleans, 1933

Junior Obregon was high as a kite. He was staggering down Louisa Street, about two blocks from the Louisa Street Wharf, singing "New Orleans Woman" in a loud, slurred voice. A teen-age colored girl named Billie Talmadge had one of his arms across her shoulders and her left arm about his waist, trying mightily to keep him from falling down. They had a crib near the corner of Louisa and North Villere streets, but it was several blocks away and her strength was failing her.

"Junior, you just gotta help me, honey," she said between pants. "You're too big for me to carry much farther, and I'm just about done."

Junior laughed drunkenly. "Don' you worry none 'bout me, sugar-tit. Jus' let ole Junior siddown a minute, he'll be awright." He laughed some more, then began snoring.

Billie pushed him across the sidewalk and propped him up against the side of a building. As she stepped back from him, Junior slid down the building to the sidewalk, his unconscious face grinning stupidly. She leaned against the building beside him, panting from her exertions. A sob escaped her throat because it was dark and foggy and she felt terribly alone.

Junior was supposed to be taking care of her, but lately all he did was get drunk or fucked up on nose candy, leaving her with the responsibility of getting them home from wherever he collapsed.

He'd lured her away from her home and friends with a lot of big promises about how great life would be for the two of them once they took up light housekeeping. The reality was a good deal different.

She didn't know how Junior made his money, but it would come in huge piles which he would then commence to drink up or shove up his nose. They lived in a damp, drafty dump, and sometimes he beat her. She thought often of going back home, but her father had told her never to come back after she took up with Junior. He'd called her a tramp and a slut and thrown her packed suitcase out into the yard before he slammed the door in her face.

There was another complication, too. Junior had started her sniffing cocaine and heroin, and although she told other people she could take it or leave it, the truth was that she needed it now. She'd thus far resisted Junior's urging to shoot up one of the potent cocaine and morphine "speedballs," but she was hooked all the same and couldn't live without the white powders.

She looked down on her lover, and wondered what she had ever seen in him. He was still a big, good-looking man with coal-black skin and eyes like jet, but his gray sharkskin suit was badly rumpled, there was a stain at the crotch where he'd wet himself, and his red, watered silk tie hung askew at his throat.

It was 2:00 A.M. and not a taxi in sight. They were too close to the waterfront for much auto traffic and too far off the beaten path for casual merrymaking. They'd been to an evil-smelling, gloomy dive off North Peters Street, where Junior had played the bigshot with the roll of bills he'd carried. When he'd drunk all the cheap bourbon he could hold, he'd gone to the back of the bar to shoot up.

Before too long, he'd begun to mouth off about the sweet thing he had with the white gangster he worked for. He'd said things even she hadn't known and wished now that she didn't. She'd realized the danger, and immediately began trying to get him to go home. It hadn't been easy, but after an hour of begging, pleading, and cajoling, she'd gotten him out into the street.

She remembered that there was a telephone booth near the corner of Louisa and Royal and, with some reluctance, left Junior passed out and began walking toward it. Tendrils of fog swirled about her feet, and every alley she passed seemed filled with her worst nightmares.

She reached the telephone booth, only to find that someone had cut the receiver wire from the box. At that moment, she was no longer a knowing woman of the streets and became once again the scared girl she used to be. She leaned against the inside of the booth and cried for her mother.

After a while, the tension in her lessened and she was able to blow her nose and shake off the fatigue and frustration she felt. She'd just have to go back and wake Junior up someway. She was getting tired of always having to be the one to clean up his messes. Putting a stern look on her face, she walked back the way she came, slowly building her anger. She didn't need Junior to get along. She could get along fine without him. If he didn't get up, she was just going back to their crib alone and in the morning she'd pack her things and get out.

As her petulance grew, she walked with an ever firmer step, her heels clicking resolutely on the cracked pavement. The fog was getting thicker, and she almost didn't see the car parked at the curb beside where she'd left Junior. Somebody was on the sidewalk, looking down at Junior. Her skin prickled with some unknown dread and she slackened her pace. She could hear voices but couldn't make out what they were saying.

She crept closer and closer, and gradually words began to float to her. She ducked into a recessed doorway and peered through the fog.

"You made a mistake, Junior. A dealer should never get hooked on his own shit."

"I ain't hooked," Junior's voice said querulously. "I just like to get high once in a while is all."

"Too bad, Junior. You get high and you talk too much. You been usin' the Big Boy's name too free, and that was stupid. The Big Boy don't like for his men to act stupid and talk stupid where other folks can hear them."

"Listen . . ." Junior began.

"No, *you* listen, fool," the other voice said. "You got a cop named Israel Daggett followin' you around and screwin' up your business since you took up with that jailbait, Billie. You can't walk down the street in this town without bumpin' into women who'll fuck your eyeballs out for a dollar and you got to go to cradle-robbin'. Man, how stupid can you get?"

Billie listened intently. There was something familiar about that voice. She'd heard it before. It was hard to see in all this fog, but that voice . . .

"Listen," Junior said reasonably. "So I got fucked up. I'm sorry. Tell the Big Boy I'll send Billie home to her mother, I swear it. Tell him I'll lay off the shit, too. Everybody there was as fucked up as I was; they won't remember nothin' I said by mornin'. I know them cats."

"Sorry, Junior," the voice said. "The trouble is, somebody there who wasn't fucked up heard everything you said and called the Big Boy. If there was one somebody there straight enough to hear, there might well have been two. I like you, always did, but the Big Boy says you're a liability now. I'm sorry as I can be, but I ain't got no choice but to do what the Big Boy says. So long, Junior."

As the young girl watched, a long-barreled gun appeared in the speaker's hand, and it exploded three times. Long jets of red-tipped fire erupted from the muzzle of the gun, seeming to point the way for the bullets punching into Junior's chest. His body heaved as the first shot struck home, then shuddered as the second and third shots hit, then he lay still. Then the figure with the gun turned, and Billie clearly saw the face of Junior's murderer.

The girl clapped both hands over her mouth and bit down hard to keep from screaming. Her body trembled and shook as she fought to keep the cries within her body. Dimly, she heard the sound of a car door slamming, the starting of an engine, and the low whine of the car departing.

When the car was gone, she leaned against the door feeling weak and sick. Eventually she found the strength to tiptoe over to where Junior lay. He remained pretty much as she had left him, slumped against the wall. His eyes were wide open now and his face bore an expression of amazement. His shirt had three ragged, bloody holes over the heart, the cloth of his shirt a bit scorched from the close proximity of the gun muzzle.

Billie knelt beside his body and she grabbed his shoulder and shook it, as if trying to shove some life back into him. "Oh, Junior, oh, God, oh, God," she said weakly. Even though he'd been about to ditch her to save his hide, Billie still found herself wanting him to wake up and tell her it was all right.

After a while she heard the sound of a siren in the distance and she looked up, her eyes shifting nervously. If it became known that she'd seen who killed Junior, her life wouldn't be worth a nickel. She rifled Junior's pockets for what was left of his roll of money, then stood up quickly, and began walking rapidly toward the building where she and Junior had lived. If she worked quickly, she could get her few possessions out of there and get a cab to the Negro YWCA before the cops could run down Junior's address. Her heels beat a rapid tattoo in the ghostly fog as she disappeared around a corner. Soon the street was quiet and empty of everything but Junior Obregon's mortal remains.

1

February 5, 1938

It was nine in the morning at Angola Prison in East Feliciana Parish, near the Louisiana-Mississippi line. It was technically winter, but as was often the case in the Deep South, the temperatures were moderate. It might have been early spring anywhere else.

A tall brown-skinned Negro named Israel Daggett emerged from the Administration Building in the company of a uniformed captain of the guards.

Around them were a number of other men, Negro and white, who were engaged in manual labor of one kind or another. Unlike these men, Daggett was dressed in an old suit, a bit small for him, and a battered snap-brim hat rather than white-and-black striped prison coveralls. The prisoners working in the yard watched the progress of the tall Negro and the captain furtively, but said nothing, and made certain to keep their eyes lowered.

Daggett might have been any age between thirty and fifty, but he was about thirty-seven years of age. His shoulders were wide, and long, ropy muscles in his arms and legs writhed like snakes under the fabric of his suit as he walked beside the captain. His face was prematurely lined from brutal work and care, and his closely cut hair was flecked with gray at the temples. He kept his liquid brown eyes straight ahead, and his stern, square jaw set. He knew from experience that until he passed the gate, the guards owned him and could delay or revoke his departure on a whim.

At the gate the captain said, "Prisoner, halt." Daggett stopped in his tracks, keeping his eyes unblinkingly to the front. "Prisoner comin' out," the captain called to the armed men at the gate.

As the gate was opened, the captain came around in front of the Negro with one hand on his butt of his holstered .44 Smith & Wesson and a long truncheon dangling from his other wrist by a leather thong. He tapped the truncheon rhythmically against his muscular leg. His eyes, blue in color, were as cold as Valley Forge, and his mouth might have been a piece of thin black thread stretched straight across the lower third of his doughy face.

"You'll be back, Daggett," he said. "You'll be back 'cause you ain't nuthin' but a no'count nigger bastard. Havin' a badge didn't make you nuthin' better'n that, and not havin' no badge'll make you worse. And you know what? I said, you know what, boy?"

"No sir, Cap'n. I don't know nuthin'," Daggett said in a flat monotone.

"I'm gonna be waitin' here for you, boy," the guard said, his mean, thin mouth curving slightly upward at the corners. "And I'll make sure you don't get out again. I'll bury you here next time."

Daggett looked straight ahead, his eyes deliberately unfocused. His arms were straight down at his sides, held in check by a tremendous act of will. He knew if they even quivered, the captain could decide it was an intimation of attack and beat him to the ground with the club he carried. He could even shoot him without fear of reprisal.

"Open the gate," the captain called, and stepped out of Daggett's path.

The gates opened slowly, rasping on their hinges, and the guards stood on either side, their Winchester repeaters held at port arms as Daggett walked stolidly past them, eyes to the front, saying nothing. Daggett was barely through them when he heard the hinges rasp again as the gates shut the sight of the world off from the men still inside.

Daggett felt a weakness grow in his legs, and his back ached from holding it so straight. He could hardly believe he was out, and was tensed for the sound of the guards' shouts, the whistle of bullets overhead, the baying of hounds at his heels. He knew they would not come, but all the same, he wanted to run more than anything in the world. Once he looked back, but by then the gate was almost out of sight.

In a lavish brick house on De Saix Boulevard, in the city of New Orleans, a muscular white man with pale skin and coal-black hair lay on his back in a large tester bed. Athwart his naked thighs kneeled a petite, light-brown woman, her hands braced on his thick shoulders as she moved her bottom in a series of intense circles over his groin. The man's hands gripped her at the waist, his thick, blunt fingers kneading the flesh as she moved over him.

Lustrous dark-brown hair hung down on either side of her face, and slanted, almond-shaped eyes, like those of a cat, glittered from within the curtain of her hair. Her lips, parted slightly, were the color of blood, with small, pointed teeth showing whitely behind.

Both the woman and the man were soundless, except for an occasional rush of breath as they strained against each other's flesh. As their moment of release drew near, a telephone on a bedside stand began to ring. The pair did not stop their lovemaking, but the man began to swear in a deep, expressionless voice. The phone kept ringing, and the man continued to curse, his voice rising slightly in pitch. The woman began to sing out, and the man's back arched violently, his eyes blaring and his teeth bared. Then it was over, and he fell back on the sheets, the woman falling against him.

The telephone continued to ring, and the man reached out a blind hand for the receiver. His questing fingers finally found the purchase they sought, and he grabbed the receiver from the hook.

"What the hell is it?" the man demanded. His heavy black brows met over the bridge of his nose as he scowled at the invisible speaker. Then he pushed up on one elbow, causing the tiny woman to slide off his chest to the side.

"I thought I told you never to call— What did you say? When?" He swung his legs over the edge of the bed and was silent for several minutes. Then he hung up the telephone and sat there staring at the wall.

The little woman shoved her hair back from her face, then reached for a package of Chesterfield cigarettes and a lighter on the nightstand nearest her. She put two of them in her mouth and lit them, then leaned over the man's shoulder and held one of the burning cigarettes out to him. He took it, put it in his mouth, and inhaled smoke wordlessly.

"What was it, Joe?" she asked finally. Her voice was deeper and huskier than her size would indicate. She kneeled on the bed and inhaled smoke, then blew it out in a long plume from between her pursed lips.

The muscular white man turned to her and propped a pillow behind his back. His face was grim. "Israel Daggett was released from prison this morning."

"So?" she said, blowing out another stream of smoke. Her catlike eyes stared at him lazily and she coiled her legs under her until the backs of her shapely thighs rested on the backs of her calves. Her body was smooth and trim, like a young boy's, except for small, rounded breasts that jiggled like mounds of Jell-O when she moved her arms.

"He was a lot of trouble when he was here before," Joe Dante said. "If he comes back, he could be trouble again."

Stella regarded him blandly as she sucked more smoke into her lungs. It appeared that she was not in the least troubled. "Big deal," she said, letting the smoke feather gently from her nostrils and the corners of her mouth. "He's an ex-con. Even if he comes back here, he can't do nothin' to you." Her eyes were hooded as she spoke, and the fingers of her left hand drummed lightly beside her knee on the sheet.

Joe crushed his cigarette end out in a glass tray at his elbow. "It was mighty lucky, him getting sent to the pen for killing Obregon. Too goddamned lucky," he said thoughtfully. He turned slightly and regarded the woman. "Y'know, Stella, I never believed he killed that punk. It was done too stupid, and for a nigger, Daggett's smart. Too smart for a sucker play like that. I think he was framed, and I'd like to know who did it."

"You wanna give 'em a medal or something?" Stella asked blandly. The word "nigger" seemed to have no effect on her at all.

He looked at her intently. "I'd like to know why they did it," he said slowly. "It wasn't a smart thing to do, because he's the kind of man who'll come back and start stirring things up until he found out who framed him. If he was somebody in my organization, like his cousin Walt, say, I'd be tempted to feed them to Daggett."

"Why's that, sugar?" Stella asked. "They did you a favor, the way I see it."

"You see wrong," Dante said bluntly. "Daggett's got friends who might help him. If one of my people did this, Daggett might just find out things I don't want anybody to find out while he's lookin' for who framed him. It's a complication I don't need, get me?"

"He's still nothin' but an ex-con," Stella said disinterestedly. "He can't even carry a gun, much less play detective. Why not just consider it a lucky break that he got sent up. Junior was a pain in the ass, and so was Daggett. You've had a free ride for five years, and you're dug in good and deep. Nothin' Daggett or anybody like him can say or do'll change that."

He shook out another cigarette from the pack between them, then took her cigarette from her mouth and used it to light his own. He pulled in a great lungful of smoke, then gave the woman back her cigarette. "You think everything's simple, baby. Our kind of life, ain't ever simple. There's always an angle to figure, and if Daggett comes back here, that's a goddamn serious one in my book. I want to be ready if he starts nosin' around where he shouldn't."

Stella inhaled the last of her cigarette and flipped the butt into a metal wastebasket a few feet away from her. "You worry too much, sugar," she said, uncoiling her body and crawling over to Joe. She lightly rubbed the inside of his thigh with her fingertips, and chuckled deep inside her chest as a flush crawled up his chest into his neck and face. *Leave the worrying to me,* she thought. *I took care of Daggett once, and I can take care of him again, permanent this time. It'll be my little secret, sugar.*

Joe lay back down on the bed, looking up at Stella as she played his body like a piano. Eventually the frown left his face, but not the troubled look in his eye.

At an office upstairs from his club, the Cafe Tristesse, a wide-shouldered man with pale gold skin named Wesley Farrell sat behind his desk smoking a Lucky Strike. Open in front of him was a ledger lying in the circle of light given off by a lamp at the edge of the desk. Farrell, himself, sat in darkness, and only the occasional red glow at the end of the Lucky indicated his presence in the otherwise darkened room. A pencil in his hand made bold, rapid strokes on the page of the ledger as he totaled and subtracted figures in his head.

He had finished his work and closed the ledger, and was leaning back in the leather desk chair when the telephone at his elbow began to ring. He inhaled smoke and let it feather out of his nostrils before reaching for the telephone. It rang twice more before he picked it up.

"Farrell," he said in a noncommittal voice.

"Do you know who this is?" a male voice asked.

"I'm too goddamned busy for kid's games, Stiles," Farrell said irritably. "What the hell do you want?"

"I was in police headquarters bailin' one of my numbers runners out and heard something you might want to know," the voice named Nate Stiles said.

"So tell me, for Christ's sake, and skip the Secret Service stuff," Farrell said.

"A body just got found out behind Audubon Park," the voice said. "A woman's body."

Farrell felt the hair on the back of his neck start to rise. "Who was it?" he asked, thinking of Savanna Beaulieu, the only woman he could immediately think of that might matter to him.

"Lottie Sonnier," Stiles said.

"Aw, Christ," Farrell said in a hushed whisper. "How? Do they know how it happened?"

"Nix," Stiles replied. "All's I know is that they found her. I ain't even got any particulars yet. I knew you was close to her once, and figured you'd wanna know."

Farrell felt sick in the stomach, and gripped the receiver so tightly it hurt his hand. "Find out everything you can. Everything, understand, and get it to me fast."

"Check," Stiles said, and broke the connection.

Farrell dropped the receiver carelessly in the cradle and leaned back in his chair. He hadn't seen Lottie Sonnier in almost two years, but ten years ago a hot fire had burned the air whenever they'd been together. It was too hot a fire to burn for long, but they'd parted friends, and he had seen her several times over the decade that followed, always with a curious gladness that she had generously returned. The world seemed a bit empty to him at that moment, and it felt lousy.

Farrell wasn't a sentimental man. By nature he was a shrewd and calculating gambler who took the losses with the wins. He'd known many women in his thirty-eight years, and didn't remember many of them. But Lottie he remembered, and he wanted to know who'd robbed her of her life, and why. He felt a burning in his throat and eyes and gritted his teeth as he filled his mind with pictures of what he would do when he found out.

2

Police Captain Frank Casey was eating a bowl of Post grape-nuts with strawberries and listening to "Don McNeill's Breakfast Club" on the radio when the call came. He frowned, knowing that if he took the call, the cereal would probably become soggy and inedible before he got back. After the third ring, he swallowed what was in his mouth, pushed away from the table, and walked to the phone in the hall.

"Casey," he said.

"Sergeant Parker, sir," the voice on the other end said. "We've got a body you might want to look at."

"Why in creation do you need me?" Casey asked, trying not to sound too grumpy.

"Because it's Lottie Sonnier," Parker said. "I knew you'd want to know immediately."

"Lottie," Casey said. He felt like he'd been kicked in the stomach. Without conscious thought, he made the sign of the cross with his right hand. "Where is she?"

"A railroad dick found her by the river on the other side of the Public Belt Railroad tracks behind Audubon Zoo," Parker said. "Initial report says it looks like a sex murder."

"Dear God," Casey said. "I'll drive over there right away."

He hung up the phone and walked in a daze back into the kitchen. Dinah Shore was a guest on the Breakfast Club, and she was singing some foolishness about love as Casey got to the table. His appetite gone, he took the bowl of cereal to the sink and flushed the grape-nuts down the drain. The sections of strawberry, caught in the trap, looked so much like raw flesh that he turned his eyes from them quickly, and went to finish dressing. Behind him, Dinah sang happily about pennies from heaven.

Dandy Walker's gymnasium on Jackson Avenue down by the river was open in spite of the early hour. Two aging fighters, no longer part of the game but drawn to the smell and sight of it nonetheless, were busily mopping the floors. Young white and black men, some of their faces already showing the wear and tear of the ring, were skipping rope, working out with Indian clubs and barbells, or performing exercises on the heavy bag and speed bags.

Dandy Walker, the tall, rawboned ex-fighter who owned the gym, was walking back and forth in front of the ring, watching the moves of the two young fighters sparring with each other. His broad shoulders were tense, and his mind was clearly divided between the action in the ring and something he was seeing in his mind.

"Damn, them boys ain't doin' nothin' but the waltz in there, Dandy," a man said from behind them. "Can't you scare 'em into hittin' each other or somethin'?"

"Huh?" Dandy said, turning toward the voice. It belonged to a ferret-faced white man dressed in a shabby khaki-colored suit that was about six months shy of its last cleaning and pressing. The man's name was Felsen, and he made a living making book on prize fights. By law, he had no business in the gym at all.

"What do you want, Felsen?"

"Wondered if you knew if your old runnin' mate was comin' back to town this week," Felsen said.

"Who do you mean?" Dandy asked.

"Iz Daggett, who else?" Felsen replied.

Dandy's eyes flattened a bit. "Sure, I knew he was gettin' out. Wasn't sure he'd come back here or not."

"He's from New Orleans, kid, as if you didn't know," Felsen said sardonically. "Nobody ever leaves here voluntarily, and they almost always come back when they can. Did he know you were thick with his woman while he was in the stir?" Felsen grinned nastily.

"He knew, 'cause I told him," Dandy said gruffly. "I wasn't doin' no back-door job on him. The guy's like my own brother, f'Christ's sake." His large hands knotted into fists, and Felsen's eyes darted as he backed up a step.

"Hey, no need to get physical, keed," Felsen said, holding up his hands. "I was just talkin' is all."

"Get through talkin' and hit the bricks, before I hit them with you. And stay out of here if you know what's good for you," Dandy said in a loud voice. Several of the fighters in the gym stopped what they were doing at the sound of Dandy's voice and looked over at the two men. Felsen turned quickly and walked to the gym entrance and out the door.

Dandy stood there glaring at the door, then shook himself, looked about at the people staring at him, then stalked back to the rear of the gym where his office was located. After a moment, everyone else went back to what he was doing as if nothing had happened.

Within twenty minutes, Casey stepped gingerly across the Public Belt tracks behind Audubon Park and walked toward the river. Morning dew glistened on the roadbed stones like diamonds among slag. An odor of oil and rotting fish swept in from the river, and the air was full of the cries of gulls.

About a dozen men were down by the river. A few were walking along the riverbank, eyes down as they searched for anything that might serve as a clue. Something was on the ground, covered by a sheet. Occasionally a breath of wind would flutter the edges of the sheet, as though some shreds of life clung to the body and sought their escape.

As he got closer to the crime scene, two of the men standing over the body turned to meet him.

"Give it to me, Snedegar," Casey said to the one nearest him.

Snedegar was a thin, worn man with a face like a carpenter's hatchet, dressed in a faded gray topcoat and hat. He said, "They found her about six this morning, skipper. They called me out, and I recognized her. Looks like she might've been raped, then killed."

Casey grimaced. "Find anything yet?"

"Not much," the other man said. He was younger than Snedegar by about ten years, had blond hair and a mustache that he had grown to make his baby face seem older. He had on a snap-brim hat made out of maroon corduroy and a belted army raincoat of olive drab. "Looks like they did everything to her someplace else, and just dumped the body here. M.E. says probably early this morning. We got some tire tracks over there, but that don't tell us much."

Casey nodded. He knelt down by the corpse and pulled the sheet away from the head. The face belonged to a Negro woman of perhaps thirty-five. Her hair was short and curled about her face in shiny black tendrils, still wet from the river. Her countenance was clean of makeup, and her eyes were fixed with a blank stare, and her mouth gaped.

Her throat was badly bruised, with the marks of a large-fingered hand clearly evident. Casey tilted her head slightly to the left and saw a single small-caliber bullet wound behind the right ear. He could find no exit wound. He lifted the sheet to the hips and examined the skin on the insides of the thighs. There was no bruising there, nor any other marks that would indicate a sexual assault.

Casey let the sheet fall and stood up, his face flat and empty. "This doesn't make any sense," he said.

"Yeah," Snedegar said in a rasping voice. "The bullet hole don't jibe, does it?"

"It seems so pointless," Casey said. "And where are her clothes? It doesn't look like a rape."

"You knew her, huh, skipper?" the blond haired dick asked.

"Yeah, Mart, I knew her," he replied heavily. "She was a social worker, and a good one. She came up in a rough part of town, but she kept clean, worked her way through school, then came back to help other kids get out into some kind of decent life. I can't understand any of this."

"If it was anybody else, I'd say it was a mob hit," Snedegar said. "Think I'll get in touch with the Negro Squad, get them started asking questions."

"Good idea," Casey said. "If somebody from the Negro community is responsible, somebody over there'll know it, sooner or later. If it was some coked-up hot-rod, he might even be bragging about it in some bar right this minute."

Casey walked away from them and over to an intense, nervous-looking man with wire-rimmed spectacles. The man was kneeling on the ground, careless of the knees of his trousers, pouring plaster into a tire tread.

"Find anything, Nick?" Casey asked.

Nick shook his head. "Whoever did this was careful. These tire prints look like B. F. Goodriches—nothing special, but I'm taking a cast anyhow. The guy who left 'em wasn't worried they'd tell us anything, or he'd have messed them up." He stood up and reached into his pocket, pulled out a small envelope, from which he removed a flat, soggy cigarette end.

"I did find this fresh butt near the tracks, though," Nick said. "It's a Wings, near as I can make out. Looks like the guy lips them when he smokes. Might be worth something later, if we get a suspect." It was clear from the tone of his voice that he held little hope of that.

"Okay," Casey said, fighting to keep the bitterness from his voice. He walked back over to Snedegar and Mart, and found them talking to a stocky, hard-bitten little man of about fifty, dressed in khaki work clothes. He wore a stubby old revolver in a belt holster, and had a sawn-off baseball bat hanging from his left wrist by a leather thong tied through a hole in the narrow end. Mart saw Casey coming and turned to meet him.

"This is Mr. Patout," Mart said, indicating the short man. "He's a yard dick with Public Belt."

Casey offered his hand, and Patout captured it in a rough grip.

"Pleased to meetcha, Captain," Patout said. "I wore a uniform on the force myself twenty years back."

Casey nodded. "That's fine. Tell me what you saw this morning."

Patout's body stiffened to attention, as though he were on parade and Casey was the commanding officer. "I got me a little handcar," Patout said, indicating a machine nearby that resembled a bicycle. It had grooved wheels and a wedge-shaped bracket that projected from the side with two more grooved wheels on it. "I pedal it down these tracks continually from the time my shift begins 'till it ends. I come from the downtown end about 5:00 A.M. and seen all these gulls flyin' around. I figgered it was some kinda dead animal washed ashore, but thought I'd take a look anyhow. I come down with my flashlight and seen her caught in an eddy near to shore. I waded out and dragged her up on dry land."

"They must've stripped her and tossed her in the river, hoping the current'd pull her out," Casey mused. "Did you see anything besides the body?"

"No, sir," Patout said. "I remembered from my days on the force that I oughtn't to mess around the crime scene. I got on my handcar and pedaled to the nearest call box, and phoned in to the dispatcher. Then I come back and stayed 'til some of your fellas come."

Casey nodded. "Anything unusual up until the time you discovered the body? See anybody along the right of way who might not belong there?"

"I seen a car driving just parallel to the tracks, heading downtown as I rounded that bend back there," he said, jerking over his shoulder with his thumb. "Looked like a LaSalle. My brother useta own one like it. A 1930 or '31 model, I think. Couldn't get no look at the driver—too dark."

"Notice the color?" Mart asked, his notebook open.

"Hard to tell," Patout said. He leaned his head thoughtfully to one side. "Mighta been dark green or dark blue."

"All right, Mr. Patout," Casey said. "It seems like you did everything by the numbers, and we appreciate your help. If we need to ask you any further questions, should we call the railroad?"

"Sure," Patout said with a grin. "They always know where I'm at." He gave Casey a casual salute, nodded to the other detectives, and strode back to the tracks. The last sight they had of him was on the bicyclelike handcar headed in an uptown direction.

"The most excitement he's had in ten years probably," Mart said with a grin.

Casey looked after the small man as he got back onto his track cycle, and tugged thoughtfully at his left earlobe. "He's pretty far below the height requirement for our department," he said. "Why would he make up a thing like that, I wonder?"

"Beats me, skipper," Snedegar said.

"Mart, when you get back to headquarters, call the personnel office and ask them to look Patout up in their records. I'd like to know what they have on him, if anything."

"Sure, skipper," Mart said. "I'll look into the LaSalle angle, too. There probably ain't more than twenty thousand of 'em around here." Mart grinned as he closed his notebook.

Casey grunted. "Yeah. I'll see you two back at the station later." He paused, and gnawed on his lip. "I know her folks. It'll probably be better coming from somebody they know."

The two detectives looked at him, at each other, then shifted their gaze at the ground or back toward the river. Casey was the only white man they knew who had friends within the colored community. It was a thing neither of them understood, but they knew better than to comment on it.

When they said nothing in reply, Casey turned on his heel and walked back toward the railroad tracks.

Israel Daggett walked along the two-lane parish highway with his thumb out for a long time before he got a bite. Most of the traffic along that route was white farmers, a group not particularly sympathetic to the idea of picking up a lone, shabby Negro. Daggett felt no particular animosity toward them. Prison had made him patient in ways that few others could understand.

About an hour and a half after he departed the prison, he heard the rattle and clank of a vehicle behind him and stuck out his thumb without looking. Within a minute, a Model T Ford pickup truck, seemingly held together with bailing wire and ten-penny nails, shuddered to a stop alongside him. The driver, a sixtyish Negro with hair the color and consistency of cotton, peered over at him.

"Need a lift inta town?" he asked politely.

"If it's no inconvenience to you, uncle," Daggett said.

"Hop on in then," the old man said.

Daggett stepped easily onto the running board, opened the door, and climbed into the ancient vehicle. He sat down on the patched leather seat and placed the small canvas grip with his few possessions between his feet.

The old Negro started off, shifted into second gear, then accelerated into third, saying nothing. After he had the truck up to forty miles per hour, he cast a sidelong look at Daggett.

"They let ya out this mornin'?" he asked.

Daggett smiled without looking over at the old man. "You don't miss much, do you, uncle?"

"I done lived in East Feliciana Parish all my life," the old man said. "Seen a lotta fellas on this road, some been in a lot longer'n you. Some been in that rathole so long that all the juice done been wrung outa them. I figger you for a short timer, no more'n five, six years, say."

Daggett nodded his appreciation of the old man's perspicacity. "Almost on the nose, old-timer. I behaved myself for five years, and they reckoned I was rehabilitated." He emitted a short, bitter laugh.

"Lookin' for work?" the old man asked. "I got some wood needs splittin'. Can't pay ya much, but I can feed ya and maybe pay ya a dollar."

Daggett leaned back in his seat, removed his hat, and ran his hand briskly over his nappy scalp. "I thank you, uncle, but I figure on gettin' back to New Orleans as soon as I can. If you can get me a little closer to the railroad station in the next town, I'll be glad to give *you* a dollar."

"Ain't no need in that," the old man said. "I'm goin' that way anyhow. Ya got friends or family back in N'Awlins?"

"No family," Daggett said. "A few friends. A woman, maybe."

"She must be loyal, waiting that long," the farmer asked. "You're lucky, at that."

"Not so lucky, uncle," Daggett said. "I was a cop once, plain clothes, and had money in the bank. I had hopes me and that woman would get married one day. Then they hung the frame on me."

"A cop?" the old man said. "I didn't know they had no colored detectives in the city. And they framed ya, ya say? Damn. There ain't no limit to the evilness of white folks, I swear it." He shook his head discouragingly. He ruminated on that for a while, then said, "Would a little nip take the edge off?" He reached behind him and came out with a pint bottle of clear glass. It had a colorless liquid rolling around inside it.

Daggett was rubbing his eyes and opened them as the bottle was handed over to him. He accepted it, pulled the cork, and sniffed it. "Whew," he said. "Smells potent."

The old man grinned. "I make it myself. Ain't bad, if I do say so."

Daggett lifted the bottle to his lips and took a long pull. The liquid raced down his throat like flaming gasoline and exploded in a fiery ball in the pit of his stomach. "Damn," he said in a wheeze. "How long you been drinkin' this stuff?" he asked.

"Nigh on to forty years," the old man replied, grinning. "I'm seventy-two now."

Daggett laughed heartily, and gingerly took another sip.

About a half-hour later, they drove into the village of Tunica. It was market day, and the town had a considerable bustle to it. The old man negotiated the narrow streets until he came to the clapboard railroad station on the opposite side of town. He pulled up, and Daggett got out.

"Thank you, uncle," he said. "I appreciate the ride and the refreshment. If you ever get to New Orleans, ask around for Israel Daggett. I'll offer you some hospitality, if I'm able."

The old man took his hand, but shook his head in the negative. "A man as old as I am ain't got no business down there. That's a town for the young and the reckless. Reckon I'll just stay out here and tend my chickens and vegetables. Maybe you'll come back this way. If ya do, I'm out on Parish Road 38. Wilbur Tatum's my name."

"Thank you, Mr. Tatum. I won't forget you." Daggett stood to one side and allowed the old man's Model T to slide past him out into traffic. He turned and saw the entrance to the depot and walked toward it, swinging his little satchel easily in his hand.

The inside of the rural depot was dim and quiet. He saw a doorway with a sign reading "Baggage Claim" across the room and strode toward it. The counter was unmanned when he entered the room, but he waited only a few seconds before a thin, irritable-looking white man wearing a green eyeshade and a pair of steel-rimmed spectacles came out. It was plain from his expression that he had no particular liking for Negroes.

"I'd like to pick this up, please," Daggett said, handing over a claim check.

The clerk scrutinized it, scowled at Daggett, then left the counter for the storage room. After a moment, he returned with a maroon leather suitcase that bore the scuffs and scars of a lot of rough handling. With some effort, the clerk lifted it to the counter and let it fall heavily.

"That'll be $3.65," the clerk said brusquely.

Daggett reached into his pocket for a small roll of bills, counted out four singles, and handed them to the clerk. The clerk took the money, opened a drawer on his side of the counter, and took out thirty-five cents in nickels and dimes which he dropped into Daggett's waiting palm. He took pains not to touch Daggett.

"Y'all have a colored washroom here?" Daggett asked.

"No," the clerk said nastily, and walked away.

Daggett stood there, clenching and unclenching his fists. For a brief moment, he weighed the pleasure of taking the scrawny little man by the neck against the certainty of being taken right back to Angola, then hefted the suitcase and walked out of the depot. Across the tracks from where he stood, he saw a small grove of trees. He stepped off the sidewalk and began walking toward it.

Finding that the trees and shrubs in the grove provided enough privacy for his purposes, he opened the suitcase and found in there new underwear, socks, a white dress shirt, and a silk necktie with red-and-black paisleys on it. Under the shirt was a paper bag containing a pair of black Florsheim wingtip oxfords. Daggett removed the clothes he'd been issued in prison and carefully dressed himself in the new clothing. In spite of his considerable muscular development, the clothing fit him like a second skin.

When he had finished dressing, he unbuckled a pair of straps and opened the suitcase's second compartment. There he found an eelskin wallet with two hundred and fifty dollars in it and a spring-clip shoulder holster of tan leather. Inside the holster was a .41 Colt Army Special with burnt bone grips and a six-inch barrel. Beside it lay a yellow cardboard carton of Peters .41 caliber ammunition. He stared at the gun for some time, not having expected to see it. He'd asked his grandma Bessie Bouchet to send the clothing and money, but had not asked for the gun, since he had no right to wear it. He fingered his chin as he looked at it, wondering why she thought he might need a gun.

He snapped the revolver smartly from the clip, opened the cylinder, and saw it was unloaded. The gun had been well cared for. The bore was clean and bright, and a faint sheen of oil could be seen on the mechanisms. Giving in to a feeling he couldn't name, he opened the box of cartridges and carefully placed one in each chamber of the open cylinder. Then he flicked the cylinder closed, restored the gun to the holster, and put it back into the suitcase. He then folded up his prison clothing, placed it on top of the pistol, and strapped the compartment closed.

After a moment's indecision, he opened his canvas valise, transferred his shaving and toilet articles and a change of underwear from it to the suitcase, then pitched the valise into the bushes. He closed the suitcase, and stood up.

He paused and looked at the battered hat he'd been given that morning, glanced down at the beautifully cut suit, then hung the hat on a tree branch. Then he walked out of the grove, back across the railroad tracks, and inside the depot to purchase a ticket to New Orleans.

3

It was about ten that evening when the brisk little black man pulled his car to a stop outside the whorehouse on Mystery Street. The little man liked the name of the street so much that it was at least half the reason he took his business here. That and the fact that a few of the whores were still reasonably young; reasonably meaning under thirty-five. Women seldom lasted longer than that, given the professional propensity for alcoholism and drug addiction and an unfortunate tendency to die during or after crude backroom abortions.

He came into the house, made his request, gave the madam, a sour old woman called Ma, two dollars, and walked up the stairs to the second floor. He knocked three times, and at a word from inside the room, opened the door and entered. A woman stood across the room from him with her back to the door. She was naked, and was washing between her legs. She had long brown hair that fell almost to her waist, and her body retained a youthful ripeness in spite of the five hard years she'd spent in the sex business.

"Just get undressed and lie down, honey," she said. "I'll be with you directly."

The little man began unbuttoning his shirt and trousers, his eyes alight with anticipation. "Man, it's been a big day outside today, Billie," he said excitedly. "Things poppin' all *over* the place."

"Yeah, Doggie?" Billie Talmadge said in a bored voice. "What happen, Huey Long get resurrected or somethin'?"

Doggie, who sometimes went by the name Dirty Dog McGee

because it sounded tough, laughed briefly as he lay down on the bed. "Shoot no, chile. This is *big* stuff. Israel Daggett been let out of prison this mornin'. Odds are six-two-and-even he'll be back here before tomorra."

Billie straightened without turning around. "Iz Daggett? He ought not be gettin' out already. He was convicted of murderin' Junior."

Doggy laughed briefly again. "Naw he wasn't. That was a manslaughter beef they convicted him of, sugar. Heard somethin' else, too."

Billie wrung out her washcloth and hung it on the little glass bar screwed to the wall over her washbasin, then turned around to him. Her full, pointed breasts swung elastically from her chest as she moved. "Yeah?" Her voice wasn't quite so bored now.

"Yeah," Doggie said. "A gal name of Lottie Sonnier got found over behind Audubon Park this mornin' early. Shot in the *head*, I mean."

Billie stopped short of the bed, her breathing almost nonexistent.

"Yeah, in the head," Doggie reiterated, looking up at her with his hands clasped behind his narrow neck. He was already fully erect, waiting for Billie's ministrations.

Billie said nothing, but crawled into bed beside Doggie and put her hands on him. He didn't need it, but it was part of the service. Doggie's eyes closed, and he began to groan. Sometimes he needed a woman to talk dirty to him to arouse him, but not today. All the street news had him plenty worked up already.

Billie's mind was far from her room, but her body was well trained. As she thought about Israel Daggett's return, and the gunshot murder of Lottie Sonnier, she straddled the little man and began to pump up and down on him. He was quickly lost in an ecstasy all his own, and couldn't see the anxious look on Billie's face.

Doc Pardee was leading his orchestra in a series of Latin tunes that night at The Cafe Tristesse, and skinny little Mario Kostelanetz was at the microphone singing "Begin the Beguine." The soft *suhshhhh* of brushes on snare drums filled the air like a tropic breeze, and muted clarinets chirped like garden crickets. Mario's baritone voice rose and fell like ocean waves caressing sand, and the women in the audience were listening raptly, their chins cupped in their hands, their dates forgotten.

Wesley Farrell was at his table on the raised section at the back of the club, drinking a vodka martini and smoking a Lucky Strike. In spite of the bad news about Lottie, he found himself smiling as he watched the enthralled women, unconsciously nodding his own head in time to the Latin beat. The house was packed tonight, and there was a lot of eating and drinking being done. He felt prosperous and nearly content.

He caught a movement in the corner of his eye, and turned his head to see Frank Casey standing in the entrance to the main floor. As usual, the redheaded cop was dressed with quiet dignity in a navy-blue suit with a pale yellow shirt and a blue-and-red regimental tie. Farrell lifted his hand and caught Casey's attention. When he saw Farrell, he nodded and started over.

Farrell snapped his fingers at a passing waiter, and told the boy to bring him another martini and a double rye highball for Casey.

"Business is good," Casey observed as he sat down at Farrell's table.

"Nights like this, I almost forget there's a Depression on," Farrell said.

"I guess people will spend money on good times, even if they haven't got it for anything else," Casey said.

"What's new with you, Frank?"

"It's been kind of a lousy day," he said, wagging his head. "Seen the afternoon papers?"

Farrell looked sharply at Casey. "You mean about Lottie Sonnier?" he asked. "Yeah, I saw it." He felt his face heat with suffused blood, and he turned his head slightly away from Casey's.

Casey noticed the change in Farrell, and observed him for a moment as he accepted his drink from the waiter. "You knew her." It was a deliberate statement rather than a question.

"I knew her," Farrell said, his jaw tight. "A long time ago we were . . . close. I saw her a few other times over the years when she would come in on social work business. She convinced me to hire a fellow to work in the kitchen a couple of years ago. The guy was an ex-con, but she sold him pretty hard. Because of her I gave the guy a break. He apprenticed to the chef and handles the breads and desserts now. She brought two other people to me later on, and I hired them, too."

"I'm sorry, kid. It's lousy to find it out in the newspaper," Casey said.

Farrell said nothing, but Casey could see the line of his mouth get tighter.

"I hope you're not thinking of getting mixed up in this," Casey said. "This is police business now."

Farrell looked at him with a bitter expression. "When a friend of mine gets hurt, it's personal business. You ought to know that better than anyone."

Casey's face flushed, and he gripped his glass a bit too tightly. "You don't have to remind me that I'd be dead now but for you," he said finally. "But that doesn't change anything. No matter what our relationship is, I'm still chief of detectives in this town, and I can't just go around breaking the rules to suit myself."

"I'm not asking you to break any rules," Farrell said. "I'm just asking you to remember that I know people in this town, people who might not talk to you. I'm not gonna let Lottie's death go unpunished because you don't know who to roust or because somebody who knows something won't talk to a cop." He crushed his cigarette out in the glass ashtray between them, and immediately placed a fresh one between his tight lips.

Casey sat back in his chair, drank half of the rye in his glass, and blew breath out quietly from between pursed lips. He regarded Farrell for a moment, rubbing his chin with his thumb and forefinger. After a few tense moments, he spoke again.

"Let's go at this another way," he said. "You've got a point. I know her family pretty well, but I don't have the connections that you do. Suppose we call a truce and make a little treaty between us."

Farrell squinted through the cigarette smoke. "What kind of treaty?"

"You beat the bushes and talk to everybody who'll talk to you," Casey said, raising a finger, "but if you get a line on something hot, you come to me before you act on it. No knives, no guns, and for Christ's sake, no killings. I had to do a lot of talking last year to keep you out of jail. I might not be that good a talker if you started leaving a trail of corpses behind you again."

Farrell's eyes were hard and his face stony as he took this in. He dropped his gaze for a second and pushed ashes around in the tray with the burning end of his cigarette. After a moment, he looked up again. "I can't promise I won't have to lean on somebody if I think they're dummying up on something."

"Swell, just don't go shooting or carving chunks out of 'em," Casey replied quickly. "I lean on guys, too, when need be, but I leave 'em in one piece. You do the same, and you've got a deal."

Farrell's face remained dark, and his eyes were filled with sparks, but finally he nodded. "Deal. What have you got so far?"

"The medical examiner says she wasn't sexually assaulted. I expect the killer stripped her corpse and threw her into the river, figuring her body wouldn't be found, but leaving nothing to trace if she should wash ashore somewhere. She was strangled to death, then for some reason shot once in the head. The only way that makes sense is if the killer was sending a message to somebody, but we don't know who, or what the message was supposed to make them do, or stop doing."

Casey got out a bulldog briar pipe, a pouch of tobacco, and matches, then packed the pipe carefully. Farrell stared at the bandstand while he did this, smoking and drinking in silence. Finally, he said, "Who was she close to? I wasn't in touch with her recently enough to know about her comings and goings."

Casey puffed on his pipe until it was drawing correctly, then said, "I'm still looking into that. I do know this: she was thick with Israel Daggett before he got sent up for the Junior Obregon kill. I don't know if they were still in touch, but Daggett was let out of the pen on good time early this morning. I'm betting he comes back here."

"I remember Daggett," Farrell said. "He was a sharp detective, and supposedly a square joe. Too square to have killed that punk like they said he did. I figured that for a railroad job."

Casey nodded. "I thought so, too, but I wasn't running things then, and couldn't do much about it."

"Kind of a coincidence, him getting out of the pen and Lottie killed on the same day," Farrell said. "Think there's a connection?"

Casey sighed and leaned back in his chair. "Anything's possible at this stage. But it might just be a coincidence. That's possible, too. I hope we find out."

Farrell's eyes flickered at Casey when he heard the "we." Casey was draining the rest of the liquor from his glass, and Farrell thought he detected a gleam in the older man's eyes, but he couldn't be certain.

"Thanks for the drink," Casey said as he stood up, stretching. "Think I'll go home and turn in."

"Sure you won't stay for another drink?" Farrell asked, feeling a bit guilty for the argument they'd had earlier.

"No, thanks. Maybe we could catch dinner at Kolb's German Tavern later in the week," Casey said. "I got a craving for some of that sauerbraten they make there."

"Sure, Frank," Farrell said. "Call me anytime."

For some time after the detective had left, Farrell sat there contemplating the almost casual nature of the relationship he had developed with Casey. No one would guess that they were father and son, a fact even they hadn't realized prior to a few months before. Farrell had become involved in a scrape with a local gangster over some smuggled diamonds the previous Fall, and after a lot of violence and death, he and Casey had discovered their kinship to each other.

And yet it was a difficult relationship to explain or define, because neither of them yet knew exactly how to treat the other. Farrell had skated along the edge of lawlessness all of his adult life, a factor that made him skittish around policemen, no matter who they were. He fought it when he was around Casey, but it was there all the same.

Added to this was another factor that had long discouraged him from a familiarity with others. His mother had been one of New Orleans's fabled *gens de couleur,* the Creoles of Color, which meant that Farrell carried Negro blood in his veins. It was probably less than an eighth, but in Jim Crow Louisiana, any Negro blood rendered you something less than human. Farrell had kept that part of his heritage a secret since leaving home at fifteen. Fewer than a half-dozen people knew it, and all were bound to him by blood or unshakable loyalty.

Farrell knew Casey wanted to assume a stronger relationship with him, but each seemed to know it was too soon for something that deep to take hold. For now, they engaged in casual meetings, off-the-cuff conversations about anything and everything, letting things happen as they might. It was only after parting company with his erstwhile father that Farrell sometimes found himself turning over in his head the connection between the two of them, and the circumstances that had brought them together again after more than thirty years.

He heard the band pause briefly, then swing into "Amapola." Bonnie Celestine, a petite girl with violet eyes and black hair, had joined Mario Kostelanetz, parroting his lyrics but singing them in a slightly different key, with a jazzy spin to them, the way Margaret

Whiting did when she sang with Bob Eberly. The audience was eating it up, and after a while, Farrell forgot about his father and Israel Daggett, and lost himself in the music.

On Rampart Street, Louis Bras and his trio were sweating bullets as they blew roaring Dixieland out into Savanna Beaulieu's Club Moulin Rouge. Savanna's joint was a club for true jazz aficionados, and the faces of the swaying, finger-snapping crowd were every shade from milk white to ebony black.

Savanna was at her private table, dressed in the strapless red sheath that was her trademark, drinking Calvert's Reserve straight up and smoking Sweet Caporals in an ebony holder. To look at her, one might think she'd been born in Casablanca or Martinique, but in truth she'd entered the world as Rosalee Ortique, and had been raised in a sharecropper's shack outside Bogalusa, Louisiana.

When she'd tired of chopping cotton and hoeing collard greens, she'd run away to New Orleans at the age of sixteen, where she lived the only kind of life available to a young, illiterate colored girl, a prostitute's life. By the age of twenty-two, she'd learned to read and keep books, and had made enough money to buy her first bar, a joint down on Telemachus Street. Eventually she worked her way up to Rampart Street, and ownership of the Club Moulin Rouge.

Louis Bras and his boys had knocked off for a couple of drinks when a woman, really more of a girl, came into the club. She was small, but carried herself in such a way that she seemed taller. Her face was heart-shaped, with a small, upturned nose, and a cupid's bow for a mouth. Her skin was the color of coffee with milk, and her hair smooth and black as a crow's wing.

She was dressed in a pale lavender suit and wore a black cape over her shoulders. The cape was damp with rainwater, as was the wide-brimmed purple hat she wore. The brim dipped down far enough to cast her eyes in shadow, but it was clear from the way she stood, moving her head from one side of the room to the other, that she was here looking for someone. By the time her gaze stopped in Savanna's corner, Savanna realized she was Lottie Sonnier's little sister.

Savanna got up and held out her hands to the woman as she approached. "Hello, Marguerite honey. It's been a long time," Savanna said.

Marguerite took Savanna's hands in her own, and looked up into the eyes of the taller woman. It was apparent immediately that something was terribly wrong. Her deep brown eyes were shiny with tears, and the pretty, round-featured face was contorted with an anguish that was near to overwhelming.

"You want to come upstairs to my apartment?" Savanna asked quickly. "It's more private up there and we could talk better."

Marguerite jerked her head up and down, but could say nothing. Savanna indicated to her bar manager with a hand signal that she was going upstairs for a while. He nodded back as he poured drinks for two customers.

In the stairwell, the young girl broke down completely, sobbing as though her heart would break. Supporting her easily in her arms, Savanna felt a surge of anger at whoever had hurt this child so much. Once they were inside the apartment, and the door shut behind them, Savanna helped Marguerite take off her hat and cape and sat the girl down on the sofa.

She went to a table in the corner with several decanters on it, and poured brandy into a small balloon glass. She brought the glass back to Marguerite, sat down, and forced the girl to drink. She choked as the brandy rushed down her throat, and coughed loudly for a few seconds. When she had stopped, Savanna took her by the arms and shook her.

"Now you tell me what's the matter, right now," Savanna said. She spoke a little more roughly than she ordinarily might, but it was enough to sober the girl, and get her to speak.

"It's Lottie," Marguerite said in a cracked voice. "Somebody . . . somebody killed her last night or early this morning."

Savanna was dumbstruck. Her hands fell from the girl's shoulders, and her mouth dropped open. "Lottie? Oh, God, no." Savanna had rubbed shoulders with some of the toughest people in the city, but the news was enough to wrench a cry of anguish from inside her breast. She pressed her hands against her mouth and bit her lip savagely to prevent herself from breaking down. After a long moment, she was finally able to trust herself to speak.

"Who did this? Why?" Savanna asked in a hushed voice.

"We—we don't know," Marguerite said, nearly breaking down again. "She said she was going out to do some case work and she never came back." The girl's fingers dug into the sides of her head, as though she fought to keep her brain from exploding.

Savanna saw she was about to fall apart again, and shook her again, hard, to bring her out of it. Savanna's own emotions were too close to the surface, and she feared Marguerite's loss of control might be contagious. "Snap out of it, honey. All that won't help anything. Had she got into somebody's face, or stepped on some hardcase's toes? Anything like that?"

Marguerite shook her head wildly. "No, no, no. She was so happy. Iz was supposed to be let out of prison today, and she'd been makin' plans to get him work when he got here."

Savanna's face went blank. "Iz Daggett? He's due back from prison? Then he doesn't know."

Marguerite shook her head miserably. "He ain't got here yet. I don't know what we're gonna tell him, I swear to God I don't."

Savanna sank back against the sofa cushions and pulled the girl into her arms. "Sweet Jesus," she said. "Have you all talked to the police yet?"

Marguerite nodded slightly. "Captain Casey of the police came this mornin' kinda early. He tried to tell us easy but—but . . ." Her voice trailed off as she dissolved once again into tears.

The crying was calmer now, though, without the wracking sobs of before. Maybe this would clean some of the grief out of her, Savanna thought. Almost unnoticed, a tear streamed down her own cheek, only to be trapped in the small gully between Savanna's lips.

"I loved Lottie like she was my own sister," Savanna said to the room. "Do you know how we met?" When Marguerite didn't answer, Savanna continued talking anyway. "I was a teenage whore, trickin' on the edge of the Quarter. When she found out I couldn't read or cipher, she spent weeks tryin' to convince me to learn. I reckon I gave in just to make her leave me alone," Savanna said, laughing a small laugh.

"I found out from her that there's always another chance, if you want it bad enough," Savanna continued. "I'd probably be just another junked-up, over-the-hill whore if not for her. I might even be dead now. We're gonna find out who did this, honey. I swear it." And I know who to ask for help, she didn't say. Somebody who won't say no to me. Then unashamed tears began to rush from her large, dark eyes, and run down her brown cheeks in rivulets.

———————

Stella walked up and down the living room of her house thinking about the news that morning about Israel Daggett, and Joe's reaction to the news. He had no idea of her involvement in Daggett's frame-up, and wouldn't like it if he did. Joe had a limited imagination where women were concerned.

She'd taken some big chances to get into his good graces, with an eye toward being something more than just a recreation to him. Stella had ambitions, ambitions that pushed her to take long chances. It was just such a chance that had gotten her into his good graces in the first place.

She'd come to New Orleans from Jackson, Mississippi, almost ten years ago, when she was eighteen years old. She was already a prostitute, wise in the ways of men, sex, and the street. There was in her, too, a streak of darkness that did not show on her childlike face, like a cat's claw hidden in the soft skin of a paw. When she unsheathed that side of herself, it was quick and brutal, and not easily forgotten. People who knew her often wondered how such a young child could harbor such meanness, but no one knew her well enough to say. She was a loner, always cruising for amusement or some kind of score.

Two years after her arrival in New Orleans, Stella met Joe Dante, and set her traps for him. He was already a big-league bootlegger with a profitable sideline in women when she met him. She was just a bottom-rung joy girl then, but she'd known him with her first look, and stalked him like a hunter, waiting for the moment to spring. She'd already learned things that set her apart from the other women he owned, and put them to use.

Her naked ambition had proved an aphrodisiac to Dante. He knew she wanted to be more than just a whore, and it gave him a strange feeling of paternalistic power to occasionally give her opportunities to prove herself.

It happened, a year or so into their association, that Dante was getting unwanted competition from a local competitor of some power. He was too strong to attack in the usual ways, and Dante mentioned to her his frustration in finding a solution. She told Dante that she could help him out. Dante laughed, and waved her off, because the man was an old queen. Women were of no interest to him.

On her own, without confiding in Dante, she found the man, and began to make herself available to him, but not as a woman. She dressed as a boy, a very effeminate boy. With her hair cut short and a dandyish suit of clothing, she began her seduction, always pulling back a bit when he became interested. Over a period of several weeks, she played him like a trout in a stream, casting her fly, and coyly pulling back.

Finally, the man was in such a state of arousal that his common sense deserted him. He ordered his bodyguards away, and invited her to his Garden District home. The night was sultry, and the man put Chopin *Études* on his Capehart phonograph. Old Madeira was poured into tiny glasses, and soon she began to work her wiles, undressing to a singlet and boxer shorts, taunting the man while she touched him in ways bound to send his blood pressure through the roof.

The moment came at last. The man let her undress him, and lay back on a divan. His ecstasy was registered in his closed eyes and gaping mouth. As she ran her nails lightly over his groin, she removed a long, slender stiletto taped to the inside of her left thigh. As the man's sighs and groans reached a crescendo, she positioned the stiletto against his left ear, and shoved it into his brain.

The man's body bucked horrendously, and his bladder and bowels exploded in the death throes. Stella jumped back just in time to keep from being fouled, her nose wrinkling in disgust. Leaving the stiletto in place, she dressed quickly in her male attire, and slipped out through a side entrance.

Later that night, she and Joe had alternately laughed at the gruesome joke and made frenzied love on his living-room floor. She'd believed that night that her future was assured, because she was no longer just a cute whore, but a woman of enterprise.

That expectation had not been realized, however. She remained a piece of property, even when she took other chances on his behalf. She had learned to be cautious after a while, because a few of her risks had not paid off, and Joe had been furious. Once, he had even beaten her. Joe's appeal had begun to fade after that. She often thought of getting away from him, and sometimes even of killing him.

In spite of Joe's qualms, Israel Daggett seemed a small danger. She'd known other men to enter the maw of Angola. The few that had returned were shadows of what they had been. Daggett was likely worse off, since he'd been sent up as a corrupt cop.

But suppose he was tougher than the rest? Suppose he knew things that he couldn't prove, and now intended to find that proof? Although she felt a fairly universal contempt for men, she hadn't gotten where she was by underestimating any of them.

Maybe she should just kill him and have done with it. It wouldn't be a murder that would engender much interest in the police. A black ex-con would be less than nothing.

She walked to her desk, sat down, and began to dial the telephone number of a man called Skeets Poche. He was one of Joe's low-level leg-breakers, but had occasionally done things for Stella without Joe's knowledge. Most men would willingly take calculated risks once they had shared Stella's bed. He answered his phone on the second ring.

"This is Stella," she said. "I got a job for you."

"I'm listenin'," Skeets said.

"Israel Daggett is supposed to've been let out the pen this mornin'. Call whoever you know up there in East Feliciana and find out where he went. Check the railroad and bus stations in the towns nearest the prison. As soon as you got a line on him, call me here."

"You ain't thinkin' . . ." Skeets began.

"Never mind what I'm thinkin'," she snapped. "Just do it."

He paused for a moment, and all she could hear was a faint crackle of static on the line. Then, "I hear you."

4

Israel Daggett sat in the Jim Crow car near the end of the train, surrounded by the heavy breathing and muffled snores of the rural Negroes who were accompanying him to the big city. In spite of the late hour, Daggett remained awake, his mind abuzz. Being framed for the murder of Junior Obregon was the worst thing that had ever happened to him, and to this very minute he unceasingly turned over in his mind the circumstances of the case, trying to fit the pieces together in a way that made sense.

Junior had been a nobody; a street-corner hustler and a pimp. But drugs were creeping into the Negro community, and Daggett was certain that Junior was involved in it. He'd been gradually building a case to bring to the commander of the Negro Squad when Billie Talmadge had come into the picture.

Billie was a sweet girl, good-hearted and pretty, and the daughter of a couple Daggett had known since childhood. She had a wild streak in her, though, and it was clear that she was getting into trouble. Junior had seduced her, and introduced her to smoking gange. Daggett feared that she might already be sniffing cocaine and heroin, and well on her way to mainlining it.

It was a terrible choice for a cop to have to make, but in the end, Daggett's loyalty to his friends took precedence over his duty as a policeman. He had taken a plant on Junior, following him openly and interfering with his illegal activities to the point that the young hoodlum could do no business at all. Daggett felt certain he was getting ready to crack, which was all he was waiting for.

But then Junior turned up dead, shot three times in the chest with a .41 Long Colt, the same kind as Daggett carried. An anonymous tip led police to Bayou St. John, where they dredged up the murder weapon, the mate to the bone-handled revolver in Daggett's suitcase, which he normally kept in his locker at the police station. The fact that Junior had been armed, himself, in addition to Daggett's unblemished record had caused the judge to downgrade the charge from second degree murder to manslaughter. It was the end of everything Daggett had worked for.

In the years he'd spent in prison, Daggett had thought long and hard about who could have framed him. During the times he was in lockdown, he'd turned the case over in his mind until he nearly went insane from it. He had many enemies in the New Orleans underworld, black and white, but very few could have engineered the theft of his gun from a police department locker room. He had immediately suspected his cousin, Walt Daggett, of the frame-up. Walt had been a cop once, but had been kicked off the force for malfeasance. Daggett, himself, had been the agent of Walt's demise. Unfortunately, Walt had had an iron-clad alibi for the time of the killing, which left Israel holding the bag.

The train was a local, and managed to stop at every pig path and wagon crossing as it crawled across the face of eastern Louisiana. Daggett had left the train only once to use a rest room and to buy a couple of roast beef sandwiches, a hunk of pie, and a vanilla cream soda from a railroad candy butcher.

He didn't have a watch, but guessed it must be near midnight. If he was right, they ought to be in New Orleans in another few hours. Once he got there, he'd get a room at the Metro Hotel on Rampart, get a little sleep, and then call Lottie.

Lottie. He'd expended a lot of effort not thinking about her for the past five years, because thinking about her made him crazy and self-destructive. Thoughts of her had caused him to pick fights twice with men bigger than he was, hoping that they'd kill him and end his misery, but the men hadn't been good enough. He'd nearly killed them instead and ended up in solitary where thinking was as corrosive as hydrochloric acid.

But now his thoughts came with an abandon, and he imagined her brown skin against a crisp white sheet, and his hands and mouth on her. The memory of that sent such a rush of blood to his loins that it shook him to the core, and he caught his breath loudly. The sound made the sleeping farmer next to him shift in his seat and grumble unintelligibly for a few seconds before he once again drifted down deeper into sleep.

Daggett felt tears spring into his eyes as he thought about the lost opportunities, the lost years. He could have married Lottie more than once, but it had been too easy for both of them to keep the relationship on a casual basis. They loved each other; had said so to each other more than once on those long Sunday afternoons they spent in his rooms. If he had married her back then, maybe things might have been different. Now, here he was, ruined, a jailbird with no resources and no particular hopes for the future. How could he ask her to marry him now?

As the despair stabbed at his heart, he reached down inside and found the strength that had sustained him through five empty years, and threw it up as a bulwark against the hopelessness welling up in his heart. *One day at a time, Iz,* he said to himself. *She's still there, and she still cares. You got more there than some other men ever have.*

It was past two o'clock on the morning after Daggett's release when the phone began ringing in the cat-eyed woman's apartment in the Broadmoor section of New Orleans. She woke from a doze on her sofa, reached over and picked up the receiver.

"Yeah," she said into the mouthpiece.

"It's Poche," a voice said.

"Well?"

"Daggett got a ride into town, and went straight to the railroad depot in Tunica," Poche said. "Somebody had sent him a suitcase that he got out of baggage claim. He changed clothes in the woods across the tracks, then came back and bought a ticket to New Orleans."

"How long ago was that?" Stella asked tensely.

"That train's a local, and is due in here around 4:30 A.M.," Poche said. "You want me and a couple boys to go pick him up and take care of him?"

Stella's red lips parted, and the edges of her sharp little teeth stood out in bold relief behind them. "No. If Daggett sees a crowd of gorillas coming for him, he's liable to start a fight. This has got to be done quiet." She paused and pulled at her lower lip with the nails of her thumb and forefinger. "I'll handle it myself, understand?"

"Whatever you say, Stella," Poche said after a brief pause. Stella heard the skepticism in his voice, but before she could respond, he hung up. She glared at the telephone for a moment. She was sick of men condescending to her. One day she'd speak and they'd jump.

Suddenly, she stood up and crossed to her bedroom. She stripped off the silk kimono she'd slept in, and quickly donned step-ins, garter belt, silk stockings, and a slip. She then chose a dark-blue long-sleeved blouse, a fashionable skirt and jacket of navy-blue wool, and a pair of low-heeled athletic shoes.

When she was dressed, she returned to the living room. From a bookcase she removed a slipcased set of Prescott's *War with Mexico* and laid it on a nearby table. The slipcase was actually a cleverly designed box with a sliding lid on one side. From the box she removed a switchblade knife with black mother-of-pearl handles and a .32 Colt pocket automatic with checked walnut grips. She raised her skirt and eased the knife into the elastic top of her right stocking. Making sure the gun was loaded, she placed it into a leather shoulder bag. Then she donned a black rubberized rain cape and a dowdy-looking felt cloche hat and left the apartment.

It was raining when she walked outside, but she gave no notice of it. She had only one thing on her mind, and that was Israel Daggett. She walked over to an emerald-green Buick sedan, got in, and cranked the motor.

As she drove off, she toyed in her mind with what she'd do if she were in Israel Daggett's shoes tonight. He'd probably be a bit off his guard, coming in so late at night. Chances were he'd be pretty tired, and not very alert. She doubted that anyone would be there to meet him at that hour, so he'd probably try to go somewhere to get a room—perhaps the Metro Hotel on Rampart, which had desk men on duty all night long.

It was nearly 3:00 A.M., and the streets were deserted of everyone but milkmen, paperboys, and working stiffs on their way to some drudgery. At about twenty minutes past three, she brought her sedan to a stop about a half block down from the Illinois Central Station near the intersection of Howard Avenue and South Rampart Street. The large granite structure was lit up like a beacon in the rainy blackness.

The rain was falling harder now, but Stella didn't bother with an umbrella. She pulled the cape around herself and walked toward the entrance with the deliberation of a panther stalking her prey.

The lights inside seemed to bounce off the marble floors with painful brightness. The place wasn't crowded, but there were enough people moving around to allow her to remain inconspicuous. A few waiting travelers were nodding on benches, and a Negro porter was busy at the doors leading to the platforms with a mop and pail, getting ready for the next onslaught of arriving and departing travelers.

Stella positioned herself on a bench within sight of the platform doors and regarded them with intense watchfulness. Some would have said it was pointless to come down this early when she knew the approximate time of arrival, but Stella was not careless about these things. When you planned to kill somebody, it was always worthwhile to get the lay of the land and see what obstacles might lie in the path of your plan. She relaxed, and emptied her mind of trivial thoughts.

It was 4:15 A.M. when the dispatcher announced over his loudspeaker that a local from the north had just arrived. Stella didn't move, but her small body tensed instinctively, like a tabby smelling a mouse. Under her cape she reached into her bag to touch the Colt automatic, but this small movement might not have happened at all to anyone watching.

A gaggle of yawning, stretching, scratching people began to stream through the large platform doors. Some were greeted by friends or relatives, and little bubbles of happy conversation echoed off the marble floors and walls. Others came through with a purposeful stride, their bags swinging in their hands. All but one.

The tall, bare-headed brown man in the beautiful blue suit walked with an elaborate casualness, one hand shoved deep in the pocket of his pants, the other easily carrying the old leather suitcase. But his eyes were constantly moving, back and forth, up and back. Occasionally he checked over one shoulder, but only Stella noticed him doing it.

Daggett seemed to briefly consider going to a telephone booth, but just as quickly he discarded this plan. He resumed his casual progress toward the street door, doing nothing that would attract any attention. When he was well past her, Stella got up and began to follow him, walking to match his pace, and no faster.

At the street, Daggett raised the collar of his suitcoat around his neck and walked in a northeasterly direction. Stella nodded to herself. It looked like he might be going to the Metro after all. She smiled, thinking how easy this was going to be. She removed the gun from her bag and held it under her cape as she followed Daggett across the broad expanse of Howard Avenue, past Julia, and over to Baronne Street.

Daggett did not walk like a man with anything to fear. His progress was steady, but measured, like that of someone with nowhere to go and nothing to do when he got there. Once or twice, some instinct caused him to pause and cast a backward glance, but that was all. Baronne seemed completely deserted. Stella's gun was out from beneath the cape now, and the safety was off. When Daggett walked under the next streetlamp, she was going to drop the hammer on him.

She was perhaps twenty yards behind him, not an optimum striking range for that kind of Colt automatic, but Stella was confident of her skill. She had practiced outside the city limits until she could shoot the pips from a playing card at fifty feet. She stopped, raised the pistol to eye level, and began to breathe in a light, controlled fashion as she waited for Daggett to reach the streetlamp. Finally, the wait was over.

Just as her finger depressed the trigger, a delivery truck took the corner at Lafayette Street a bit too fast. Daggett, reacting to the sudden noise and light, faded quickly into the shadows as the explosion from Stella's gun sounded. Even with the truck noise, Daggett had recognized the high-pitched crack of a light-caliber pistol. He leaped wildly around the rear of the truck, ducking as the crack and whiz of a second shot went by him.

Stella ran to the corner, her eyes searching for a target, but Daggett was nowhere in sight. "Goddamn it to hell," she said aloud, her voice cracking with anger and frustration. But Stella hadn't lived so long by being careless. She knew the shots would likely bring a beat patrolman to investigate, so she shoved the gun into her bag and quickly retraced her steps to the railroad station.

Her exotic features were blurred with disappointment. The failure rankled, but she consoled herself. Daggett was here, and what Stella could find once, she knew she could find again.

Daggett stood huddled in the recessed doorway to an apartment building, a cold sweat standing all over his dark brown face. Somebody had laid for him and tried to kill him without warning. That meant somebody was worried about his return—somebody with something to lose if he managed to clear himself. If he'd had any doubts about his decision to return home, they were gone now.

Watching the street carefully for movement, he unlatched his suitcase, unbuckled the second compartment, and found the cold, hard weight of his .41. He removed it from the holster, shut the suitcase, and tucked the bone-handled revolver into his waistband over the hipbone. He knew he was taking a chance by carrying it. If he was caught, it would violate the terms of his parole and he'd be shipped right back to Angola in leg irons.

Checking carefully before leaving his shelter, Daggett satisfied himself that, for now, his assailant was gone. He picked up the suitcase with his left hand and continued through the darkened city streets until he reached the Metro Hotel on South Rampart Street.

There were several drink-and-dance joints in that neighborhood, and even though the hour was late, he found foot traffic and heard the melancholy sounds of clarinets and saxophones leaking desultorily from the open doors he passed. The Metro's door was almost always open, and the yellow neon sign over the entrance glowed like a friendly firefly.

A dapper-looking Negro with straightened hair combed straight back and parted in the middle stared fixedly from behind the desk. He looked like he was in a daze, but when Daggett approached the desk, he blinked and became instantly alert.

"Iz? That is you, ain't it?" the desk man asked. Teeth like pearls gleamed from beneath his Duke Ellington mustache.

"What's left of him, anyway," Daggett replied. "How are you, Arthur?"

"Gettin' older and not rich," Arthur replied. "I didn't know they let you out. You just get into town?"

"Yeah," Daggett answered. "I just got in on the local from Tunica and walked over here. You got any rooms with a bath available?"

"Right as rain, cousin," Arthur said, turning the registration book so he could sign in. At the same time, he reached behind him and took a tagged key from a rack behind him. "Take room twenty-five," he said. "It looks out on the street. Be a good way to ease back into city livin'. What you plannin' on doin', Iz? I mean, we got an opening for a hotel dick, if you're interested."

Daggett dipped a bank pen into an open inkwell, and signed his name carefully. He put the pen back into the tray and looked up at the hotel man. "Thanks, Arthur. I don't know yet. Lottie Sonnier said she had a few job interviews scheduled for me, so I guess I'll see what they have to say."

At the mention of Lottie's name, Arthur's face got a stiff, shocked look to it, and he rubbed his right hand roughly over his mouth and chin. Daggett saw the look, and felt a strange thrill run up his spine.

"What's the matter, Arthur? I say something wrong?" Daggett asked, puzzled.

"I—I guess you ain't heard, since you been on the train all day," Arthur began. "Lottie's . . . that is, I mean to say, Lottie was . . . killed yesterday."

Daggett's large body reeled as though struck a heavy blow. His large hands gripped the edge of the registration desk and his eyes seemed to blur. He closed them, holding his breath, then opened them again. Arthur was still there, looking at him with that damned pitying expression. "Dead? How?" was all Daggett could say.

"Nobody knows all of it," Arthur said quietly. "But she was found shot over behind the zoo this mornin' early. Leastways, that's all was in the papers."

Daggett reached out a numb hand and captured the key that Arthur had laid in front of him. Once, a long time ago, Daggett had been shot in the side, and the numbness of the blow had gradually given way to terrible, burning pain. This news had the same effect on him as the bullet wound, and he knew he had to go somewhere until the pain subsided. He reached into his pocket and found the roll of bills there. He peeled off a five-dollar note and handed it to Arthur.

"Get me a quart of bourbon and send it up with some ice," he said. "Get it up there as quick as you can."

Arthur took his eyes from Daggett's ashen face, and moved the note around in his fingers. "Sure, Iz. I'll get it for you right now."

Daggett picked up his suitcase and walked to the stairs. He stumbled as he walked up them, but could not feel his feet hitting the treads. Room twenty-five was about halfway down the hall, and he found himself weaving as he got there. He inserted the key in the lock, pushed the door open, and walked inside, dropping the suitcase as he walked heavily to the bed, where he sank down with his head in his hands. He was still in that position when Arthur appeared with the bottle of whiskey and the bucket of ice. He did not appear to notice when Arthur walked quietly out and pulled the door closed behind him.

When the night began to fade into the small hours of the morning, Wesley Farrell left the Cafe Tristesse and ventured out into the darkened city streets. In spite of Casey's proviso, he had his Italian spring-blade stiletto strapped to his left forearm and his German Solingen steel straight razor in a special pocket sewn into the lining of his gray flannel suit. They were a part of his wardrobe, and he wore them without thinking.

He strolled out of the Quarter and walked through the darkness until he reached Rampart. This was primarily a Negro entertainment district, but white men and women were frequent visitors to the jazz bars and strip clubs up and down the street. As he passed open doors, he heard snatches of jittering clarinets and the gut-bucket moan of saxophones. Shills stood outside the entrances of striptease joints, praising the charms of the naked dancers within. Occasionally a door would be open just enough for a curious passer-by to get a glimpse of bare, jiggling flesh—enough, perhaps, to draw him inside to the bar.

After walking much of the length of Rampart, Farrell saw a sign he was looking for and turned inside Fat Man Murphy's Bar. He stepped to the side as he passed through the door, letting his eyes adjust to the gloomy interior. Pale lights shone over the bar, and the scratched and cracked mirror behind reflected the empty faces of the men and woman scattered around the room. Small neon signs advertising beers and liquors festooned the walls, giving the place an unearthly glow.

He found the man he was looking for in the corner, and walked toward him. The man was heavily proportioned, and his even features in a light brown face suggested some white blood in his family tree. The size of his body gave the illusion that his head was a bit small for the rest of him, sufficient reason for people to call him "Little Head" Lucas.

Lucas looked up from a small chessboard in front of him as Farrell approached. "Dull night at your place, Mr. Farrell?" the Negro asked in a smooth baritone.

"I'm prowling," Farrell said.

Little Head Lucas's dark brows moved upward, but the rest of his face remained neutral. "For men or women?" he asked.

"I don't know," Farrell said, hooking a chair with his foot and sitting down across from the other man. "I'm trying to find out what happened to Lottie Sonnier."

Lucas's brows elevated again, and his mouth pursed and twisted thoughtfully. "That was a damn shame," he said. "You and her was friends once, 'less I disremember."

"Nothing's wrong with your memory," Farrell said. "I don't like it when friends of mine get hurt. I want to know who did it."

"Lotsa the rest of us wanna know, too," Little Head Lucas said. "If I knew, I'd be glad to hold 'em for you while you cut 'em into dog meat."

Farrell's face, largely in the shadow of his hat, was invisible to Lucas, but his bowed head spoke eloquently of his feelings on the matter. "What can I do to help you?" Lucas asked finally.

"Lottie spent a lot of her time counseling prostitutes, helping abandoned wives and children, and working with the poor in the colored sections of town. But the bullet behind her ear is gangland stuff. What could she have been doing that would get her in trouble with a gangster?"

"Hmmm," Little Head Lucas said, fingering the white rook as he considered Farrell's words. "I can only think of one thing, but I can't give you nothin' definite."

"Tell it," Farrell said, leaning slightly in Little Head Lucas's direction.

"They's enough heroin and morphine comin' into town to float a battleship," Lucas said. "Most of it's endin' up in the colored sections of town. Holdups, robberies, and burglaries in that section are drivin' the police Negro Squad nuts. They's always a connection between property crime and drugs in our side of town. Lottie was askin' a lot of questions about it, tryin' to keep it out of the hands of poor kids and some of the weaker brothers and sisters."

Farrell silently fingered his chin as he considered Lucas's assessment. It might mean something, but he had to find a way to tie Lottie to it in some way before it explained the killing. "So maybe she talked to the wrong person and it got her killed. But who?" he asked finally.

Little Head Lucas's mouth turned up sardonically at this. "Now you're askin' something. You know how Lottie got around. She might talk to a hundred people in a day."

Farrell nodded. "Who do you know who might be connected to the narcotics?"

Little Head Lucas stared at his chessboard for a moment, then moved a white knight to check the black king. He left his finger on the knight for a moment, pursing his lips before he took it away and looked up again. "You're edgin' up to some dangerous shit, Mr. Farrell. I won't be doin' you no favor if I help you."

"Let me worry about that," Farrell said. His voice had dropped to a low, sibilant whisper that caused the hair to stand up along the backs of Little Head Lucas's arms and neck. Like everyone with a line to the underworld, he knew of Farrell's reputation, and also the reputations of the men he had killed. He felt his hand shaking, and dropped it softly into his lap.

"I only know one name, and I can't back it up with anything solid," Lucas said. "You know who Walt Daggett is?"

Farrell's face was still in shadow, but his head nodded imperceptibly. "Israel Daggett's cousin. He was bounced from the cops, wasn't he?"

Lucas nodded his seemingly small head wisely. "Caught in a hotel room with a seventeen-year-old chippie, both of 'em coked to the gills. Gettin' thrown off the cops didn't seem to hurt him none. He's been livin' nice ever since for a guy with no visible means of support."

"Lottie was Israel Daggett's woman," Farrell said.

"That's right," Little Head Lucas replied.

Farrell got up, and for the first time, a shaft of light fell across his face, and his pale eyes glowed whitely from under his hat brim. "If you ever need anything, Little Head, let me know, all right?"

Little Head Lucas waved a diffident hand. "Don't worry 'bout it. Let me know how things shake down, hear?"

Farrell touched a forefinger to the brim of his hat and disappeared from the bar like smoke.

5

The next morning Captain Frank Casey sat at his desk on the second floor of headquarters reading the coroner's report on Lottie Sonnier and the crime lab reports on the findings at the scene. His mouth was stretched into a bitter line as he reflected on how little they had. He had just put the reports back into their folders when his secretary buzzed him.

"Sergeant Snedegar's here with another gentleman," she said.

"Send them in," Casey said, getting up from his desk.

The door opened and Snedegar stood aside to let the little railroad detective precede him into the room. Patout was dressed in a cheap brown corduroy suit that probably hadn't seen a pressing since Prohibition was repealed. He had a cap of the same shade and material as the suit in his gnarled and work-roughened left hand.

"Have a seat, Mr. Patout," Casey said, indicating one of the two chairs in front of his desk. Patout sat down in the left-hand chair with an expectant look on his face. Snedegar took the right-hand chair, his hatchet face sharp and interested looking.

"Mr. Patout, you told us yesterday about having been on the police force a number of years ago," Casey said.

Patout's eyes got a cloudy look on them, but he nodded. "Yes, sir, but it was a long time ago. I was just a kid."

"You're a little under the size of a regular police recruit," Casey said, "and that made me curious, so I looked into it." Casey leaned his arms on the desktop and clasped his hands as he stared at the railroad detective. "It isn't quite true that you were a policeman, is it?"

"Well, I . . ." Patout scratched the back of his head, and his face seemed to fall apart.

"You tried to enlist, but you were too small, so you got a job as a guard in the Parish Prison," Casey said. "They had you over in the women's part of the prison where you proceeded to force three women to have sexual intercourse with you. Isn't that right?"

Patout's face had gone white, and his shoulders slumped.

"They gave you the opportunity to resign instead of firing you," Casey went on. "Which was a lucky break for you. You should have been arrested, tried, and sent up the river. You had a cousin in charge over there at the time, and he got you out of the soup, right?"

"Ye-yeah," Patout said stupidly.

"I'll tell you what bothers me, Mr. Patout," Casey said. "We got a victim with her clothes torn off, which might have been the lead-up to forcible rape. Could be it went bad and that's the reason she was killed. Maybe it was you, and maybe it wasn't, but I'm going to have you detained until we can look into this a bit more. Unless you can offer any evidence in your own defense, or an alibi of some kind."

Patout's face was the color of milk, and his mouth worked without any sounds coming from it. Casey had taken him completely by surprise.

"Okay, if that's the way it is," Casey said. "Take him downstairs and book him, Snedegar."

Snedegar, anticipating Casey's orders, had already gotten up and pulled the smaller man to his feet. He went over him quickly, and removed a cheap, nickel-plated Forehand and Wadsworth .32 from his belt, and a braided leather sap from his hip. "Let's go, pal," he said.

"You—you got me all wrong, Captain," Patout protested. "I ain't done nothin', I swear, I ain't done nothin'." His voice was shrill, and he struggled in Snedegar's grip.

"Pipe down, you little creep," Snedegar said as he twisted the smaller man's hands behind him and snapped cuffs on his wrists.

Casey watched silently, his brow furrowed. He said nothing as Patout was dragged protesting from the office. It all seemed too pat for some reason, and he found himself wondering if there was more to it than this.

The air was full of chilly drizzle that morning when Wesley Farrell got out of bed. He stood at the window overlooking the small parking area behind his club and made a face at the bleak gray sky and the incessant pocking of the puddles beneath. He hunched the collar of his thick flannel robe up around his neck and shivered before turning back to the kitchen.

He was just turning the fire on beneath his coffeepot when he heard the sound of the buzzer at the rear door. Checking his watch first, he walked back and opened it to find Savanna standing there. Her face had an expression on it that he couldn't read.

Farrell stood back from the door and waved her in. "It's kind of early for you to be out visiting, isn't it?" he asked as he closed the door.

Savanna came in without a word, and took off her raincoat and hat. Underneath the coat she was dressed in a beige suit and a pale yellow blouse with lace at the cuffs and throat. Her hat looked like a big inverted saucer made of beige felt. When she'd draped the hat and raincoat over Farrell's coatrack, she turned, wrapped her muscular arms about his waist, and kissed him like it was the last kiss ever to be allowed on earth. There was an urgency and need in that kiss that went beyond sexual desire, and it surprised him.

"Better let me turn the coffeepot off," Farrell said when she let him come up for air. But she kissed him again, and led him to the sofa. Soon Farrell forgot all about his coffee.

"That's not what I need you for," she said finally, tracing the line of his jaw with her fingers.

Farrell took a deep breath, and pulled her closer to him. "Damn, that's too bad," he said fervently.

"I need to talk to you about something important," she said, pulling herself back slightly from his embrace.

"Now?"

"Yeah, it won't wait," she said firmly.

Farrell sighed, and with some reluctance let her go. "Want some coffee?" he asked as he trudged back to the kitchen.

"No," she said.

When he'd poured his coffee and brought it into the living room, he sat down beside her and said, "Okay, I'm listening."

"A friend of mine was found dead yesterday morning," she said.

Farrell looked at her strangely. "Was Lottie Sonnier a friend of yours?"

Savanna's eyes widened. "How'd you know about that?"

"A guy I know was in police headquarters when the word about her came through," Farrell replied, sipping his coffee. "He called and told me about it."

"What was Lottie Sonnier to you?" Savanna asked, watching him carefully. She knew as she asked the question that she might not like the answer, but she asked anyway.

"We were friends once," he answered.

Savanna folded her arms under her bosom and gnawed the side of her lower lip. "Friends?" she asked finally.

He sipped his coffee, and watched her through hooded eyes. "I wasn't a virgin when I met you," he said. "It was a long time ago when she and I were both younger. You couldn't have been more than a kid at the time."

"Lottie was a friend of mine, too," she said a bit hesitantly. "I never knew . . ."

"How could you?" he asked, leaning forward to put his cup and saucer on the coffee table. "It was ten years ago. She didn't know everything about me that you do, so it isn't likely she'd talk about a love affair she was having with what she thought was a white man."

"I . . . I came here to ask you to find out who killed her—and why," Savanna said a bit hesitantly. For a reason she could not quite put name to, she felt at a terrible disadvantage, and embarrassed beyond measure.

"I'm doing that now," he said. "It's been a long time since . . . since Lottie and I were together, but she meant a lot to me once, and I don't like what happened to her." He sank back and rested his right arm along the back of the sofa. His eyes were cast down at his cup and saucer, and he seemed as remote as the planet Pluto.

Savanna felt her insides fall and twist as she sat there. She fought to keep the hurt in her from showing on her face, and to quell the irrational feeling of jealousy that threatened to engulf her. It was several minutes before she could trust herself to speak again.

"What can I do to help?" she said finally.

"Stay out of it," he replied. "I'm stepping all over cop business as it is. I might be able to talk myself out of any trouble I get into, but I wouldn't be able to talk you out of any. Besides, I don't need any help."

"The hell you say," she replied angrily, jumping up from her seat. "Not too long ago, a group of crooked white men put your ass in the fire, and you needed all the help you could get, then. *I* helped you pull it out, remember?"

Farrell turned his face away, and got up to walk to the window. He did remember, all too well. But Savanna had taken a bullet meant for him, and nearly died. He'd taken his revenge, but Savanna's injury still weighed heavily upon his conscience, particularly given the new intensity of their relationship.

As he stood there remembering all that, the silence in the room became oppressive. He could pretend to be angry, throw Savanna out, and try to crawl back into self-imposed isolation, but he knew better. The minute he'd told Savanna about the Creole blood in his veins, he'd left that isolation behind. She was as special to him now as Lottie had been ten years ago. Besides, he reminded himself, Savanna had her own contacts in the city. She could be a help to him, if he could keep her from sticking her neck out too far.

He remembered something else, too. Once, long ago, his mother had been isolated and in need of help, and there had been no one to give it. A connection to the rest of the world meant giving up the lone wolf act, and taking the hand of a friend when it was offered. He turned back to Savanna, his face wiped clean of its misgivings and irritation.

"Okay," he said with a sigh. "You're right, and I'm sorry. If I'm going to find out who killed Lottie, I'm going to have to trace her movements and know who she saw up to the time she was killed. Who'd know all that?"

"I'm not sure," Savanna said, her face softening. "I guess we could start with her mother and sister."

"Okay," Farrell said again. "Let me change clothes, and we'll go over there."

Savanna walked over to Farrell, put her arms around his neck and kissed him softly. "Thank you."

"For what?" he asked, smiling.

"Nothing," she said. "Everything."

His eyes searched hers for a moment, then he smiled again and broke away to get dressed.

The Sonniers had a house on Leonidas Street in the Carrollton district, near the river bend. According to Savanna, old Mrs. Sonnier, known to almost everyone as 'Tee Ruth because she was so small, had been making a living as a cook for a wealthy family on Versailles Boulevard for twenty years. Marguerite, the younger daughter, was studying to be a pharmacist at Xavier University, the Catholic Negro college across town.

The rain had temporarily subsided by the time Farrell eased his Packard to a stop in front of the Sonnier household. The house was a typical three-room New Orleans shotgun cottage, with a front yard about the size of a man's pocket handkerchief. The small yard was enclosed behind a wrought-iron fence, painted black, and was filled with red, pink, and white rosebushes. In spite of the cool weather, most of the bushes were in bloom.

There was black crepe on the front door, a bit wilted from the rain. Savanna led the way up to the porch and knocked on the door. Within the space of three breaths, the door opened and Marguerite stood there.

"Rosalee," she began, then, "Oh . . ." She fell speechless when her eyes fell on the tall man with pale golden-hued skin standing beside Savanna. Clearly this was something she hadn't expected.

Savanna stepped into the breach with the aplomb of an English butler. "Marguerite Sonnier, this is my friend, Mr. Wesley Farrell."

"Oh, yes," Marguerite said, working quickly to recover herself. "Won't you . . . won't the two of you come in?"

They walked into a modest room with a sofa, two armchairs, and a coffee table grouped in front of a small fireplace that had been converted to a gas log. The fire was on, and the air in the room was warm and dry.

"Mr. Farrell is going to try to find the ones responsible for . . . for what was done to Lottie," Savanna said. "He wanted to ask you and 'Tee Ruth a few questions. That is, if you're up to it."

Marguerite, still a bit taken aback by the appearance of a white man in Savanna's company, fumbled around for the right things to say. "Mama's resting in the back. Please, have a seat—there," she said gesturing toward the sofa.

Farrell removed his Burberry overcoat and draped it and his gray Stetson on an umbrella rack beside the door. As he helped Savanna off with her rain cape, he noted an old Atwater-Kent radio in a Chippendale cabinet with a needlepoint picture over the speaker baffle in one corner. On the wall over the fireplace was a framed lithograph by John McCrady of the soul of a woman being welcomed into heaven in the sky over a Negro sharecropper's cabin.

A crucifix hung in the midst of the wall opposite, and on the wall to his right was a hand-tinted photograph of Pope Pius XII. A sepia-toned photographic portrait of a woman who resembled Marguerite, dressed in a graduation gown and mortarboard, rested on a table opposite the door to the next room. Farrell felt a catch in his throat as he recognized the picture was the young, fresh Lottie he had known a decade before.

"I—I'm glad to meet you," Marguerite managed to say as she took a seat in one of the chairs opposite them. "Would you like some coffee?" she asked quickly. "I've got a fresh pot on the stove."

"No, please don't trouble yourself," Farrell said before she could get up again. He could sense her discomfort, and knew once again that vague feeling of guilt he always got when dealing with Negroes. The careful part he played never failed to make him feel a bit ashamed at such times. To mask it, he leaned forward quickly and said, "What can you tell us about Lottie's movements before she was found yesterday?"

Savanna immediately noted the difference in him, and pitied him for a moment. Sometimes she wished he would quit pretending, but that was a decision he'd have to make in his own time and in his own way. Right now they had other fish to fry.

"I've thought about it quite a bit since the police came to question us," Marguerite said. "She didn't act like anything was any different than usual. She was so excited that Israel was coming home." She frowned. "I was expecting to hear from him by now—he must've had trouble getting here or something."

Farrell's eyes flickered. "You haven't heard from Israel yet?"

"No," Marguerite said. "Did you know he was due back?"

"Yes," Farrell answered. "I knew."

Marguerite's face took on a distraught look as Farrell spoke. "What am I gonna tell him about Lottie. What?" She covered her face with her hands, and her shoulders shook with silent sobs.

Savanna got up and went to her, and began to make soothing noises. Farrell got up and walked about the room scowling. He felt utterly useless, and he wasn't used to feeling that way. He wasn't a detective. What did he hope to do, anyway?

He was staring out the window when he felt someone come into the room. He turned and saw a short, stout old woman standing there. Her reddish-brown skin was so full of wrinkles that it resembled a field plowed in red dirt.

"You must be Mrs. Sonnier," he said. "I'm Wesley Farrell." He held out a hand, and after a moment's scrutiny, the old woman took it in her own.

"She can't stop cryin'," the old woman said softly. "I did mine already. There ain't any tears left."

"I'm sorry," he said, impressed by the strength radiating from the old woman. "I used to know Lottie. I came to see if I could help."

"Help how?" the old woman asked bluntly. "What can you do?"

"I'd like to help find whoever killed your daughter," he answered.

"What good will that do?" she asked, shrugging, her eyes cast down. "Nothin' can bring Lottie back."

"But we can get the man who did it, and make him pay for it," Farrell replied, an edge growing in his voice. He heard it and checked himself to keep from upsetting the old lady.

She shrugged again. "I'd kill him myself if it would do any good, but it wouldn't bring her back. I'm a church-goin' woman, Mr. Farrell. 'Vengeance is mine, saith the Lord.'"

"He can have it, ma'am," he said with a small smile. "I'd just like to give him a hand."

She looked up into his face, saw something she liked there, and returned his smile with one of her own. "C'mon back to the kitchen. I got some coffee on."

Farrell looked at Savanna. She saw his look, nodded to say she was all right for now, then jerked her head in the direction of the kitchen.

He followed in her shuffling footsteps through a bedroom with two chifforobes, an oak sleigh bed with a chenille bedspread, and curtains of unbleached muslin. The second room they tramped through must have been the old woman's. It had a single cast-iron bed with a patch comforter on it, a cedar wardrobe, and a crucifix on the wall over the door.

The kitchen was painted red, and had a spotless gas stove and a fairly new Coldspot refrigerator. A curly maple dining table stood in the middle of the small room with four gingham place mats on it. Four straight-backed chairs were neatly in place. The old woman gestured for him to sit down, and he took the one opposite the stove. She took two cups and saucers from a cabinet, and filled them with coffee and hot milk from a pan heating on the stove.

"You like sugar?" she asked.

"This way is fine," he said.

She put both cups on the table, then took the seat across from him.

"Seems like I know your name for some reason," she said over the rim of her cup.

"I've been around for a while," he said, smiling back. The old woman was cagy, and he found he liked her.

"No, it's not that. I knew Marie. We grew up together." She sipped coffee, and gazed placidly at him.

It gave him a bit of a start for her to mention that name, but he kept his face neutral. Marie Turnage had run his cathouse on Soraparu Street, and had been killed by Emile Ganns's men the year before. "Marie was a good woman," he said.

"Too good for what happened to her," she replied. "You took care of the ones did that, didn't you?"

Farrell nodded. "All of them, Mrs. Sonnier."

"That's real fine," Mrs. Sonnier said. "Call me 'Tee Ruth. Everybody else does."

"Call me Wes," he said.

"Just one thing I want, Mr. Wes," 'Tee Ruth said. "I want to know why. Why somebody had to kill my baby, and use her the way they done."

He nodded. "If I can find out who did it, I'll make sure they tell me. I won't let them go until they do."

"Good. What can I tell you?"

"What do you know about where she went the day she died?" he asked, blowing on his coffee to cool it.

The old woman squinted as she tried to find the doorway in her memory. "She was a goin' girl, always had a million places to get. I know she had some people in Gert Town she was helpin' to get a children's recreation center started. Man over there named Merton Diaz is in charge of it."

"Gert Town can be a rough place," Farrell observed.

Ruth nodded her agreement. "Scared me for her to go there, but she wasn't afraid of nothin'. People over there respected her, too. They knew she was there doin' good for people who needed it. I b'lieve if anybody over there tried to bother her, a bunch of them people woulda beat the black right off'n him." She emitted a dry cackle.

"Okay, I'll try over there," he said, laughing a little himself. "Where else would she have been going that day?"

"Hard to say," the old woman answered. "She started each day with a schedule she got from her office downtown. She might not follow it to the letter, 'cause she had little projects of her own, but that'd be a place to start. She worked for the Community Service Agency on Camp Street. She worked for a Mrs. Sallie Taylor."

"Okay," Farrell said.

The old woman suddenly looked tired, and hung her head. "What will I tell Israel? This gonna be a terrible blow to that man. He and Lottie was sweethearts goin' way back."

Farrell lowered his eyes to hide the look he knew was in them, and shook his head. "There's no way to turn away from it. He's a pretty tough guy—he has to be to've survived five years up at Angola. He'll make it through somehow."

"You talkin' about the kind of tough that means fightin'. Lotta men can fight what they can lay their hands on, but this is different. You can't hit loss. You can't shoot it or knock it down. It just crawls inside you and eats your heart. I've known men to go crazy and die from somethin' like this. I fear for him, Mr. Wes, I swear I do."

Something in her distress touched him. She could stand the pain herself, but she worried about a man not even related to her. Impulsively, he reached out a hand and placed it on her wrist. After a moment's hesitation, she put her other hand on top of his, and squeezed down on it.

"I ain't never met a white man like you," she said finally.

"No," he said. "Probably not."

They left the kitchen and went back out to the living room. Marguerite had regained control of herself, and she and Savanna were talking in low voices.

"I think I'm through," he said. "We can go whenever you're ready."

"I'll be outside in a minute," she said.

He nodded, and retrieved his hat and overcoat from the rack.

After he closed the door behind him, the three women were silent for a moment. Finally Ruth spoke.

"That's some man you got there, Rosalee."

Savanna's head snapped up, and she fixed the old woman with a blank stare.

"Be glad you got somebody like that," Ruth continued. "It ain't no shame."

"Really, Mother," Marguerite said a bit sharply. To Savanna, she said, "Do you think he can do anything?"

Savanna turned and smiled at her friend. "He has a way of stirrin' things up," Savanna said. "And when he does, something or somebody's gonna rise to the top. Then it'll be time to duck."

It was nearing noon when a tall, lean Negro stumbled inside the grimy tavern on City Park Avenue. His excessive thinness was emphasized by the way he had his camel's hair overcoat wrapped tightly around him. He had an expensive Wilton snapbrim jammed down on his head against the wind, and his face was gray with the cold.

The nameless tavern was empty but for the bartender, a small, narrow-skulled brown man who stood there desultorily polishing shot glasses with a faded towel. The gray-faced man walked unsteadily to the bar and placed his hands flat on the bar in front of him.

"Kinda nippy out there, eh, Walt?" the bartender said.

"God *damn* the weather in this shithole of a town," Walt said hoarsely. "If you ain't sweatin' buckets, you're drownin' in rain. If it ain't the rain, it's that wind cuttin' into you like a knife. Gimme a shot of I. W. Harper, Mel."

Mel cocked up an eye from his glass polishing without stopping his chore. "Ya got cash, Walt? Ya know I can't serve ya without ya pay somethin' on that tab of yours."

Walt, still hunched in his overcoat, fished around in the right-hand pocket and came up with a roll of bills. He peeled off a note and dropped it in front of Mel. The wizened little barkeep put down his towel and flattened the creases from the note.

"God *damn*, Walt," Mel said. "You strike it rich or somethin'? I ain't seen a twenty in here since last month. You want I should use fifteen of it to clear the tab?"

"Yeah, but bring me the bourbon first, and leave the bottle,"

Walt said, unbuttoning his coat. The heavy steam heat in the bar seemed to be finally getting its way into his chilled bones.

Mel turned and got the bottle of I. W. Harper from the shelf behind him, smiling to himself. Walt Daggett had more money than Creosus, but he'd nickel and dime you to death, buying on credit, then taking a month to pay what he owed. Mel found something humorous in the spectacle, otherwise he'd have told Walt to hit the bricks and not come back.

When Mel put the bottle and glass in front of him, Walt poured a shot into the glass and threw the whiskey down his throat in a single dose. Then he filled the glass again, and sipped it slowly. His face had the look of a man experiencing an epiphany.

"So, Walt," Mel said, back to polishing his glasses again. "I hear Iz is outa the pen. Got out on good behavior. Some shit, huh?"

Walt's hand froze in the act of lifting the glass to his mouth again. "What's that?"

Mel cocked an eye at him again. "What, ya ain't heard? Easter Coupe sent me a card from up at Angola. You know, Easter's serving a five-to-ten for armed robbery up there. Said Iz was bein' released day before yesterday. Bet he stopped in the first town he got to, found him a woman and been wallowin' in her ever since just to get used to havin' it again."

Walt's gray face was perfectly still except for the nerve under his left eye that had begun to jump. He finished lifting the glass to his mouth and poured the rest of the whiskey into it. Very slowly, he lowered the glass to the bartop and put it down.

"He'll come back here," Walt said, his voice no longer hoarse. It had a peculiar clarity in the still, stuffy room, like the sound of a mason's hammer hitting marble. Mel looked up sharply, feeling a chill run down the length of his backbone.

"Somethin' wrong, Walt?" he asked.

"No, nuthin'," Walt said. He turned and walked back toward the entrance.

"Hey, Walt, you got change comin'," Mel said to his retreating back. But Walt didn't answer, and walked out the door into the biting February wind.

6

Sleepy Moyer rarely slept at all. He got his name for the fact that his eyelids were always at half-mast, due to some neurologic dysfunction in his facial muscles. He was a short, thick-set brown man of about twenty-eight or 'nine, with a nose that had stopped too many punches and thick lips that looked always on the verge of a smile. That was a false impression, too. Sleepy only smiled when he was hurting someone.

He was already half awake when the telephone started to ring. He raised up on one elbow and caught the receiver before the second ring came. He hated the sound of bells.

"Yeah," he said noncommittally.

"Iz Daggett's back in town," a man's voice said.

"So?"

"So? That all you can say?" the voice asked incredulously. "What do you think's gonna happen when he finds out Lottie Sonnier's dead? He's liable to tear this town apart brick by brick until he finds out who did it. If I end up goin' down, the rest of you go, too. I done my part by y'all, now y'all can stick by me."

Sleepy's blunt fingers tightened on the receiver, and his rubbery lips curled cruelly. The light in his muddy brown eyes gleamed like a freshly sharpened straight razor. "That kinda talk could get you killed," he said. "And you wouldn't die easy. There ain't a soul knows why or how she been killed, much less by who. He's just one man, and an ex-con on top of that. He can't do nothin', and the cops don't give a shit about a dead nigger nohow. You just keep still, and keep doin' what you're told." He hung up the phone and sank back onto his pillow. He stared at the ceiling for a few minutes, then raised up again, picked up the telephone receiver, and dialed a number. It rang twice before it was picked up at the other end.

"Hello," a woman's voice said.

"It's Sleepy, Stella."

"What the hell do you want?" Stella asked, her voice dripping contempt.

"I just got a call from one of your li'l friends," Sleepy said. "He's gettin' the runs 'cause Iz Daggett's back in town."

"That weak-kneed sack of dogshit," Stella said. "Will he crack?"

"I told him he was worryin' about nuthin'," Sleepy said, "but I warned him what would happen if he went off the beam. I think he'll stay shut, but you better watch him, case he gets religion or somethin' and lets his mouth run away with him."

"Jesus Christ," Stella said. "Just once I'd like for a man to be good for somethin' besides causing me grief."

"I'm good for somethin', baby," Sleepy said. "Just call me some time, and I'll give you a sample."

Stella slammed the telephone down and broke the connection. Sleepy grinned lewdly and placed his own receiver down.

The nude, tan-colored woman beside him began to snore. The sounds coming from her mouth were like those of a file rubbing a piece of wood. Sleepy was wide awake now, with no chance of going back to sleep. He also found himself in a state of intense arousal, so much so that he could not think of anything else. He grabbed the sleeping woman's shoulder and shook it several times, but she continued to snore loudly. They had killed a quart of Old Crow the night before, and she'd had the lion's share.

With a disgusted frown on his face, Moyer rolled to his side, pulled her hips into him, and entered her roughly from the rear. He copulated with her for perhaps five minutes before a grunt like a rooting hog's escaped his throat. He gave a sigh and fell back onto his side of the bed, panting.

After a few moments, he got up, washed himself at the basin, then began dressing himself in a beige shirt, red silk tie with a rising sun on it, and a gray hound's-tooth check suit. After tying the laces of a pair of black bluchers, he put on his overcoat and hat. A Luger automatic rested in the right-hand pocket of the overcoat, and his hand instinctively sought it, the fingers curling around the butt. He had killed three men with that particular gun, and he felt an affection for it that was akin to a boy's love for a painstakingly built hot rod.

He left the room and walked down creaking stairs to a shabbily decorated parlor. A Negro woman of about thirty-five with thick, dark-brown hair sat in a platform rocker, knitting an afghan. A cup of chicory coffee sat at her elbow, and the room was full of the smell.

"Well, you finally through, Sleepy?" she asked.

"I reckon, Alice, for the time being, anyhow," he said.

"I need some money," she said. "You keep me on too short a leash here. I ain't got no food in the house, neither."

"If you'd lay off the liquor, you'd eat better," he said without sympathy. He reached into his pocket, pulled out a crumpled roll of bills, and peeled off two tens. He handed them to the old woman, who shoved them into the bosom of her housedress.

"Come again," she said, cackling. It was an old joke, but she could never resist using it on anybody who'd been upstairs.

Sleepy sneered at her and left the bordello, pulling his hat down until the brim almost touched his flat nose. He walked up Annunciation until he reached Louisiana Avenue. That part of Louisiana was empty except for an old man who sat on the corner with a pile of newspapers at his feet. Sleepy walked over to him and picked up one of the papers.

The old man looked over at him tiredly and said, "Five cent, mister."

Sleepy shot a mean look at the old man over the top of the paper, and then continued reading.

"Them papers cost five cent, I said," the old man said a bit louder.

Sleepy was about to kick the old man when he came to the article about the death of Lottie Sonnier. His eyes narrowed, and he read the article all the way through, twice. As he'd predicted, the police had not a clue as to who had killed her, or why. When he lowered the paper, his lips were bent into a travesty of a smile, and he stared off at the horizon like a man seeing a vision.

"You cain't just take a paper without you pay for it," the old man said peevishly. "This is how I make my bread, mister. Gimme five cent, or gimme back my paper."

Sleepy's lazy gaze flicked over at the old man, and he reached through the slit in his overcoat pocket to his pants. He came out with a quarter, which he flipped to the old man. While the coin was in the air, he threw the paper down on the stack, causing the sections to fly apart. He sneeringly watched the old man shuffle the paper back together for a few seconds, then walked across the street to his car.

The thick gray clouds scudding overhead made the midafternoon sky almost like eventide as Walter Daggett stepped off the bus on lower Washington Avenue in the Broadmoor section. A freezing wind cut through his expensive overcoat like a jagged icicle, and he had to hang onto his Wilton with one hand while he clenched the collar of his overcoat close to his throat with the other. His eyes were fixed in a baleful stare as he walked two blocks down from the bus and into the neighborhood of middle-class homes and apartment duplexes.

With unerring steps he went directly to a two-story building with a beige stucco finish, and large windows with points at the tops like those in a gothic cathedral. He pushed the bell to the lower apartment and stood there shivering in the cold rain waiting for a response. He remained there staring at the door for two full minutes before the door opened.

"What the hell do you want, Walter?" the cat-eyed woman said, cutting him with her slanted eyes. She was wearing a wrapper of watered silk decorated with peacock feathers. It was plain she wore nothing under it, but she stood there oblivious to the cold while she waited for his answer.

"Iz came back to town," he said in an accusing voice. "Why didn't nobody tell me?"

"You're big enough and ugly enough to find things out for yourself," Stella said carelessly. "I didn't take you to raise."

"You sure got a short memory, Stella," he replied, curling his lip. "Before that white man came along, I gave or got for you everything you had. I never treated you bad, and never raised a hand to you. He don't treat you that good. I've been told." But his sneer couldn't hold while talking to her. His eyes became soft and liquid as he looked at her. "One of these days you're liable to remember and want to come back where you belong."

"Where I belong?" she snorted. "Joe put me on top of the world. I was never anybody when I was with you 'cause you ain't nobody. With him, I'm somebody, and don't you forget it."

His eyes flashed, and one large hand shot out and captured her wrist. "One of these days you'll push me too far," he said with a voice grown blurry around the edges. "Don't get the idea that my not havin' white skin makes the Big Boy better'n me. I can show him, and show you, too."

Her slanted eyes got a humorous look in them, and one corner of her delectable mouth turned up as her gaze dropped to his hand, then back up to his face. "It don't take much gumption to rough up a woman. Why don't you go home and play with yourself for a while?"

"Let me in, woman," he said. "I ain't the mailman. I don't talk to people on their porches." Some of the fire had gone out of his eyes, but she could see he wouldn't be put off.

She lowered the lids over her eyes as she considered for a moment, then stepped back from the door and held it for him to come inside.

The room was warm with steam heat, and expensively furnished with heavy Victorian furniture. Stella sat down on a chaise longue covered in crushed velvet and leaned back, allowing the silk wrapper to fall open and reveal a lot of leg. The bodice gaped open over her breasts long enough for them to become almost completely exposed before she smiled provocatively, and pulled it closed with a thumb and forefinger.

Walter saw the display of flesh, and clenched his jaw in impotent rage.

"Now, Walter honey, just what is it you want, anyhow?" she asked lazily.

"I wanna know what you're gonna do, now he's back," he said. "If somebody don't hit him hard, he's gonna start knockin' everything and everybody down until he finds out what happened to Lottie."

"You worry too much. Anyway, he's a walkin' dead man," she said. "He just don't know to lie down yet. I almost got him two nights ago, but a truck spoiled everything. It's just a matter of time before I get to him."

"You ain't that good," Walter said contemptuously. "You think he's the kind of man to just keep takin' shit. He knows he was framed, same as you, and he's probably got some idea who was behind it. And now his woman's been killed. This is more shit than any man's gonna take lyin' down. Suppose he finds what he's lookin' for before you get him? Flappin' in the breeze, woman, that's where we'll all be. And Joe won't like it."

"Did you kill his woman?" Stella asked, staring at him through heavy-lidded eyes.

Walt Daggett started, half turned, and stared at her. "Hell, no, I didn't kill her. I expect it was that goddamned Sleepy squarin' accounts with her. But that don't help me none. Iz has plenty of reason to hate me, and he's liable to suspect me whether I did or didn't. I can't afford to wait on you to handle this."

Stella yawned, got languidly up from the chaise, then walked over to a small writing desk. She opened the drawer and pulled out a hammerless .38 Smith & Wesson revolver with a squeeze safety in the grip. She tossed it to Walter, who caught it clumsily. "If you're that nervous, take that and go lookin' for him. He can't possibly know anything yet, so you got the edge over him." She walked back to the chaise and lay back on it again, propping her head on one hand so she could see his face.

Walter looked down at the blunt shape of the revolver in his hand, then raised his eyes to hers. There was a look of pity on his face, and he tossed the pistol on the chaise beside her.

"You just don't get it, do you?" Walt said wonderingly. "The end of the world's comin', and when it does, Joe's gonna blame it on you, and throw your cute li'l ass to the sharks. You'll come to me then, I reckon, 'cause you won't have noplace else to go. I'll probably even take you back, 'cause that's the kind of goddamned fool I am. Look out for yourself, baby. I wouldn't want you to get hurt."

Then he turned and left the room. She remained on the chaise until she heard the door slam, then got up to go to the window. Daggett was walking back toward Washington Avenue. His back was straight and his hands were thrust deeply in his overcoat pockets as he walked. She felt a chill run down her spine, and walked quickly back over to the fire.

Israel Daggett lay on his back in the room at the Metro Hotel dressed in only in rumpled, sweaty underwear. The quart of Jim Beam that Arthur had brought for him lay empty on the carpet, and the bone-handled .41 Colt was cradled in his right hand. His eyes, the whites striated with burst capillaries, stared emptily at the ceiling in the room. The sound of a trombonist fooling around with the tune to "Little Brown Jug" could be heard dimly from the street, but Daggett seemed not to hear it.

A knock sounded at the door, but Daggett did not stir, nor call out. The knock sounded twice more before the person tried the knob. A tall, rawboned man with a long, angular face stuck his head in the door. In the dim light, he could have been Daggett's brother.

"Iz? Iz? It's me, Dandy Walker. Can I come in?"

Daggett said nothing, and did not stir. After a few seconds, Dandy came into the room and closed the door quietly behind him. He walked softly across to the bed and stood over the ex-detective. He saw the revolver gleaming in Daggett's slack fist and reached down to take it from his hand. When he had it in his hand, he broke the cylinder and emptied the six .41 caliber cartridges into his other hand and dropped them into his pants pocket.

"Leave me alone," Daggett said distinctly. The voice had weight and resolve in it, which contrasted oddly with his beaten look.

Dandy shook his head. "What kind of a friend would I be if I let you do anything with that gun? You can't do nothin' with it but hurt yourself or end up back in the stir."

"What's the difference?" Daggett asked. "Lottie's gone, and there ain't as many reasons for me to hang around as there used to be."

Dandy hooked a chair with his foot and dragged it to the side of the bed, where he sat down on it. "I know this is bad, partner, but we been through worse. You been through worse. 'Tee Ruth and Marguerite are prob'ly at the house waitin' for you. Why don't you get up, clean yourself up a li'l, and go over there with me?"

"No," Daggett said. "Couldn't stand to look at 'em. Not now."

Dandy hung his head, and his face fell into shadow, unreadable to Daggett where he lay. When he spoke again, his voice was mournful. "Listen, we all loved Lottie. I reckon I loved her as much as you. The only way we gonna get through this is together. Once we say good-bye to her, then we can try to live again, you know what I'm sayin'?"

Something in Dandy's voice made Daggett's eyes shift to where his old friend sat. He could not see his face distinctly, but he could see Dandy's head hanging slackly between his wide shoulders and hear the soft sound of sniffling. He sat up then, and swung his bare legs over the bed. His head ached dully, and a dry belch escaped his mouth.

"Okey, kid," Daggett said with forced jollity. "While I shower and shave, go downstairs and get another quart of this Beam. I need a little hair o' the dog to brace me. Maybe you could use a belt, too." He rummaged in his pants pocket and came up with two dollars, which he put in Dandy's hand.

"Reckon I could, at that," Dandy said. He got up at the same time as Daggett, and the two men faced each other in the dim light. "Glad you're back, partner. It ain't been quite the same without you."

"Good seein' you, too," Daggett said. He began to strip off his undershirt, and Dandy left the room.

In about fifteen minutes, Dandy returned to the room, and found Daggett standing naked in the floor, toweling himself vigorously. The snow-white towel contrasted sharply with his muscular, dark-brown flesh. Daggett had a small piece of tissue paper fixed to the point of his chin, and he grinned foolishly when he saw Dandy looking at it.

"I got a little careless with the razor. Nicked myself," Daggett said.

"Good thing it weren't one of them cutthroat razors," Dandy said, returning the grin. He pulled a bottle of Old Granddad from a paper sack and set it on the bureau. There were two glass tumblers standing mouth-down on a bamboo tray. He set them upright, and poured two slugs of whiskey into them. "They didn't have no Beam, so I got this bonded Granddaddy. Hope you don't mind."

Daggett wrapped the towel around his lean flanks and took one of the glasses. "I reckon a hundred proof whiskey's all right. It'll get you where you want to go quicker." He drank half of the liquid in his glass, and rolled it around his mouth before swallowing it. His eyes gleamed brightly for a second.

Dandy sat down in his chair again and drank some of the liquor. "What you gonna do now that—now that Lottie's gone?"

Daggett opened his suitcase and removed the clean prison underwear, socks, and a clean white shirt, and began to dress. The whiskey had made him feel better, and he moved with his customary speed and economy of motion. "I thought of comin' back here to try and clear myself," he said as he buttoned the shirt. "I ain't sure it matters anymore without Lottie." He turned and looked at Dandy steadily. "You and she were going around a little, I heard."

Dandy's face turned to stone, and he drank the whiskey in his glass without meeting Daggett's eyes. "It wasn't nothin' big," he said after a silence. "I'd known her as long as you. Nobody knew when you'd get out, or if you ever would. I reckon she just wanted somebody she knew to go out and kick up her heels with once in a while."

Daggett nodded, his eyes hooded. "I can see that. Lottie told me herself in a letter that you'd been good to her, and that I shouldn't take it wrong. I trusted her, like I trust you. Up until a month ago, it didn't matter anyhow. That's when the parole board decided I might deserve a break. I didn't come back here necessarily thinkin' I could take up where I left off."

Dandy chewed his lower lip and shook his head. "It's right good of you to take it that way. A lotta men wouldn't.'"

"You and I grew up together, Dandy, you and me and Walt. I ain't holdin' no grudge, understand?"

Dandy stood up as Daggett pulled his suspenders up over his thick shoulders, and shoved his feet into the black wingtip oxfords. "You got a car?" he asked.

"Downstairs," Dandy said. "The wake's tonight, but I reckoned you might wanna go over to 'Tee Ruth's house and say somethin' to her and Marguerite."

Daggett went into the bathroom and brushed his teeth and tongue vigorously with his prison-issue toothbrush, and gargled the water and toothpowder mixture to rid his mouth of the foul taste the liquor had left there. When he came out, he put on the coat to his suit and led Dandy out into the hall.

"What time is it?" Daggett asked as they descended the stairs to the lobby.

"About four in the afternoon," Dandy replied. "We got a few hours before the wake begins."

"That's fine," Daggett said. "Somebody took a shot at me when I got off the train early this morning." He said this as someone might say "the sky is blue."

Dandy's eyes flickered over at him and became nervous looking. "You know who?"

"No, but I figure it's somebody who's worried that I might start nosin' around. It's good news, in a way." Daggett said.

Dandy's eyes got large. "What the hell's good about it?"

"If I'm important enough to kill," Daggett said, "then somebody's afraid my being here'll cause the truth to get out about Junior's murder. It can't mean anything else."

Dandy said nothing, but Daggett noticed the skin around his

mouth was tight and his eyes flickered nervously. He started to say something to his friend, but thought better of it.

They got into Dandy's late-model Chrysler sedan, and drove away from the Metro.

"How's everything working out down at the gym?" Daggett asked after they'd been silent for a while.

"Not bad," Dandy replied. "I got the mortgage paid off, and got a few fighters who look promising. If I have any luck, I'll be a rich man one day."

"That's fine," Daggett said. "You must've worked damn hard to pay off that mortgage. Money's been hard to get since the Depression hit. I heard some other gyms here in the city closed up while I was in the stir."

"Yeah," Dandy said. "Those boys didn't have no luck. I just played my cards right, is all."

"I'm right glad things worked out for you, buddy," Daggett said. "I might have to ask you for a job."

"Anything for you, Iz," Dandy said.

Wesley Farrell maneuvered his convertible through puddles big enough to float a pirogue on the downtown end of Tchopitoulas Street as he looked for a certain building in that district of warehouses, shipping businesses, and supply houses. He'd never met the man he was going to see, but a contact said the man might know something about Walt Daggett, so Farrell was determined to see him.

The smell of coffee hung heavy in the air as Farrell found the building he was looking for. It was a three-story warehouse made of blocks of Indiana limestone. Steel-framed windows ran all along the sides from the top to the bottom. A printed wooden sign over the door said "Piaget Coffee Importers and Roasters, Inc." Farrell pulled to a stop in front of the entrance and cut the engine. The wind cut into him like a jagged icicle and he turned up the collar of his Burberry, shivering as he walked to the door of the building.

The smell of roasting coffee was a lot stronger inside, and the air was warm and dry. Gratefully he unbuttoned his coat and luxuriated in the heat. He heard sounds deeper in the building, and moved in that direction.

He walked down a corridor until he found an open door on his left. The heat was more intense here, and as he looked through the door he found a half-dozen Negroes grouped around several coffee roasting machines, checking temperatures, shoveling roasted beans into burlap sacks, and sewing the filled sacks closed. The aroma of coffee was so thick that the air had a faint oily taste to it. Farrell stood in the door until one of the men happened to look up and see him. As the man stood upright, several of the others noticed and turned toward Farrell, too. After a moment, one of them spoke.

"Help you, mister?" The speaker was lean and of medium height with skin the color of burnt ochre. His face was narrow and V-shaped. His hair grew to a wooly widow's peak on his forehead. His arms were hairy and sinewy, and he had a long knife at his belt.

"I'm looking for Wendell Gautier," Farrell said, taking a cigarette from his mouth.

"Who's askin'?" the man asked. The other Negroes remained still, their eyes fixed on Farrell's face and their hands loose at their sides. Several of them also wore knives on their belts.

"My name's Wes Farrell," he said. He noticed a flicker of recognition in several sets of eyes, but the man with the V-shaped face appeared unfazed by it. "Tiny Giteau sent me," Farrell concluded.

The man's hands relaxed at his sides and he stepped forward. The other men turned back to their work. "I'm Gautier," he said. "What you need?"

Farrell jerked his chin at the door, and the two of them went outside into the corridor. Farrell turned so he could keep the door to the coffee roasting room in sight, and offered Gautier a cigarette. The man took one, stuck it in the corner of his mouth, and accepted a light from Farrell.

"Thanks," he said, blowing the smoke out of his nose. "Tiny's my cousin. Why'd he send a high roller like you over to me?"

"Know Walt Daggett?" Farrell asked, watching the other man's eyes closely.

Gautier inhaled smoke and blew it out of his nose again. His eyes narrowed to slits and his face become unreadable. "Yeah, I know him. I've known him way too long."

Farrell nodded. "That mean you don't mind answering a few questions about him?"

"I know who you are," Gautier said with a trace of a smile. "He an enemy of yours?"

Farrell regarded him for a moment, dragging on his own cigarette.

"I don't know him at all, but he might know something I want to know."

Gautier looked down at his feet and moved them about on the floor before he looked back up again. "Will what I tell you go past this room?"

"No. And not to the cops, either, if that's what you mean."

"Shoot then," Gautier said, dropping his butt on the floor and grinding it out with his heel.

"Word has it that Walt Daggett's been involved for some time in bringing narcotics into the city and then distributing them throughout the Negro community," Farrell said. "Any truth in it?"

Gautier stoked his chin with a lean hand before speaking. "Walt's had his hand in just about every kinda filthy way to make money there is. Sure, he's mixed up in it. But I don't know much more than that."

"How much more might you know?" Farrell asked.

"Well," Gautier said, hesitating for a moment. "I think he's hooked up with a white gangster named Dante."

"You think?"

Gautier looked up and grinned. "It's kinda complicated. Walt used to go 'round with the damnedest-lookin' woman. She had these slanty eyes, like a pussycat's, and the prettiest tan skin. You just wanted to lick it every time you seen her."

"Negro girl?" Farrell asked.

"Yeah, but I heard she came from some of them Filipinos that come into Louisiana back in the 1880's, settled upstate, and then mixed in with some of the coloreds up there."

"She got a name?"

"She calls herself Stella Bascomb," Gautier said, "but a person can call themselves anything they want if they ain't from around here."

"You say he used to go around with her," Farrell said. "What about now?"

"She left Walt and took up with Dante," he replied. "But Walt hung around, maybe to be near her, I don't know. He started runnin' Junior Obregon's territory after Obregon got killed five or six years ago. I know for a fact that Junior worked for Dante, so if Walt took over his territory, he's gotta be workin' for Dante, too."

Farrell nodded. "What was your connection with Walt?"

"I ran numbers for him for a while, trucked in booze during

Prohibition, stuff like that," Gautier said. "I drew the line at dope. That stuff's pure evil."

Farrell's eyes dropped to the knife at Gautier's belt. "That's some pig sticker you got there. Can I see it?"

Gautier's gaze went to his belt. He drew the blade, flipped it lightly so the blade ended up in his hand, then offered the hilt to Farrell. "A blacksmith made it for me out of an old hinge. It's sweet, though."

Farrell took the knife. It had a broad, leaf-shaped blade, a cross-guard of hammered brass, and a pair of shaped and checked mahogany scales for a handle. It had a beautiful balance. Farrell flipped it, caught it by the blade, then snapped his wrist. The knife flew through the air, turned over one and a half times, and struck the door post blade first. It quivered there, buried two full inches in the wood. Gautier's eyes followed the blade, and he whistled admiringly as he turned back to Farrell.

"Nice," he said.

Farrell held out a hand with a five-dollar note folded in his fingers. "Thanks for the information. If you hear anything else about this, call the Cafe Tristesse, and leave word for me."

"Will do," Gautier said. He walked over to pull his knife out of the wood, and when he turned around again, Farrell was gone.

7

Frank Casey was getting ready to go to lunch when the telephone on his desk rang loudly. "Yes," he said into the receiver.

"Sergeant Tripoli of the Negro Detective Squad," Casey's secretary, Mrs. Longly, said.

"Put him on," Casey said, sitting back down behind the desk.

"Sergeant Tripoli, sir," a bass voice said. "I thought you'd like to know we've traced Israel Daggett."

"Where is he?"

"He's put up at the Metro Hotel on Rampart," Tripoli said. "According to the desk man, he checked in, found out about the Sonnier murder, and locked himself in his room with a quart of bust-head."

"Poor guy," Casey said half to himself. "Just in case, put a man down there to watch for him."

"You want us to bring him in?" Tripoli asked.

"No, just keep him under surveillance. My guess is he'll be at the wake tonight. I'll try to talk to him then. He's probably in no shape to talk to anybody right now."

"Right, skipper," the sergeant said, and hung up.

Casey had his coat on when the telephone rang the second time. Grumbling under his breath, he turned back to his desk and picked up the receiver again. "Yes."

"Nick Delgado from the crime laboratory, Captain," Mrs. Longly said.

"Put him on."

"Detective Delgado, sir," a voice came on.

"What is it, Nick?"

"The coroner sent up the bullet from the Sonnier body. We compared it with that Forehand and Wadsworth Patout was carrying, but it doesn't match. The slug's a copper-nickel jacket, probably fired from one of several European automatics. They searched his place for another gun and found a Mauser. Looks like a war souvenir or something, but it's no match, either. The guy's not a smoker, either. Dips a little Beechnut snuff, but no Wings cigarettes at his place or on his person."

Casey made a face. "All right, Nick, I'll have him released." He hung up the telephone and made a face at it. Back to square one, and almost nothing to go on. None of the investigating detectives had been able to find a thing, not even a sighting of Lottie during the day before her murder. He wondered if Farrell was having any luck.

Gert Town was a mean, hardscrabble of weathered shotgun cottages resting in a triangle bounded by the Washington Avenue Drainage Canal, Carrollton Avenue, and Fountainbleau Drive, between Uptown and Mid-City. Somebody said once that Gert Town was where dreams went to die. Farrell doubted that the people who lived there had ever had any dreams at all. It was strictly nightmare town.

The Gert Town Community Center was on North Genois Street, about three blocks back from Washington Avenue. Xavier University's brick and Indiana limestone gothics shone like jewels in dish of field peas above the tin-and-asbestos shingle roofs of the surrounding neighborhood.

The center was a two-story clapboard building that might once have been a grocery store or some other kind of emporium that had fallen on hard times. It needed paint like a man in the desert needs water, but the street and area around it was spotlessly clean, the windows gleamed, and a hand-painted sign reading "Gert Town Community Center" in red letters swung from a steel bracket over the porch. Farrell parked his car and went inside the building.

The front room was bright, and a half-dozen Negro children of about thirteen years were nearest the largest window behind easels holding canvas. Farrell could see that they were working in oils, and were very intent. A pretty young brown girl with a long, graceful neck and black hair that hung past her shoulders sat for them on a barstool. From upstairs, Farrell could hear someone energetically playing a Beethoven sonata on a slightly out-of-tune piano.

He was walking down a hall toward the back of the house when a rugged-looking dark-brown man with smooth, black hair combed straight back from his forehead came through a door and saw him.

"Can I do anything for you?" he asked in a pleasant baritone.

"I'm looking for Merton Diaz," Farrell said.

"I'm Merton Diaz," the other man said. "And you are . . . ?"

"My name's Farrell, Wesley Farrell," he replied. "I understand that Lottie Sonnier did a lot of work with you."

Diaz frowned, his thick, black brows forming a solid line across the bridge of his nose. "Did. Yes, Lottie was a wonderful woman. What happened to her was despicable. If I could . . ." It was plain what was in his mind by the way he clenched and unclenched his big-knuckled hands.

"I want to find out who killed her," Farrell interjected. "Her mother, Ruth Sonnier, asked if I could look into it."

"And do what when you found out?" Diaz asked with a raised eyebrow. "Whoever did this was an animal. It was probably—" He stopped talking abruptly, and turned his face away from Farrell. He cleared his throat several times, and played with the knot of his wine-red tie.

"Probably who?" Farrell asked. "If you've got a suspicion, why not share it?"

Diaz stopped playing with his tie, and turned his face back toward Farrell. "Let me make myself clear," he said. "You're obviously a person of sincere intentions, but you're out of your depth in this part of town. Social workers and well-meaning white people don't have any idea of the squalor and brutality we live with every day here. There are men in this part of town who'd kill you for the change in your pocket. How do you expect to find Lottie's killer, much less do anything about it?"

Farrell fought to keep the emotion from his face. He knew Diaz was judging him on what he could see—a well-off white man with a do-gooder streak—and it galled him in a way that few other things had. A tart rejoinder sprang to his lips, but before he could utter it, the irony of his situation struck him, and he calmed down, forcing his arms and hands to relax at his sides.

"Don't be too sure that what you're seeing is all you get, Diaz," he said. "I came up in streets like this, and I know as well as you what goes on. The trouble is, I don't think Lottie just ran into a rough heister or happened to be in the wrong place at the wrong time. She was strangled, then shot once in the head. I'm thinking that somebody was shutting her up, and sending a message to anybody else who might know what she knew."

Diaz's face lost its look of polite contempt and became thoughtful. "But Lottie was just a social worker. What could she know that would interest a gangster?"

"That's what I'm trying to find out," Farrell said. "Her mother and sister said she worked extensively with you and that you knew what went on in this part of town. If you know anything, even have a vague suspicion, it's worth hearing. Don't you want her killer found?"

"Of course I want the killer found," Diaz said with exasperation. "I just don't know why I should tell you anything. You're not from the police."

Farrell paused for what he hoped was dramatic effect, then, "Have any policemen been to see you yet?"

Diaz looked down, his jaw muscles working. "No. Not so far."

"I've got connections with the police," Farrell said in a softer voice. "If I can find something out that looks useful, they'll investigate it. You have my word on it."

Diaz looked up, chewing his bottom lip. He stared into Farrell's face for a moment, then said, "Come back to my office." He turned on his heel and Farrell followed him down a hallway to a small office with a window covered by dusty burlap curtains. After Farrell came inside, he closed the door and gestured toward a battered and nicked mahogany side chair. Diaz took a similar chair behind a scarred desk and began to talk.

"Sorry I acted like that," he said. "Lottie's death has been a real blow to me."

Farrell nodded. "I can see that. An accident would have been bad enough, but this was no accident."

"No," Diaz said. "And I can think of only one person rotten enough, cruel enough, to have done something like this. His name is Sleepy Moyer." Unconsciously, perhaps, Diaz had lowered his voice as he spoke Moyer's name, as if he feared the man might hear him in an adjoining room.

Farrell nodded. "I've heard the name. He's a gun punk, a heroin pusher, a pimp—just about every rotten thing a man can be and still stand up on two legs. What makes you think he might be the killer?"

Diaz's face, in spite of its craggy ruggedness, reflected the struggle of a man trying to keep a lid on his fear. His jaw muscles bunched several times, and he blinked rapidly as he spoke. "There were a few girls who came here that this Moyer was trying to corrupt. He had begun following them as they'd leave the center, offering them Coca-Colas at the corner store. A couple he'd given silver charm bracelets to."

"Lottie found out about it?" Farrell ventured.

"She heard some of the other kids talking about it, and she began watching. One day he was out there, smiling at them, taking hold of some of their hands and making over them. Well, Lottie went wild," Diaz said, offering a sick grin to the memory. "She went outside with a corn broom, started giving him hell. I didn't even know she knew language like that. He offered to slap her, and she took the broom and began smacking him with it. She was a pretty good-sized woman, you know, and he isn't that tall."

He paused a moment, and rubbed a shaky hand over his brow. "He tried to get the broom away from her, but she began punching him in the ribs with the handle. He didn't have a chance. I stood on the porch watching. I should have helped her. I should have gone out there and knocked him down." He face was working and he had one hand pressed against his mouth. His eyes were screwed into a squint of pure anguish. "But . . . but I was afraid. I wasn't as good a man as that woman." He turned his face to the window, and looked through it while tears welled up in his eyes.

"So you think Moyer might have laid for her, and killed her for making him look bad," Farrell said.

"Who else could have done it?" he cried. "They loved her in this part of town. She'd brought things to every child in this godforsaken place. She'd comforted every pregnant woman, she'd helped men get jobs—I can't believe anyone who lived in Gert Town would have killed her like that. Everybody had been touched by her, everybody."

"Well, I'd say that was pretty interesting stuff," Farrell said after a moment of silence. "I appreciate you giving me so much of your time. I'll keep in touch." He got up from his chair.

Diaz turned and got up quickly. He reached across his desk to Farrell, the fingers groping blindly. "Please don't tell anyone I talked to you. Please don't." His face was twisted with shame, but his eyes pleaded for Farrell's promise.

Farrell looked at him. "Nobody will know about it from me," he said. Then he turned and left the room, but as he reached back to close the door, he saw Diaz, his elbows propped on the desk and his face buried in his hands.

Farrell walked past the painting class and outside to his car. He didn't notice Sleepy Moyer standing in the doorway of a corner grocery across the street. Moyer's dark eyes lit with recognition as Farrell's face became visible, and he stroked his chin thoughtfully. When Farrell's car pulled away from the curb, Sleepy got into a green LaSalle, started it, and pulled away in pursuit.

Billie Talmadge got off the bus on Florida Avenue, near Bayou St. John, and pulled her cheap, threadbare coat closely around her. Mardi Gras was only about two weeks off, and it was still colder than the south end of a northbound frog. She shivered, and walked briskly down a side street. About two blocks in, she came to an elaborately constructed shotgun single, painted canary yellow and covered with intricate gingerbread trim. She went up on the porch and knocked at the door. After a moment, the door opened and Walt Daggett stood there with a heavy-caliber Astra automatic in his right hand.

"What do you want?" Walt asked gruffly.

"Can I come in? It's cold out here," Billie said, dancing around as a gust of chill wind hit her bare legs. Walt stood aside, scanned the street, then closed the door behind her.

Billie saw that the gas log in the small fireplace was going, and walked over to it. She turned her backside to the fire and rubbed her arms vigorously with her hands.

"How are you, Walt?" she asked as he walked into the room and sat down in an armchair.

"What do you want?" Walt asked again, his voice irritable.

"Israel's supposed to be back in town," she said. "Doggy McGee told me last night when he came in to get his ashes hauled. I thought you'd want to know."

"That's old news, baby sister," Walt said. "Why you think I'm walkin' around with this?" He hefted the heavy Spanish automatic, then placed it on the arm of his chair.

"You ain't got nothin' to worry about," Billie said. "You didn't do nothin' to him."

"How would you know?" Walt asked scornfully.

" 'Cause I saw Junior when they hit him. I know it wasn't you done it."

Walt's body bucked upright, his eyes showing white all around and his hands quivering. "What'd you say?"

"I know lots of people think you framed your cousin 'cause he got you fired off the police force," Billie said. "Prob'ly Iz thinks so, too, but I know different."

Walt's head turned quickly toward her. He looked at her sharply, his gaze intense, his thumb fingering the safety on his gun. Finally, he said, "If you know who done it, why'd you let Iz go to prison?"

" 'Cause I was scared," she said impatiently. "Why the hell do you think I stayed clammed up? The cops wouldn't of paid no mind to a whore, and as soon as things quieted down, the killer would of come for me. My mama didn't raise no fool."

"Then why come to me?" Walt asked, pacing the room. "It's nothing to me."

"I'll tell you why," Billie said. "I'm tired. Tired of the life, tired of workin' from one fix to another. I'm only twenty, but I look thirty-five. Pretty soon, nobody's gonna want me. I want to be taken care of by somebody'll do me right. What I know oughta be worth that much." She paused for a moment, and then struggled to put a friendly smile on her face. "You and me useta get along pretty good before your cousin found us together that time. I still like you, Walt. We could be friends again, couldn't we?"

Walt looked at her thoughtfully. "Anybody know you came here?" he asked.

"Not a soul. I told Ma that I was goin' out to buy some hairpins and perfume. If I don't come back, she'll just hire some new chippie to take my place."

Walt scratched his head and looked thoughtfully at her. "All right, you can stay here for a while. But I want you to do one thing. I want you to write down everything you saw that night. As good as you can remember it."

Billie smiled way back in her jaws, the same smile she used on the men who came to see her. It was a smile that reached down into the groin and around into the hip pocket. "Okay. Whatever you say. You won't be sorry, Walt honey," she said.

Wesley Farrell pulled to a stop outside a five-story office building on Camp Street. The purple-and-gold Mardi Gras banners and tinsel that had begun to sprout in various places as the early parades began to roll looked forlorn in the bitterly cold wind that swept down from the northwest. He shivered and turned up the collar of his coat as he walked toward the building entrance.

The Community Service Agency was located on the top floor, so Farrell entered the elevator cage and asked the young Negro woman operator to take him up to five. He got out and found himself standing in pile carpet so deep that he left footprints in it as he walked.

The agency's reception desk was just across from the elevator, so he walked over.

"I'm Wesley Farrell, a friend of the Sonnier family," he told the young brunette receptionist. "I wonder if I can talk to Mrs. Taylor?"

"I'll see if she's free," the young woman said. Within a few seconds she had the agency director on her intercom, and announced Farrell's arrival. She lifted her head and said to him, "She'll see you now. Her office is just down that corridor on the left." She pointed with a slim, manicured hand, and Farrell touched a finger to the brim of his hat as he walked away.

The rooms and corridors were painted an immaculate white, and their simple elegance was broken only occasionally by an oil painting or an Audubon print. Furniture was strictly utilitarian, with no frills or architectural statements being made. He saw a woman standing in the hall as he approached. She was tall, slim, and sophisticated looking, dressed in a dark-blue skirt and jacket and a cream-colored blouse with a floppy bow tied at the neck.

"Mr. Farrell? I'm Sallie Taylor," she said. "Please come in." She gestured to an open door, and allowed him to precede her before she closed the door behind them.

"The receptionist said you were a friend of the Sonnier family," she said without preamble. "How can I help you?" She was all business.

Farrell unbuttoned his topcoat but didn't remove it. He sat down in a leather chair across from Sallie Taylor's desk, and placed his hat on the floor beside him. "I'm looking into Lottie's death at the request of the family," he said. "I was wondering if you could give me some idea of her movements on the day she disappeared."

"Are you with the police?" she asked dubiously.

"No, but I work with them sometimes, and pass along anything that I get," he said in what he hoped was a persuasive tone. He was deviating further and further from the truth with each interview, but he was determined to find Lottie's killer no matter how many lies he had to tell.

She looked at him levelly, and after a moment nodded as though she'd made up her mind.

She opened a pad on her desk and consulted it for a moment. "According to her assignment sheet for yesterday, she was supposed to visit Gert Town Community Center, then make some home visits in Mid-City with three unwed mothers, and if time permitted near the end of the day, she wrote down that she had a young prostitute she was counseling."

"A prostitute?" Casey said. "Any name?"

Sallie Taylor looked down at the pad briefly, then shook her head. "She doesn't say here, but I remember speaking to her about it earlier, and I got a strong impression that she knew the woman, or had known her at an earlier time."

"Hmmm," Farrell said. "If she was trying to get a girl out of the life, she could have made a bad enemy out of the woman's pimp. Is there any way we can find out the name of this woman?"

"Possibly," Sallie Taylor said. "It'll require some looking. Lottie was an excellent social worker who made a lot of progress in the projects she tackled, but unfortunately she was less meticulous in her paperwork. Sometimes reports on her assignments got filed well after the resolution came. I'll have to look through her files and see if she did any preliminary paperwork on the case."

"I'd appreciate it," Farrell said, handing her a card. "You can reach me or leave a message at one of those numbers. Can you tell me anything else about her, her movements, her life outside the office?"

"She didn't have much life out of the office," Sallie Taylor replied. "I remember that she was involved some years ago with a Negro police officer who had been sent to prison for killing a man. He was supposed to be getting out about this time and returning here. More recently she was seeing another man, but I don't know his name." She stopped talking for a moment, then her eyes flickered with a sudden recollection. "Excuse me for a moment. I just thought of something."

She got up and left the room. She was gone for several minutes before returning with something in her hand. "I remembered seeing this out on her desk, but for some reason she'd put it in one of her drawers, and it took me a while to find it."

She handed the picture to Farrell, and he saw it was a candid photograph taken at a negro nightclub called The Brown Fedora. Lottie was there, laughing, in a strapless cocktail dress. Sitting beside her, also laughing happily, was Dandy Walker. Farrell nodded, handing the photograph back to Sallie Taylor.

"Anything else you can think of?"

Sallie Taylor's face lost some of its professional polish, and some of her emotions began to register. "No. I wish to God I could. I liked her a lot, and admired her for what she'd done in the colored sections of town. There's no telling what she could have accomplished if she hadn't . . . if she'd lived."

Farrell nodded. "Yeah. Thanks for your time, Mrs. Taylor. If you can find anything on that prostitute, please call me day or night." He got up and picked up his hat from the floor.

"I will. I hope you get the louse who did this," she said, her face crumpling a bit. She turned away quickly, and began straightening some papers as Farrell left the office.

Sleepy Moyer sat with his hat tipped down over his eyes across the street from the Community Service Agency. According to his gold watch, Farrell had been in there for a half hour. His trips to Merton Diaz and Lottie Sonnier's place of work could only mean he was interested in Lottie's death.

Sleepy knew just enough about Farrell to know that he could be a problem. Nobody knew why a rich white man like Farrell had so many interests and friends in the colored community, but whispers about the things he had fixed and the small injustices he had corrected, sometimes by force, had been floating around the underworld for years.

Sleepy's hand went to the Luger in his pocket. It might be that the simplest thing for everybody was to pick him off right now, before he got to be a problem. Stella wouldn't like it that he didn't call her first, but that was just too damn bad. Once Farrell was out of the way, there was no need for her to know anything about it. What was it his grandma had always said? 'Least said, soonest mended.'

He removed the Luger from his pocket, worked the toggle, and fed a fresh cartridge into the breech of the German automatic. He then turned the ignition switch and let the La Salle idle. He took good care of it, and it idled like a purring cat. Farrell had to be out soon, so all he had to do was be patient. It was easy to be patient when you got to put the pencil on somebody at the end. He grinned at the thought.

It was a bit less than ten minutes later that the glass doors to the building opened and a tall man came out buttoning his overcoat. Sleepy instantly recognized that it was Farrell. He placed his left forearm on the open window ledge, then extended his right hand with the Luger out until it was braced on the left arm. He gazed down the length of the barrel, breathing lightly as he gently squeezed the trigger. The Luger roared and bucked in his hand, and he saw Farrell's hat fly off his head and the tall man go down behind his car.

Before he'd even touched the wheel, Sleepy had the La Salle in gear, racing uptown on Camp at a high rate of speed. His heart was pounding with excitement, and the smell of burnt cordite was like perfume in his flared nostrils.

8

Dandy Walker and Daggett arrived in front of the Sonnier house a few minutes before 5:00 P.M. Israel got out and stood for a moment looking at the house, as if searching for a memory to which he could not put a name. He remained there until Dandy touched his shoulder. He looked at his old friend and saw the lines of his face blurring as Dandy struggled with some strong emotion.

"Reckon we oughta go inside now," Daggett said. For the moment he felt as though his grief had burned up inside him, and he opened the gate and led the way up to the porch.

At his knock, Marguerite opened the door. He stared at her, somewhat surprised to see how mature she was. When he'd left for prison, Marguerite had seemed like a child to him. "You've grown up, little girl," he murmured.

Marguerite placed her hands on his deep chest and laid her head against them. "I'm glad you're home, Israel," she said, her voice a bit muffled by the fabric of his coat.

She let go, and stood back to let them in. When she looked at Dandy, her face lost the sweet, vulnerable look with which she had greeted Daggett, and became stiff and formal. "Good afternoon, Dandy," she said. Her voice was cool. Surprised, Daggett searched her face, and then Dandy's, but saw no explanation in their expressions.

Dandy stood stiff and upright, his face devoid of emotion. "Afternoon, Marguerite," he said.

Further conversation was interrupted by the entry of 'Tee Ruth into the room. She walked up to Daggett, grasped his shoulders, and hugged him. "Welcome home, son. I wish you didn't have to find things like they is." Her eyes were shiny, but she kept the tears inside. "Hello, Dandy. You comin' to the wake with us?"

"Yes, ma'am, if it's no trouble," Dandy said in an inflectionless voice.

"That's fine," 'Tee Ruth said.

"If it's all right I'll let Iz ride with you so he can catch up on things, and I'll go over separate in my own car," Dandy said. "I'll leave now, and see you over there."

Marguerite spoke. "Thank you, Dandy. That's real kind. Thank you for bringing Israel home to us." She was still coldly formal, and Dandy's face remained stiff and blank. He nodded, and left the house.

Daggett could feel the level of tension in the room lessen as soon as Dandy left. He looked at Marguerite and Ruth in the hope of gaining some understanding of what was going on, but the young woman stared at Dandy's retreating figure and said nothing. Ruth was busy pinning a black pillbox hat and veil on her gray hair.

"I hope this won't be too hard on you, son," Ruth said as she picked up her coat. Daggett took the heavy garment and held it for her.

"I got to go, 'Tee Ruth," he said. "I want to see her once more before . . ." He couldn't finish.

"I'm right glad, Isr'al," Ruth said as she turned back to him and began buttoning her coat. "She don't look bad at all. She looks just like she's sleepin'."

Daggett nodded dumbly and turned to Marguerite. She was shrugging into her own coat. He stepped over to help her, and she looked over her shoulder at him with a winsome smile. "Would you mind driving?" she asked. "I don't feel completely up to it."

"No," Daggett replied. "Not at all. Where are they having it?"

"It's at the Christ's Majesty Funeral Parlor on Dryades Street," she replied. "You know the way?"

"Yeah," Daggett said.

"I'm glad you're back," she said, reaching up a hand to touch his cheek. As her hand made contact with his skin, he closed his eyes. She held it there until he opened them, and saw she wore a small, sad smile. He returned it with one of his own.

The telephone rang in the cat-eyed woman's apartment, and she answered it. "Yeah," she said.

"It's Poche," a man's voice answered.

"What you got?"

"Daggett's holed up in the Metro Hotel," Poche said, "but he left there late this afternoon and went to the Sonnier house with Dandy Walker. We figure he's goin' with the mother and sister to the Sonnier broad's wake. What do you want to do?"

"Keep a tail on him," she replied. "We can't hit him at the wake. There ain't no tellin' how many people might be there, and we can't risk getting him with a bunch of witnesses." She thought for a moment, and Poche waited silently at his end of the line. He knew better than to press her. Finally, she spoke again.

"The best thing to do is to keep him in sight until he goes back to the Metro. Put a couple of men in his room to wait for him. No guns, understand?"

"Look, Stella," Poche said, his voice uncertain and conciliatory at the same time. "Joe would—"

"Don't tell me what Joe would do," Stella flared. "I'm handlin' this to keep Joe from worryin' about it, understand?"

"If this gets fucked up and turns into a mess," Poche said, "he's gonna be more than worried. He's liable to tear chunks offa me and you, too." His voice had gone flat, but it was plain. He didn't want to back her up.

"You chicken-shit bastard," Stella said in a cold, hard voice. "This is my business, not Joe's. If you want to cross me, I'll find a way to let him know you were sniffin' around me. Now do it, and don't come back until it's finished." She slammed the telephone down on the cradle and walked from the room. In the hall, she stood and fumed for a moment. Then she thought of someone she should call. Someone who could make certain things went off without any hitches. She went back to the desk and began dialing.

The Orleans Parish Prison was a forbidding granite structure just off Tulane Avenue behind the courthouse. It had the aspect of a medieval keep that was emphasized by the drear sky and the sheets of rain that lashed its smooth gray skin. Casey found a parking place near the entrance, and managed to get only half soaked on his way in.

Like most of the institutional buildings in the city, the jail had steam heat which took the chill out of his bones very quickly after he gained entrance. He checked at the chief deputy's office and surrendered his .38 Police Positive and the flat leather sap he carried in his hip pocket. From there he was escorted by a uniformed sheriff's deputy to an interview room with a scarred oak table and four ladder-backed oak chairs. Casey draped his wet overcoat and hat over one chair, then took up residence in another. He was packing his pipe with Sir Walter Raleigh when the door opened again.

Another uniformed deputy gently pushed a second man ahead of him. The man was of medium height and build, with an elegant carriage that contrasted oddly with the drab suit of prison overalls he wore. His face had the high cheekbones of an Indian brave, and merry green eyes that measured and inspected everything in his path. He had coal-black hair, and a neatly trimmed mustache over a mouth full of strong, white teeth. His eyes brightened when he saw Casey.

"Hiya, Frank," he said happily. "Come over to see how the other half live, eh?"

Casey stood up and took Murphy Culloz's hand and shook it. He smiled warmly, as if greeting an old friend, which in a way he was. "You're looking good, Murph. Jailhouse chow must agree with you."

"Hey, we get grits and bread every morning except Sunday, when they let us have an apple with it, beef stew every other day for lunch, and fried chicken on Saturday. It's just like home, except the sheets don't get ironed." Murphy hooked a chair with his leg and sat down across from Casey.

Casey signaled to the deputy that he could leave, and brought out a package of Old Gold cigarettes which he passed across the table.

"Mmmm," Culloz sighed appreciatively. "Tailor-made cigarettes. I miss them the most of all. Thanks, Frank." Culloz tore off the cellophane, tapped a cigarette from the pack, then leaned over the table to accept Casey's light. When he'd pulled in a lungful of smoke and expelled it luxuriously, he said, "Okay, Frank. You got me softened up. Now what do you want?" He grinned over at the red-haired detective.

Casey leaned back and sucked on his pipe as he measured the

man across from him. Murphy Culloz had been a detective sergeant once, before the Gus Moroni scandal broke. An internal investigation had turned up about a dozen officers involved in corruption of one kind or another, and Culloz had been one of the last to fall. He was in Parish Prison waiting for sentencing before being transferred to Angola.

"I just wanted to see how you were doin', Murph," Casey said. "I get lonesome for you every once in a while."

"Bullshit," Culloz said with a grin. "If it wasn't for you, I wouldn't be rotting in here now. What's the pitch?"

"Remember Israel Daggett?"

"A shine dick, and a good one," Culloz said. "I was still riding high when that case broke. The old man handled it himself," he said as he fingered his black mustache. "What about him?"

"They let him out two days ago," Casey said. "Word is, he's coming back here."

"Oh, yeah?" Culloz said with a breath of smoke. "I wish him well, the lucky stiff."

"Not so lucky," Casey said. "His old girlfriend was murdered two nights ago. It's a strange coincidence, wouldn't you say?"

Culloz's face became sober. "Damn. That's rotten luck. I feel for the guy."

"Murph, you and I used to be friends of a sort," Casey said after a brief pause. "I want to make you an offer."

Culloz's black eyes got bright and alert. "Make your pitch."

"I want to know if any of you guys in with Moroni had anything to do with pinning the Obregon kill on Daggett," Casey said. "I know how Moroni felt about Negro cops, and I know he wasn't alone in those feelings."

Culloz regarded Casey for a moment, his face a stone mask but his eyes flickering like fingers on an adding machine. "What's in it for me if I help you out?" he said finally.

"You're looking at a five-to-ten-year stretch at 'Gola," Casey said. "Choppin' cane and dodging rattlesnakes, and any con up there with a shiv and a grudge against cops. Talk straight to me, and when your case goes before the pardon board in eighteen months, I'll go up there and tell them you willingly helped me on an important case."

Culloz gave Casey a sidelong leer, and scratched the back of his neck as he leaned back in his chair. "You ain't offerin' much, ole buddy. Can't you do more than that?"

Casey shook his head. "I can't and you know it. The pardon board's made up entirely of bible-thumpers from upstate who think we're Sodom and Gomorrah down here. All you got going for you is my reputation as a straight cop, so take it or leave it."

Culloz's eyes twinkled merrily, and he laughed at Casey's serious mien. "You can't blame a guy for tryin', Frank." He paused and scratched his neck again. "Obregon was nothing but a punk. Gus might've stepped on his face if he was lying in front of him, but he wouldn't've walked across the street to do it."

"What about the others?" Casey asked.

"Daggett broke a couple big cases after they put him in plain clothes, which was some trick for a nigger cop with no inside track to anything big. It didn't bother me, but some of the other guys didn't like it much. Me, I never saw any percentage in hating a guy because he had black skin, but everybody ain't as enlightened as I am." He laughed, then lit a fresh cigarette off the butt of his first one.

"Can you see any of them tying a can on Daggett's tail just because they hated Negroes?" Casey asked.

Culloz observed him with a sly grin, then shook his head. "Frankly, I can't. We were interested in making as much money as we could from graft. There was nothing in it for any of us to cause Daggett that much grief. Besides, he couldn't have hurt any of us. We had protection—that is, until you and that gambler turned Gus's lights out."

Casey nodded and drew on his pipe for a moment in silence. "What's your slant on how Daggett's gun got out of the locker room? How tough would that have been?"

"Well, the colored cops got their own locker room, and so far as I know, no white cop's ever gone in there. You know as well as I do that a white man goin' into a nigger place would be noticed by somebody. Whoever swiped the piece had to be a nigger, himself, is the way I'd look at it." Culloz smoked a while in silence, then Casey saw a light come into his eyes. He'd been rocking back on the rear legs of his straight-backed chair, but he came forward quickly.

"You look like you just got an idea," Casey said in a wry voice.

"Walt Daggett," Culloz said. "You remember, Daggett's cousin? The one got thrown off the force after he got caught with that coked-up jailbait?"

Casey took his pipe out of his mouth and raised his left eyebrow.

"Daggett, himself, made that arrest, and testified at Walt's hearing, didn't he?"

"Damn right," Culloz said in a triumphant voice. "He'd have known the layout at headquarters, and about his cousin's spare gun. Suppose he came in dressed in a uniform and walked back there between watches? Who'd have paid him any attention? All those guys look alike anyhow, 'specially if you put 'em in the same uniform. Christ, he could've gone in there and stolen things out of half the lockers in the place. Killing Obregon with Daggett's gun would have been a sweet way to pay him back for busting Walt off the force." Culloz's eyes were wide, and his face intense. He and Casey might have been two detectives in harness again, working on the same case.

Casey nodded, smiling a little. "It's a good idea, Murph, except they checked Walt, and he had an iron-clad alibi for that night. But some other Negro might have done it. Daggett had enemies." Casey paused and drew on his pipe for a moment. "You were a good dick, Murph. I wish I had you out here helping me on this."

"Hell, let me out for a couple days," Culloz said, feathering smoke out of his nostrils. "I could wrap up the case, put the real killer in jail, then you could get me a pardon right away. A pretty good deal, I think." He rocked back on his chair again, and grinned. He looked a lot younger, sitting there with his touseled hair and a cigarette burning cockily in the corner of his mouth.

Casey stood up and offered Culloz his hand. "I wish I could, Murph. Watch your back up there. It might be rough for a while."

Culloz's face sobered as he stood up to take Casey's hand. "Thanks, Frank. I'll be as careful as I know how. Drop me a card once in a while, will you?"

"Sure. I'll send some Old Golds up there, too."

"See ya around, kid," Murphy said, his face suddenly white with strain.

The door to the interview room opened, and the heavyset deputy came into the room. He took Culloz by the shoulder, and pushed him gently out into the corridor. Casey waited for a couple of minutes, then he followed, leaving the room vacant but for a cloud of tobacco smoke.

Wesley Farrell lay on the cold concrete sidewalk with skyrockets going on and off in front of his eyes. He reached up a hand and felt around his head. When he brought it back down to eye level, he was relieved to find no blood there. The shot had been so close it was like a dynamite kiss. He sat up quickly, and peered through the driver's side window of his car at the street, and could see nothing. Because of the weather, few people were out walking around, and the single shot hadn't been enough to bring anyone outside to investigate.

He looked around and found his hat, and found the crown shredded where the bullet had taken it off his head. Farrell's hands were shaking, and his mouth was like a desert. He got up, dusted off his overcoat, and got into the Packard. After he started the engine, he opened the glove compartment and brought out a Smith & Wesson revolver with a four-inch barrel and checked hard rubber grips. He broke the cylinder and saw the brass heads of six .32–20 cartridges reflecting light back at him. He laid the gun on the seat beside him, and drove away from Camp Street.

As he drove, he diverted his mind with what he'd learned so far. The story about the prostitute was interesting for any number of reasons. Sleepy Moyer was a pimp, and might have had a connection to the young whore.

Then there was the business of his humiliation at Lottie's hands in Gert Town. Being beaten by a lone woman with a broom would have been all over the city before the next morning's breakfast— reason enough for him to want to exact revenge.

Above and beyond that was what had just happened. Farrell knew he had enemies, but none with enough of a grudge to have him stalked and executed in broad daylight. He could not prove it, but his instincts told him there had to be a connection with the questions he was asking. He wondered who it was, and how they'd found out his involvement so quickly. It suggested to him an intelligence with a broad reach, something that only a big-time gangster like Dante might be able to bring together. It was an unpleasant thought.

For now, he had a breathing space, because his attacker surely thought he was dead for the time being. Farrell couldn't know how long that might last, so he knew he had to make the most of it.

Farrell headed across town to St. Claude Avenue. The street was a thriving commercial district with many Negro businesses on it, and not a few taverns and bars. A couple of calls had wised him to the fact that Sleepy did a lot of traveling on this street, and was well known there.

He parked on the street across from Levin's Department Store, and put the revolver in his right-hand overcoat pocket. Then he got out and strolled along the street with his overcoat buttoned and his collar pulled up against the gusty wind. Hatless, his thick, reddish-brown hair blew about his head, and he had to keep shaking it out of his eyes.

There weren't many white people along here, but the weather was too bad for anyone to pay him much attention. He strolled along, unconcerned by the weather until he found the place he was looking for. A sign in the shape of a policeman's head with a whistle in his mouth swung jerkily from a bracket, and below it swung a smaller sign that read, "The Whistle Stop." Farrell pushed open the door and stepped inside.

The tavern was already dim and smoky, and quite a few men were engaged in conversation or shooting pool. Farrell moved to the end of the bar, and stood there quietly until the bartender noticed him and strode toward him. The bartender was in his sixties, but moved with the cat-footed grace of a younger man, and his thick shoulders and chest stretched the fabric of a spotless white shirt almost to bursting. When he got closer, Farrell said, "Hello, Sarge."

Sarge squinted, then thrust out a huge, meaty hand. "Mr. Farrell, ain't it? By damn, it is. How are ya?"

Farrell took the paw and tried not to wince at the pressure of Sarge's grip. "Glad to see you, Sarge."

Sarge's mouth opened, and provided Farrell with a pearlescent display of large white teeth. "You're a sight for sore eyes. Have a drink." He reached under the bar and brought out a bottle of bonded Old Forester and two glasses. When he'd filled them, he pushed one over to Farrell, and lifted his own. "Here's how." He downed the hundred proof liquor like it was apple juice, and set the empty glass on the bar.

Farrell took a drink, and nodded his appreciation. "I could use a little information, if you've got it."

Sarge got a cagy expression on his face, and leaned over the bar toward Farrell. "Cop stuff?"

Farrell took out a package of Lucky Strikes and shook some out of the package. Sarge took one, and accepted Farrell's light. The old man inhaled half the length of the cigarette in one draw, and expelled enough smoke to screen a squadron of destroyers.

"You hear about Lottie Sonnier?" Farrell asked.

Sarge nodded, grim faced. "Yeah. A lotta people are gonna miss that girl."

"Her mother and sister asked me to look into it," Farrell said. "I said I'd try to help."

Sarge nodded. "A little out of your line, ain't it?"

"A little," Farrell admitted, "but I know a lot of people, and I figured if I asked enough questions, somebody might accidentally let something slip."

Sarge nodded again. "You got any ideas yet?"

"I heard a story earlier today about how Lottie caught Sleepy Moyer trying to turn some young girls out over in Gert Town, and beat him up with a broom. Sleepy's a bad actor, and I decided to run it down."

"That little skunk," Sarge said. "He might have just enough guts to kill a woman. I know of some he has hurt, plenty, although he didn't kill any of 'em."

"So you don't think the idea's all wet," Farrell said.

"Damn right," Sarge said. "He likes to hurt things, and I reckon he could kill pretty easy. I'm almost sure he killed a rival pimp. Shotgunned him and his woman in bed. But I couldn't prove it. It wouldn't be easy to pin anything on Sleepy. Punks like him are usually dumb, but he's different. He's careful and shrewd."

"If he killed Lottie, he was pretty careful this time, too," Farrell said. "Frank Casey said they had practically nothing to go on."

"Reckon Israel Daggett's back in town yet?" Sarge asked, abruptly changing the subject.

"Probably. I heard he was coming," Farrell replied. "He and Lottie were supposed to be pretty close."

"Lottie was a lot of woman," Sarge said. "She was loyal to Daggett in her own way, but she liked to kick up her heels too much to enter the convent. I've seen her in here with several fellas over the past few years."

Farrell looked up with a gleam of interest in his eyes. "Such as who?"

"Well, let's see," Sarge said, stroking his chin. "Coupla years back she was keepin' Gil Boudreaux pretty busy. He's a lawyer. There was a clothing store owner, too, Waterston was his name. Owns that place way down on Claiborne Avenue."

"Anybody else?"

"Last time I saw her, six months back, she was pretty thick with Dandy Walker," Sarge said.

"The prize-fighter?" Farrell asked, playing dumb.

"That's the one. Has a gym now, and trains fighters," Sarge said. "Has a youngster he brought over here from Lake Charles who might be a contender, they say."

"Well, Sarge," Farrell said, scratching the back of his neck. "Not much gets by you, does it?"

"Not much," the old man said with a smug grin.

"This thing with Walker. Was it serious, you think?" Farrell asked.

"Can't say from her side, but he followed that gal like a pupdog on a leash," Sarge said. "But she was some woman. Any number of guys would've been willing to follow her anywhere. Reckon he's pretty cut up about her death, as close as they been."

Farrell stared at the bar for a moment, then his eyes brightened as he thought of something. "Sarge, you ever hear of a woman named Stella Bascomb? Supposed to be a looker with cat's eyes."

Sarge got a sardonic grin on his face. "Now you're talkin' about something."

"You know her?" Farrell asked.

"No, but know plenty about her," Sarge replied. "She came to town six or eight years ago; I forget. Anyhow, I figured her for just another cute baby whore, but she must've had somethin' special the men liked. A lotta men wanted to take that gal home in their pockets, but she was as dangerous as all get-out. She got arrested on a cutting beef—damn near took a man's arm off with a cutthroat razor, but the guy wouldn't press charges. Can you beat it?"

"What's she doin' now?" Farrell asked.

"Moved up in the world, I hear," Sarge said. "She was too cute and too wild to keep whorin' for nickels and dimes."

"Any chance she's mixed up in narcotics traffic?"

"Who knows?" Sarge said, shrugging. "She was a wild girl— maybe she still is."

Farrell nodded. "Hmmm. Okay, Sarge. Thanks for the information. I'll see you around." He shook hands with the ex-police sergeant, and walked out of the bar, hitching up his coat collar around his exposed neck and ears as he walked.

Sarge began wiping the bar with a clean towel, a scowl on his face. He'd liked both Israel and Lottie, and the hard luck that had befallen them troubled him greatly. He was so deep in his ruminations that he failed to notice a tall, thin, tan-colored man get up from the bar about ten feet from him and walk to the telephone booth in the rear of the bar.

The man dialed an Uptown exchange number and dropped in his nickel. The line buzzed twice before somebody picked up.

"Yeah," Stella's voice said.

"Stella, this is Mops," the slender Negro said. "You know a white man name of Farrell?"

"Wesley Farrell?" she asked. "What about him?"

"I'm at the Whistle Stop havin' a few drinks when this Farrell comes in. Sarge drops everything and greets him like a long-lost brother."

"Go on," she said, interest mounting in her voice.

"Farrell and Sarge talked about that Sonnier broad who got killed day before yesterday. Talked about Sleepy Moyer maybe bein' responsible."

"They don't know a thing about it," she said unconcernedly. "But why is this Farrell mixin' in this?"

"He asked Sarge about you, too," Mops said.

"What?" the voice said.

"He wanted to know was you mixed up in any dope business," Mops explained.

"What in the hell would put him on that?" Stella asked, her voice edgy and unsure. Before Mops could reply, she said, "Get after him, see where he goes. When he lights somewhere, you call me quick, understand?"

"I'm gone," Mops said. He hung up the phone and left the bar.

9

The visitation at Christ's Majesty Funeral Parlor on Dryades Street was quiet and solemn, and the wake that followed was little different. Lottie's friends and the people she helped came in throngs to pay their respects and express their sympathies to Ruth and Marguerite.

Israel sat with them, his face turned to stone and his eyes as glazed as a drunkard's. He would take the hands of the people who offered them, but his eyes and ears seemed to register none of the sights and sounds directed to him. Life seemed to have departed his body, leaving behind only a thing that occasionally moved, and looked vaguely like Israel Daggett. Dandy Walker stood at his shoulder, shaking hands with many of the same people. He, too, seemed pulled within himself, and his face was as empty as a cue ball.

Frank Casey entered the wake with his hat in his hand and his wet overcoat unbuttoned. A lock of gray-shot red hair fell like a comma over his right eyebrow, and his blue eyes darted around the room like they had lives of their own. He walked over to the family and offered his hand to 'Tee Ruth.

"How are you, 'Tee Ruth?" he asked quietly.

The skin around her mouth and eyes was tight and strained, but she answered him with the placidity of one who believes staunchly in the mysterious symmetry of life and death. "I am as well as can be, Mister Frank," she replied. "It's the others I fear for." She moved her head almost imperceptibly in the direction of Marguerite and Israel, who sat like statues beside each other, and Dandy who stood

behind. Marguerite was a pretty, vivacious girl under other circumstances, but tonight her manner was listless.

Casey nodded to the old woman, and walked over to them. He
offered his hand to Daggett. "Hello, Marguerite. Hello, Dandy,
Israel. It's a poor excuse for a homecoming, but I'm glad to see
you again." Dandy and Marguerite were shaken from their trances
sufficiently to nod and smile to Casey.

Daggett looked up at him, and recognition dawned slowly on his
long face. "Inspector Casey," he said, taking the other man's hand.
"How are you?"

"It's captain now," Casey replied. "Not bad, I guess. Unhappy
about this. Do you feel like talking to me for a moment?"

Daggett stood up, and followed Casey to the edge of the room,
his hands hanging loosely at his sides.

"I'm sorry as I can be about this," Casey said. "She was a wonderful person. I aim to find who did this and hurt them as much as I'm
able when I do."

Daggett stared at him, nodding slowly. "I'd like to help you, but
I'm . . ." His voice trailed off, testifying to the helpless inertia he felt
just then.

"I hate to ask you this, but is there any chance she was killed to
hurt you?" Casey asked.

"I was in prison until two days ago," Daggett said. "I been out
of circulation so long, I can't imagine why anybody'd care to hurt
me. Seems like they'd've hit me in the pen long time ago, if they
was gonna."

"Let me try something else on you then. I hear she had a fight
with Sleepy Moyer and humiliated him not long ago," Casey said.
"You ever have any run-ins with Moyer?"

Daggett nodded again. "I licked him once for cuttin' a whore.
But that was ages ago." However, his eyes gleamed strangely, and
Casey could see him seriously entertaining the idea that Moyer could
be involved. Prison hadn't drained away his policeman's instinctive
suspicion of the criminal class.

"Think about it when you get the chance," Casey said. "I've got
a few more leads to run down before I begin to take anybody seriously,
but he's bound to be on the list of suspects." He paused and tugged
at his earlobe. "If it means anything, I never believed you were guilty
of killing Junior Obregon. I'm going to try and have the case reopened

and to see if we can clear you. You were too good a cop to have done what they said."

Daggett's eyes looked at Casey as if actually seeing him for the first time. "Thanks, Captain. I appreciate your faith in me."

"Go on back over there with 'Tee Ruth and Marguerite," Casey said. "I'll talk more to you after all this is . . . later." He grimaced as he struggled to find neutral language.

Daggett nodded, and walked back to the family table and sat down beside Marguerite. Casey noticed that as he did so, Marguerite reached for his hand, and he let her take it. They sat very still beside each other, saying nothing and not looking at each other.

Before he turned away, Casey noticed one of the funeral parlor employees come to Dandy Walker, whisper something in his ear, then lead him away from the family group. Casey knew Dandy had been seen out with Lottie, and realized that he might be handling some of the funeral business for the family. The Sonniers and Daggett were lucky to have a friend at a time like this.

Casey felt hungry, and moved to a buffet table full of fried soft-shell crabs, gumbo, crawfish etouffe, and other Creole-style delicacies. He hadn't eaten all day, and made himself a crab sandwich and a plate of gumbo. After he got himself a glass of beer, he sat down at a vacant table and began eating. He was chewing a bite of sandwich when a young Negro man approached his table.

"Are you Captain Casey of the police?" he asked in a cultured voice.

Casey blotted his lips with a paper napkin, stood up, and replied, "Yes. And you are . . . ?"

"Michael Dixon," the young man said. "I work for Community Service Agency, and knew Lottie quite well."

"Sit down," Casey said, gesturing to a vacant chair across from him. Without further talk, the young man sat down. He was of medium height and build, with aquiline features and crisp black hair. He wore a gray suit with a white shirt and red velvet tie, and wore a college ring on his right ring finger.

"What can I do for you, Mr. Dixon?" Casey asked when they were seated.

"I'd like to help you find Lottie's killer," Dixon said.

"You have some information?"

Dixon cast his eyes down, and gnawed briefly on his bottom lip, then he said, "Lottie was a courageous woman, but she often delved into things beyond a social worker's realm of effective action." He cast his eyes down for moment. "She confided some of her suspicions to me, and I asked her to go to the police before continuing. I wish she'd listened to me."

Casey put down his sandwich and looked closely at Dixon. "What were those things Lottie was looking into, if you don't mind."

"Narcotics," Dixon said. "Flowing into the Negro community at a shocking rate. We've seen numerous youngsters subverted by narcotics, and then adopting criminal behavior. Petty theft, robbery, murder, and prostitution have claimed a number already."

Casey nodded. "I get reports on that from the Negro Detective Squad all the time now. What had Lottie found?"

"She told me something recently that I dismissed at the time, but her death caused me to think of it again," Dixon said. "There's a white gangster in the city named Joe Dante. Lottie said she knew of some Negroes working with him that she believed were helping him channel illegal operations into our part of town. She was trying to find out more about them before she was killed." He shook his head sadly. "I begged her to take what she knew to the police, but she didn't feel she had enough information."

Casey's eyes seemed to grow larger, and he pushed his plate of food to one side as he leaned across the table toward Dixon. "Did she give you any names?"

"Walter Daggett was one that she mentioned," Dixon said. "I think he was a policeman at one time, and I know he's the cousin of Israel Daggett." He nodded in the direction of the Sonnier family table.

"Any others?"

"She told me of a woman she'd heard of, a Negro woman involved in prostitution, and worse things Lottie suspected her of. She mentioned her several times, but never told me the woman's name."

"Damn," Casey said. "Did she mention anything about her, beyond her suspicions?"

Dixon scratched the back of his neck while he thought, then he looked up suddenly. "She said the woman had slanted eyes, like a cat's. Once or twice she referred to her as 'the cat-eyed woman.' "

"Hmmm," Casey said. "That's a lot more than I had when I came in here, Dixon. I appreciate it very much. Here's one of my cards. If you think of anything else, or hear something from the street, please call me at either of those numbers."

Dixon took the card, glanced briefly at it, then slid it into the breast pocket of his gray flannel jacket. Then he stood up. "I hope you get the ones who did this. Lottie was . . . special. I'm going to miss her very much."

Casey stood up, too, and offered his hand to Dixon. "Lottie was a friend of mine, too. We won't give up on this one, I promise."

Nerves were dancing along the planes of Dixon's face as he shook Casey's hand. Then he nodded, and walked away quickly.

"Lottie, you sure had a power," Casey said to himself. He wondered how many other men in the crowd around him had been in love with her. He looked around until he found an employee of the funeral home, and walked over to him. He casually removed his leather folder and opened it discreetly so that the man could see the gold shield pinned inside.

"I'm Captain Casey of the police," he said. "I wonder if you could let me use a telephone for a minute or two."

The employee, a well-dressed man with skin the color of old parchment, said, "Just this way, please," and led Casey out of the large room into a corridor, and down the corridor to an office. They met Dandy Walker coming out. His eyes were sad and drawn down at the edges. He stood to one side, and allowed them to pass.

The office must have been the parlor owner's, because it was nicely furnished with a mahogany desk and chair, a sofa of purple damask, and two leather-upholstered wing chairs in front of the desk.

"No one will disturb you here, Captain," the funeral employee said. "Use it for as long as you want."

Casey nodded his thanks and picked up the receiver. It was still warm from someone's hand, probably Dandy's. He dialed the main headquarters number. When the desk sergeant answered, he asked for Inspector Grebb.

"Grebb," the man said at the other end.

"This is Casey. "What have you got on Joe Dante? Anything concerned with narcotics traffic?"

"Suspicions, but not much else," Grebb said. "He's got quite an organization built up with at least six layers between him and his distributors and street dealers. We've hauled people in several times, and most of 'em don't even know Dante's name. We spent time trying to help 'em remember, too, skipper, you can believe that."

"I'm at the Lottie Sonnier wake," Casey said. "One of her social work colleagues said she'd found something that connected Walt

Daggett to Dante. She also mentioned a woman described as having slanted eyes, like a cat's. Got anything on either of them?"

"Daggett's dirty," Grebb said, "and we've been watching him, hoping he'd get stupid and lead us to Dante. Hasn't happened yet, though, and might never. Daggett's gotten a lot cagier since he got thrown off the force. The woman I don't know about, but I'll check and see if any of my people know of her."

"Thanks," Casey said. "I'll check with you later."

"Gotcha, skipper."

Farrell was getting tired. He'd been all over the city today, been rained on and shot at, and hadn't had anything since the cup of coffee he'd had when Savanna came in the door that morning. He thought about going back to the Cafe Tristesse for some hot food and a shower, but had a thought. There was one more place he might try tonight before packing it in.

A half-hour later, he was on Louisiana Avenue below St. Charles Avenue. Ahead on his right was a large, well-lit building with a neon sign in the shape of a man's felt hat. Over the hat winked letters spelling the Brown Fedora. He pulled to the curb about a half-block down from it, and once more got out into the blustering winds.

He began hearing the music before he got to the door, and walked into the vestibule in time to hear Anna Lou Hamer and Lonnie Perez break into "Nobody Knows the Way." Anna Lou was the undisputed queen of Negro female vocalists in New Orleans, and was as cute as a bug's ear besides. Farrell stood in the entrance of the Negro nightclub tapping his foot and nodding his head as she sang notes up into the ceiling.

After a time, he gave his overcoat to a passing check girl, ran his fingers through his disordered hair a few times, then strolled into the large room. A wizened little brown man with steel-rimmed spectacles behind the bar spotted him, and raised a hand to catch his attention.

Farrell went over to the end of the bar and shook hands with the man. "How's it goin', Pops?" he asked with a grin.

"Man, I think the Depression must be 'bout over," Pops said. "Since I got Anna Lou in here, I got 'em standin' in line in the rain just to get in. What you doin' so far from your patch?"

Farrell leaned closer to the old man and his face went sober. "I'm mixing in the Lottie Sonnier murder. I've been around town trying to see what I could stir up."

"Anything floatin' to the top?" Pops asked.

"Sleepy Moyer, Walt Daggett, and Joe Dante," Farrell said. "Anything in that combination ring any bells with you?"

"What would a gal like Lottie be doin' with any of them?" the old man asked incredulously.

"Word is the three of them are mixed up in the dope traffic in the Negro sections of the city. Lottie was supposed to have been turning over rocks to find out about it."

"Jesus, Mary, and Joseph," the old man said. "I don't know anything much, 'cept Sleepy and Walt are a pair of trash who oughta be in jail, but that ain't news."

"Well, keep your ear to the ground, will you?"

"Sure," Pops said. "How's about a drink?"

"Tell you the truth, I could do better with some food. How's the gumbo tonight?"

"Best in town, like always," the old man beamed. "Stay where you are. I'll get a waiter to bring you somethin' here." Without asking, he mixed a vodka martini and placed it in front of Farrell with a flourish before walking over to one of the waiters.

Farrell sipped the martini and let the tension fall from his body. His mind was abuzz with all he'd heard that day, and he was having trouble assimilating it all. Lottie might have done all kinds of things, but so far nobody had told him any specific reason why she should have been killed the way she was. From what he knew, it had the look of something that hadn't been planned well. Maybe the killing had been done by somebody who hated her, or whom she had threatened in some way. The bullet behind the ear and subsequent attempt to lose the corpse in the river was either a ruse to make it look like a gangland hit, or just clumsiness by somebody not used to making enemies disappear.

He turned these thoughts over in his mind until a waiter brought an enormous bowl of chicken-andouille gumbo and a basket of bread and butter. Farrell fell onto the food and began eating it with relish.

He was nearly finished when he heard a voice at his elbow.

"The service here used to be better than this," a woman said. "Leastways they never used to make people eat at the bar before."

Farrell turned, and found himself looking into a pair of exotically slanted eyes set into a beautiful tan face, and felt his heart jump. "I came in and asked the bartender for a handout," he said with a grin. "They didn't want me sitting with the paying customers." He heard alarm bells going off in his head and felt the hairs on the backs of his hands stand up. His belief in coincidence, never strong to begin with, evaporated completely as he looked into Stella's face.

"Then come to a table with me," the cat-eyed woman said. "And I'll entertain you proper."

Farrell left his bowl and allowed the woman to lead him to a table near the stage. Anna Lou and the musicians were taking a break, and the club was filled with the murmur of happy voices. He held a chair for her, and she sat down with a smile of gratitude. She was dressed in a strapless dress of pale yellow silk, and had diamond studs set into her earlobes, a decoration that seemed to make her more exotic than ever. A matching diamond necklace glittered above her plunging bodice, and her dark brown hair was pulled into a French twist.

"My name's Wesley Farrell," he said after they were seated. "What's your name?"

"Stella Bascomb," the woman said. "I don't often see white people in this club." It was a bold observation, but then her invitation had been bold, too, and had caught the attention of some of the other tables. He pretended not to notice.

"I run a club myself, and sometimes I go around to hear the other acts," Farrell said, taking out a package of cigarettes and offering them to her.

She took one, placed it between her lips, and leaned over for him to light it. As she inhaled to get the cigarette going, her eyes smiled at him from beneath her lashes, and a faint aura of sandalwood drifted up toward him. *I know you and everything about you,* she seemed to say. *I know you and I'm not scared of you or anybody like you.*

She leaned back and expelled a long plume of smoke into the air between them. Her lips toyed with a smile, and her eyes glittered. In spite of himself, Farrell felt blood collecting in the lower part of his body. "I've heard of you and your club. It's called the Cafe Tristesse, isn't it?" she said, still playing with a smile. "What does that mean?"

"My French isn't too good," Farrell said. "I think a rough translation would be 'the sad cafe.'"

"Hmmm, and are you ever sad?" she purred. "Surely not."

"Not usually," he said. "The guy who owned the place before me named it. I'm not sure he spoke any French at all." *You're cool as a cucumber, aren't you,* he thought. "What do you do when you're not here rescuing beggars from the bar?" he asked, lighting a cigarette for himself.

"This and that," she replied. "I have some property, and it gives me enough to live on."

"It must do a lot more than that," Farrell said, eyeing her diamond necklace.

She caught his gaze, looked down at her chest, and laughed in a light, deprecating way. "A friend gave me this," she said, raising a hand and allowing the diamonds to sift lightly through her fingers.

"You make the right kinds of friends, sugar," Farrell said. "I admire a woman of enterprise."

Before she could reply to his remark, Anna Lou and Perez's orchestra came back to the bandstand, and Anna Lou began to sing "Blue Moon," but in a way the composer hadn't thought of. It was jazzy and full of improvisation, and the orchestra played the piece in foxtrot time. Stella got up, reached for Farrell's hand, and pulled him onto the dance floor.

Even though she was a full foot shorter than he, Farrell found her wonderfully adept on the dance floor. He had not danced with anyone in years, but the movements of the foxtrot came back to him in a rush. She followed his movements like a shadow, and he could feel her body thrumming with an animal excitement next to his.

Anna Lou ended "Blue Moon," and swung into "Deep Purple" without missing a beat. The music slowed for the romantic ballad, and Farrell moved effortlessly into a waltz with Stella a bare half-step behind him. Her exotic eyes blazed up into his, and Farrell recognized the woman's raw power and sensuality. Here was a woman to whom few men, if any, could say no. "You're good," he heard himself say.

"Yes," she replied, smiling so he could see the sharp, white incisors behind her red, full lips.

Farrell smiled down at her, fully enjoying this moment. He'd known other women like this one, and knew how thin the veneer of civilized behavior could be. The dangerous glint in her eyes was all the reminder he needed that someone had tried to kill him earlier that day, and that she probably was connected to it. He was almost sorry, because the dancing was nice. It was just the right time to shake things up a little and see what happened.

"I guess you don't get out to dance much," he said.

"What makes you say so?" she asked. Her eyes had a hardness growing behind them, and Farrell felt her left hand gripping his right a bit too tightly.

"Joe Dante's probably not much of a dancer," Farrell said. "He's got his mind on too many other things, all of them connected with money." As he watched her face, her smile disappeared, but her eyes remained fixed on his. The intense stare made it plain to Farrell that she was poised on a knife edge, sizing him up and probing him for some weakness to exploit.

Her smile was gone now. It was nothing now but a display of teeth. The cat had decided playing with the mouse was no more fun—it was time to bite off the head. He decided to push her a little harder.

"C'mon now. Everybody in town knows about Joe Dante and his cat-eyed girl," Farrell said, grinning insolently down into her face. "I just figured he never let you out of his sight." Farrell pulled her toward him closely, and moved her aggressively about on the dance floor. Her body was no longer thrumming, and instead became tight and hard next to his.

"I don't belong to nobody, white man. I go where I want, and do what I want, when I want," she said in a soft, even voice. "You want to follow me home and let me show you? Maybe while we're there, you'll find somethin' out about me. Maybe somethin' about yourself, too."

Farrell's insolent smile remained fixed, his eyes bright and hard. He could hear the alarm bells again, but he wasn't about to let her go that easy. "Sure, honey, why not? It's too cold and wet to go home alone. Is it warm at your place?"

She said nothing, but her smile was back again. "What a silly question," she said.

They released each other at the same moment, and she left the dance floor. He followed at a brief distance. By the time he got to the table, she had picked up her purse and the fox cape she had left in one of the chairs, and was walking away. He followed her, stopping long enough to get his overcoat from the bar.

He was playing all of this by ear now, not certain whether he'd done something smart or something stupid. One thing he knew, he had bothered her by knowing so much about her. He had to think of a way to exploit that.

It was raining again, and the street was slick and shiny with reflected street light. She led him to a Buick sedan, and he walked around to help her get behind the wheel. As she cranked the motor, he walked around to the other side of the car and got in. He was turning his head to speak to her when something hit him behind the left ear. *God, are you stupid,* he thought as the blackness swept over him.

Stella and Mops had the last run of the Jackson Avenue Ferry to themselves, just as Stella had hoped. One deckhand was below in the engine room, and the other had gone up to the pilot house for a moment. She looked at Mops and jerked her chin at him.

With no wasted motion, the man pulled a door of the green Buick open and dragged Farrell's limp body from the backseat. Mops was slight of build, but he handled the bigger man's body easily. With Stella keeping watch, Mops dragged Farrell to the port side rail, draped him over it, then flipped him headfirst into the swirling waters of the Mississippi.

Stella went to the rail, and looked behind them. There was no sign of Farrell. "That's one nuisance taken care of," she said to Mops.

Mops's eyes were large in his dark face. "I hope you're right," he said in an undertone. "I don't want him comin' back after us."

"Don't be a chump," she said impatiently. "He was out cold and the current's really runnin' hard tonight. Nobody could survive in this cold for very long. Let's get off on the other side, drive over to Algiers Point, and take the ferry back. I got some other things to do before the night's over."

"Whatever you say, Stella," Mops said.

"You got it, boy," Stella replied, her sharp teeth glinting in the pale moonlight.

10

Mops was silent as he and the cat-eyed woman drove through the dark winding lanes of New Orleans's West Bank. Few people lived in this semirural area, so there was no traffic to watch for. Stella's mind got fuzzy and her thoughts diffuse. It was a thing that happened when she had killed, and she had learned not to fight it. She had killed five people in her relatively short lifetime, and found that it got easier for her.

Most of the people she'd killed had been trying to do her hurt, and she rationalized that they'd had it coming. A couple had been strictly business; obstacles to money or advantage that she needed or simply wanted. Over time, killing had become just a tool, like sex, that she found useful. She was untroubled by feelings of guilt or remorse. Those had been bled out long ago.

For some reason, she found herself thinking back to the sharecropper cabin over in Winn Parish where she'd grown up. She'd been a very unworldly little girl, unaware of the things that went on between her father and mother, content to feed chickens, gather eggs, and help her mother with cooking, cleaning, and canning.

Then her mother had sickened when she was in her thirteenth year. They didn't know what it was about, and couldn't afford a doctor. The fever perplexed both the Negro midwife and the rural herbalist, and killed her mother within a month. Her childhood had ended at that moment, because from then on she was enslaved to caring for the needs of her father and three brothers. She was up by 3:00 A.M. every day, including Sunday, on an exhaustive round of cooking and cleaning, which ended around eight every evening, rain or shine, winter and summer.

The first time it happened was a year later. She was in the barn tending to their lone milk cow when her father came up behind her, standing very close. At first she didn't realize what was going on when he put his hands on her boyish hips and budding breasts. Then his caresses became more demanding and urgent, and he pushed her to the ground, with her protesting and crying. He'd pulled her bloomers down around her ankles, fumbling with his overalls at the same time. He was large and ugly down there, resembling some large, misshapen root. He entered her so roughly that she'd screamed, and then plunged against her for several moments before finally falling heavily on her with a loud groan.

After a moment, he managed to push himself to his knees, crying piteously. He begged her forgiveness, and promised not to do it again. It was only because he was so lonely for her mother, he'd said. He'd pulled a small purse from the pocket of his overalls, and removed from it a silver quarter dollar, which he gave to her. *Don't tell your brothers,* he'd said. *They wouldn't understand. But I don't understand, either, Daddy,* she'd answered, choking on her ashamed tears.

After that, she would often find him looking at her, a mixture of cunning and fear in his eyes. She made an effort to keep from being in a room with him alone. It wasn't easy, but somehow she managed to keep him at bay for months. But finally, inevitably, her vigilance flagged, and he caught her again.

This time it was a Saturday afternoon. He'd given her brothers a dollar and told them to walk into town and get a beer. When she saw them walking down the road together, skylarking and yelling the way young men will do, she knew she was in trouble.

He found her in the kitchen where she'd been chopping vegetables for a stew. The look on his face was unlike anything she'd ever seen, such a look of naked hunger. She backed away, but he caught her in a corner and ran his hands up under her dress.

"No, no, please, don't do it!" she'd cried.

"It's all right," he replied, panting in his urgency. "I'm your daddy, it ain't bad, it ain't."

"No," she cried, pushing at him. "It's wicked, it's wrong."

But the struggles and appeals to reason were for naught. He tore her clothes from her, pushed her onto the floor, and mounted her.

Holding her wrists immoble with his large, calloused hands, the old man copulated with her for forty-five minutes before he managed to flush the pent-up lust from his loins. Then he'd fallen away from her, sighing in his relief, his forearm up over his eyes as he lay on his back.

Gradually she came back to herself, and felt his mess trickling down the insides of her thighs. She raised up on one elbow and looked down on his prostrate form, contempt and hatred for him burning up every other emotion she had.

She staggered to her feet, and dragged her bruised and naked body to the kitchen sink to wash his scum and stink from between her legs. It was then that she saw the knife. It was a crudely designed butcher knife made by a local blacksmith. It was twelve inches in length, with a swollen belly of a blade and a pair of rough hickory scales for a handle. She reached out and picked the knife up.

She could tell from his light snoring that her father was deep in sleep. She went and knelt beside him, her naked breasts heaving with fear. Holding the huge knife in both hands, she positioned it over his heart and thrust it down with all her might. She felt the sharp point puncture skin and spread the ribs in its path. Her father's body bucked completely off the floor, his eyes wide open and a huge chuff of surprised air escaping his gaping mouth. She got up quickly, backing away from him, a sick, scared feeling almost overwhelming her.

Now that it was done, the enormity of it struck her with full force. She was a murderer, and could be hung for what she'd done. She had to get away now, before her brothers got back.

Without bothering to wash, she picked up her dress and saw it was too badly torn to wear again. She dropped it, and ran up to the loft where she had her pallet and few possessions. She found a clean shirt that had belonged to one of her brothers, a denim skirt, and a pair of boy's brogans. She hurried into the clothes and shoved the brogans on her feet, then ran back down the ladder.

She knew she'd need some money and some food, and began ransacking cabinets. In the pie safe she found half a loaf of bread, a piece of fat bacon, and four raw turnips which she wrapped in a piece of clean rag and shoved inside an empty flour sack. Her father kept his money inside a piece of hollowed-out firewood, held together with wooden pegs. She tore the firewood box to pieces until she found the right one, and smashed it several times on the floor until it burst open. In a leather pouch were ten one-dollar bills, a five-dollar gold piece, and a handful of silver coins—a veritable fortune to her eyes.

She put the folded dollar bills into her shirt pocket and the pouch of coins into the flour sack, then thought of something else. Suppose the parish sheriff came looking for her. A posse would begin looking not long after her brothers found their father's body. She went into her mother and father's room, and opened a handmade cypress chest. Under the blankets, way in the bottom, was an old nickel-plated revolver. On the black rubber grips was a medallion with an owl's head embossed on it. She vaguely remembered hearing her father speak of his "owl's head six-shooter." She didn't know how to break the gun open, but by looking at the end of the cylinder, she saw the silver noses of five cartridges. At least now she could fight for her life, and if necessary kill herself rather than be taken prisoner.

As she walked out into the sun, a hot, dry breeze wafted through the yard, burning the sweat from her skin and creating little swirls of dust around her feet. It seemed to her that she was in some kind of horrible dream, and the world appeared to be going by her at a painfully slow rate of speed.

She walked in the opposite direction of town, knowing of a railroad crossing where the Illinois Central stopped on the way to New Orleans once a day. She knew she could make it, if she pushed hard. She didn't look back.

She smiled when she thought of how naive she'd been until that day. Many men had tried to take advantage of her since then, and most had lived to regret it. Wesley Farrell had not had time to exploit her—she had fooled him with her eyes and her smile, and she felt a sense of accomplishment. He was supposed to be more cunning then most. He had been overrated. If he had discovered who killed Lottie Sonnier, and why, there were other things, just as dangerous, that he might also have found. That danger was over now, and she yawned tiredly. She would rest easy tonight. Maybe she'd take Mops home with her to help her sleep.

Dark—air—need air—choking. Wesley Farrell felt himself tumbled about in a foreign environment where light and air didn't exist. He fought to keep his mouth and nose closed, and to ignore the terrible desire to inhale air into his burning lungs.

His overcoat was wrapped around him, and inhibited his control of his arms. He began fighting to get it off, and every second he fought it he felt himself grow weaker. He was about to give into the frigid embrace of the water when his arms came free and he kicked his powerful legs in an effort to reach the surface. He kicked and kicked—pushing water behind him with his arms, giving every ounce of his one hundred seventy-five pounds of muscle and sinew to the effort.

He burst through the surface of the water like a torpedo, and immediately flopped back to the surface, blowing and gasping for oxygen. He turned quickly onto his back, trying to keep from being dragged under by the vicious crosscurrents. The waters, rushing from ice-bound streams hundreds of miles to the north, seemed to suck the warmth from his body like an insidious leech. He knew that if he couldn't escape the grasp of the river soon, he was as good as dead.

He could see lights around him, but they might as well have been on the opposite side of the moon for all the comfort they gave. He could see no boats on the river anywhere near him. The current maintained its death grip on him, and he couldn't break free, even with the adrenaline of fear and desperation rushing through his veins.

As he threw back another hopeless glance, he saw something black racing to overtake him. As he watched it grow larger, he realized with a thrill of horror that it was a huge tree stump, with roots trailing from it like the snakes of Medusa. He thrashed to get out of its path, and felt something pluck at him. As he kicked in terror, he felt himself pushed to one side by some trick of the current.

Without thinking, one of his hands caught at a branch projecting from the side of the waterlogged juggernaut, and he felt himself dragged along with it. It came to him in a blinding flash that here was a way to stay above the current. He could worry about getting out of the river later—now he needed to stay afloat, and alive.

The stump was roughly twelve feet long, and was perhaps as much as three feet across, undoubtedly the remnants of some damaged tree that had been undermined and then swept along by the river's raging current. With the river still pulling at him, Farrell used his last strength to pull himself alongside, then upon the huge floating derelict. The rough bark was as welcome as a mother's touch at that moment. He collapsed full length upon it, occasionally looking through the tangle of roots and branches ahead of him.

The current was moving at perhaps thirty knots. In no time at all he would be miles from the city and any means of help. It occurred to him, in his half-frozen and traumatized state, that he could be swept out into the Gulf of Mexico if he could not find a way to bring himself closer to shore. It was almost more than his mind could deal with. He was so cold—colder than he'd ever been in his life. He felt his mind growing fuzzy, and fought to remain conscious.

He raised up again, and all around him was darkness. Despair began to crowd the corners of his consciousness. He'd lost his gun, which he might have used to signal for help—except there was no one to signal out here. He thought about Frank, and about things he wished he'd been able to say to him. He felt a flush of warmth in his frozen body, which he had just enough presence of mind to know was a bad sign. As he fought to keep his eyes open, he saw his mother's face. She seemed to be reaching out to him. He held out his hand toward her, and felt consciousness slip away from him.

Savanna had not heard from Farrell since she'd taken him to the Sonnier house, and she wondered what progress he was making. Savanna had gone to him because she believed he'd get results, but she was an independant woman who seldom looked to anyone for help. It occurred to her that she might try asking her own questions, and perhaps quicken the pace of this unofficial inquiry into Lottie's death.

She began phoning people in town who owed her favors, and called in all the markers. Sometime in the early evening the telephone in her apartment began ringing.

"Hello," she said.

"Savanna, this is Grady Badeaux," a hoarse male voice said. "I hear you been askin' around 'bout Lottie Sonnier."

"Hello, Grady. I want to know where she'd been lately, and who she might've seen. If I knew that, I might be able to find out who killed her."

"Damn, girl," said Grady. "Lottie got around. You could be lookin' over the shoulders of 'bout two hundred people."

"That's my problem," Savanna said. "Just tell me what you've heard."

"Hmmm. Now alla this prob'ly ain't gospel," Grady said. "Leastways, I ain't bettin' my life in the hereafter on it."

"I'm not askin' for your soul, fool," Savanna said impatiently.

"Well," Grady began, "Lottie was goin' into a lotta places where they don't usually see no social workers. She been askin' a whole lotta dangerous questions, too."

"About what?"

"Well, last coupla years, been a lotta smack and M comin' into certain parts of town. They's some brothers mixed up with Joe Dante, sellin' it in our part of town, is what I hear, and they's a lotta money changin' hands."

"You know any names?" Savanna asked.

"The man makin' the biggest killin' in this is Walt Daggett," Grady replied. "He took over Junior Obregon's territory after Junior got penciled out, and he been makin' money hand over fist ever since, they tell me."

"Who's this 'they' you keep talkin' about?" Savanna asked testily.

"Sheeeit, girl," Grady said. "You didn't just get off no banana boat. The street's got eyes, ears, and tongues, but no names. People pick stuff up, and they pass it along if they think somebody's interested. One thing I know, Walt lives nice to have started out as nothin' but a cop. He owns property all over town, drives a big Cadillac when he ain't too cheap to put gas in it. I'd change places with him in about a half second."

Savanna mulled this over, then had a thought. "Here's another question for you," Savanna said. "If Walt profited the most from Junior's death, what's the chance he had Junior killed and set up his cousin to take the fall?"

"Iz Daggett was so clean he was almost white," Grady said. "Even if he wasn't, he ain't big enough fool to kill somebody with his own gun and then throw it where the cops could find it. Settin' him up for the fall took brains and gall. Walt's got the brains, but he had an alibi cast in steel for the night of the killin', though."

"Hmmm," Savanna said, clearly interested in Grady's words. "Get back to Lottie."

"I was in Mama Lester's Homestyle Bar and Grill couple nights ago and she was there," Grady replied. "I got to talkin' to a few of the cats after she left, and one o' them said he heard her chattin' up the bartender, name of Harvey Prado. Said she was yankin' Harvey's dick a li'l, makin' him think she was interested in him. He was talkin' to her about Junior Obregon and Walt Daggett."

"This was the night before she got killed?" Savanna asked.

"Right as rain, Mama," Grady said.

"You got any idea where she might've gone after leavin' Mama Lester's?" Savanna asked.

"No soap there," Grady said. "Maybe one o' the cats over there could tell me, if I asked."

"No, I think I'll go over there myself and see what I can see," Savanna said.

"Baby, you ain't thinkin' of goin' over there alone, are you?" Grady asked, his voice worried. "Mama Lester's ain't exactly the kind of place where a lady goes unescorted, you know what I'm sayin'?"

"Good," Savanna said. "I don't want anybody there to think I'm a lady. It might get in the way of my askin' questions."

"Baby, you oughta let me tag along, 'cause I'm scared for you to go alone. I wouldn't feel right about it," Grady said, mounting concern evident in his voice.

"That's right nice of you, Grady, but I'll be all right, you hear? Thanks a lot for everything." She hung up before he could argue with her any further.

Within fifteen minutes, she had dressed herself in a suit of needle-fine blue-and-white pinstripes, a snow-white blouse buttoned to the neck, and an off-white show handkerchief with three perfect points thrusting from the breast pocket of the jacket. Her feet were shod in pale blue heels that added two extra inches to her five-foot-eleven-inch height. She completed her ensemble with a dark-blue low-crowned hat with a wide brim snapped down in front, and a flowing rain cape.

When she'd finished dressing, she went to her desk and opened a drawer. From it she removed a nickel-plated .38 Colt Banker's Special with a two-inch barrel and ivory grips. Along the backstrap of the handle someone had engraved SAVANNA in flowing script. Farrell had given her the gun some time ago, and it was one of her prized possessions. Savanna knew that when a man like Farrell gave a woman a tarted-up firearm, it had more significance than a five-carat diamond ring. She flicked open the cylinder, checked the loads, then placed it inside her shoulderbag of blue calfskin.

It was a bit before 8:00 P.M., and beginning to drizzle when Savanna eased her electric-blue Mercury coupe to the curb outside the tavern at Tchopitoulas and Annunciation streets. She hadn't been in this neighborhood for a long time, and saw that the Depression hadn't done it a bit of good. The unpainted houses and rusting automobiles veritably shouted out the hard times people there were suffering.

Mama Lester's Homestyle Bar and Grill had been in the neighborhood since the 1910's, and was still a favorite hangout of the Negro "sports" who traversed the black underworld of New Orleans. It was also frequented by colored bougeoisie who enjoyed the thrill of slumming in a place where gamblers and hoodlums were known to drink. Savanna knew what to expect the moment she stepped inside, and braced herself for it.

The joint was only moderately crowded, since it was still early in the evening, and the hum of low-pitched voices wasn't quite enough to overwhelm the sound of Lady Day singing "Can't Help Lovin' that Man of Mine" on the jukebox.

Throwing the damp raincape back, Savanna walked boldly into the room, giving a raffish swagger to her broad shoulders and gently rounded hips. The eyes in the room turned and locked on her like artillery sights, and the place got a bit quieter. A smile touched Savanna's lips as she moved deliberately toward the bar.

The bartender, a tall, good-looking, tan-colored man with pomaded hair and a trimmed mustache the width of a needle eased himself toward her, and gazed at her body with lustful admiration. " 'Lo, baby," he said in a soft burr. "Whatever it is, I can help you with it." His smile revealed strong white teeth.

"That's a big promise, Harvey," she murmured, looking straight into his eyes. Her faint smile issued a challenge to him that she knew he'd accept with the entire bar watching.

Harvey's grin deepened as he heard her use his name. He was thinking that this must be a place he'd been before, and figured he'd play it cool in order to get there again. Even though he didn't remember her, he was sure the occasion would come back to him once he had her stripped in the back room and draped over the top of his desk.

"This is a high-class establishment, li'l honey lamb," he said. "Nothin' but the best here—of everything. What'll it be first, a drink or some more talk?"

"Got any brandy back there?" she asked.

Harvey reached under the bar and removed a bottle of three-star

French cognac that was wrapped in a fine wire mesh. He brought out two small snifters and set them in the bar. Then he carefully drew the cork from the bottle, poured two healthy measures, and offered one to Savanna. "Here's to happy memories, baby sister," he said, raising his glass.

Savanna's smile grew bolder as she accepted the glass, touched it gently to his, then swallowed her dose in a single bite. Harvey looked at her in amazement, then quickly swallowed his own. The brandy's heat pulled the breath out of his lungs like a vacuum pump, and he had to clear his throat loudly several times to keep from coughing.

"Now let's talk, Harvey," Savanna said when he had his breath back.

"Sure, honey," Harvey replied, beginning to be a little annoyed that he couldn't place her in his sexual past. He didn't like her having that advantage over him. "Come on in the back and we'll do all the talkin' you want." He leaned aggressively toward her, until his face was only inches from hers. Savanna didn't move, didn't blink. *Damn,* thought Harvey, *this is a live one.* His hands began to grow a bit damp, but he stayed himself from wiping them on his pants legs.

"Lottie Sonnier was in here three nights ago," Savanna said suddenly. "She was talkin' to you."

Harvey's body stiffened, and his smile wavered under his mustache. This wasn't part of any love game he knew. "So what? Lotta women come in here to talk to me. I get around a lot, know what I mean?" He affected a pose of nonchalance, and buffed his nails clumsily on the front of his shirt.

"Yeah, I know what you mean," Savanna said in a low, mocking voice. "You're one of those guy who uses his dick in place of his brains, thinks he's a real stud horse, prob'ly comes on the second push. I know about three hundred like you."

"Who the hell you think you are, woman?" Harvey demanded in a hoarse whisper, his eyes hot. His eyes darted about the room, and it was plain he was worried that his humiliation might be noticed by other patrons of the bar.

"I'm the person's gonna come back here with some boys I know," Savanna said with quiet intensity. "They'll tear this place apart and rip you a new asshole while they're at it. One'a them's got an eleven-inch jalop . . . he'll fall in love with you at first sight."

Havey had never heard a woman talk like this one, and her threats took all the starch out of him. "You ain' got no call to talk to me thataway," he said, his whisper almost becoming a shrill. He reached across the bar and grabbed one of her wrists. As he did, Savanna eased the little Colt halfway from her bag, and let him see it pointing at him.

"Let go of me, you stinkin' piece of rat meat," she said. "Unless you want me to blow those useless balls from between your scrawny legs."

Harvey paled visibly, and withdrew his hand from her wrist quickly. The rest of the bar, used to Harvey's frenetic love life, seemed oblivious to their quiet wordplay.

"Let's try again, Harvey. I know Lottie was here that night, and within a few hours somebody killed her. I want the sonofabitch who did that. I want him more than I ever wanted anything in my life, and I might just do anything to get him, understand?"

Harvey, his eyes as big as silver dollars, leaned across the bar, his voice dropping to a hoarse whisper. "I don't want to get mixed up in nothin', Mama. I could get killed just talkin' about this."

Savanna curled her lip. "You could get killed if you don't," she said, flicking a glance down to the gun.

"She wanted to know who Junior hung with before he was killed," Harvey whispered urgently. "I told her that Junior's runnin' mate was a man named Walt Daggett. They useta come in here sometimes with a coupla broads."

"Tell me the name of those broads," Savanna said.

"I—I dunno," Harvey said, avoiding her eyes as he tried to loosen his collar.

"Bull," Savanna sneered. "Ain't a woman come in here in the past five years you don't know her height, weight, birthday, and the number of moles on her ass."

Harvey's eyes flickered up to hers, down to the gun, then back up to her face again. "A-a—all r-right," he said. "Junior was runnin' 'round with a piece of jailbait named Billie Talmadge. He hooked her on smack, and she became a hooker after he died. I still see her here and there."

"Yeah, go on," Savanna said.

"Walt's woman was class all the way, a real looker with the damnedest eyes," Harvey said hurriedly. "They was all slanty, you know, like a cat's. She could look right through you with 'em, I swear."

"What's her name?" Savanna pressed.

"Stella Bascomb is what she calls herself," Harvey said. "She ain't with Walt no more."

"Oh?" Savanna said. "Who's she with now?"

"She's layin' pipe for white meat now," Harvey said with a sneer in his voice. "She's Joe Dante's chippy."

"You tried her and she shucked you off, didn't she, Harvey?" Savanna said with an amused note in her voice.

Harvey's face crumpled, and his eyes slid quickly away from hers.

Savanna laughed very quietly down in her throat, and pushed her gun back into her bag. "Thank you, Harvey. Thank you very much. If we're both real lucky, neither one of us will ever see the other again. Keep your nose clean, you hear?"

Savanna eased off her stool, swept the tavern with her eyes, then swaggered through the dimly lit room and out into the street.

The wake was winding down, and Israel Daggett was glad. The aura of tragedy and suffering that hung over the gathering was suffocating. There was almost no room for his own grief when that of so many others crowded in on him. He glanced to one side, and saw Marguerite rubbing her eyes with a thumb and forefinger.

"How you doin', Maggy?" Daggett asked in a soft voice.

She turned to him with a wan smile. "Don't call me Maggy. That's what you called me when I was a little girl. Call me Marguerite."

"Okay, Marguerite," he said, smiling back at her. "Tell me something."

"What?" she asked.

"When Dandy Walker came with me, you were a little offhand with him. What was that all about?"

She shrugged. "It's all ancient history now."

"Come on," he persisted. "I'm curious. I know he was going out with Lottie while I was away. You don't have to keep anything from me about that."

Her face relaxed a bit, but her face was far from happy. "He was pushing her to get married all the time," she said. "Lottie went out with men while you were away, but I don't think she ever let any of them take your place. When the word came that you were getting out of prison, Lottie was trying to cool things off between the two of them. He took it kind of bad."

Daggett sank back into his chair, his expression bleak. "Oh. So it was like that."

"There's no need in cluttering your mind with it," Marguerite said. "Lottie's gone now, and all we've got are our memories of her. He's not part of that."

"I reckon you're right," Daggett replied heavily. "I guess we can go now."

They got up, and one of the funeral parlor managers brought Ruth and Marguerite's coats and hats to them. Daggett helped Marguerite into her coat while the funeral parlor man helped 'Tee Ruth.

Daggett got into an old overcoat and hat that had belonged to 'Tee Ruth's late husband and walked out into the rain to get Ruth's old car.

There was a great deal of traffic in front of the parlor, and it took about ten minutes of fuming and jockeying before he finally got Ruth's old Hudson to the front of the funeral home. When he had them in the Hudson, he walked back long enough to talk to Dandy.

"I reckon I'll take them home and then go back to the Metro," Daggett said. "You want to catch a drink with me before you turn in?"

Dandy was in front of the funeral parlor's porch lights, and his face was a dark blur. "Sure, Iz. Want me to follow you around to 'Tee Ruth's and pick you up?"

"Yeah. I'll just make sure they get into the house okay, and then I'll be ready to leave."

"You feelin' all right?" Dandy asked.

"I don't know," Daggett said. "I never had much grievin' to do before this. I feel all busted up inside."

Dandy nodded. "I know. I'll see you over to the house." He turned and walked out into the street.

Within another five minutes, Daggett had gotten both women into the car and then turned the car out into the rain-swept street. They were all silent for several blocks, then Daggett heard quiet sniffling coming from Marguerite.

"You got to buck up, child," 'Tee Ruth said. "Lottie'd want us to get back to the business of livin' right away, not stand around makin' ourselves sick."

"I . . . I can't help it," Marguerite said in a muffled voice. "I'm not strong like Lottie . . . I'll never be that strong."

Daggett, jarred from his own grief, reached out a large, work-roughened hand, and placed it over Marguerite's. "She was proud of you, Marguerite," he said. "Her letters were always full of what you were doin', and what a success you were gonna be. Don't be talkin' that way about yourself."

Marguerite captured Daggett's hand in her left, and pressed a handkerchief to her mouth with the other hand, but she stayed quiet after that. She held Daggett's hand until the next time he had to shift gears at an intersection.

They turned off Claiborne Avenue to Leonidas, slowing when the light on Ruth's porch came into sight, then Daggett cut his engine and coasted to a stop. He did not see Dandy's car, and assumed his friend had been held up in traffic somewhere.

He got out and helped Marguerite, then her mother, out onto the sidewalk. After holding the gate open for the two of them, he preceded them up the stairs and opened the front door for them. He followed them inside, and took off the old hat and unbuttoned the overcoat.

"Is there anything I can do for you tonight, 'Tee Ruth?" he asked.

"No, son," she said. "I'm just gonna go to bed and try to sleep. Thanks for bein' with us today. Thanks for everything." The old woman came and hugged him briefly before disappearing into the rear of the shotgun cottage.

"What will you do tonight, Israel?" Marguerite asked as she took off her own coat and hat.

"Dandy's supposed to follow me over here. I guess we'll get a drink somewhere and turn in," Daggett said. "I'm about done in myself." He shook his head as though he couldn't clear it.

"Would you like to sit down?" she asked.

"Dandy's sure to be comin' directly," he replied. "I thought I'd stand here at the window and watch for him. If you'd like to go on to bed, girl, I'll lock up behind myself as I go out."

"No, I'll wait with you," she said. She walked to the door where he stood and looked out at the dimly lit street. "What will you do now?"

"I don't know," he said after a pause. "I really haven't had all that much time to think about it. A friend at the Metro Hotel offered me a job as house dick yesterday. Might be I'll take that."

She hesitated, then said, "So you think you'll be staying?"

"New Orleans is the only place I've ever known. It's my home," he said. "I don't reckon there's anyplace else I want to go."

"I—I'm glad you'll be staying," she said. "It hasn't been the same with you gone." She wrapped her arms about his waist and hugged him. After a moment, he cupped her head in one of his big hands and patted her shoulder with the other, feeling a strange heat in his chest. Then she let him go, and disappeared into her own room.

Within another five minutes, Dandy's car pulled up outside the house. Daggett switched off the lights, then set the deadbolt and left. He was grateful for the wamth of Dandy's car.

"Want to go back and hit that bottle I got for you early today?" Dandy asked. "I ain't in the mood for some noisy bar tonight."

"Yeah, I know how you feel," Daggett said. He pulled away from the curb and headed toward Claiborne Avenue.

11

Dandy and Daggett drove in silence for several blocks, each seemingly lost in his own thoughts and private grief. Finally, Daggett spoke for the first time.

"Why didn't you tell me that you'd asked Lottie to marry you, Dandy?" he asked.

Dandy didn't answer right away, and Daggett saw his hands tighten convulsively on the steering wheel. The tension in the car became a live thing, flopping at the end of Daggett's words like a fish suddenly jerked from the water.

"I—I didn't know how to tell you," Dandy said. "I felt like a louse anyhow. What with Lottie bein' dead . . . well, I just couldn't see no sense in bringin' it up."

"It ain't like you to keep things from me like this," Daggett said. "What'd you think I'd do? Shoot you, maybe?"

"I don't know," Dandy said, his voice quavering. "Jesus God, I don't know. I never felt like anybody the way I felt about her. It ain't somethin' I planned, you know? She was so full of life, and I got to thinkin' I couldn't live without her is all. Christ Jesus . . . I'm . . . I'm sorry, Iz. I love you, too. None of this was supposed to happen."

His voice broke then, and for the first time, Daggett could see the depth of the pain his friend was in. *Why, he feels worse than me,* Daggett thought with some surprise. *I should be the one all torn up by this, but he's so much worse off.* Unconsciously, as he mulled these thoughts, Daggett reached over and kneaded his friend's blocky shoulder with his left hand. "We need that drink pretty bad, don't we, old-timer?" he said. Dandy, his shoulders heaving, said nothing, and kept his eyes fixed on the wet concrete rolling under them.

About forty-five minutes after they left Christ's Majesty Funeral Home, Dandy pulled up across the street from the Metro. He was trembling all over, and his eyes looked sunken in their sockets. "I don't reckon I want that drink after all, Iz. Think I'll just go on home."

"Nothing doing," Daggett said. "We both feel rotten, but I reckon for tonight we'd be better off with each other than sitting in rooms all by ourselves."

"No, really, I—"

"Look, Dandy," Daggett said, taking his friend by the shoulder again, "The stuff about you and Lottie don't matter now. I'm askin' you as a friend, as a brother, to come on upstairs with me. We'll kill that bottle, and get another one if that ain't enough. Now, no more arguin'." He reached over and cut the engine, and took the key out of the switch. Before Dandy could protest, he was outside on the sidewalk, tossing the key up and down in his right hand. Dandy, favoring him with a sick grin, eventually got out and joined him.

As they entered the Metro, Arthur came out from behind the desk to greet them. "Hey, Iz, Dandy. How you fellas makin' it?"

"We feel like two sticks of well-chewed gum," Daggett said in a poor attempt at a joke. "Figured we'd just have a few drinks before hittin' the sack."

"Well," Arthur said, fingering his carefully trimmed and shaped mustache, "don't do so much drinkin' that you forget where you at, hear? It's late for any carousin', cousin."

"Don't worry," Daggett said. "We ain't in the mood for any carousin'. We just want to be left alone for a while."

"Okay," Arthur said. "Ring the desk if you need anything, hear?"

"Sure, Arthur. 'Night." Daggett said, turning away. Dandy, who had remained wordless throughout the interchange, looked bleakly at Arthur, then followed Daggett to the elevator. When they had the elevator moving, Daggett made attempts at small talk.

"Arthur offered me a job here as house dick," he said. "I guess it wouldn't be a bad job at that. The Metro don't attract many people on weekend marriages or folks going on a five-day drunk. After five years in the pen, the quiet might be good for my nerves." He made a halfhearted chuckle.

They got off on Daggett's floor, and walked down toward the

front of the building where his room was located. When they reached the room, Dandy stood back a bit to allow Daggett room to get his key in the lock.

As the key turned, Daggett felt his skin prickle unpleasantly, and he half straightened, every sense in him alive to danger. As the tumblers fell in the lock, he realized what it was—cigarette smoke. He didn't smoke, and the only other person who'd been in the room with him that day was Dandy, who also didn't smoke. Yelling a warning to his friend, Daggett threw his shoulder into the barely opened door, and felt it smash into something soft on the other side.

Reaching around the door, Daggett's hand met material and hard flesh. His fingers gripped it, and he dragged the owner around to where he could see him. As he did so, he felt, rather than heard, something swish past his head, and he ducked, feeling his hat knocked forcefully from his head. He struck out with his free hand, and felt the immense satisfaction of cartilage squashing under the bones of his fist.

As the man fell away from his hand, something sharp traced a burning arc across the left side of his face. He yelled for Dandy again, and grabbed at the hand holding the glittering knife as he and the other man fell to the floor. As he grappled with the man, he saw the point of the knife fall to within inches of his face. His strong left arm was all that kept it from plunging into him, and he felt the muscles there quivering as they fought to keep the cold steel at bay.

Daggett's right hand was trapped between their bodies, and he heaved and struggled to get it free. As the man pushed himself into a position of greater advantage, he slid upward. Daggett felt the other man's knee pressing down painfully on his thigh, bearing him down. Daggett's hand, trapped between the thigh and his own body, reached downward, found the man's groin, and squeezed the testicles as hard as he could. The knife man roared with pain, giving Daggett all the opportunity he needed to heave him off.

He threw himself atop the man, warding off a blow to his chest as he did so. Daggett grabbed the knife arm by the wrist with his left hand and held it steady, pounding the man's face with his right fist, again and again. But the man was tough. The blows seemed to enrage him. He captured Daggett's left wrist in his right hand, and used the strength of both arms to push the knife at Daggett's chest. Daggett grabbed at the tangle of hands and arms with his free hand, and a tremendous test of strength and wills ensued, each man thrashing and heaving, trying to gain an advantage. Daggett's teeth were clenched, and breath whistled through them as he fought.

Then the man managed to break free, and as he rose to flee, Daggett captured one of his ankles and dragged him back. The man fell heavily, gasped once, then lay still. Daggett, stunned by the silence, moved cautiously to where the man lay, and turned him over. In the pale light filtering in from the hall, he saw the handle of a huge spring blade clasp knife buried in the man's chest to the hilt. Sobered by the sight, Daggett stared transfixed for several seconds before he remembered his friend.

"Dandy! Dandy, you all right?"

"Here, I'm here," the ex-boxer said weakly from the hall.

Daggett cut on the lights, and saw the curtains standing out in the breeze from his open window. A quick check showed the fire escape was vacant, and there was no sign of anyone on the street. He turned and saw Arthur standing there with a cocked .38 in his right hand.

"Jesus Christ on a bicycle," he exclaimed. "What the hell you all doin' up here?"

"Two men waiting for me in here," Daggett said between gasps for breath. "Looks like one got away. This one wasn't so lucky." He looked down at the dead man, and Arthur came over to look at the upturned face.

"Skeets Poche," Arthur said.

"You know him?" Daggett asked.

"A bad boy," Arthur said with some awe in his voice. "I reckon he'd kill his own mother if there was fifty cents in it. Look at the size of that goddamned knife."

"I don't need to," Daggett said, dabbing at the cut oozing blood on his face. "I felt it go by." He turned and walked to the hall, where Dandy lay propped against the wall. Several people had been roused by the fight, and the hall was full of their murmuring voices. Daggett knelt beside his friend.

"Did he cut you anywhere?" Daggett asked solicitously, running his hands over Dandy's body as he talked.

"I think I caught a sap on the back of the neck or somethin'," Dandy said a bit woozily.

"You see who the second man was?" Daggett asked as he helped Dandy to his feet.

Before Dandy could answer, loud voices began to reverberate from the opposite end of the hall.

"Straighten up, y'all. Police comin' through."

The crowd in the hall parted as two tall Negro patrol officers made their way toward Daggett.

"What's goin' on here?" the first one demanded.

"My friend and me just got back from a wake, and two guys were waitin' in my room," Daggett said. "Looks like they were here to kill us."

The uniformed officer shot Daggett a penetrating look. "Ain't you Sergeant Israel Daggett?"

"Just Israel Daggett now, officer," Daggett replied.

"Who's this guy?" the cop asked, pointing at Dandy.

"My friend, Dandy Walker. He runs a gymnasium here in town."

"Sure," the second cop said. "I remember when you fought Jersey Joe Walcott and Walcott won by a decision. You was robbed that night, brother."

Dandy, still looking a bit knocked about and frightened, looked wide-eyed at the man, but seemed incapable of a reply.

The first cop had walked past them into Daggett's room, and switched on the lights. Daggett walked over to where he had knelt beside Skeets Poche's body. "Well, well, ole Skeets come to call. Sonofabitch, would you look at that knife. It's a Ka-Bar Grizzly Bear. You don't give no manicures with one'a them. It's about time somebody jerked the rug out from under this weasel."

He stood up and turned to Israel. "I'm gonna phone this in to headquarters, see if one of the Negro Squad detectives'll come down and take care of this without me havin' to drag you in. Your story listens right to me, and if your buddy can confirm it, that'll be enough to satisfy whatever dick they send down."

"Thanks, officer," Daggett said in a voice suddenly gone shaky. If the wrong cop had caught this squeal, he might be back on his way to jail now. He was suddenly thankful that his name still carried the weight of trust with other Negro cops. He went back and got Dandy, and got him into a chair in his room.

Wesley Farrell came back to himself in slow blurs. He remembered riding the tree down the river, and thought at times he was still on it. Each time he tried to grasp a moment of consciousness, it was snatched away from him.

"He gonna die?" he vaguely heard somebody ask. If there was an answer, he couldn't hear it.

Some time later, his eyes opened for the first time. There was a sickly yellow light coming from somewhere, but it was such an effort to turn his head that he soon forgot about it. Wherever he was, there was a peculiar rocking motion to the place, which lulled him back into sleep. Maybe he was dead, and was floating on a cloud. *Funny, I always figured to go the other place,* he thought.

When he opened his eyes again, he saw pale light filtering through a round window over his head. He still didn't feel like moving, but watched the round window with a strange fascination.

"Well, so you decided to live after all," a voice said.

Farrell turned his head slightly, and saw a long stringbean of a man with curly red hair peeking out from the edges of a black knit watch cap. His nose was long and beaky, like that of a sandhill crane, and two humorous bright blue eyes sat on either side of it. He was dressed in a black turtleneck sweater and black denim trousers. He had a thick china mug in his hand, and steam rose from it gently.

"Where am I?" Farrell asked.

"You're on a barge tug on the Mississippi," the man said wryly. "Where'd you think you was?"

"Heaven," Farrell said.

The man laughed. "You looked like you was reachin' for it when we spotted you on that log, but I don't reckon there's a one of us could even make it *to* the Pearly Gates, much less through 'em. Who are you and why was you ridin' that chunk of tree in the river last night?"

Farrell pulled a hand from out of the blanket he was wrapped in and brought it to his head. It was tender and pulpy at the back. "I was sapped in New Orleans last night. I don't know what happened after that. They threw me in the river, I guess."

"Well, you was wearin' the prettiest suit I ever did see, messed up awful, so we reckoned you didn't decide to take a cruise on your own. Suit's wrecked, more's the pity."

"Where are we now?" Farrell asked.

"Nigh on to Pilot Town at the mouth of the river," the man said.

Farrell sat up, wincing. "I got to get back to New Orleans," he said, noticing for the first time that he was stark naked underneath the blanket. "Anybody got any clothes I could borrow?" he asked.

"We'll be tyin' up in about another half-hour," the seaman said. "Guy has a general store near there. He might be able to sell you somethin'. You managed to hang on to your wallet, and all the money's still in it. Quite a roll for a guy too cheap to buy a steamship ticket." He grinned at Farrell.

Farrell grinned back. "What's your name?"

"Cap'n Daniel O'Neil. Danny to my friends. And you?"

"Wesley Farrell. I run a nightclub in New Orleans."

"Damn," O'Neil said. "I never knew the music business could be so rough." He handed the mug of coffee to Farrell, who accepted it gratefully.

The rain fell steadily as Savanna negotiated streets with as much as four inches of water standing in them. She drove slowly to keep from throwing water up into her engine compartment and flooding the motor out. Thunder rolled in the distance, and flashes of lightning occasionally lit the rain-swept streets. She tried not to look directly into them, because she was having enough trouble seeing as it was.

Savanna knew that Walt Daggett was Israel's cousin, and also knew about the trouble he'd been in that had gotten him fired from the police department.

Savanna wondered about the woman, and was struck by the fact that Harvey Prado was in such awe of her. Women had no doubt turned him down before, but Harvey's ego was legendary. This cat-eyed woman must be formidable, as well as good-looking. It was of no small interest that she was now the mistress of Joe Dante, a man who could have any woman he wanted.

Savanna felt that this connection had to mean something to Israel Daggett's case. Junior Obregon's associations were shadowy, but there was nothing to say that he hadn't worked for Dante then, or had been a threat to him otherwise. She debated trying to contact Farrell, but the little clock set into her dashboard said that it was already well into the small hours of the morning. He was probably out on the street, shaking trees of his own. No, the best thing was to follow this trail and see where it led. It had occurred to her, after leaving Mama Lester's, that there was one other place where some information might be had, and she headed the Mercury in that direction.

As Savanna turned off South Carrollton to Orleans Avenue, she saw lights of the Sassafrass Lounge glowing like a ship's beacon in the distance. The lounge was everything that Mama Lester's wasn't— a slickly designed two-story club with a lot of glass brick on the outside. A striped canopy projected from the entrance to the street, and a Negro doorman in a Scots Guards uniform stood underneath to help people from their cars. Over the entrance was a large neon sign in the shape of a martini glass with a sprig of sassafrass, and the name of the lounge spelled out in green letters. Savanna eased her car up to the door and got out under the umbrella the doorman held for her.

"The keys are in it," she told him as she walked under the canopy to the door.

Inside, the club was doing a fair business, considering the state of the weather. Bones Melancon's Sextet was on the bandstand doing a rendition of "It Don't Mean a Thing," and the dance floor was crowded with well-dressed Negro couples. Savanna checked her damp hat and rain cape with the hatcheck girl, and moved around the perimeter of the main floor to the bar.

She took a stool at the bar and scanned the room for people she knew, but found no familiar faces there.

"What's yours, mama?" a silken baritone said behind her.

She turned to find a wide-shouldered ebony-black barman standing across the bar from her. His hair was clipped close to his round skull, and a part was carefully razored on the left side. She recognized him immediately.

"Hello, Big Lucy," she said. "I heard you were workin' over here these days."

Big Lucy shrugged and favored her with a grin. "I got sick of duckin' punches and razors, honeychile. I was gettin' too old for it. Here, the most I get is a tipsy lawyer once in a while."

Savanna nodded. "Sass in tonight? I don't see him on the floor."

Big Lucy's grin got some teeth in it, and a brief gust of laughter escaped his big chest. "Believe the bossman's up there entertainin' a lady, but he oughta be 'bout finished. Have a drink on the house, and I'll check upstairs in a little bit."

"Make it a brandy," Savanna said. "It's a cold night out there."

"Woman like you ought not ever be cold," he said with a grin as he reached for a bottle behind him. He poured out a double into a small balloon glass and handed it to her with a flourish. "What else can I do for ya?" he asked.

She smiled back and nodded to him as she lifted the glass. When the brandy was warming her stomach, she looked at Lucy for a moment. He got around—he might know something. "What do you know about Walt Daggett?" she asked.

Big Lucy gave the bar in front of Savanna a leisurely wipe with a spotlessly clean bar towel, giving the task his full attention. "Walt's good at mindin' his business," he replied idly.

Savanna ran her index finger lightly around the rim of her glass. "I hear he's connected to Joe Dante. Anything in that?"

Big Lucy folded his towel very meticulously, and placed it on a shelf behind the bar, then he looked up at Savanna with a wide, candid gaze. "Sugar, Walt Daggett's a punk, but he's up to his eyeballs sellin' horse and M. I reckon he's pushed enough to get every nigger in this town high."

Savanna smiled lazily, and lowered her lashes down on her cheeks. "That's mighty interesting, Lucy. What else you know about old Walt?"

Lucy's eyes narrowed, and he put each of his hands flat on the bar and braced his powerful arms on them. "Savanna, it ain't good for nobody to know too much about the doin's of a man like Walt. He's hooked up to some very big, very dangerous people. More'n that you don't wanna know."

Savanna's face lost the fluttery, girlish look she'd been offering the man, and the skin of her face stretched tautly over her cheekbones. "Somebody killed Lottie Sonnier a couple days ago. It's known she was gettin' in the hair of some people with things to lose. I think Walt knows somethin' about it, and I wanna know what he knows."

Lucy's black face became as impenetrable as a concrete wall, and he stepped back slightly from her. "Then go ask him yourself, mama. I don't know nothin' about that, and I'll tell you somethin' else. I don't wanna know." He drifted away from her like smoke on a breeze, and Savanna found herself staring at her own reflection in the mirror behind the bar.

The sextet had shifted into "Take the A Train," and as some couples sat down for a rest and others took their places on the dance floor Savanna picked up her brandy glass and walked around the edge of the dance floor and back to the lobby. Her mind was abuzz with what she'd heard that night. She was tired and worried, and more than anything else, she wanted to hear Wesley Farrell's voice. He'd know what to do right now, far better than Savanna, herself.

The rest of the club was happily engaged in the talk and emotion that go with liquor and good times. Savanna, her face sober, was like a smooth stone splitting the current of a frothing mountain stream. She saw a telephone booth off to the side, and walked over to it, reaching into her shoulder bag for a nickel. After she got into the booth and had closed the door, she dropped the nickel into the slot and asked the operator for the Cafe Tristesse.

"Cafe Tristesse," a man's voice said.

"Harry, it's Savanna Beaulieu," she said.

"Miss Savanna," Harry said. "How ya doin'? The boss ain't in right now, so can I do somethin' for ya?" Savanna knew from experience that Harry's deference to her, although out of character for a white man addressing a Negro woman, was unfeigned. He must have known, or sensed, that Savanna was more than a casual business acquaintance of his boss's, and treated her with a rare respect.

"Do you know where he is, or where he might be reached?" she asked.

"No, not really," Harry replied. "He went out early today and said he didn't know when he'd be back. You want me to take a message?"

Savanna gnawed her lip in indecision. Finally, she said, "If he calls in the next thirty minutes, tell him I'm at the Sassafrass Lounge. Tell him I'm on to something, and could use his help."

"The Sassafrass Lounge, and you're on to somethin'. Right," Harry said. "I'll make a coupla calls. Somebody mighta seen him somewheres."

"Thanks, Harry. I'll talk to you."

Savanna hung up and stared at the dead receiver for a moment, not quite sure what else she could do there. She was staring when a rap at the door jarred her abruptly from her thoughts. She jerked her head around to the door, heart pounding with fright, and saw Big Lucy's round, black head staring in at her. She pushed the booth open.

"The boss is free, li'l lady," he said. "You still wanna talk to him?"

Savanna knew that very little went on in the shadowy world of the Negro underworld that Sassafrass DeLatte didn't know, and decided to see what she could pump from him. She got up quickly, and said, "Thanks for looking for me, Luce."

"No problem," he rumbled. "Follow me."

He led her across the lobby to a door, and the door opened to a staircase. Lucy held the door for her and said, "Second door on the right at the head of the stairs. Watch your step, sugar."

Savanna nodded her thanks, and walked up the stairs. The building was well soundproofed, and Savanna could hear nothing of the music that was being played below her.

Sleepy Moyer was sitting in a cubbyhole office in the back of a whorehouse he owned on Annunciation Street down near Louisiana Avenue, listening to Louis Armstrong and his Hot Seven combo on a little radio. It had been a quiet night with no problems. His girls were keeping up a steady trade, and there were no rumbles to deal with.

Sleepy was a little bored, if truth be told. He liked for a john to get out of hand once in a while so he could get some exercise. He was idly opening and closing the blade of a razor he normally kept down in his sock, occasionally whetting it on the sole of his shoe, when the telephone rang.

"It's your nickel," he said laconically. He'd heard that line in a movie, and used it whenever he could.

"We got trouble," Walt Daggett's voice said at the other end. Sleepy smiled, knowing that whatever it was couldn't be that scary, not to him, anyway. He tipped his hat onto the back of his head with a lazy forefinger.

"Sheeit," he said with a chuckle bubbling in his deep chest. "Trouble just needs a troubleshooter, cousin. Toss me the rattle."

"There's a woman named Savanna Beaulieu. She's been askin' questions about me at Mama Lester's, and Big Lucy just called from Sassafrass's joint to say she's there right now."

Sleepy almost snorted, thinking how easy it was to worry Walt sometimes. "Questions about what, Walt?"

"She's tryin' to make a connection between me and Lottie Sonnier's death. We can't afford to have her go around askin' any more questions about that."

"Well, what you wanna do about it?" Sleepy asked, folding his razor and sliding it inside his shirt pocket.

"What the hell you think, fool? I want you to go out and do what I pay you for," Walt said before he slammed the receiver down on the hook with an angry clatter.

Sleepy shook his head, still laughing. He got up from the desk, straightened his tie, and shrugged back into his jacket. He got his overcoat from the rack and slipped that on next, then took out his Luger and checked the magazine. Satisfied that he was ready, he turned off the light on his desk and left the room.

Frank Casey had been sitting in his office reading case reports when a call came in from the officer in charge of the Negro Squad about the fracas at Israel Daggett's room. When he'd heard the report, he told the officer he'd be going over to conduct the interrogation himself. Pausing only long enough to strap on his .38 and get his hat and coat, he was out the door.

Twenty minutes later he was at the Metro, where three other cars and a morgue wagon were already in attendance. Parking across the street, he walked past the uniformed officer at the hotel entrance with his gold star-and-crescent shield in his upraised right hand.

With a word from Arthur Bordelon, the night manager, Casey was able to find the right floor. A trail of colored policemen, Negro newspaper reporters, and other assorted hangers-on led him to the room Israel Daggett had been living in. He walked to the sheet-covered body on the floor, lifted the edge nearest the head, and studied the face. Lifting the sheet a bit higher, he saw the knife, still buried in the dead man's chest. After a moment, he dropped the sheet and turned to the medical examiner's man standing near by.

"What we got, Doc?"

"Nothing special, skipper," the doctor replied. "Negro male, about thirty-five, some contusions about the face and head, and six inches of carbon steel right through his breastbone and into the aorta. Death was near instantaneous, I reckon. I can probably have an autopsy for you late tomorrow, unless you need a rush on it."

"No suggestion of anything other than a fight and the tables getting turned, eh?" Casey asked.

"Look at Daggett's face and clothes," the pathologist said, jerking his chin at where Daggett sat, talking to Willie Meraux, a Negro Squad detective. "He's been in a hell of a scrap. He's probably lucky he ain't the one laying there."

Casey nodded, and walked over to where Daggett and Meraux were. Meraux got up and threw Casey a salute. Casey returned it, then focused his attention on Daggett.

"Tell me the story, Daggett, from the beginning," Casey said. Then he listened patiently as Daggett talked, nodding occasionally, tipping his hat to the back of his head and rubbing his chin. He remained silent until Daggett reached the end, then he drew a long breath and blew it noisily from pursed lips.

"Somebody doesn't like you being here, Daggett," Casey said.

"I reckon not, Captain," Daggett said. "This is the second time somebody's tried to ice me in the last couple days."

Casey started. "The second? When was the first?"

Daggett explained about the shots fired after he left the railroad terminal, and Casey's eyes got a hungry gleam in them.

"You're scaring somebody to death," Casey said. "I've got a good mind to put you in protective custody."

"Nothin' doin', Captain," Daggett said, folding his arms. "Whoever this is slipped up tonight. If I'd had two cents worth of luck, I'd have grabbed the second man, and we'd know who's behind this. Maybe we'd know who really killed Junior Obregon."

"And if *he'd* had one cent of luck, you'd be laying here with a knife in your guts instead of Skeets Poche," Casey said angrily. "I don't need anybody's permission to put you in protective custody, Daggett, not even yours."

Daggett came closer to Casey, lowering his voice and exerting every ounce of persuasiveness he could muster. "Give me a break, Captain," he said. "I got a chance to get my life back. If you put me in jail, all that means is I lose that chance. I just spent five years in 'Gola for something I didn't do. Let me have this chance to clear this up and maybe get my badge back. Please."

Casey turned his shoulder to Daggett, and rubbed his chin as he thought. He'd never believed Daggett was guilty of Obregon's murder. Somebody was scared that Daggett was going to find out who did. Casey admitted to himself that Daggett had a point—it was his life that had been ruined, and this was perhaps the only opportunity he might have to redeem that life. He turned back to Daggett.

"All right, I'll leave you free, but stick with me. I've got to keep you alive somehow. Did you get any indication of who the second man was?"

"No, I had hold of him for a minute, but I lost him in the struggle,"

Daggett said. "I didn't get any indication of what he looked like, even. He was hiding behind the door, and I hit him with it as I came in."

"What about Walker? Did he see or hear anything?"

Daggett looked at Dandy, and Dandy looked up at Casey with a dazed look on his face.

"No, sir, Captain," Dandy said. "I got hit with somethin' and it stunned me."

"Where did they hit you?" Casey asked.

"Feels like the back of the neck," Walker said. "I been hit lots of times in the ring, but never like that."

Casey went over and pulled Dandy forward by the shoulders, and examined the back of his neck, touching it lightly with his fingers. "They didn't break the skin. A glancing blow, maybe." He pushed Dandy back in his chair and regarded him for a moment. "Where were you when the fight started?"

Dandy licked his lips, and looked up into Casey's face. "I was right behind Iz," he said. "He was unlockin' the door, then he put his shoulder to it and smashed it into the wall. I ran in after him, and that's when I got clubbed."

"Neck still hurt?" Casey asked.

"Yeah, like a toothache," Dandy said, nodding.

"Better get some ice on it before it swells up," Casey said. "Come on, Daggett. I expect you could use a little sleep. You go home, too, Walker."

Casey turned toward the hall door, and Daggett followed. After a few moments, Dandy got up and left the room, too.

Walt Daggett was sitting in his living room with the curtains drawn and the gas heater in his fireplace glowing red. He had a glass of scotch in his left hand, and his right hand lay beside the nine millimeter Spanish automatic on the chair arm. Billie Talmadge sat on the rug in front of the gas fire, wearing nothing but a pair of step-ins as she toasted herself.

"God, you don't know how good it feels to be warm," she said with a purr in her voice.

"Yeah," Walt said absently.

"Junior never had no heat in that dump we lived in, and most of the other places I lived didn't have no heat neither. Not since I left Ma and Pa, anyway."

"Well, enjoy it then," Walt said, taking a drink of his scotch.

"You look worried, Walt," she said, crawling across the rug and putting a hand on his knee. "If I could maybe have a li'l fix, I bet I could make it better."

"Stop, I ain't in the mood for that right now," he said peevishly. There was a time when he'd have taken Billie up on it. She wasn't too bad-looking, but she was a whore, and Walt felt above such things now.

"C'mon, Walt," she coaxed. "In just a coupla minutes, I can make you forget whatever's on your mind. Gimme a chance."

Walt stood up quickly and walked over to the window, where he peeped at the street through a crack in the curtains.

"I thought my tellin' you about who killed Junior would make things easier for you, baby," she said petulantly. "You been jumpy as a cat since I come to live here."

"I let you come here to keep you from tellin' anybody else," he said.

She got up and walked up behind him. "Who could I tell, honey? I ain't interested in gettin' killed, and the cops'd prob'ly put me in jail if I went to them. Ain't nobody gonna find out nothin' from me, honest."

"You stupid whore," Walt said as he swung around to her. "Don't you think they'd find a way to make you talk if they found out about you? All they'd have to do would be to lock you up without a fix. You'd talk, all right. You'd sing like a robin."

"Gee, I never looked at it that way," she said. She started rubbing the inside of her left arm, and walked restlessly about the room. "Maybe I should get outa town while I still can."

"The hell you are," Walt said. "You're stayin' right here, where I can keep an eye on you. Half the town's out there askin' too many questions about too many things. If anybody got to you, everything'd go to hell in a handbasket. You'll stay right where you are."

"What questions, honey?" Billie asked.

"Things," Walt said evasively, keeping his eyes out on the street.

"Everybody's real upset about Lottie Sonnier," Billie said suddenly. "Somebody killed her. They oughtn't to've done that. She was real nice to me. She was gonna help me get clean, get out of the life. I wish . . ."

"Shut up," Walt said. "You're gettin' on my nerves with all that talk. Shut up about Lottie Sonnier, too. It's her own damn fault she's dead. She shoulda minded her own business."

"What do you mean?" Billie asked.

"Shut up!" Walt shouted. He turned on Billie, his eyes glaring with some emotion apart from anger in his thin, dark face. His hand with the gun in it was shaking, and Billie drew back from him, covering her bare breasts with her arms.

"You're scarin' me, Walt," she said in a small voice. "I ain't done nothin'."

"Then shut up and leave me alone," Walt said, lowering his voice.

"Walt, I ain't feelin' so good," Billie said. "You think I could have a fix now?"

"Yeah, I reckon you can."

Billie got her spoon and syringe from her purse, and Walt took them from her. As he turned to get the morphine from the kitchen, he momentarily considered giving Billie a deliberate overdose. She was a liability to him and everyone else, and he couldn't keep her hidden forever. If Stella found out, she'd likely come over here and make Walt kill the girl. No. More likely kill her, herself, and leave the mess for Walt to clean up. No. He had to think. There had to be a way out of this without any more killing. He just had to sit still and think on it some more.

As he prepared Billie's fix and then fed it to her, he found himself thinking what a great life he and Stella could have had if Dante hadn't taken her out of that bordello. Walt would've married her, and they could be living somewhere else by now. But they were two different people now. He wondered if it could even be possible after all they'd done to get where they were. As Billie began to nod from the shot, Walt almost envied her the oblivion the morphine had given her.

12

Savanna knocked at Sassafrass's door, and heard a male voice call out to come in. The doorknob turned at her touch and she entered the room.

She found Sassafrass sitting behind his desk, dressed in a maroon silk smoking jacket with a huge panatella between his pale, sensual lips. He looked at Savanna, his big bald head shining in the light and one side of his mouth turned up into a grin.

"Well, well, if it ain't li'l Savanna," Sass said in a full bass voice. He removed the huge cigar from his mouth and blew a long plume of blue-gray smoke from between pursed lips. "I ain't had a real woman up here until now. This is a special occasion."

"Save the applesauce, Sass," Savanna said. "I didn't come up here to entertain you. I wouldn't if you were the last dick wavin' on the North American continent." She knew all about Sassafrass and what he spent most of his time doing up here. She also knew the only way to get his respect was to talk as roughly as she knew how.

"And what did you come for, Chicken Little?" he asked, his eyes still appraising her.

"I'm trying to find out who killed Lottie Sonnier," she said.

"Hmmm," he said, cocking an eyebrow at the ceiling. "Seems like I know that name."

"Don't play dumb," she countered. "You know what happened to her two nights ago. You probably knew five minutes after it happened."

He chuckled. "Life is full of sudden stops, li'l sister. What makes you think I know anything?"

"Like I said, you know everything," she said with a seductive smile. "Sometimes even before it happens."

He emitted a small snort of a laugh. "Then why didn't you come here first, 'stead of goin' over to see what you could scare outa Harvey Prado? All his brains is hangin' betwixt his legs."

"I heard from somebody else that a person I was lookin' for hung out in there," Savanna said. "I figured it wouldn't do any harm to see what Harvey'd say about her."

"What 'her' was that?" Sass asked.

"A woman with cat's eyes," Savanna said. "I don't know her name, but I'll bet even money she knows all kinds of things I want to know."

Sassafrass stretched out his arms, then folded his hands behind his hairless neck, squinting at her from behind a small cloud of cigar smoke. "What makes you think she or anybody else's gonna talk to you about what you wanna hear, girl? You're stickin' that pretty nose into things that already got one woman killed. You wanna end up in the graveyard with her?"

Savanna felt cold all over, and her fingers played self-consciously with the catch of her bag. Farrell had always warned her to keep the gun close to hand when she carried it, but even in her lap, it didn't seem quite close enough at that moment.

"I told you Lottie was a friend of mine. I can't just let it lie," she answered in a tight voice.

"Got-*damn*, but you're hardheaded," Sass said, sitting up suddenly. "Go on and get outa my place. This ain't none of . . ." He stopped speaking abruptly as the telephone began to ring. He gave Savanna a hard look, and picked up the receiver.

"Yeah," he said roughly. "Uh huh. Yeah. No. Are you crazy?" His dark face got tight and shiny as beads of perspiration began to stand out on his broad forehead. "Y-yeah. A-awright." He hung up the telephone receiver heavily, his eyes still focused on it.

Savanna could feel something electric in the air, a smell of fear so tangible she could almost touch it. With focused deliberation, she unlatched the clasp of her bag and drew the Colt from inside. As she did, she stood up, every nerve in her body poised to fight or run. Her movements registered on Sass's brain, and he looked up at her slowly, a sick look spreading across his broad features. Savanna raised the gun to shoulder level, pointed it at his head, and cocked it. As the gunlock's final click died in the hushed room, the lights went out.

Thrust into total darkness, Savanna fired the gun, then stepped quickly to one side, firing on either side of where her first shot had gone. She was turning to find the door when something grabbed her arms from behind and pinioned them. She kicked out, gasping for breath, then kicked out again and heard a cry as she felt her assailant's grip relax. She was grinning, turning to shoot him when something hard and unyielding struck her over the temple, and her world dissolved in a welter of exploding lights.

It was no later than 6:00 A.M. when the river tug *Eustace Tilley* tied up at Pilot Town, the last civilized piece of Louisiana before you hit the Gulf of Mexico. Captain Danny O'Neil loaned Farrell a set of coveralls and some brogans, and led him over the gangplank to a ramshackle clapboard building on the other side of the road. It had a long gallery running the length of the front, and nailed all over it were rusty tin signs advertising the likes of Royal Crown Cola, Sun Drop, Beech Nut chewing tobacco, and Merita bread. Even at that early hour, a trio of loafers were already sitting on a bench out front, yawning, whittling, and spitting into the dust.

The inside was dim, warm, and dry, and everywhere were shelves, counters, and glass cases containing everything from sour pickles and peppermint sticks to ladies' foundations and curtain rods. A fat little man was behind the main counter, squinting through a pair of wire-rimmed spectacles as he worked some figures on a clipboard.

"Mr. Jeeter," O'Neil said from the entrance. "I got a man needs to do some business with you."

Jeeter's eyes jumped from the clipboard to the two men who advanced upon him. "Well, Danny, you're better'n a newspaper advertisement. What do you need, mister?"

"Better ask what he don't need," O'Neil said with a grin. "We fished him outa the river last night, ridin' an ole tree like it was a buckin' bronco in a rodeo."

"I need some clothes and a place to wash up, if you've got one," Farrell said.

"What kind of clothes?" Jeeter asked.

"Underwear, socks, shirt, a suit if you've got one. Just pants and a jacket if you don't. Oh, and some shoes," Farrell said.

Jeeter's eyes appraised Farrell as he walked out into the store. He went to a shelf and took a large white box, which he brought over to Farrell. "Fishing boat skipper ordered this from New Orleans last year for a weddin'. The gal jilted him and he didn't need it no more. Looks to be about your size."

He opened the box, and revealed a gray flannel suit with narrow pinstripes. Farrell took it from him. Jeeter led him around the rest of the store, dumping in socks, underwear, a white shirt, and a gaudy yellow tie with red paisleys all over it. From under another counter, he found a pair of brown oxfords with toe caps, and a belt. Farrell took everything over to the counter, and told Jeeter to talley everything up.

"There's one other thing I need, if you happen to have one," Farrell said as the other man began adding up his purchases.

"What's that?" the man asked in a distracted voice.

"A gun."

The man flicked his eyes up at Farrell, then over to O'Neil, who merely grinned.

"A gun?"

"A pistol of some kind, and some cartridges for it," Farrell said.

Jeeter tried to keep his face neutral, and pursed his mouth up as he thought about it. After studying Farrell's face for a few moments, he went to a chest behind the main counter, got out a key, and unlocked it. From it he took a parcel wrapped in oilcloth, and brought it back to where Farrell and O'Neil waited.

"Back durin' Prohibition, we had a lotta fireworks 'round these parts," Jeeter began. "Knew an ole boy who ran rum past the Coast Guard boats purty reg'lar. Well, when Repeal came, he was out of a job. Didn't need this no more, so I bought it from him for thirty dollars. I'll let you have it for fifty."

Farrell untied the string that held the parcel together, and removed the oilcloth wrappings. Inside he found a black leather spring clip shoulder holster. He removed from it a Colt .38 military automatic with a long barrel and a lanyard swivel on the left side of the grip. Farrell snapped out the empty magazine, worked the slide, brought the gun to eye level. He sighted along the barrel, and pulled the trigger. "I'll take it," he said.

O'Neil, who had watched his movements with an interested eye,

nodded approvingly and took something from his hip pocket. "Seein'
as you thought you'd need that, reckon maybe you'll want these
back, too. Might come in handy when you find out who threw you
in the drink." He handed Farrell his spring-blade stiletto and the
Solingen steel razor that he had thought lost. Both had been wiped
dry and clean, and had a sheen of oil on the metal parts.

"Thanks," Farrell said with a small smile. "Now how do I get
back to New Orleans?"

The new day dawned with gray clouds scudding across the drear
February sky, and Frank Casey had his full share of worries. He'd
tried several times to reach Farrell, but no one had seen him since
the previous day. Harry, his bar manager, told him that Savanna
Beaulieu had called the previous evening looking for Farrell, and
had sounded both worried and excited about something.

Casey sat thinking about that for some time. Savanna had not
been at the wake, but he had a hunch she might be involved with
the Sonnier family in some way. He pulled his telephone toward him
again, and called the Club Moulin Rouge. He got Savanna's bar
manager, Nathan Pargeter, and asked for his boss. Nathan reported
that he hadn't seen her since the previous afternoon. He didn't seem
concerned, because he knew she sometimes kept late hours, and
didn't show up until the next morning.

Casey broke the connection and sat back sucking on his teeth.
Something smelled fishy to him, and he felt mildly worried for reasons
he couldn't quite explain to himself. While he sat at his kitchen table
stewing, Daggett walked in, with a bit of shaving lather still adhering
to his left earlobe.

"Good morning," Casey said. "Sleep well?"

"Pretty well, considering," Daggett said with a tired grin. He still
had a face towel over his shoulder, and used it to wipe the errant
blob of soap from his ear. "Anything happening?"

Casey cocked an eye at the ex-policeman. "Yes and no," he said.
"Wes Farrell's been out prying into things on your behalf, and he's
gone missing. You know who Savanna Beaulieu is?"

"Sure," Daggett said. "I knew her when she called herself Rosalee
Ortique. I still think of her like that. She's a friend of Lottie's and
her family."

Casey nodded. "I suspected that. She's missing, too."

Daggett leaned back in the kitchen chair he'd taken, and looked at Casey blank-faced. "Think it's got anything to do with last night's mess?"

"Yes," Casey said. He got up and walked to the electric icebox. "I'm going to fry up some ham and eggs. Can I interest you in any?"

Daggett nodded. "Thanks. I didn't eat last night, and I could eat a wet mule this mornin'. What are you planning to do today, and can I help?"

"First we're going to go down and see Lottie's boss at Community Service Agency and see what she can tell us. After that, it's kind of up in the air. Things look to be heating up a little, though. I think something might break today, if we have a little luck. Put some water in this pot and let's get some coffee going. My head's still a little fuzzy."

The two men cooked and ate enough food to carry a troop of cavalry, then Daggett finished dressing while Casey shaved and brushed his teeth. By eight-thirty they were out on the street.

It was nearing nine when they pulled up in front of the building that served as headquarters for Community Service Agency. In less than five minutes they were in the office of Sallie Taylor.

"Good morning," she said to them. "You must be Israel Daggett."

"Yes, ma'am," Daggett said.

"I'm terribly sorry for what's happened," Mrs. Taylor said. "Lottie was a wonderful person. I still can't believe it happened. Have you spoken to Mr. Farrell at all?"

Casey tried to keep his face neutral. "No, not recently. He's been here already, then."

"Yes," she replied. "He was interested in knowing about a prostitute Lottie had been counseling before she was—"

"Prostitute?" Casey interrupted. "What's her name?"

"I couldn't remember it when he was here, but I've found it in Lottie's files. It's Billie Talmadge."

Casey and Daggett exchanged a knowing look.

"Do you happen to have an address for Billie?" Casey asked.

"Yes," Mrs. Taylor said, handing him a slip of notepaper. "She was working in a bordello on Mystery Street. That's the address on the paper. Do you think it's important?"

Casey looked at the paper and nodded. "I think it might be. Is there anything else you've uncovered that might be useful in this investigation?"

"I don't know if this is of any use, but she left a list of names in her desk drawer. Billie's name is on there, so I thought there might be some connection."

She handed over a second piece of paper, which Casey unfolded and looked at for several seconds. Daggett looked curiously at the police captain's face, but nothing registered there that told him anything. After a while, Casey folded the two pieces of paper and placed them in a leather case he removed from an inside breast pocket.

"Thank you, Mrs. Taylor," Casey said finally. "You've been an enormous help. I'll let you know how this all turns out. C'mon, Daggett."

As they walked from the suite of offices and got on the elevator, Daggett looked over at Casey. "Captain, I been out of harness for a while, but not so long I don't recognize that look on your face. What did she give you in there?"

Casey's face remained impassive as they walked out of the elevator and through the building entrance to the street. "It's too little to go on right now. Let me get a few balls in the air and see if it comes to something first. It might be nothing."

"Okay, Skipper. You're the boss."

They got into Casey's police cruiser and drove downtown until they came in sight of a telephone booth. Casey pulled the car to the corner, left the motor running, and got out. When he got into the phone booth, he dropped in a nickel and dialed headquarters. When the desk sergeant answered, Casey asked for Sergeant Snedegar.

"Snedegar here, Captain. What do you need?" the hatchet-faced detective asked.

"I need you to put somebody on a little research down at Notorial Archives and at one of the banks." He gave Snedegar some names, and gave specific instructions on what he was looking for. Snedegar told him he'd put Detective Fred Schwarz on it. Schwarz was a college graduate, and a natural for that kind of research, Snedegar assured Casey.

"Okay, Daggett," Casey said. "Now let's go talk to Billie Talmadge, if we can find her."

They drove through downtown traffic until they hit Canal Street, then followed Canal as far as Decatur. Decatur took them along the riverside edge of the French Quarter, which was alive with a duke's mixture of savory, sweet, and utterly foul aromas wafting from the docks.

On the other side of the Quarter, they picked up Esplanade, once the showplace of Creole life, and drove down as far as Mystery Street, a little cul-de-sac that butted up against the fence of the Fairgrounds Race Track. The house he was looking for was near the dead end of the street, which made him smile. The image of getting your ashes hauled while the fairgrounds announcer described the progress of the ponies was ridiculous enough to be a scene from a Marx Brothers movie—if the Hays Office allowed such things.

Ma Blanchard's place was a tall, white three-story Victorian with a green tile roof, a big front porch, and a carefully tended front lawn. The walk was lined with trimmed boxwoods that were almost mature enough to start forming a little hedge.

Casey Daggett mounted the stairs and knocked briefly at the door, then waited to see who would open it. Casey'd never met Ma Blanchard, herself, but he bet himself a nickel that the white-haired old lady with too much rouge on her lips and cheeks had to be her.

"Mrs. Blanchard?" he asked hopefully, holding his hat brim in both hands like a bashful cowpuncher.

Ma's eyes surveyed him and Daggett from head to toe, her face giving away none of her thoughts. "Yeah?"

Casey opened his badge case and held it up for her to see. "We're looking for a girl who's supposed to live here. Billie Talmadge?"

"Whaddaya want with her?" Ma asked.

"Just a few questions," Casey said. "And it's not a roust. We're not from Vice."

"No?" Ma said, unbending a little. "Well, I reckon y'all can come in then." She held the door and stepped away so he could enter. "She ain't here. Took off day before yestiddy and ain't come back yet."

Casey took off his overcoat, and draped it and his hat over the back of an overstuffed wing chair upholstered in olive-green corduroy. He sat down in another just like it and crossed his legs. Daggett stood behind his chair, still wearing his coat and hat.

"You got any idea where she might have gone?" he asked.

"These young girls, who knows where the hell they go," Ma Blanchard snorted. "They ain't got no loyalty, no loyalty at all."

"She have any friends here who might know anything about her?" he asked.

Ma scratched her white head, and thought a minute. "Terrie might know somethin'. Lemme go fetch her." She got laboriously to her feet, and shuffled over to the stairs. Casey listened to her halting progress, and wondered if his beard would grow before she got back. Daggett came around and rolled his eyes, and Casey grinned back at him.

After several very long minutes, the sound of the old woman's shuffle returned, followed by a lighter tread. A bit later, the old woman came in, accompanied by a woman with skin the color of old ivory who might still have been in her early thirties.

"This is Terrie," Ma Blanchard said, jerking her thumb at the other woman. "Tell Captain Casey what you told me, honey."

"Well, I don't know about talkin' to no cop, Ma," Terrie said in a nasal voice. "I don't want the kid to get in no trouble." Terrie was tall and wide across the hips. She wore a tattered housecoat, and her hair needed brushing. Casey wondered momentarily how she went about transforming herself when she was working into something more desirable.

"He ain't from vice," Ma said.

"I want to help her," Casey said. "I think she's in danger."

Terrie's eyes got wider, and she hugged herself suddenly with her arms, as if she felt a chill. "Well, she'd been actin' kinda funny lately. She was talkin' to this social worker named Lottie somethingerother. Was talkin' a lot about gettin' outa the life."

"Yes," Casey said. "Go on."

"Anyhow, this Lottie somethingerother got killed the other day, and Billie got to actin' funny, ya know? She kept talkin' about knowin' something that mighta got the woman killed."

"Did she say what that might be?" Casey said, trying to keep his excitement from showing.

Terrie scratched her unkempt hair, and assumed an elephantine look of thoughtfulness on her face. Finally, she said, "She said somethin' about tellin' the social worker about this guy who killed her pimp, Junior, years gone back. But she didn't tell me the guy's name, not that I would've wanted to know." She shuddered.

Casey felt chagrined, and sank back in his chair. He looked at his watch. "Would there be any way I could have a look at Billie's room?"

Ma looked up at Terrie, who shrugged. Then she turned back to Casey. "I guess it's okay. Just don't go actin' too much like a cop, willya? I don't wanta spook none of the customers."

Casey grinned. "Sure, we'll behave. Can Terrie show us the room?"

"Sure, honey," Terrie said. "Just follow me, okay?"

Business seemed light that morning, but it was only about ten in the middle of the week, with Friday payday yet to come. Casey heard a few muffled voices and creaking bedsprings as he passed by each door, but otherwise the house was quiet.

Terrie stopped in front of a door on the third floor, and opened it for Casey. Casey stuck his head inside, and found the light switch. A single bulb hanging from the ceiling without a shade cast a harsh yellow glare about the room. The bed was neatly made, and what little the girl had possessed was neatly stowed away.

Terrie sat down on the bed and watched silently as Casey and Daggett began to canvass the bureau, chifforobe, and a few shelves. Billie hadn't accumulated much in her life. There was the usual assortment of underthings, lace handkerchiefs, dime store perfume bottles, and cheap costume jewelry.

A little mantelpiece over a bricked-up fireplace had a half-dozen historical romances still in their gaudy jackets, five or six little glass animals standing in a group, and an old-fashioned ring-handled brass candlestick. Daggett began riffling the pages of the books, and feeling around the mantelpiece for a hiding place of some kind.

A cardboard box under the bureau caught Casey's eye, so he dragged it out and began sorting through the contents. There were snapshot photographs of many people not recognizable to him, and a few embossed cardboard display folders bearing the names of Negro nightclubs, among them the Sassafrass Lounge and the Brown Fedora down on Louisiana Avenue.

Casey opened them, and immediately recognized Junior Obregon and Walt Daggett. They were accompanied by two women. One of the women caught his eye. Whoever she was, the camera loved her. The others in the photo were laughing and behaving foolishly, but the woman faced the camera directly, a lazy line of cigarette smoke rising from the butt in her hand up alongside her exotic features. Her slanted eyes gazed indifferently from beneath half-lowered lids.

Casey held the photo up so Terrie could see it. "You know this woman?"

Terrie's lip curled. "Stella."

Casey's eyes narrowed. "What about her?"

"She's a bitch. She likes to act like she's somethin' better'n a whore."

"You know her last name?"

"Bascom. At least that's what she told us. I never believed it. She's just a little country nigger gal with dust between her toes. She had a north Louisiana accent you could cut with a knife when I knew her, but I bet she's got rid of it by now. She was makin' up her life as she went, prob'ly hidin' from somethin' or somebody."

"Where is she now?"

"Around," Terrie said. "I seen her once in a while, drivin' a big Buick automobile. Dressed in real expensive clothes. She's with some white man now, some big shot."

"Hmmm," Casey said, laying the photograph to one side. There was a third photo from the Brown Fedora, which he casually flipped open. The tableau was a bit different this time. Stella Bascomb, and Walt Daggett, and Sleepy Moyer were there, but a third man was in the picture with his back turned to the camera. He was wide-shouldered and tall. There was no clue as to his identity.

Casey removed the picture from the cardboard folder and turned it over. There was a date from sometime in 1932, but nothing else. He turned it back over and noted a five-pointed star embossed in the lower left corner. He put this photograph into his inside coat pocket, and put everything else in the box, and returned the box to its place beneath the bureau.

Casey stood up, and saw Daggett looking at him. The tall Negro made a shrugging motion with his shoulders and hands, and looked blank.

"I guess we're finished," Casey said.

Terrie got up without a word and led him back down the stairs. They found Ma Blanchard still sitting in the parlor. "Thanks, Mrs. Blanchard. I appreciate your help."

Ma waved a diffident hand, and they left the house.

"You still got that look, Captain," Daggett observed as they got back in the car.

"Let's just say that my curiosity is mounting," Casey said. Before he could elaborate, the police radio crackled from the dash.

"Inspector 37, calling Inspector 37."

Casey unclipped the microphone and keyed it. "Inspector 37, go ahead."

"A Mr. Wesley Farrell requests you meet him at headquarters, over."

"Tell him we're on the way. Thirty-seven out."

Stella Bascomb entered Joe Dante's office in the Hibernia Bank Building with some nonchalance, but the nonchalance evaporated when she saw the thick-bodied man standing beside Dante's desk. The man, who had the heavy features and reddish skin of the Red-bone, had sticking plaster in three places on his face, and the skin under his left eye was dark and bruised. He looked at Stella balefully.

"Nice you could drop by, baby," Dante said with heavy irony. "I sent for you two hours ago. Where you been?"

"I was up late last night," Stella said, feeling her stomach flip. "What's the panic?"

Dante laughed bitterly. "I'll tell you what the panic is, you little chisler. You been steppin' way out of line. So far out you're just about to step right out of the world. Who said you could order any hits on people?"

"What're you talkin' about?" Stella asked with cool nonchalance. She hadn't seen Joe like this many times, but when she had seen this side of him, somebody had usually gotten slapped down, hard.

"Don't play innocent with me, you dumb twist," Dante said viciously. "You sent Poche and Ridau here to take out Israel Daggett last night. Poche didn't come back. If he's dead, that ain't so bad, but if the cops've got him, your tit's in the ringer."

"Don't you call me a dumb twist," she snarled back.

"Shut up," he ordered. "If you talk again before I tell you, I'll get up and slap you into the middle of next week, get me? What the hell do you think you're doin', sending men out to kill somebody without tellin' me about it first?"

Stella shrugged diffidently, narrowing her eyes to slits. "You acted worried about Daggett comin' to town, so I thought I'd just get rid of him. I had it all set up to take him in his room at the Metro. Those assholes must've fucked it up some way."

"Goddamnit, why didn't you ask me first?" Joe yelled at the top of his lungs. "You know what's liable to happen if Poche ain't dead? He's liable to crack and send the cops right in here, you stupid little bitch. For me." Joe's reddened face was contorted with fury. Even

Stella felt the power of his anger, but she held herself perfectly still, hoping he'd give her a chance to talk her way out of it.

"Don't you think if Poche could talk, the cops'd be here already?" she asked quietly. "I sent them out late last night."

Joe's temper had cooled as he vented his anger, and he sat there with his chin cupped in one hand, drumming the fingers of the other on his desk blotter. His coal-black hair gleamed like patent leather in the sunlight filtering through the window behind him. "What else have you done, Stella? What other brilliant schemes have you let loose that could break my back, huh?"

Stella knew she dared not confess to having killed Wesley Farrell. Even though that went off without a hitch, Joe wouldn't be in the mood for it right now. "Nothin', honey. Nothin' at all. I was just tryin' to help."

Dante hadn't moved, and his fingers still drummed restlessly on the desk. "You got too much ambition, baby. You're real cute, but you got too much ambition for a whore. If I was you, I'd stick to what I was good at, and leave the heavy work to me and the boys. I've let all of them know that they don't do anything without my personal orders, so don't think you can pull this shit behind my back again, understand?" He stared at her with unblinking eyes, letting her know that this was no joke—that her life might depend on complete understanding between them.

Stella felt a flush crawl up her body from the belly to her face. She had not felt such hatred for a man since her father had raped her more than ten years before, and her fingers itched for the touch of blue steel. She'd taken a lot from him over the years, always telling herself that one day it would pay off. Now he was making it plain there would be no payoff—that she was just a piece of property that he kept around for amusement.

After a few moments of complete silence, Joe spoke again. "Go home, honey. And stay there. I'll let you know when I want you again." He let his gaze fall to the top of his desk as he picked up a fountain pen and began writing something on a sheet of paper.

Stella left the office without another word, her small body on fire with hate. It was getting time to cut her losses. The thing that needed doing was to get rid of Joe. She couldn't do it alone, but she knew somebody who'd help her. She stopped at the elevator and pushed the button. As she waited, she turned and stared back toward Joe's office door. He'd regret the things he'd said to her, and soon.

13

Casey and Daggett found Farrell pacing up and down in Casey's outer office. Although he was dressed in clothing far too inexpensive and sedate for his normal style, his neat appearance clashed vividly with the marks his desperate ride down the river had left on his face.

"Where have you been?" Casey asked as he walked in with Daggett at his side.

"I went dancing last night, and ended up in the river with my head split open," Farrell said.

Casey's eyebrows shot skyward. He looked over at his secretary and said, "Hold all my calls for the time being. I think I'm about to be busy." She smiled and nodded, but he could tell from the look in her eyes that she would make him miserable until he told her the whole story.

The three men went into Casey's office, removing their hats. After Casey closed the door behind him, he said, "Wes, this is Israel Daggett. Daggett, Wesley Farrell."

As the two tall men met in the middle of the room, each made an eyeball inventory of the other. The mutual appraisal lasted only a fraction of a second before each stuck out a hand and gripped that of the other. "I've heard of you," Daggett said. His eyes were fixed on Farrell's. They were not the eyes of a Negro watching the eyes of a white man in search of a threat or insult, but the eyes of a strong, confident man meeting those of an equal. Farrell could not help but be impressed.

"I've heard of you, too," Farrell said. "And I know you got a raw deal. I'd like to help you straighten things out."

Daggett's eyes gleamed, and he nodded in response to Farrell's profession of faith in him.

"Okay," Casey said. "Get to talking, and don't leave anything out."

"I started out talking to a guy down by the docks that knows Daggett's cousin, Walt," Farrell began. "He told me that Walt was sweet on a prostitute named Stella Bascomb, and that the two of them were connected to Joe Dante's drug operation. Later I went to Gert Town and talked to a man who runs a settlement house named Merton Diaz. He told me about a fight Lottie got into with Sleepy Moyer."

"I know most of that," Casey said.

"Here's something you didn't know," Farrell continued. "I went down to Community Service Agency later that day, and found that Lottie had been trying to get a prostitute out of the life when she was killed. I didn't get the name of the prostitute, but on my way out of there, somebody took a shot at me and missed my head by a thread."

"We've been to see Mrs. Taylor," Casey interjected. "The prostitute's name is Billie Talmadge. The same Billie Talmadge who was Junior Obregon's girl when he was killed. Probably not coincidentally, the same girl who got Walt Daggett thrown off the police force. We traced her to a whorehouse off Esplanade Avenue. The girl had cleared out, but she left something behind that I'm following up on."

Daggett shot a sharp look at Casey, but said nothing. Farrell noted the look, and nodded imperceptibly.

"After I left Community Service," Farrell continued, "I drove over to St. Claude and talked to Sarge Gallapoli at his bar. He knew who Stella Bascomb was, and said he believed she was hooked up with Joe Dante now."

"The woman with cat's eyes," Daggett said, speaking up for the first time.

Farrell nodded at him. "There's some who know her that way."

"I talked to another of Lottie's colleagues at the agency at her wake," Casey said. "He said Lottie was snooping around the Negro community, trying to find the source for all the drugs. He mentioned Walt's possible connection to that, and to the Bascomb woman."

Farrell's pale gray eyes were bright with anticipation, and he traded a look with Daggett. "I'm not sure how you fit into all this, but there are too many lines coming to a point, and you look more and more like the center."

"It's getting clearer and clearer that Junior Obregon's death and Lottie's are connected somehow," Casey said, "which suggests to me that my original opinion that you were unjustly framed is a correct one." He turned to Farrell. "You might be interested to know that Daggett and Dandy Walker were attacked at Daggett's hotel room last night. One of the assailants, Skeets Poche, fell on his knife, but the other man got away. Skeets worked a lot of free-lance leg breaking, but the Negro Squad says he was known to work for Walt Daggett. Walt's dropped out of sight, too. I find that damned interesting." Casey paused for a moment, then said, "But I still want to know what that crack about being in the river was about." He looked at Farrell pointedly.

"I ended up at the Brown Fedora last night," Farrell explained. "I was talking to Pops Meachum, having a little late supper when the Bascomb woman came in. She made a beeline for me, and we ended up at a table together. She's a hell of a dancer, Frank," Farrell said with a tight grin.

"Huh?" Casey said stupidly.

"We got to talking, and I braced her up about Dante," Farrell continued. "For some reason, that didn't trouble her. She invited me to her place for what I thought would be some fun and games, but she was ahead of me. When I got into her car, somebody black-jacked me. When I came to, I was at the bottom of the river. I'm fuzzy about it all, but I managed to hitch a ride on a big chunk of tree that was caught in the current. When I came to again, I was on a tugboat headed for Pilot Town. Funny thing, Frank," he said.

"Yeah, what's that?" Casey asked.

"There was a point when I thought I was at the end of the rope. The last thing I remember is my mother reaching out to me."

Casey's eyes flickered momentarily. He cut his eyes at Daggett, who was picking at one of his thumbnails, then back to Farrell. "After that, what happened?"

"I got some clothes and hitched a ride up here. It took me about four hours to get to your office, and here I am."

"Well, now we've got something to work with," Casey said. "I'll have the Bascomb woman picked up, and then I'll turn her over to the wrecking crew until she starts talking." Casey stopped, and began rubbing his chin as though trying to think of something. Then his eyes lit, and he snapped his fingers.

"I knew there was something I wanted to tell you," Casey said. "I tried to get in touch with Savanna Beaulieu while I was looking for you. She never got home last night, and Harry said she'd called you from the Sassafrass Lounge and needed your help."

Farrell's face registered nothing, but his eyes narrowed as he took in what Casey had said. "What would she have been doing at the Sassafrass Lounge?" he said finally. But inside, he knew she'd gone off by herself to help him, and now was probably in trouble. He fought to keep his uncertainty from his face.

"I don't know," Casey said, but it might be connected to the rest of this mess. Almost everything and everybody else is. Excuse me while I go check on something I've got one of my other detectives working on. You can use the phone if you want."

Casey got up and left the room, leaving Daggett and Farrell to themselves. Daggett was watching Farrell sharply, and after a moment, he spoke. "You a friend of Rosalee's, too, Mr. Farrell?" The question was asked without inflection, but Farrell could hear the curiusity behind it.

"Yes," he said.

"I know what you're thinking, Mr. Farrell. If you want to do anything about it, I'm your man. Rosalee's a friend of mine, too."

Farrell's head turned and his eyes lit on Daggett's face. Daggett could see a vein in his forehead pulsing. "I'm thinking of going over to see Sass DeLatte, and ask him what Savanna was there after. You want to come?"

"If you don't mind stoppin' by my room first," Daggett replied.

"No, why?"

"I'd like to pick up my gun," Daggett replied. "I'm the only one in this fracas that ain't heeled, and I'm tired of feeling left out."

"Frank isn't gonna like this," Farrell said warningly.

"You only live once," Daggett replied.

Farrell drove the Packard like it was a six-horse hitch with a band of murderous Apaches on its trail. He left downtown, miraculously without hitting anybody, and slewed the corner at Canal Street on two wheels. Traffic lights he ignored with a blatant contempt.

"If a cop stops us, we're cooked," Daggett opined casually. "It won't do you a bit of good to have an ex-con with a gun in the car."

Farrell said nothing, but it was clear that he understood the unspoken warning. He throttled back to thirty-five miles an hour, and tried not to run the lights after that.

"What's your plan?" Daggett asked as the roar of the engine lessened.

"Don't have one," Farrell said. "I thought we'd get there and play it as it lays."

At the turn to Orleans Avenue, they could see the concrete-and-glass-brick spire of the Sassafrass Lounge projecting ahead of them like a church steeple. Farrell cut his engine two blocks away, and let momentum guide them to a stop about a half-block from the entrance awning. The two men got out, and met at the front of the car.

"I'm going in the front door," Farrell said. "Go around back, and sweep your way forward. If you hear shooting, take care of yourself first. If anything happens to me, this'll all be up to you."

Daggett nodded, unable to think of anything to say to a statement like that. He turned and walked around the building out of sight. Farrell pulled his hat down low over his eyes and walked to the entrance. The doorman pulled the door open and Farrell passed through without a word.

It was past 2:00 P.M., and the lobby was largely deserted. The sound of a trombonist playing with the tune to "The Woody Woodpecker Song" emanated from the big room. Farrell cast his eyes from one side to the other as he made for the door he knew led upstairs.

"Do somethin' for ya, Mister Farrell?" a voice said from behind. Farrell turned and saw the dark bulk of Big Lucy standing there. Lucy was dressed in a white shirt with black trousers and a black bow tie. The sleeves of his shirt were rolled up to the elbow over his massive black forearms.

"I want to see Sass, Lucy," Farrell said tonelessly.

"I don't reckon he wants to see you, Mr. Farrell," Lucy replied quietly. "Y'all best go on home."

"I'm going upstairs," Farrell said. "Don't get in the way."

Lucy's round black face wore a pained expression. "I get paid for doin' what Sass tells me," he said. "He said nobody goes upstairs, so that's the way it has to be. Go on home, else I'll have to hurt ya."

Farrell half turned, and Lucy moved in front of him with a remarkable lightness of foot for a man so large. Farrell could see the other man's eyes become opaque, and his face flatten out. Farrell stepped in close and hit Lucy on the hinge of his jaw as hard as he could. The shock rode past his wrist and up into his shoulder like he'd hit concrete. Lucy absorbed the punch, then shook his head as if to clear it, and waded into Farrell's space.

The big man had been a professional fighter in his youth, and a professional leg-breaker after that. If he had any fear of physical pain, he had learned not to show it. He blocked Farrell's left jab with his arm, and drove his own left into Farrell's ribs. Farrell grunted, covered, and fell back. As Lucy moved toward him, Farrell let go two fierce right jabs into the other man's nose. He felt cartilage squash and break, and blood spurted onto his hand.

Lucy shook his head again, and his face became more determined looking. He threw a right into Farrell's forehead, snapping his head back, then came in with two swift jabs to the ribs. Farrell fell, rolling across the floor. Faster than Lucy could believe, he rolled back to his feet, the golden skin of his face flushed with blood, and his pale gray eyes glittering like chips of ice.

The big man moved in quickly to end it, but Farrell feinted and moved inside his reach, pounding Lucy's face with short, vicious jabs to the eyes, mouth, and the already-broken nose. Lucy grunted with pain, tried to cover and back up, but couldn't get outside Farrell's reach. The blood lust was on Farrell now, and he no longer saw a man in front of him, just an obstacle to overcome. By the time the fifth blow fell, Lucy was staggering, no longer covering. Farrell worked on the big man's torso and felt it grow softer with each blow. Finally, Lucy just folded up like a piece of wet cardboard, and fell senseless at Farrell's feet.

Farrell saw his hat laying on the carpet. He bent down, grabbed it, and jammed it back on his head. He stepped over Lucy's unconscious form, and took the stairs two at a time until he reached the top. The door was closed, so Farrell grabbed the knob, felt it give, and pushed the door open.

The suite appeared to be empty, but somewhere in one of the rooms Farrell could hear a radio faintly playing the Dorsey Brothers' version of "Tangerine." He smelled something heavy in the air, and recognized it as the smell of cordite. Someone had fired a gun in here recently.

He moved silently through the adjoining rooms, scanning each with his eyes as he went. He saw a kitchen ahead of him, and the sound of the radio grew louder. At the doorway, he found Sass, standing at the counter biting into a meatloaf sandwich.

When Sass saw him, he put the sandwich down on the counter, and spit the bite he'd just taken into the sink. "What the fuck you think you're doin' in here?" he demanded.

Farrell saw no need for any talk. He walked up and sank a hard left into Sass's gut. The big, bald man gasped for breath as he bent over, then Farrell grabbed him by the lapels of his vest and threw him bodily out of the kitchen.

"Where is she?" he asked in a dry, whisper of a voice.

"You fuckin' whore chaser, what're you talkin' about?" Sass asked, his voice a wheeze.

Farrell grabbed his vest, jerked the man to his feet in a single clean motion, and slapped him open-handed with his right hand. The slap cracked like a gunshot, and shook Sass to his ankles.

"Where is she?" Farrell asked, his voice louder.

"I don't . . ." Before he could finish, Farrell began slapping the bald man forehand and backhand until the harsh cracks fell into a rhythm that rang in Sass's ears. By the fifth slap, Sass's legs had turned to jelly, and his face was swollen and dark with ruptured capillaries. By the seventh slap, he could no longer stand at all, and had fallen completely out of Farrell's grasp.

Farrell went to the kitchen, and found an empty pitcher on the counter. He filled it with cold water, then carried it back to where Sass lay. He kicked Sass's ribs lightly for several seconds until he was certain the other man wasn't faking, then upended the pitcher into his upturned face.

The bald man gasped and sputtered as the water went down his nose and throat, and turned from side to side to escape the stinging stream. Painfully, laboriously, he pushed his body onto his side, and came up on one elbow. "No. No more. No more," he moaned.

Farrell reached into his clothing and the air filled with the metallic rasp of the razor opening in Farrell's hands. "Sass, you know me. I don't bluff, and I don't make promises I won't keep. Savanna's a friend of mine. If anything's happened to her, you better get ready to fight, run, or die. Now tell me where she is."

"Sleepy," Sass said, raising a weak hand in front of his face. "Sleepy come here for her. He made me stall her so he could get at her."

Farrell's face turned the color of bone. "Sleepy? Sleepy Moyer?"

"Yeah, yeah," Sass said in a small voice.

"Where'd he take her?" Farrell demanded.

"I—I don't know," Sass said, wailing in dispair.

Farrell knelt beside the bald man, grabbed him by the throat, and laid the cold steel of the razor along the jugular vein. "You better think of something then, 'cause I'm just about out of the need for you." He pressed the blunt edge of the razor into Sass's neck.

"No, no, no," Sass said, weeping like a child. "He's got a whorehouse on—on Annunciation, near L-Louisiana. Yellow p-paint. I—I d-don't know where else he mighta took her."

"Did he hurt her, Sass?"

Sass could not stop weeping. Farrell had broken everything in him that had been a man.

"Did he hurt her?" Farrell screamed in the other man's face.

"He—he sapped . . . her," Sass said.

"You sonofabitch," Farrell said in a voice that he didn't quite recognize as his own. "I ought to . . ."

Before he could complete the sentence, an explosion sounded behind him, and Farrell threw himself away from Sass's body, registering the heavy smell of burnt gunpowder as he rolled into a crouch.

Sprawled in the door, his left hand clutching his bloody right shoulder, was Big Lucy. Lying a bit in front of him was an old-time .45 frontier Colt, still cocked. Behind him, Israel Daggett stood with his gun in his hand. "Big Lucy," he said, "you're the luckiest sonofabitch I know. If I'd been in better practice with this shooter, you'd be layin' there holding your stupid head right now, 'stead of your arm."

Farrell got up a bit weakly, his hands trembling and his face pale. "I owe you that one," he said.

"Forget it," Daggett said. "You squeeze anything outa that worm?" He gestured with the muzzle of his gun at Sassafrass.

"Something," Farrell said. "What it's worth, I don't know." He walked over to where Sassafrass lay, and tapped him in the ribs with his toe until the bald man looked up at him.

"If I find out that you warned Sleepy, I'll be back for you," Farrell said. Sass could do nothing but nod, his swollen face contorted with pain.

"Let's go," Farrell said, picking up his hat and Lucy's gun. The two men left the room.

Savanna came back to consciousness in a dark room. She found that her wrists and ankles were tightly bound, and nearly numb. She could feel a hot place over her ear that ached dully, and nausea swept over her when she tried to move. She heard a moan escape her throat, and she bit down hard to keep from doing it again.

She tried to remember what had happened, and found only a confused series of images. She had been with Sassafrass DeLatte . . . in his suite at the Lounge. She'd been talking to him about Lottie. A telephone rang, yes, she could remember that, and Sass started to look funny. After that things were vague. Somebody had hit her, but she didn't know who, and now she was here in this dark room, only God knew where. She felt sick and scared.

Light erupted into her world, and she shut her eyes tightly to keep out the painful rays. Her head started hurting again, abominably, and her stomach roiled as the pain swept over her. She heard footsteps on a wooden floor, and opened her eyes a slit. Her vision was blurred, but she could make out the shape of a man.

"Welcome to hard times, baby sister," a man's voice said mockingly. "You done bit off more than you can chew this time."

Savanna forced her eyes to open wider. She saw a face she recognized. Sleepy Moyer. "You dirty bastard," she said hoarsely. "Wes Farrell's gonna cut you like a steer and make you eat the leavin's when he finds you."

Sleepy laughed contemptuously. "He ain't even alive, baby sister. And even if he was, which he ain't, he still wouldn't scare me none. I butted heads with a passel of white boys in pretty suits in my time, and I'm still here." He laughed again.

"You stupid little prong," Savanna said. "Nobody you know is good enough to kill him. You're dead and don't have sense enough to lie down."

The laughter drained out of Sleepy's eyes like water disappearing from a sink. He reached into his shirt pocket and brought out a straight razor with black celluloid handles. He jerked the blanket back from Savanna, and as she tried to squirm away from him, he began to systematically cut the clothing from her body. Her eyes grew wide as she watched the razor work, and she began to realize that she'd said too much.

Sleepy whistled "Chatanooga Choo-Choo" a bit off key as he

worked, his eyes gone flat and hard. When he had cut through her clothing and pushed the ragged pieces to the side, he folded the razor and put it on a table beside the bed where she lay. Then he began to unbutton his clothes, still whistling. It was only then that she realized he was going to rape her, and her throat grew hot and dry. She fought to keep the loathing out of her eyes, and began to breathe shallowly. When he was completely undressed, he crawled over her, and began to violate her body every way he could think of.

Nobody had touched Savanna in years who she hadn't wanted to touch her. When she'd fought her way out of prostitution, she'd found her self-respect again, and now this vicious little animal was stealing it away from her. In self-defense, she blanked her mind and tried not to scream.

When Casey returned to his office and found Farrell and Daggett gone, his face flushed to the color of his hair. He charged out to where his secretary was, and said, "Where did the two men in my office go?"

Mrs. Longley looked up at him from some typing she was doing. "They didn't say, Captain. But they were in a hurry."

Casey turned from her and stalked back into his office, uttering every foul word he knew under his breath. One of his recurring nightmares of late was of having to arrest and imprison his own son for a serious crime. Worse yet, Daggett had gone with him, undoubtedly placing his own freedom in jeopardy. Damn it, and they were so close to cleaning this mess up.

He thought of following them, but decided against it. Instead, he picked up his telephone and called the commander of the Negro Detective Squad.

"Sergeant Tripoli," a baritone voice said.

"This is Casey," he said. "Get a couple of detectives and a squad car with some uniformed men over to the Sassafrass Lounge. You know the place?"

"Yes, sir," Tripoli said. "Took my wife there on her birthday last month. Something happening there?"

"Maybe. I don't know for certain," Casey said. "I don't want you to go in there. Just keep the place under surveillance, and step in if anything untoward happens. Is that clear enough?"

"Yes, sir. You want me to play it by ear, and not break any of the crockery while I'm at it," Tripoli said.

Casey laughed out loud. "Sergeant, sometimes I get the feeling that you fellows don't really need me. You've already got it all figured out. Go to it."

"Yes, sir."

Now that he had that covered, Casey decided to run something down that had been on his mind since the night before. Now that he didn't have Daggett with him, he was free to do it.

He looked up the number for the Brown Fedora, and dialed it. It rang three times before anyone answered.

"Brown Fedora, Pops speakin'."

"This is Captain Frank Casey of the City Police," he said. "Is your photographer in this early in the day?"

"Carol Sue usually don't come in 'til six, Cap'n," Pops said. "Can I help you with somethin'?"

"I got a photograph taken in your place sometime back in '32," Casey said. "I wanted to ask her to help me identify somebody in the photo."

"Well, I don't reckon Carol Sue'd be the one you wanta talk to," Pops said. "Back in those days, Sid Richards was the house picture-taker. Called himself 'the photographer to the stars,' and always stamped a little star down in the corner. He got a better job at the *Louisiana Weekly* a few years ago and went to work over there."

"Thanks a lot," Casey said. "I'll check over there."

After hanging up, Casey quickly found the number for the newspaper, and dialed the telephone. Someone answered on the third ring.

"*Louisiana Weekly.*"

"This is Captain Frank Casey of the New Orleans Police. Is Sid Richards there by any chance?"

"Yes, sir, he's up in the darkroom. Shall I ring up there for him?"

"No, but would you please tell him that I'm on my way over, and to please not leave before I get there."

Casey hung up the phone and left.

Billie had gone to sleep after injecting the mixture of cocaine and morphine known in the underworld as a "speedball," and was in a bedroom at the back of Walt's house. Walt paced the floor, wracked with indecision. His instincts told him to cut his losses and get the hell out before somebody came looking for him.

The killing of Lottie Sonnier, the arrival in town of his cousin Israel, and the sudden appearance of a live witness to Junior Obregon's murder had him feeling like the man in the myth with the sword hanging over his head.

For the first time in his life, he felt like just running away from everything. He'd worked hard and taken some big risks to get where he was, but he was sitting on a time bomb, and he didn't want to be around when it went off. For all his faults, Walt was a shrewd man. He knew that the events of the past few days would bring everyone concerned to a disastrous confluence. Anyone connected to Dante was at risk, perhaps especially Walt, himself.

He finally sank down in his chair, exhausted from the pacing and worrying, and fell into a doze. He didn't know how long he slept before he heard the light tapping on the door. He came immediately awake, his hand seeking the Astra automatic. He pushed off the safety with his thumb, and looked at the clock on the mantel. It was after 4:00 P.M.

He walked cautiously to the door, stood well clear of it, and said, "Who's there?"

"Stella. Let me in."

Stella. The sound of her voice at his door produced both anticipation and dread in him. He'd never stopped wanting her, but their meetings always left him feeling diminished. He pulled the bolt and opened the door.

Stella walked in as if she owned the place. Her eyes fell briefly on the gun, then came lazily back to his face. "That for me?" she asked.

No matter what passed between them, he always ended up feeling foolish. "No," he said. "But there's trouble out there." He shoved the pistol into his waistband and closed the door.

"What I'm gonna say ain't easy," she began. "I know I ain't treated you right. I've been a bitch, and I'm sorry," she said as she sat down in one of his chairs.

"What?" Walt asked, his stomach fluttering.

"Joe's a louse," she continued. "He slapped me around, and accused me of double-crossing him. Sleepy's been tellin' him lies about me. Said I been cheatin' on Joe with you behind his back."

"Sleepy?" Walt said. "What's he got against you? Or me, for that matter. He works for me, and I always treated him right."

"Sleepy got ambitious," Stella said wearily. "He figures it's time he took over your territory. The only way he can do that is to get rid of you. Maybe I gave him the opening he needed."

"How?" Walt asked, his heart melting at her distress.

"He tried to get me into bed with him yesterday," she said. "I chased him off with my gun. He must've gone to Joe, 'cause Joe beat me and said he was gonna have you taken care of. I got out of his place as soon as I could, and come here to warn you. And to tell you I was wrong to you. I wanna make it up to you, if you'll let me." She walked to him, and reached out with one small hand and slid it sinuously up Walt's chest. Then she came closer, and he could smell the sandalwood she was wearing. "You're more of a man than Joe ever was. I see that now."

Walt's breath was coming in short, ragged gasps. It was all too much to take in. Stella wanting him back, and Sleepy double-crossing him. Sleepy was about to get a big surprise, the dirty little pissant. Sleepy was good, but Walt knew he was better, particularly when he had a reason, and now he had one. "Don't you worry, baby," he said. "I'll take care of Sleepy. And then we'll do something about Joe, too. I'll teach him to put his hands on you."

Stella put her head against his chest, then put her arms around his waist and pulled her hips into him. The smell and touch of her was overpowering, and Walt began to tremble. He lowered his face hungrily to her waiting mouth.

14

The news of the fracas at the Sassafrass Lounge didn't take long to reach Joe Dante at his house on De Saix Avenue.

"What do you want, Sass?" Dante asked. "I'm busy."

"Fuck you and your busy. You and me are quits," Sass yelled. "Farrell knows Sleepy took the Savanna dame outa here last night. He's a crazy man, and I ain't gonna let him kill me for you nor nobody else."

"What the hell are you talkin' about?" Dante hissed between his teeth. "I didn't tell Sleepy to do anything."

"Ram it, white boy," Sass said. "Jam it in sideways, you greasy dago fuck. Somebody told Farrell the bitch was here. He done beat me and Big Lucy like we was nothin' but cur dogs, and then Iz Daggett shot Lucy when he was tryin' to help me. I didn't want nothin' to do with the mess you and Stella is up to, and now I'm out of it. Money is good, but you can always get money. You can't get no other life, and Farrell's a lifetaker."

"You can't talk to me like that, nigger!" Dante yelled. "I don't even know what you're talkin' about."

"Like hell," Sass roared back. "First that Beaulieu woman comes in here askin' a lot of questions about Lottie Sonnier, then Sleepy calls and takes her out of here. For all I know, she's as dead as Lottie Sonnier, and that's too many dead bodies for me. You and Stella and Sleepy and Walt can just kiss my ass, 'cause I'm gettin' away from here before Farrell or somebody else comes back in here with a gun."

"What'd you tell him?" Dante demanded in a shrill voice.

"I didn't tell him nothin'," Sass said, " 'Cept Sleepy sapped the woman and took her outa here. I sent him to Sleepy's house on Annunciation. If you're real lucky, he'll find his woman and kill Sleepy before he talks too much. I'm through, Dante. Finished." He hung up the telephone without another word, leaving Dante standing there, slack-jawed with the dead receiver in his hand. After a long moment, Dante dropped it back into the cradle, and sagged in his desk chair.

One of his bodyguards, a Swedish ex-seaman named Lars, stood there with a quizzical look on his face. "You want I should do something for you, boss?"

Dante ignored him and dialed Stella's number. It rang for fifteen times before he gave up and replaced it in the cradle. He wasn't sure just what was going on. He didn't know anything about Wes Farrell or Savanna Beaulieu, although he knew who they were. What they had to do with Sass, Sleepy, or anybody else was a mystery to him.

It was clear that now they were somehow involved in this mess over the Sonnier woman, which was something he knew nothing about. Was this some more of Stella's conniving behind his back? He came to a rapid decision that it was time to get rid of her, and maybe the others, too.

He pulled the telephone toward him and dialed the number of Sleepy's apartment. It rang many times before he broke the connection and dialed another. He dialed three more numbers, none of which responded. He looked up at Lars and said, "Call Marco and get the car. We're going to hole up at the club on the Old Hammond Highway until some of the shit stops falling."

"Yah," Lars said, then went off to do Dante's bidding. Dante opened the drawer to his desk and took out a pearl-handled .38 Smith & Wesson with a two-inch barrel. He checked to see that it was loaded, then put it in the pocket of his jacket.

He reached for the telephone and dialed a number. It rang three times before anyone picked it up.

"Ridau, this is Dante," he said into the mouthpiece. "You wanna pay Stella back for the shit you and Poche fell into the other night? Fine. I want you to find her and get rid of her. She's got the whole town in an uproar, and if we don't move fast, everything I've got is gonna fall down around my ears. You know where she lives? Good.

Make her disappear, permanent." He slammed the receiver down on the cradle and got up from the desk.

Walt was in his bed with the lights out, feeling the pressure of Stella's body lying in the crook of his arm. He remembered anew how much he'd loved her in the past. They'd had a nice thing going before she met Dante and he took her out of that brothel where she was working. He should have killed Dante then, but Stella made it clear she wanted to move up in the world. Well, that was over. If Stella wanted him back, he'd buck Dante and six more like him. He was good with a gun, damn good. It was the only thing about being a policeman he'd excelled at.

After he got Sleepy, he'd hit Dante's bodyguards, then take Dante out afterward. He particularly wanted to kill that Swede, Lars. He'd taken a lot of shit from that fish-faced motherfucker.

Stella sighed in her sleep, and moved closer to him. The feel of her skin on his was like an electric current going through him, and he felt aroused all over again. He turned slightly toward her, and felt his lips brush her thick, dark hair.

"You awake, honey?" he asked in a soft voice.

She yawned, and said, "Uhm, humm." Then, "My, my, my, we ain't ready to play again already, are we?" She ran her fingers lightly over his stomach and down to his groin. He could see hot yellow flashes in front of his eyes and groaned softly.

"I don't know why I ever let you go, Walt," she said as her fingers played across his body. "You were the best, and you always treated me right. To Joe I was just another whore."

Walt felt his anger at Dante flame into high heat as she said this, and he pulled her closer. She chuckled and put her arms around his waist. Soon they were rocking to an age-old rhythm that took Walt's mind off everything but Stella. Later, he lay there gasping for breath with Stella resting on top of him. After a while she spoke.

"We need to get the show on the road, sugar," she said. "Sleepy's probably over at that whorehouse he owns on Annunciation Street. You could go over there and take care of him now while it's still dark. It's so late that probably nobody would see you come and go. You got a silencer for your gun?"

Walt felt cold all over. Now that the lovemaking was over, he faced the reality that he really had to kill some people, if he and

Stella were going to survive. Even so, he'd never had to kill anyone before. His belly was doing a swan dive. He sat up quickly and pushed the cover back from him.

"Don't worry, baby," Stella said, seeming to intuit his sudden case of nerves. "Sleepy would never think you'd try to kill him. He'll be completely off guard. I brought along a gun with a silencer you can use." She pushed back the covers and stood up, her boyish figure just visible to him from light filtering in from the living room.

She put on her step-ins and pulled a slip over her head, then found her purse among the debris of their hastily shed clothing. She sat down on the bed, opened the bag, and pulled out a small, flat pistol.

Walt turned on the bed lamp and examined the gun. It was a slim-barreled Browning .32 automatic. Screwed to the end of the barrel was a six-inch tube of stainless steel with numerous holes bored in a symmetrical pattern all over its surface.

"I had that silencer specially made, baby," Stella said. "It's good for four shots before it has to be repacked with steel wool. It won't make any more noise than somebody snappin' their fingers on a dance floor. Sleepy and Joe won't know what hit 'em. God, I wish I could be there to see it." Her voice was low and thick with barely suppressed excitement.

Walt pulled back the slide, and saw a fresh cartridge slide into the breech. He set the safety and laid the gun aside. Stella crawled to him and sat astride his lap, taking his face in her small, soft hands.

"This is gonna be the beginning of something big, sugar," she said in a tender voice. "We're on the way to runnin' things in our part of town without no white man tellin' us what to do." She kissed his mouth, and ran her tongue slowly about the contours of his lips. He could feel himself getting hard all over again, in spite of the fatigue and nervousness he felt.

She got up then and dressed quickly in the rest of her clothes. When she was finished, she put her bag over her arm and walked around to Walt's side of the bed. He was buttoning his shirt, and having a hard time doing it with his quivering fingers. He stood up and looked down on her with mixed feelings of tenderness and disquiet.

"I'll be at my place in Broadmoor when you're finished," she said. "Come over there and we'll decide what to do next."

"All right," he said, following her to the living room.

She turned at the door and laid a hand on his face, looking at him with such love that he felt his legs get weak. Then she opened the door and left him standing there with the silenced Browning hanging from his right hand.

Billie's eyes came open in the dark, and her body tensed. Something, some sound, had awakened her, and she sat up. The drowse brought about by the speedball had passed, and she felt sharp and alive with the drugs in her veins. There was the sound again. She got up, still wearing just her step-ins, and padded barefoot to the door. There was nothing in the room directly adjacent to hers, so she walked through it to the next room.

She heard the unmistakable sounds of two humans making love, and the sounds brought her up short. Walt had been alone when she'd taken the fix, and so far as she knew, he lived alone. She stood back from the open door, and listened to the whisper of limbs on sheets until climactic cries emanated from the bed.

She heard them talking, and there was something about the woman's voice that was familiar to her. A lamp came on in the room, and she pressed herself close to the wall and listened. She heard the woman talk to Walt about killing Sleepy and Joe Dante, and the words shook her. Walt had always seemed like such a nice man, too quiet to be going up against people as dangerous as Sleepy Moyer and Joe Dante.

Wait—what now? The woman rummaged in a purse and brought something out which she heard described as a gun with a silencer on it. The woman was speaking loud enough for Billie to hear everything.

Then she knew the voice. It was Stella. Billie's blood turned to ice in her veins, and she put a cautionary hand to her mouth to prevent any sounds from coming from it. She backed away from the door and went back to the room where she'd been sleeping. She'd thought she was safe with Walt, and now Stella was here sending him out to kill. Billie's stomach roiled.

Her first thought was to run, but to where? She had no real friends, and had very little money. She got back into the bed and lay very still in the hopes that she could clear her mind and think. After a time, she heard Walt go into the bathroom. Water ran in the tub, and she could hear him washing himself. When she heard the loud gurgling of water going down a drain, she pulled the covers up to her chin and turned on her side, facing the wall opposite the door.

The sounds of Walt's footsteps came and went for several moments. Then he came to the door of her room, and stood there quietly. After a while, he walked away. Within a minute or so, she thought she heard the front door open and close, then she got cautiously from the bed, dressed, and shoved her feet into her worn red shoes.

She crept room by room to the front, and got to the living-room window in time to see Walt's car leave the curb. Now she gave in to complete despair and sat on the floor, crying like a lost child.

Stella was poison, and Walt was as good as dead, for even if he lived through his confrontations with Sleepy and Dante, Stella would dispose of him when she had no further use for him.

Billie's well-developed sense of self-preservation kicked into gear, and she quickly got dressed. Then she began rummaging through the house looking for money. After a period of fruitless search, she came to Walt's desk, but it was locked. She found a heavy steel paper knife lying on the desk's surface, and used it on the lock. The wood was heavy and thick, but Billie's panic lent her strength. By bearing down, she was able to pop the latch from the mitered slot in the wood.

The middle drawer held nothing but paper, pencils, and a bottle of ink. Two more drawers held a myriad of useless items. The third drawer contained something that brought her up short. It was a folder made of soft, expensive leather, secured by a small belt and buckle that encircled it. Curious, she unbuckled the belt and opened the folder. It unfolded into four walletlike sections, three of which contained papers that meant nothing to Billie. However, the fourth wallet contained over a thousand dollars in fifties and hundreds. Billie almost wept with joy. She was saved.

She happened to glance into the still-open drawer, and saw the black shape of a little .25 caliber Colt automatic. She didn't like guns as a rule, but she was in deep, and couldn't see daylight yet. She snatched the little gun up and shoved the drawer closed.

She pushed the money back into the wallet, folded it back together, and secured it with the buckle. She walked quickly back into her room, pushed the folder into her large purse, and ran back to the front with her coat over her shoulder. She didn't bother to close the door after herself, and left the porch at a dead run.

Frank Casey's eyes felt like the sockets were filled with sand. *I'm getting too damned old for this,* he thought as he pulled his police cruiser to a stop outside the offices of the *Louisiana Weekly* on Howard Avenue. The unassuming nature of the two-story building belied the importance of this Negro weekly newspaper. Casey knew from other newspapermen that it was the premier Negro newspaper in the Deep South, and had a national readership.

He entered the lobby yawning and rubbing the back of his neck as he walked. He saw a young black man of perhaps twenty-five years going over a sheet of copy with a pencil held in the fingers of his right hand. He seemed very intent, and didn't notice Casey until the policeman stopped in front of him.

"Yes, sir," the young man said as he looked up. "Sorry, I was so busy proofing that I didn't hear you come in."

Casey held out his gold shield. "No apologies necessary. I called earlier about Sid Richards. Can I speak to him?"

"Sure, you're Captain Casey," the young man said. "Thought I recognized your voice. Just let me call upstairs."

"Thanks," Casey said with a smile. The young man was very self-possessed. Casey had shown his badge to many another Negro over the years, and the sight had almost invariably caused consternation, no matter how hard Casey had tried to appear nonthreatening.

Within a moment, the young man was back. "Sid's in his office darkroom on the second floor. Take the stairs and follow the corridor all the way back."

Casey touched a finger to the brim of his hat. "Thanks." Then he walked to the staircase.

Upstairs, he found the door at the end of a long hall open and filled with light. Casey stuck in his head, and called, "Mr. Richards?"

A neat, medium-size brown-skinned man wearing a white shirt, red tie, and a brown wool vest and trousers rose up from behind a pile of paper and photographic prints. He wore a mustache flecked lightly with gray, and his hair was long and smoothed back with pomade. "You Captain Casey?" he asked.

"Right," Casey said. "I've got something I want you to look at." He opened the cardboard folder and showed the photograph he'd found at Billie's room.

Sid Richards came forward, pushing his unbuttoned shirtsleeves higher on his forearms, and took the photograph. "Sure, I remember this. That was some hot mama," he said, grinning appreciatively.

"I was wondering if you could tell me who this man might be," Casey said, pointing at the man with his back to the camera.

"Hmmm," Richards said. "I might have another print of that. Sometimes people don't want their pictures taken, or even turn their heads at the wrong moment. Seems to me that was what happened that time. Let me look in my negative file. This was a few years ago."

Richards walked deeper into his file-cabinet-crammed office and began pulling drawers open. On the third drawer, he said, "ah, ha," and pulled a manila folder from the drawer. He removed a handful of negatives, and began holding them up to the light. Finally, he found what he wanted, and waved it.

"I think we got what you want here," he said. "Have a cup of coffee, and I'll have a print for you in a jiffy." He pointed over Casey's shoulder to a large, stained metal urn that rested precariously on top of yet another filing cabinet. Occasional perking noises and the hiss of steam emanated from it.

Casey found a thick, handleless china mug with U.S. Navy markings that seemed reasonably clean, drew coffee from the urn, and sat down in one of the few chairs not piled with material. He sipped the coffee, and gratefully emptied his mind for a few moments.

Fifteen minutes later, the coffee was gone and Casey was feeling pleasantly relaxed. He heard a sound, and turned his head to see Sid Richards walking toward him from the darkroom. In his hand he held a damp print fresh from the fixative.

"Think I got what you need here," he said. "I probably would've remembered this guy, except for the woman. She's the kind makes you forget your own name." He grinned, and held the print out to Casey.

"Holy Mother of Jesus," Casey said. The one thing he needed to confirm a day's worth of suspicions was in his hand. "This is interesting, indeed. Can I keep this?" he asked.

"Sure," Richards said. "I got plenty more where that came from." He stretched his arms wide, and swung them in a semicircle.

Casey laughed, and touched a finger to the brim of his hat as he left the cluttered office.

———

Dandy Walker left the noise of Rampart Street and entered the lobby of the Metro Hotel. He saw Arthur behind the desk, and walked over to him.

"Is Israel Daggett in his room?"

"No, I think you missed him," Arthur said. "He was gone last night and most of the day, but he came back here a few hours ago, went upstairs, and came right back down again. He didn't have any messages, so we only spoke for a moment. He didn't say where he was headed, or when he'd be back. You want to leave a message I can give him if he phones in?"

"No, that's okay, I reckon," Dandy said. He shoved his hands into his trouser pockets, and walked back out on Rampart Street. His eyes roamed up and down the long street, taking in the flickering neon lights and hearing the faint chitter and wail of trumpets leaking from the closed doors of a dozen bars and nightspots.

When he was young, he'd thought Rampart Street the greatest place in the world, even better than Lenox Avenue in Harlem. He'd seen and done a lot, and he was grateful for those chances. He felt a bit melancholy, though, remembering all those good times. He wondered what had happened to them all, and what turns of fortune had left him an aging athlete, reduced to training boys to compete for the titles he'd been unable to achieve. There were other things he'd hoped to achieve, too, but now they were gone, too, forever. He cursed himself, and clenched his fists until the nails cut into his palms.

He drifted down the street until he heard snatches of a song he liked drifting from a bar. He turned into it, and sat down at the bar. When the bartender looked at him, he asked for a glass of Schlitz and a shot of Early Times to go along with it. He drank the shot right off, then chased it with a swallow of the good, cold beer.

The place wasn't much by Rampart Street standards, but the quiet was good for his nerves. They were shot. He reached into his pants pocket and brought out a crumpled package of cigarettes. He shook one out, laid the pack on the bar, and lit the one in his mouth with a match from a paper book lying beside the ashtray. He didn't like to smoke all that much, but sometimes, when his nerves were really frayed, he found that the nicotine had a marvelous calming effect on him.

He was as upset as he'd ever been, and wondered if he'd ever be all right again. Everything seemed wrong, and there seemed no way to fix them. He drew in a lungful of smoke, then let it out slowly as he reached for his beer glass and took a sip.

As he sat there, two men came into the bar. One was a brisk-moving, small man he vaguely knew as Dirty Dog McGee. He didn't know why the man was called that, and thought it a bit imprudent for such a small man to have such a bad-sounding name. The other was taller, but slim to the point of emaciation. Dandy knew his face, but not his name. The pair sat down the bar, and he paid them no particular mind.

"I'm tellin' you, there must be a full moon out 'er somethin'," the small man said emphatically. "They was a big fight in the Metro last night, and Iz Daggett's supposed to have killed a man. Skeets Poche was his name. A bad man, Skeets. I seen him cut a man to death over to Lafayette three years ago, then walked down the street and ate two hamburgers and a plate of pork and beans afterwards."

The excessively skinny man laughed briefly, and then drank from a pilsner glass full of beer. The little man continued talking as though the other man was breathless with impatience for the rest of the story.

"Earlier today, I heard Daggett and this white man named Farrell went over to the Sassafrass Lounge, beat Sassafrass 'til his face looked bee-stung, and then shot Big Lucy. Can you dig that? Big Lucy ain't never lost a fight I heard of. I done heard plenty 'bout that Farrell, though. He kilt six men out by the Lakefront last fall, 'cludin' Gus Moroni, that po-lice captain. That was one man nobody's gonna miss."

Dandy sat up straighter and began listening intently to the talkative little man's story. When the small man paused to gulp some of his beer, he turned toward him.

"Hey, Doggie," he said. "Was you just talkin' about Iz Daggett?"

"Who is that? Dandy Walker?" Doggie asked. "Sure it is." He hoped off his bar stool and walked over to pump Dandy's hand. "Gladtaseeya, man," he said.

"You was talkin' about Iz Daggett," Dandy reminded him.

"Sure was," Doggie said with a big grin. "He been *raisin'* hell since he got back to town. He a friend of yours?"

"I grew up with 'im, and we did some fightin' together before he went on the cops," Dandy said. "You know where he went after he and that Farrell fella left Sass's place?"

"Somebody who talked to Big Lucy at the emergency room said they took outa there lookin' for Sleepy Moyer," Doggie said.

Dandy's face flattened as he took in Doggie's words. He got up from his stool, and Doggie stepped back, a little nervous at Dandy's change of attitude.

"You all right, man?" Doggie asked in a quiet voice.

Dandy said nothing, and turned and left the bar, his cigarette pack left on the bar. Doggie raised his hand preparatory to calling him back, but Dandy was already gone. After a second, Doggie scooped up the cigarettes, frowned disapprovingly at the brand, then put them in his shirt pocket and went back to his friend.

Now that Stella had set Walt in motion, she felt a curious sense of satisfaction. The ease with which she'd manipulated Walt into killing Sleepy renewed her confidence in her own powers. She knew that once Walt had taken Sleepy out, his confidence would harden, and then he'd turn his attention to Dante. She wished she could be there when that happened. She wanted to see Dante on his knees begging for his life to a black man.

She turned into her street enjoying the picture she'd conjured, and slowed as she neared her house. The street was dark and deserted but for a few cars. She did not know any of her neighbors, but the cars were vaguely familiar to her. All of them but one, that is. She eased her car to the curb across the street from her house, a bit past the far end of her lot, but left the motor running.

It was a large black Chrysler. She stared at it for several seconds, trying to place it, but gave up. Probably somebody visiting across the street or something, she thought. She was getting too jumpy. What she needed was a long, hot bath and to sleep until noon. She'd need the rest, because after Walt cleaned house for her, she'd be busy for a while, solidifying her new position.

She was fishing in her purse for her house key when something about the house caught her attention. Through one of the large, cathedral-shaped windows, she could see the drapes askew, and a dim light shining from between them. She knew she hadn't left any lights burning, and would never have left the drapes like that. She slid to the opposite side of her car, and got out through the passenger door, being careful not to make any noise as she opened the door.

She crept down to the strange automobile, and opened the passenger door just wide enough to slither into the front seat. There was enough light from a streetlamp for her to get a look at the registration tag hanging from the steering column by a leather strap. The name on the registration was that of Jules Ridau.

Stella sat up straight, her face flat and her mouth open. Her body shook convulsively, and tears of panic almost overflowed her eyes. There could be only one reason Jules Ridau's car was parked there—he was waiting inside for her. She slid quickly back to the open door, and out to the sidewalk, leaving the door open. Her eyes flickered up and down the street, and she pulled her Colt automatic from her bag.

Moving with feline grace and speed, Stella made it back into her own car in the space of two heartbeats. It took all of her strength not to vomit from the panic she felt. Joe. That sonofabitch had sent Ridau here to kill her. And he chose Ridau because he knew Ridau would still be smarting from his narrow escape from Israel Daggett's hotel room. God damn that dago bastard to hell with his back broken.

She laid the Colt in her lap and eased her car away from the curb, not trying to gain too much speed until she reached the corner. Once out of sight of her house, she turned back to Broad Street, and headed downtown. She was in the soup now, and had to find a place to lay low. The trouble was, Joe knew all of her haunts, and might have people out there covering them, too. Walt was her only hope, and she didn't even know where he was. *God damn,* she thought, nearly breaking down. *He's trying to kill me, he's really trying to kill me.*

She swiped at her tearing eyes with the back of one gloved hand, and bit down on her lip until the pain shocked her out of the terror that threatened to engulf her. She had to stay calm, stay loose, and even more, stay on the move until she could hook up with Walt again. Oh, Jesus wept, she thought as she floored the accelerator, driving as fast in the opposite direction of her house as she could.

15

Annunciation Street was a sight less grand than its name would have you think. Only one street back from the warehouse-and-wharf-lined Tchopitoulas Street, it was a lengthy expanse of aging shotgun cottages owned by working-class blacks and whites. Sleepy Moyer's yellow whorehouse was about three buildings uptown from the Louisiana Avenue intersection.

Unlike most of the other houses in the neighborhood, Sleepy's place was a two-story building of substantial size, with heavy drapes covering all of the windows facing out on the street. Drapes were as foreign to this street as French champagne, so even a schoolchild could tell instantly that this was no ordinary household.

Farrell pulled his Packard to a stop just two doors down from the yellow house and cut the engine.

"Think Sass called him?" Daggett asked casually.

Farrell shook his head. "Dunno. Could be he figured that tipping Sleepy off would be a swell way to pay us off for stomping him and Lucy. It's a chance we've got to take."

Daggett removed the .41 Colt from his shoulder holster, replaced the empty cartridge with a fresh one, then snapped the gate shut. He twirled the big revolver easily on his finger and let the bone grips settle into his palm with a crisp snap. "Wanna handle it the way we did at Sass's joint? Me at the back, you at the front?"

"Sleepy's probably got the back door locked," Farrell said. "You knock on the door, and I'll keep out of sight until you can get your foot inside."

"That sounds fine," Daggett said as he slid the long-barreled revolver back under his arm. They got out of the car and walked up to the porch of the house.

When Farrell was positioned beside the door, Daggett knocked loudly several times. After a moment, a Negro woman of about thirty-five, dressed in a print housecoat, opened the door. Her thick, brown hair was piled carelessly atop her head, and she held a glass half filled with amber liquid in her right hand.

"Well, well, *well,*" she said with a grin. "A fine-lookin', lonesome-lookin' man, and me just sittin' here wishin' for somethin' to do. C'mon in, sugar, and we'll just fix you right up."

She reached out with her free hand, grabbed Daggett by his lapel, and dragged him through the door. As he went, Farrell darted from cover and through the door behind him before she could shut the door. As he pushed the door closed, both he and Daggett drew their guns.

"Keep real still, mama," Daggett said softly, punctuating his syllables with the muzzle of the .41. "And nobody'll get hurt."

"Wha—what d'you'all want?" she asked in a quavery voice. She still had hold of the liquor glass, but she shook so badly that some of the liquor slopped over the rim.

"We're looking for Sleepy Moyer," Farrell said. "Where is he?" His voice had become thick and husky, and his golden complexion was flushed with dark blood.

"He—he ain't here," the woman said. "Honest, mister, I don't know . . ."

"You run this place for him?" Daggett snapped.

She'd heard that kind of voice before. It had "cop" written all over it. "Y-yeah."

"What's your name, woman?" Daggett demanded.

"A-A-Alice Y-Yoakum," she stammered.

"Alice, we want Sleepy, but we don't want you, get me?" Daggett said. "We know he's kidnapped a woman, and we wanna know where he's got her. Kidnapping's a federal beef. If the Feds get called in, you can kiss this place good-bye, 'cause they'll tear it to pieces and send you up to the pen in Detroit as an accomplice."

"A-accomplice?" she said, dazed by Daggett's machine-gun patter.

"I'm gonna ask you again, Alice, is he here, and did he bring in a woman who might've been drugged or tied and gagged? This'll be the last time I ask nice," Daggett said.

"No, no," Alice said. "I swear it. I ain't seen Sleepy since yesterday sometime. "He ain't been back here that I know about. That's gospel, mister, honest to God."

"I think she's tellin' the truth," Daggett said," but I'd feel better if I checked the other rooms."

"Go ahead," Farrell said. "I'll stay here and watch her."

The woman sank gratefully into a chair, her eyes wide and dazed looking. She seemed to notice for the first time that she still held the glass of liquor, and gulped it quickly. She shuddered as the raw whiskey flamed down her throat, but she calmed visibly afterward.

Within five minutes Daggett was back. "Nothin' upstairs but a bunch of girls haulin' people's ashes," he reported. "I checked every room, and nothin' shakin' in any of 'em but the usual."

Farrell turned again to Alice Yoakum, and stared at her. His new pistol was still in his hand, held muzzle down along his right leg. "This can't be the only place Sleepy has. Where would he hole up if he needed to?"

"God, mister," Alice said. "Sleepy don't tell me nothin'. I don't reckon he's ever told a woman any of his business in his life."

"He never tells you where to find him if there's trouble of some kind, or if you need him quickly?" Farrell asked skeptically.

"I could think a li'l better if I had some whiskey," Alice said, looking mornfully at her empty glass.

Daggett's mouth turned up into a loopy grin. He saw a bottle of Peter Dawson scotch on a sideboard along one wall, walked over and got it. He came back, and poured Alice a drink with the aplomb of an English butler, then stood while she drank it.

"Man, that's better," Alice said. Some of the boyancy they'd seen when she opened the door seemed to return to her now.

"Start talking," Farrell said, "then you can forget you ever saw us."

"You gonna kill Sleepy?" she asked quickly. "I don't wanna get mixed up with no killin'."

"If you been workin' for Sleepy," Daggett cut in, "you been mixed up in more killin' than you can ever know. Look on the bright side, Alice. If Sleepy gets killed, all of this becomes yours. Not a bad payoff, huh?" Daggett swept his arms wide and twisted his body gracefully to include the entire room.

A crafty gleam came into Alice's dark-brown eyes, and something akin to a smile threatened to bend her lips. "Well, I'm just rememberin' somethin' Sleepy told me once," she said with a laughable attempt at subtlety. "Sleepy has him a boardin' house over to Dumaine Street, the other side of Rampart. It ain't got no boarders and never did, so far as I know, so it'd be perfect to hide somebody out in."

Farrell nodded. He'd been studying the woman carefully since Daggett spoke, and her mounting enthusiasm convinced him she was telling the truth. Her half-buried streak of capitalistic enterprise had wiped clean any fear she might have had of Sleepy Moyer. To her, Moyer was already dead. She had probably already picked out the shade of new curtains she'd buy for the parlor.

"Sleepy have any men over there that you know about?" Daggett asked.

"I reckon," Alice said, her face clouding a bit. "I done forgot about that."

"About what?" Daggett asked.

"Well, Sleepy got him a man over there named Huey, who looks after the place and runs people away when they get too close or too nosy," Alice said. "He's kinda big and mean, and not too bright. I'd watch out for him, if I was you."

The skin around Farrell's mouth had gotten white with strain, and his eyes darted from Alice to Daggett. Daggett caught the look, got the address from the woman, and they left the yellow house.

"Reckon we'll need any help?" Daggett asked when they were back in the Packard.

"I wouldn't know anybody to ask," Farrell said as he let in the clutch. Before he could take off, however, a car rolled up in front of them. Farrell had his Colt out from under his arm before Daggett grabbed his wrist.

"That's Dandy," Daggett said with surprise. "What's he doin' here?" He opened his door and got out into the street. Farrell followed suit.

Dandy got out of his automobile and walked over to the other two men. His jacket was unbuttoned, and Farrell noted the saw handle of an antique .38 Colt Lightning in his waistband.

"What the hell you doin' here, man?" Daggett asked.

"I was in a bar down on Rampart and I heard Dirty Dog McGee talkin'. He'd talked to somebody in the emergency room at Charity

Hospital who said you'd busted up Sass DeLatte and were out lookin' for Sleepy Moyer. I figgered to come along and give you a hand."

"This ain't no time for amateurs," Daggett said. "You go on home and put that gun away before it blows up in your hand."

Dandy shook his head stubbornly. "I wasn't able to help you when you got into trouble years ago, but I can help you now. Where you goin'?"

Daggett looked at Farrell, and Farrell shrugged as if to say it was up to him what happened. Daggett turned back to Dandy.

"Sleepy Moyer's supposed to have a boardinghouse over on Dumaine. We think he's got Rosalee held over there against her will," Daggett said. "We're goin' over there to see about gettin' her out."

"Got room in the car for me, or you want me to meet you over there?" Dandy asked.

"Get in," Farrell said. "We're wasting too much time."

Frank Casey drained the dregs of coffee from the cardboard container he'd brought from the diner across the street from headquarters. He felt like a man waiting for the end of the world. On the plus side of the coin, he'd gotten the research back from the Notorial Archives, and Detective Schwarz had done some checking with the Whitney National Bank. Casey had hold of some very interesting information, but he needed some questions answered, and only one man could answer them. The trouble was, he'd dropped out of sight. Casey had men out looking for him, and it was only a matter of time before they found him. When the questions got answered, Casey believed he'd have a good bust to take home.

On the minus side, his son was somewhere on the street with a gun, and everyone connected with this case seemed to be out there with him, hell bent to oblivion.

Savanna Beaulieu's disappearance was a wild card the game didn't need. The last time somebody had hurt that woman, Farrell had reduced the population of New Orleans by a considerable number. It had taken a hell of a lot of talking on Casey's part to keep him out of prison, and he hoped he wouldn't be put in that position again.

He got up and paced the room, too tired to sit, and too jangled to sleep. The telephone rang, and he walked quickly to the desk to answer it.

"Casey," he said.

"This is dispatch, Captain," a voice said. "The officers reporting from the Bascomb woman's house reported finding the back door jimmied open. They went inside and found two Negro males there. Both armed."

"Who are they?" Casey asked.

"Detective Barnes says their names are Jules Ridau and Vince Devine."

"Those names don't mean anything to me," Casey said.

"Detective Barnes says they worked for Junior Obregon some years back, and he believes they've been taking orders from Walt Daggett lately."

"Which could mean Dante," Casey said half to himself. "I'll bet you even money they were there to kill her," Casey said. "They probably broke in the back and were there waiting. If there's been a contract taken out on her, she might be real happy to have a policeman's shoulder to cry on about now. Have an all-points bulletin put on out Stella Bascomb. Whenever they pick her up, they're to bring her directly to my office, understood?"

"Going out now, sir," the dispatcher said, and hung up.

Casey cradled his telephone receiver, and drummed his fingers on the top of his desk. Things were heating up, and the expense in lives looked to grow heavier. He had a feeling that the break he needed was coming soon, but more than anything else, he wanted to know where Farrell was. He'd already nearly been killed, and was out there somewhere, probably armed to the teeth and looking for trouble. Casey rubbed his face and leaned back to wait. Making captain hadn't made him any better at that than he'd already been, which is to say lousy.

Walt Daggett's mouth was as dry as the dust bowl of Oklahoma, and his tongue felt like a piece of dessicated leather as he moved it around trying to generate some spit. The Astra pistol under his arm seemed to weigh fifty pounds, and in spite of the cool weather, he was sweating inside his overcoat.

The farther he got from Stella, the more afraid he got. He had spent his whole life trying to stay out of trouble, and now he was rushing toward it like a juggernaut. He took his hands off the steering wheel and wiped them on the front of his coat. He tried not to think of what he was about to do, but it was impossible. It was like a sore tooth that nagged at him incessantly. He wondered if killing Sleepy would make the ache go away.

Annunciation Street was quiet when he rolled into it. Lights were on in the cathouse Sleepy owned, and Walt steeled himself for the confrontation he felt coming. He parked his car and got out. He pulled the silenced .32 from his pocket, checked it over, then pocketed it again, keeping his hand wrapped about the grip, his thumb near the safety.

When he opened the front door, Alice was dancing by herself in the center of the room as a singer with a pansy voice sang "I'm a Ding-Dong Daddy from Dumas." She was pretty drunk, and had a loony smile on her face. Either there wasn't very much business, or all the customers were upstairs with the girls.

"Where's Sleepy?" he asked. When Alice didn't seem to hear, he spoke louder. "Where's Sleepy, I said."

Alice turned and looked at him, but the loopy smile remained. "He might be on the way to meet his maker, if we're real lucky."

Walt stiffened. "What do you mean?"

"They was two men here not long ago with guns in their hands," she said. "They seemed to want ole Sleepy real bad."

"Why? Who were they?" Walt gripped the gun tightly, and his head felt all dry and brittle inside, and confusion made his stomach roil.

"They looked like cops to me," Alice said. A white one, and a colored one." She stopped, took a drink, and closed one eye while she thought. Then she opened her eye and looked almost intelligent when she turned her gaze back to Walt. "I'll be damn'. You know, I b'lieve the colored one was your cousin, Iz Daggett. I thought he was up at 'Gola er somethin'."

"Goddamnit woman!" Walt fairly shouted. "What did they want with him?" He drew the gun and waved it at her.

Alice stepped back, dropping her glass of liquor on the floor. She looked at the gun, then back up at his face, her eyes level and sober. "If'n I had to reckon on it, I'd reckon they was lookin' to kill 'im."

But suppose they weren't, Walt found himself thinking. Suppose they took him alive and he started talking. What then?

"Where did you send them?" he demanded, waving the gun muzzle in Alice's direction again.

"I told 'em I figgered he was over at that old boardin' house of his on Dumaine," she replied in her sober voice. "He's supposed to've kidnapped some woman and took her somewheres."

Walt turned and almost ran out of the parlor. He was gone so quickly that Alice wondered for a second if she'd dreamed him being there. After a while, it ceased to matter. She got her glass from the floor, refilled it from her bottle of Peter Dawson, and went back to dancing by herself.

16

Savanna dreamed of herself as a little girl named Rosalee Ortique, dressed in a red dress with yellow flowers and a new straw hat with a red ribbon. She was holding her father's hand as they walked down an unpaved country road. Dust rose from the road as they walked, but the air was cool and the dust didn't cling to her dress or shoes.

Her daddy had his guitar slung over his shoulder, and was singing "Skip-to-my-Lou," a song he knew Rosalee liked in particular. She began to skip in time to the music. Light reflected in the distance, and she stopped skipping to get a better look. As the shape neared them, she saw it was a large black coach drawn by a huge black draft horse. The heavily built horse trotted lightly in spite of his burden, but as he drew near, she saw his eyes were white and wild looking, and his flared nostrils and lips were the color of blood.

Rosalee tried to slacken her pace, but her father, still singing "Skip-to-my-Lou," kept on, dragging the little girl along with him. As they walked, the black coach and horse drew nearer, but Rosalee's father did not give ground, nor did he step to the side of the road. Rosalee was frightened now. "Stop, Pappy, stop!" she cried. He kept on singing, dragging her nearer and nearer to the oncoming coach. She pulled and pulled at his hand, and in her struggle she looked up, and it wasn't her father at all, but the leering face of Sleepy Moyer, reaching down with his open mouth and his heavy-lidded eyes.

Savanna cried out, and the cry brought her back to consciousness. Her body was bathed in sweat, and she ached all over. Her ankles and wrists were bound, and tied to the bed she was in, but the sweat seemed to have loosened the rope at the left wrist, because she found she could move her wrist within the circle of rope. She began testing it, trying to work herself free. She was covered by a thick, coarse blanket, but she could tell that she hadn't dreamed the destruction of her clothing. She was nearly naked underneath.

The room was dark, and it was impossible to know if it was day or night. She found herself wishing she knew how long she'd been here. Farrell would certainly be looking for her, but there was no way to know when, or even if, he might show up. Wait. Sleepy had said Farrell was dead. How could that be true? It couldn't be, but suppose it was? The thought turned her knees to water.

The possibility of rescue seemed remote now. If she was going to get out of here, she was going to have to work at it herself. Even alone as she was, she realized she had a powerful ally: hatred. Sleepy had tried to take from her the only thing that mattered—her self-respect. He had treated her like something less than a whore—a piece of furniture that he could use as he saw fit. She trembled all over with rage at the pimp, and revulsion for what he had done to her. She clenched her jaw to keep from crying, and prayed for the chance to kill him.

She heard a noise, and immediately stilled her efforts. Across from where she lay, light fell into the room from an open door, and with it came the noise of a shuffling gait on a wooden floor. She forced herself to stay still, and closed her eyes to slits. A shape approached her, a shape far too large to be Sleepy Moyer.

Whoever it was breathed heavily, as if he had run up a high hill. He walked around the bed slowly in the same shuffling gait as when he walked in. Then it stopped, and Savanna felt the blanket being lifted. Although terrified, she forced herself to remain still, and kept her breathing regular. The only sound in the room was the deep breathing of the man beside her. Then he dropped the blanket, and shuffled back toward the door to her room.

Savanna chanced opening her eyes, and saw in the pale light coming through the open door a man as large as she'd ever seen. He looked like a mountain from the back. She felt a cry rising in her throat, and bit her lower lip to stifle it.

When the door closed, Savanna began working at loosening the rope around her left wrist, and gradually, painfully, she felt it give enough to allow her to pull herself free. She almost sobbed with relief, and reached across her body to work on the rope around her right wrist. After several moments and two broken fingernails, her hands were free, and she could sit up.

She pushed the blanket aside, and managed to wriggle her body up to where the ankles were tied. Soon all the ropes were in a pile in the floor. Her legs and arms were full of pins and needles where the circulation had been cut off, and stung horribly as she attempted to stand up for the first time. She danced from foot to foot, shaking her wrists as she moved, her breath coming in ragged gasps. Finally, she was ready to get out of there.

Although her clothes had been cut to ribbons, a few shreds remained that could be tied or buttoned back together. The effect was ludicrous, she knew, but it was better than being naked. Her feet were bare, but that was a blessing. She had to get out without making a sound, and shoes would be a bother.

Savanna found the door, and cautiously worked the knob until she discovered elatedly that it wasn't locked. By millimeters, she eased the door open sufficiently for her to peek out. Before her she saw a deserted hallway, with several other closed doors in her line of view. She could hear nothing, but a ray of very dim sunlight trickled from a small and rather dirty windowpane directly ahead.

She held her position for a full minute, holding her breath as she listened for the slightest sound of a board creaking, or the shuffle of the big man's footsteps. Finally, she could wait no longer, and pulled the door wide. On her toes, she entered the hall as a bead of icy sweat traced a line down her back.

She could hear faint sounds beneath her, and she realized that she must be in the upstairs floor of a large house of some kind. She trod the hall with a light foot, her eyes searching for a staircase, and her ears cocked for the slightest sound. Then she heard it. A heavy tread on steps. It was ahead of her, rather than behind, so she turned and retraced her steps back the way she came. At a bend in the hall, she found herself at a dead end, and halted there with a sinking feeling in the pit of her stomach.

Close to hand was a heavy oak ladder-backed chair. Savanna picked up the chair by the back, and pulled it to her. For the first time in several minutes, Savanna was calm. She was no longer tied down, and she had a weapon. She knew what she would do when the moment came.

The shuffling of feet came closer and closer, then the sound of a door opening around the corner. The shuffle continued as before, then a sudden stop, followed by more rapid steps. The air around Savanna seemed charged with something electric, and she felt the fine hairs on her arms and body rise as if to meet it.

Small, unintelligible cries of confusion and upset came to her. They were not sounds she had ever heard come from a human being. Savanna felt her stomach dip and rise, and she bit her lips to keep from screaming. The steps were coming again, still a shuffle, but faster, like the progress of a huge snake. Savanna raised the chair over her head, her muscular arms tensed and ready.

The big man rounded the corner so quickly it almost took her by surprise. She brought the chair down on his head with every ounce of her strength, and felt the shock run up her arms into her shoulders. He cried out, a high-pitched bleat that sounded more like that of a rooting boar than a man.

The sound horrified Savanna, but she was in the fight now, and that was all that mattered. She pulled back and swung the chair at his knees, and saw him stoop and stagger. As he bent forward, she bunched her shoulders, brought the chair up again, and smashed it down on his broad back. He went to his knees, but was far from out. Part of the chair had broken off, and what remained was rickety and far less solid than the weapon she'd started with.

The big man got to one knee, his breath coming in fierce grunts. Panic and fear warred with her fighting spirit as she began smashing what was left of the chair at his head. At the third blow, she heard a cry of pain come from him, and saw that a splintered chair rung had pierced his skull, but still he came to his feet, one hand tugging at the splintered wood, the other reaching for her. His eyes were those of wounded bear surrounded by baying dogs.

Savanna, her bludgeon reduced to a few useless sticks, backed into the dead-end hall, her eyes hypnotized by the jagged piece of wood protruding from his forehead, now slippery with bright red blood. Her back hit the wall, and she tensed to throw herself at his head, and either drive the wood in further or tear out his eyes with her nails. Her face was fixed in a rictus of horror, her knees bent for the spring, and suddenly four shots racketed from the other end of the hall, then two others, heavier than the first four.

The big man stopped, raised up. His horrible eyes rolled back into his head, and he crashed face forward to the floor. Savanna screamed and screamed, her hands tearing at her hair as she jumped away from the toppling body. And then she saw Farrell and Israel

Daggett standing there, staring over barrels of their drawn guns. Slightly behind them, his eyes bright and his face contorted with shock and horror, stood Dandy Walker.

Farrell ran forward, grabbed the body by the shoulder and lifted it partway from the floor. He stared into the dead eyes for several seconds, his lips drawn back over his teeth as if hoping the man wasn't yet dead. Then he looked up and saw Savanna nearly collapsed against the door, her clothes reduced to rags. In that instant, he knew what had been done to her and his heart felt squeezed in a vise. He rushed up and caught her up in his arms as her legs gave out.

There were so many things she wanted to say to him, but she could not make her brain and mouth work together. Only cries and gibberish came from her. Farrell pulled her to him and crushed her body against his, seeming to know instinctively that she wanted to hide, and that his body was the only shelter in sight.

"God damn," Israel Daggett said. "That sonofabitch's got a piece of wood as big as my thumb driven into his skull."

Dandy Walker had turned the body over, and was inspecting and probing it for life, it seemed. His face was still stiff with fear, and he seemed unable to talk.

Farrell swept Savanna up and turned to Daggett. "Let's get out of here and keep score later."

"Wait," Daggett said. "Don't be hasty."

Farrell turned, his eyes blazing. "Wait for what?"

"We want Sleepy," Daggett said. "He's bound to come back here. Let's just hang back, if she's not too banged up."

"He's right, Mr. Farrell," Dandy said earnestly. "He's bound to've been in on everything from the start. Could even be he's the one killed Junior."

Farrell's face relaxed. He eased Savanna in his arms so he could see her face. "Savanna. Savanna. Are you okay? Did he hurt you?" Farrell immediately felt what a stupid thing that was to say to a woman who'd probably been raped, but before he could rephrase it, Savanna shook her head in the negative. "I want him," she managed to say.

Daggett disappeared for a moment, then came back with a blanket, which he helped Farrell wrap around the barely clothed Savanna. They walked downstairs, and found a room furnished with a table, chairs, a bed, and a radio. A small kitchen was just off the room, with an icebox and a two-burner stove, and shelves of various groceries.

Farrell put Savanna down on the cot and sat beside her. Daggett could be heard rummaging around in the kitchen. He emerged with a bottle of Calvert's Reserve and a glass. He poured some of the whiskey into the glass, and gave it to Farrell.

"I'm gonna go out to the front and keep watch," he said. "When I spot Sleepy coming, I'll come back and tell you."

Farrell nodded, then raised Savanna's head so she could drink from the glass. When she'd drunk it all, he laid her head back on the pillow and stroked her head. Soon the room was as quiet as a mausoleum. Dandy stood silently in the hall, his eyes cast down to the floor.

Casey was still pacing the room when a call came in.

"Casey," he said said.

"This is dispatch, Captain. The Negro Detective Squad just reported Billie Talmadge apprehended at Illinois Central Terminal. They're requesting instructions."

Casey wasn't sleepy anymore. Adrenaline was bursting through his middle-aged veins like the Colorado River through the Grand Canyon. "Request the detectives to hold her at the scene. I'll drive over to the station now, be there in about fifteen minutes."

"Understood," the dispatcher replied.

It took Casey less than twelve minutes to make the large railroad terminal, and he left his black Dodge police cruiser at the front entrance curb.

The terminal police office was on the second floor, and Casey took the steps three at a time in his haste. When he burst into the sparsely furnished office, he found a white uniformed sergeant at his desk, and a woman who could only be Billie sitting glumly in a chair flanked by two Negro officers in plain clothes. The older one with the mustache turned and spoke.

"Detective Wallace, Negro Squad, sir," he said. "Detective Andrews and I responded to a tip from one of the ticket sellers that a young woman with an urgent desire to leave town paid cash for a ticket to Chicago with a new fifty. The woman said the girl looked frightened and skittish, so we walked around until we saw her."

The younger detective, Andrews, spoke at this point, saying, "The suspect asked to use the rest room. We figured it for a runout, so Wallace went around the side and found her trying to crawl out the window. We found these things on her." He pointed to the leather folder, a pile of cash in fifties and hundreds, and a .25 caliber Colt automatic pistol.

Casey saw some papers alongside the cash, and took a few moments to look at them. As he did so, he nodded, as though he'd found something he already knew was there. He put the papers back in the folder, pocketed it, then turned back to the girl.

"All right, young lady," he began. "Your name is Billie Talmadge, if I'm not mistaken."

Billie's eyes were large, and her skin shiny with sweat. She rubbed the inside of her left arm incessantly now, and sniffled loudly. Casey noticed that there were no tears.

"Well," Casey said, frowning down at her.

"Yeah, yeah, yeah, my name is Billie Talmadge," she said in an unnecessarily loud voice.

"Where did you think you were going with all the money, Billie?" Casey asked.

"It's mine. I was leaving town to start over in Chicago," she said bitterly. "This town is for shit. All I ever got was kicked around here."

"Your mother and father didn't kick you around, honey," Casey said in a softer voice. "If you'd left Junior Obregon all those years ago, you'd still be with them now, probably married to some decent, hard-working man. You made all your own trouble, and now you're sitting here in the soup, needing a fix real bad, am I right?"

Billie's face turned to him sharply, surprised that he knew so much about her. Her eyes were scared, and her lip quivered.

"You can dig yourself out of some of this if you'll talk to me," he said, not unkindly. "Where's Walt Daggett? He's the one you got the money and those papers from, isn't he?"

"Mister, please, I'm sick. I need a shot," she whined.

"Talk to me, and we'll see what we can do," Casey said, letting his voice go flat.

"Leave us take her outside, skipper," Wallace said with a nasty smile. "She'll get to talkin' pretty damn quick then."

Billie turned her scared face to Wallace, then back to Casey. "Please, mister. I'm sick. You promise you'll help me?"

"I promise, but you've got to tell me all you know," Casey said. "No holding back, because you're in a lot of serious trouble. You're already guilty of felony theft and breaking and entering."

"That ain't true," Billie protested. "I asked Walt Daggett if I could stay with him, and he said I could."

"Then why did you steal from him?" Casey demanded harshly.

"Because . . . because . . ."

"Tell him quick, girl," Wallace snapped. "Stop wastin' our time."

"Because Stella came and sent him out to kill somebody," Billie blurted. Then she began to cry hysterically, like a small child who's hurt herself.

"Who? Kill who?" Casey asked in a softer voice. "Maybe we can get to them in time."

"She told him to go out and kill Sleepy," she wailed.

"Sleepy Moyer?" Casey asked.

"Yes, yes," Billie cried. "She said they could take over everything if he'd kill Sleepy."

Casey turned away from Billie to Wallace and Andrews. "What could killing Sleepy Moyer get anybody?" Casey asked sotto voce. "He's just a two-bit pimp and a leg-breaker."

"Beats me," Wallace said. "Unless he's tied into something bigger than we know."

Casey turned back to Billie, who was wiping her face with a tissue the desk sergeant had given her.

"Stella is the cat-eyed woman, isn't she?"

"Yes."

"Is Walt hooked up with her and Dante?"

"Yeah, I think so."

"What does Walt do with them? Drug distribution?"

"Yeah, yeah," she said, a bit calmer. "Walt runs just about the biggest drug operation in the colored part of New Orleans. What I took from him ain't a patch on what he's got. He's got more money than Carter's got liver pills."

Casey turned to the desk sergeant. "Get on the horn and tell dispatch to put out an all-points bulletin for Sleepy Moyer and Walt Daggett. They'll both be armed, but I want 'em alive if possible."

The sergeant moved to obey, and Casey turned back to the two Negro detectives. "Book her with felony theft, carrying a concealed weapon, and possession of narcotics and narcotics apparatus, then take her to Charity Hospital to the prison ward, and tell the doctor she's a heavy user. He'll be able to take care of her."

"We're on the way," Wallace replied.

Sleepy Moyer walked back to the boardinghouse feeling the satisfaction of a good dinner in his belly. He had a toothpick in the corner of his mouth, and the taste of fried ham, candied yams, and collard greens still on the back of his tongue. He paused at the corner and looked up and down the dark street, then crossed to the entrance of his house, his eyes shifting vigilantly back and forth. Everything seemed as usual. He felt a vague itching in his groin, and entertained the notion of going back upstairs for another little session with Savanna. She was some hunk of woman—far better than he was used to.

There were only a few lights on the house, two upstairs and only one on the ground floor. That seemed like usual. Huey wasn't afraid of the dark, and liked roaming around the empty corridors. That Huey was strange, but he sure had his uses. Should've told him to leave the woman alone, Sleepy thought. He might get ideas.

Sleepy inserted his key in the lock and walked through the door. "Huey?" he called. "Where you at, anyhow?" He closed the door behind him, walked a few steps into the hall, and suddenly felt a tremendous blow that came out of the shadows and connected solidly with his jaw. He fell to the floor, everything whirling around him at a dizzying speed.

He was vaguely conscious of someone grabbing the lapels of his coat and dragging him into a lighted room. As though in a dream, he could see Israel Daggett looking down on him from a great height, and the Savanna woman glaring hatred at him from on the bed. His eyes roamed skyward, and he found himself staring up into the face of a man with skin the color of old gold and eyes that glittered like chips of pale ice. *God damn,* Sleepy thought. *You sure take a hell of a lot of killin'.*

Standing next to Daggett with an antique Wild West pistol in his hand was Dandy Walker. Sleepy wondered why he was here with that silly gun. Dandy looked scared, which Sleepy thought funny under the circumstances.

The gold-skinned man bent down and began going over his body. He felt the Luger leaving his pocket and heard it thud dully on the floor behind him. The man tore open his coat, found his razor, and held it in front of his eyes. The man made the handle and blade of the razor do a chittering, scratchy dance in his fingers before closing it again.

Some time went by, and Sleepy heard voices speaking, but the words meant nothing to him. He was as one paralyzed until he felt himself hauled up once again by his lapels and thrown into a chair. The movement seemed to bring him back to himself again, and he shook his head stupidly.

"What'd you hit me with?" he asked.

"You're lucky I didn't knock your damned head right off," Farrell said in a loud voice.

Sleepy's rubbery lips slipped into a half-grin. He wasn't scared of the gold-skinned man. He'd been hit that hard before, and had lived to talk about it. There was still a chance he could turn things around. "That woman over there belong to one of you?" he asked. "She sure is one juicy bitch." He laughed then, a rich, thick laugh of pure enjoyment. Farrell slapped him open-handed, and nearly knocked him from the chair.

"Sleepy, you remember me?" Daggett asked as Sleepy shook his head to clear it.

Sleepy shook his head, then turned it slowly toward Daggett's voice. "So, they let you out, huh? You musta licked the warden's boots every day for the last five years, Iz."

Daggett grinned amiably. "It's all comin' apart, Sleepy. Y'all managed to frame me into the pen, and you been poisoning our kids with that shit you bring into town, but it's all about to fall apart. We know about you and Walt and Stella and Dante. The police are huntin' the others down right now. You'd do yourself a favor if you'd tell me what you know right now."

"Shit, why should I help you?" Sleepy asked arrogantly. "I laughed my ass off when they sent you up. I ain't forgot the time you beat me up over that whore I cut."

"You're a sorry excuse for a man, Sleepy," Daggett said in a kind voice. "I can tell you from bein' there that 'Gola can be mighty rough on a man, particularly if that man's used to women doin' all his heavy work for him. Little as you are, they gonna turn you out to trickin' inside of a week."

Sleepy's eyes narrowed to slits, and the rubbery lips peeled back to bare his teeth. "Hey, fuck you. Nobody makes Sleepy Moyer act like a fuckin' woman. Nobody!"

Daggett laughed quietly. "Bein' Sleepy Moyer ain't gonna be

worth shit up there, my friend. The little fellas always get broken in quick, while they still tender. You'll be wearin' lace pants by the time they get through with you." Daggett removed his hat and ran his hand over his bristly scalp, grinning hugely. Farrell watched him, keeping his face flat and emotionless. Daggett was doing a good job.

" 'Course, there is a way you can get yourself off the hook, maybe get sent to one of the prison farms upstate. It ain't so bad in them, and you get worked so hard, nobody thinks much about gettin' laid when the lights go out."

Sleepy's face had gotten gray as Daggett talked. With both Farrell and the ex-detective in the room with guns, he knew he didn't have a chance to break away. He'd heard of some of the things that happened to men in prison, but nobody had made it as graphic as Daggett—and he'd just come from there, a factor that lent some credence to the picture he was painting. Sleepy's eyes flickered at Dandy, but the ex-prize-fighter only stared back nervously.

"Bullshit," Sleepy said halfheartedly. "You just tryin' to shake me up is all."

Daggett laughed hugely. "And gettin' there, Sleepy honey. You oughta see your face right now." Daggett fluttered his eyelashes at Moyer, and puckered up his lips in an obscene parody of a kiss.

Sleepy's face blanched and fell completely apart. Sweat broke out on his forehead, and his small hands convulsed into fists. "Knock it off, goddamnit, knock it off, or—"

"Or what?" Daggett said, leaning over with his teeth bared in a snarl. "We own you, boy. If you want a break, you better start talkin' right now."

"You guys ain't cops," Sleepy said uncertainly. "What good's it gonna do for me to tell you anything?"

"Mr. Farrell over there's got connections to the cops, and Captain Casey says he can prove I was framed," Daggett said with a straight face. "Whatever you tell us will go straight to Casey, and he'll buy it. How's about it? You wanna save your worthless ass before you have to peddle it? 'Cause you goin' to 'Gola, come what may."

Sleepy licked his lips. "Okay," he said. "Okay, I'll talk."

"Who killed Junior Obregon?" Daggett snapped. "The truth."

Sleepy's eyes flickered from Daggett to Farrell to Dandy, then back to Daggett. Farrell and Dandy both held their pistols like they'd like to use them. "I—I don't know for certain, but I think it was

Walt," Sleepy said. "He still had his police uniform, and prob'ly used it to sneak into the station and get your gun."

"You think," Daggett said nastily. "You better do better than that, boy."

"Walt was the one said he needed to be killed," Sleepy blurted. "He was gettin' fucked up on the shit he was sellin', then walkin' all over town talkin' 'bout his connection to Dante. Walt decided he had to be hit, and hit hard. I was in the room when he gave the word. I swear it in God's name."

"I wouldn't be callin' on God if I was you, Sleepy," Daggett said. "I don't reckon he even knows your name after all the hell you raised. Did Walt give anybody an order to make the hit, or did one of you draw lots to see who'd get to do it. Answer me, goddamnit!" Daggett slapped the top of the table with his hand, and it cracked like a whip.

Sleepy jumped in his chair, his eyes sunken in his face. "I swear, Iz, I don't know who he told to do it. I'd tell you if I knew, on my honor I would."

"Daggett, I think he needs persuading," Farrell spoke up. He reached up his sleeve and removed his spring-blade stiletto. His thumb moved imperceptibly and five inches of steel popped open in his hand.

"Cut him like a steer," Savanna said from the bed. Her hair was wild about her head, and her eyes had smoke in them. She was a beautiful woman under most circumstances, but now she looked like a murderous banshee.

"I reckon he's talked too much already," Walt Daggett said from the hall. He pressed the trigger on the silenced Browning twice. The slugs put an extra pair of eyes in Sleepy's forehead. He didn't even have time to be surprised before he died and fell off the chair.

Daggett and Farrell had guns in their hands before Walt stopped shooting, and fire jumped across the room as they traded shots with him. Daggett grunted in pain, then a wild shot knocked out the light overhead and the room plunged into darkness.

17

Walt drove through the evening stillness with a sick heaviness in his chest. The Browning automatic, still warm to the touch, lay on the car seat beside him. Sleepy had needed killing, and Walt was glad to have done it.

He was less happy about the way the rest of the fracas had gone. He realized that he'd left witnesses behind, but their being there at all was a surprise, and he didn't know how he could have handled it differently. Farrell and his cousin were his equal or better with firearms, and he doubted he could have bested both of them at once. Dandy Walker's presence there startled and surprised him. There was no love lost between the two of them for quite a few reasons, and it was an added complication finding him mixed up in this business.

It weighed on his mind somewhat that he had killed his cousin. He told himself that Israel, sooner or later, would have to've been eliminated if he and Stella were to know any peace. Left alive, Israel would just have continued to hang around, stirring things up until some piece of damaging evidence floated to the surface. Walt couldn't afford that, not after all that had been done. Not if he wanted Stella back in his life.

Walt passed a Catholic church, and, as was the fashion in Catholic New Orleans, half-consciously made the sign of the cross over his breast. He recollected that he had not been in church for a very long time, nor to confession for a lot longer. He was privy to things that no man could confide to a priest.

Temptation had always loomed large in Walt Daggett's life. He lacked many of his cousin's natural abilities and talents, and continually found himself sucking hind tit. Envy and avarice had ridden on his shoulders since childhood, and those things had eventually led him to involvements with street-corner hustlers, back-alley craps games, experimentations with muggles and morphine, and worse.

He had joined the police force with the hope of finally besting his cousin at something, but his spiritual impoverishment was already too great for him to place his own base desires behind the demands and duties of a policeman. He was always looking for that kick that might stand between him and the black despair that threatened to engulf him from one day to the next.

Stella had been both the high and low points of his life. When he'd been with her, he'd always felt more alive than he ever had. There was a danger and excitement about her that magically transferred itself to him, and he became somehow a bigger, more formidable man. She made him feel special.

Stella was both ambitious and, if truth be told, driven by greed. There was only so much Walt could give her, so when Dante had come along, waving money, clothes, and fancy apartments, there was little Walt could offer that could counteract such lavish temptations.

He tried to tell her that Joe was just using her, and that sooner or later he would tire of her; he had told her those things, not quite believing that they were true. They had quarreled, and Stella had walked out of his life. Their interactions had been few and far between after that, and usually filled with acrimony, as they had less than two days ago.

But now she was back; the old Stella who had trusted him; looked to him for help and comfort. It was strange, almost beyond belief that her opinion should change so radically in just a few days time. If he hadn't been so hungry for her touch, he might have questioned it.

But he had not, and his desire for her, and the life they'd once had, had overwhelmed any doubts or questions he might have had. Joe couldn't have hurt her very much, because Walt couldn't remember any bruises or cuts on her, and he'd seen every inch of her body in his bed. Perhaps Joe's abuse had been largely of a verbal kind, and he'd administered only a mild slap or two. That would be more than enough to raise Stella's ire, as proud as she was.

Anyway, Walt had killed Sleepy and his cousin, too. There was no turning back now. He would have to find Joe and kill him now before the white gangster got wise, and put the pencil on him. There was also Dandy Walker, and the fierce-looking man with pale gold skin to deal with. Dandy wouldn't be a problem, but the other man—his eyes were enough to melt another man's backbone.

Walt felt tired and a little frightened. Stella was at the end of all this—he had to keep his eyes focused on the prize. It was worth all the risk and the killing. He had to remember that, and not bother himself with questions about Stella's motives. She had come back and given herself to him. That was what mattered now.

Walt's jaw grew tight, and he pulled his hat lower on his forehead as he pressed his foot down harder on the gas pedal toward Stella's.

Farrell heard Walt Daggett run through the house, and jumped to his feet to run after him. "Daggett, stop!" he yelled. Walt threw back two more shots, causing Farrell to flatten himself along one wall. By the time he made it to the front of the house, a car was pulling away rapidly, its taillight winking at him in the distance.

"God damn it to hell," he swore. He slapped the wall with his hand in frustration. He had no idea where Walt might be going, and couldn't pursue. He thought he'd heard Daggett cry out in pain, and he didn't know how Savanna was. He turned and walked rapidly back to the room.

He found the room lit by a floor lamp, and Israel Daggett flat on the floor. Savanna, barely covered with the rags of her clothing, bent over him, trying to tear the seam along the arm of his shirt. Blood stained the white cloth over his shoulder, and his eyes were bright with pain. Dandy Walker stood over them, watching. He still had his antique gun in his hand, and was shaking like a leaf in a November wind. His mouth kept opening and closing, but he couldn't seem to force any words out. Farrell shook his head. Dandy was good in the ring, but nothing there could prepare a man for what had happened here.

"How bad is it?" Farrell asked.

"Went clean through," Daggett said through clenched teeth. "Missed the bone. It won't slow me up much. What about Walt?"

"Forget it," Farrell said, his voice full of chagrin. "Walt's five miles from here by now."

"Damn," Daggett said.

Farrell pulled a large white handkerchief from his hip pocket and gave it to Savanna, then he bent and tore away the arm of the bloodstained shirt. Between the two of them, they managed to cover the bullet hole and staunch the blood.

"We've got to get out of here," Farrell said. "There's been too much going on here, and sooner or later the cops are going to show up. There're too many questions we can't answer yet, and too many dead bodies to explain away."

"Where to?" Dandy asked, breaking his long silence.

Farrell thought for a moment. "We'll go to 'Tee Ruth's," he said finally. "I want to get Savanna out of harm's way for the moment, and we can clean up that wound there."

Daggett looked worried. "I don't want to bring more trouble down on them. How about someplace else?"

"Walt came here to kill Sleepy, and he probably thinks he's killed you. Sooner or later it'll dawn on him that he has to hunt the rest of us down and eliminate the witnesses to Sleepy's murder. 'Tee Ruth's is the last place he'll think of going."

Farrell crossed the room to where an old candlestick-type telephone sat. He removed the receiver, then rattled the hook several times until the operator came on. When she answered, he gave her the number of the Cafe Tristesse.

"Cafe Tristesse," Harry answered.

"This is Farrell."

"Geez, boss, I been worried sick," Harry said. "Captain Casey's lookin' for you, and nobody knows where Miss Savanna is."

"Calm down and listen," Farrell said. "I've got Savanna, and she's all right for now. Get hold of Marcel, tell him to get my gun from the desk drawer and the DeSoto from Julius's garage, and meet us at Ruth Sonnier's house on Leonidas Street. Tell him to rush it. Things are happening."

"Right." Harry hung up.

"Okay," Farrell said. "Let's get the hell out of here."

Joe Dante was pacing the floor of his office at La Belle Epoque. He was dressed in a beautifully cut nubby tweed shooting jacket with chocolate-brown suede patches at the elbows and right shoulder, and brown gabardine trousers with a crease like a knife edge. His face was a bit flushed from drink and worry, and a lock of his shiny black hair had fallen over his right eyebrow.

The telephone on his desk rang, and Lars reached for it. "Yah," he said. The person at the other end of the phone was doing a lot of talking, but Lars's pale, square face and ice-blue eyes had no more expression than an egg. "Yah," he said again, then held the telephone receiver out to Dante. "It's Detective Matty Paret. He wishes to speak to you."

Dante crossed the room and snatched the phone, glaring at Lars for waiting so long to give it to him. "Hello," he said belligerently.

"Somebody's let the cork outa hell, Joe," Paret said.

"What the devil's that supposed to mean?" Dante said in a truculant voice.

"For starts, Inspector Grebb's men raided your house and took everybody there away with 'em," Paret said genially. "For another, them two guys you sent to get Stella are in jail."

"Jail?" Dante said stupidly.

"Casey sent some uniforms there after Stella and took 'em by surprise," Paret said. "They're talkin' their heads off."

"Shit," Dante said feelingly.

"Don't hang up yet," Paret said. "I was down by the dispatcher a few minutes ago. Somebody iced Sleepy Moyer in a house over on Dumaine sometime this morning. Two slugs in the face he took. And that cretin he used for a watchdog's there, too."

"Dead?"

"They don't get no deader," Paret said. "Listen, I'm takin' a chance stayin' on the phone with you so long. I'm not riskin' my badge for you any longer. If I was you, Joe, I'd get in the car and start drivin' north. They tell me the weather's nice in Saskatchewan this time of year." Paret broke the connection.

Dante stood there staring with the dead phone in his hand. He didn't hear Lars speak to him, and he seemed not to notice when Lars took the dead receiver from him and replaced it in the cradle. Lars said "Boss?" three times before Dante began to register things.

"What you gonna do, boss?" Lars asked.

Dante walked to a chair and sat down in it heavily. Everything was crumbling around him, and he could only figure out one reason why. Stella. Stella was walking through his world like one of the Four Horsemen of the Apocalypse. One little colored whore was bringing everything down on him. If somebody had written a magazine story like this, Dante would've laughed and thrown the magazine in the trash. Finally, he spoke.

"Call all the boys you can find and tell them to get out here with everything they can carry. We'll drive up to Baton Rouge until all this shit settles down. Tell them to hurry."

Lars looked at Dante for a moment with that empty, dispassionate stare, then came over and began using the telephone.

Casey had no more than finished with Billie when the news of Sleepy Moyer's death reached him. Wearily he got back into the car and drove across town to the abandoned boardinghouse. He found Snedegar and Mart there, along with people from the crime laboratory.

"What we got?" he asked.

"Looks like the end of the world in there," Snedegar said. "Sleepy Moyer's got two small-caliber bullet holes in his face, and a guy who looks like the side of a mountain's upstairs with six more bullets in him, and piece of wood driven into his skull."

"Killed by the same gun?" Casey asked.

"No," Mart said. "Looks like at least four of 'em were from a .38 automatic. We found the shells on the floor. Nobody with any sense would've tried to use a .32 on that guy, anyway. Slugs that small would've just made him mad."

"What else have you found?" Casey asked.

"Somebody got shot who walked away," Snedegar said. "We found bloodstains on the floor, and bloodstained cloth that looks like it might've come from a man's shirt."

"You talked to anybody in the neighborhood?" Casey said.

"Seems like most people were asleep," Mart supplied. "I don't think the shots inside woke anybody up. Apparently there was some shooting outside, and a sedan was seen pulling away at a high rate of speed."

"I don't suppose anybody got a make on the car or the license tag," Casey said.

"No," Snedegar said, "although somebody we talked to said that about five minutes after the shooting died down, three or four people come out of the house real quiet-like, walked down the street, and got into another car and drove off. No model or license on that, either. Too dark, they said."

"Great," Casey fumed. "Think I'll take a little walk around the building myself, since it doesn't look like I'm gonna get any sleep."

He took a flashlight from his pocket and began walking up the stairs. Wherever he found an electric light switch, he turned it on and investigated the rooms. He'd been inside four or five when he came to a room with some scraps of cloth on the floor beside the bed. As he bent to examine them, he noticed ropes tied around the head and foot rails.

The scraps of cloth appeared to come from a woman's dress, and he could smell the lingering traces of perfume on them. He gathered them into a little pile, and got up. His eyes tracked the rest of the room until he noticed a closet. He walked to it, tried the knob, and found it locked, but the lock didn't look like much. He walked back to the entrance, checked out in the hall, then closed the door.

Back at the closet, he removed a heavy clasp knife with a thick, blunt blade from his pocket. He opened the blade, inserted it into the space between the door and the latchplate, and exerted pressure on it. The dry wood cracked and popped, and then the door jumped free of the latch.

On the floor he found a woman's blue hat, a pair of low-heeled women's shoes, and a blue leather shoulder bag. He picked up the bag and began to inspect the contents. The first thing he found was a little Colt revolver with ivory grips and the name "Savanna" engraved along the backstrap of the handle. Casey's heart sank. He found a wallet, opened it, and discovered a Louisiana driver's license made out to Savanna Beaulieu.

Quickly, Casey gathered the scraps of cloth and shoved them into the bag with the gun. He picked up the shoes and placed one in each pocket of his overcoat, shoved the hat down in the waistband of his trousers, and tucked the bag under his coat. He buttoned the coat over the bag and hat, and walked back down the stairs. No one noticed that he went outside, opened the trunk of his car, and deposited his finds inside the trunk before closing it again.

He was without doubt that Savanna had been held prisoner there, and probably given a bad time. The fact that the house was full of dead men suggested to him that Farrell had been there, and probably Israel Daggett, as well. Now he was guilty of supressing evidence to protect them. He'd seldom felt any lower than he did at that moment.

He walked back into the house tapping his flashlight lightly against his thigh, trying to think what to do when Snedegar walked out the door and down to where he was.

"This has been a hell of a few days," Snedegar said. When's the last time you had any sleep, skipper?"

Casey rubbed the bridge of his nose. "Seems like a week, but I know this has only been going on a few days."

"Go on home then," Snedegar said. "We'll wrap this up. We don't have anything much to go on yet anyway, and may not unless the lab people come up with a fingerprint or something. Seems like all of this started with the Sonnier murder, doesn't it?"

Casey had been looking past Snedegar at Sleepy Moyer's boardinghouse, but the mention of Lottie Sonnier made him think. If Farrell was looking for an out-of-the-way place to take his friends for protection and help, what better place than the Sonnier house? 'Tee Ruth would say so, herself.

"Think I will go home and grab some shut-eye," Casey said. "Don't call me unless something big breaks. I may be out for a while. Guess I'm not as young as I used to be."

"Okay, skipper," Snedegar said. "Good night, or I guess I should say good morning."

"Right. I'll talk to you later," Casey said. Within another minute, he was two blocks away in his police cruiser.

18

Farrell had no sooner pulled to a stop outside the Sonnier house when an old black DeSoto sedan coasted to a stop behind them. Farrell got out and walked toward it. A trim, good-looking octoroon kid in a tailored gray tweed suit got out and walked over to him. It was Farrell's young second cousin, Marcel Aristide, whom Farrell had taken in after the youngster had gotten into some trouble the year before.

"Mornin', Wes," he said in a soft voice. "What's the panic?"

Farrell's face was drawn with fatigue, and his eyes were bloodshot. Reddish-brown bristles covered his cheeks. "We found Savanna in a dump Sleepy Moyer owned over on Dumaine. She's pretty shook up. Before we could get Sleepy to tell us who he was covering for, Walt Daggett came in, shot Sleepy, and put a bullet in his cousin, Iz. Before I go looking for him, I wanted to put Savanna and Daggett where they'd be out of harm's way. I want you to hang around and make sure things stay quiet."

"I guess that's why you said to bring the gun," Marcel said with a grin.

"You catch on quick," Farrell said with a tired smile.

Farrell went back to his Packard and helped Savanna out, then carried her to the porch where 'Tee Ruth stood with the door open. Daggett got out of the backseat, followed by Dandy Walker. Daggett had undone a couple of shirt buttons, and had his wounded arm resting in it as though it were in a sling.

Marguerite had joined 'Tee Ruth on the porch, and had pressed her hands to her mouth when she saw Savanna and Daggett. "Dear God," she said in a hushed voice. "What has happened?"

"I'll tell you about it later," Farrell said as he carried Savanna inside.

Marguerite's eyes lit on Daggett's injured arm as he gained the porch, and she rushed over to offer him support into the house. 'Tee Ruth turned to follow them in, and Dandy and Marcel followed at a short distance.

Farrell took Savanna into Marguerite's bedroom, and laid her on the bed. Her eyes were sunken in the sockets, and her brown skin had turned ashy.

"Are you gonna go after Walt?" she asked as he knelt beside her.

"Have to, I guess," he replied. "Sleepy, Walt, the cat-eyed girl— they're all mixed up in Lottie's murder some way. All I need is one of them in a condition to talk."

Savanna looked at him, and saw that the pale gray eyes had a hard brightness in them. She knew what he wasn't saying, and nodded.

'Tee Ruth bustled up with a washcloth, a basin of warm water, and a cake of Ivory soap. She placed the basin and soap on the nightstand, and dropped the cloth into the basin. "Why don't you go on back to the kitchen," she said. "I'll see if I can't clean her up a little, and find her a nightgown."

Farrell looked at her, and she could see in his face his reluctance to leave. She smiled briefly. "You can come back once I've cleaned her up, now go on and get some coffee."

Farrell got up finally and nodded, then left for the kitchen.

'Tee Ruth pulled back the blanket Savanna was wrapped in, and began to help her take off the pitiful rags she was wearing. "Who done this to you, child?" she asked as Savanna eased her shoulders out of the ruin of her blouse. She noticed the marks of teeth around her breasts, and sucked her breath in sharply.

"Sleepy Moyer," Savanna said as she lay back down. "The only thing I'm sorry for is that somebody else killed him before I could."

'Tee Ruth found it difficult to talk, and busied herself by carefully soaping Savanna's body, wringing out the cloth, then rinsing. "Did he—?"

Savanna's eyes blared with hate, but she turned them from the old woman. "He didn't take nothin' that wasn't already gone, 'cept— 'cept . . ."

" 'Cept what, Rosalee?" 'Tee Ruth asked softly.

"Nobody's touched me that I didn't want in nearly ten years," Savanna said in a husky voice. "I had self-respect even when I didn't have nothin' else. Now, that li'l bastard . . ." She found she couldn't talk anymore, and kept her eyes focused on the ceiling. A shine in them grew, but she kept it from overflowing.

The old woman sighed heavily, and continued carefully washing Savanna's battered body. "That ain't something a man can take, once you got it," she said. "He might've bruised it some, but it can't be stolen from you, Rosalee. Our women have been mistreated like that for two hundred years, but we still here, still goin' on. Don't forget that." Savanna couldn't talk anymore, but she nodded her understanding.

In the kitchen, Farrell sat across from Daggett while he sipped at a cup of thick black coffee. Daggett had his coat and shirt off while Marguerite cleaned his wound and dressed it with gauze and sticking plaster.

"It isn't a big wound, and it seems clean enough," Marguerite said. "If not very much cloth got carried into the wound, you should be all right in a couple of weeks."

"Lucky it was such a small bullet," Daggett said through his teeth. He kept his eyes turned from Marguerite in an effort to keep her from seeing the painful brightness in them.

Farrell got up and put his coffee cup into the sink, then ran his fingers through his hair a couple of times. Then he leaned over the sink, ran the cold tap, and cupped his hands under the spigot. When they were full of water, he brought the water to his face and rubbed it in several times. When he raised up slightly, Marguerite put a clean dish towel in his hands and watched while he patted his face dry.

"What are you going to do now?" she asked him.

Farrell shook his head like a man who's absorbed too many punches. "I don't know. A lot of this is coming together, but I still don't know who killed Junior or Lottie. Until I do, we got a handful of nothing."

Marguerite looked back at Daggett, who shook his head. "I think I'll go see if Mother and Rosalee need anything." She left the two men alone.

"Mr. Farrell?" Daggett said.

"Yeah," Farrell said in a dull voice.

"This is maybe none of my business, but—have you known

Rosalee a long time?" Daggett kept his eyes forward, and his tone light and conversational. What he was asking would be a grave impertinence under most circumstances.

Farrell's eyes flickered briefly. He hadn't expected that to be the question. "I've known her a while," he said. "Why?"

Daggett scratched his stubbled chin with the back of his hand. It made a dry, whispery sound. "I don't mean to be crackin' wise by askin'. It's just that colored people don't normally expect a white man to get that involved in their problems, particularly scuffle-town colored people like me and the Sonniers and Rosalee. We ain't exactly Urban League types."

Farrell's mouth turned down slightly at the edges, and his mouth got dry. This was territory he'd rather stay clear of if he could find a way to steer it in another direction. However, his mind was too fuzzy and full of care to be evasive just then. "I'm not an Urban League type, either," he said.

Daggett shook his head. "No, I reckon not." He paused for a moment, and brushed at his nappy scalp. "I guess I just wanted to tell you I'm sorry if my troubles have caused you and Rosalee any hurt. I can tell that . . . that she means something to you."

Farrell turned his eyes at Daggett, unable to find the right words to answer this man who he was beginning to think of as a friend. The lousy feeling he always got at times like this assailed him, and he felt a burning of shame in his guts that wouldn't go away. Sometimes he got so tired of pretending; so tired of living a life in the shadows where trust was a thing doled out like watery soup at a Salvation Army soup kitchen. Afraid to speak, all he could do was nod his head.

"Mr. Farrell."

"Yeah?"

"I just had a thought," Daggett said. "I remembered a minute ago that I used to be a detective."

"I'd forgotten that, too," Farrell said, glad to have the conversation steered back to the problems at hand. "You got an idea?"

"Yep," Daggett said. "Look, the place where Walt and Sleepy and the cat-eyed woman all meet is Joe Dante's, right?"

"Right."

"Shit is hittin' the fan right now, and none of it's good," Daggett reasoned. "People are gettin' shot up, and kidnapped, and I don't know what all. That ain't good for any man's business, particularly if that man's Joe Dante."

"You got a point," Farrell said.

"If the world was shakin' under your feet, and you were Joe Dante," Daggett said, "what would you do?"

"Well," Farrell said, staring out the window at the early-morning sky. "If I had a place that was hard to hit, I'd go there and fort up, until the mess got straightened out, one way or another."

"What kind of place like that has Dante got?" Daggett asked.

"Hmmm," Farrell said with a smile. "He's got a roadhouse out in Jefferson Parish with a lot of open ground around it. He just might go out there."

Daggett folded his arms across his chest and nodded his head sagely. "That's where I'd go, too, speaking strictly as a detective."

"Damn," Farrell said. "You might be a swami *and* a detective."

The two men got up and walked to the front. As they were about to pass through the room where the women were, Farrell thought to clear his throat before entering. "Everybody decent in there?" he asked.

"We all covered up," 'Tee Ruth said. "Come on through."

They walked into the bedroom and found Savanna covered to her neck with a clean white sheet. With her face washed and hair combed, she looked quite a bit better. "She'll be all right?" Farrell asked.

"I reckon," 'Tee Ruth said. "Takes a lot to hurt one of us. We had too much practice at it."

Farrell looked at Savanna, and she returned it with a small smile and a nod. 'Tee Ruth got up, and she and Daggett went out to the living room. Farrell went to the bed, and knelt down beside it.

"Was it bad?" he asked, laying a palm on her forehead.

"Bad enough," she said. "He told me you were dead, and that was a lot worse than what he did to me. It was so hard to believe . . . but when you didn't come, I began to be afraid he was tellin' the truth. That was the worst thing, thinkin' you were gone and I'd never see you again."

"I know," Farrell said softly. "I was afraid I'd lost you—again. I'm sorry it took me so long to find you. You'll never know how sorry." His eyes were moist, and his mouth was stretched into a thin, agonized line.

She took one of her hands from under the sheet, and reached out a palm to his face. His face bent to meet it, and his eyes closed as her soft hand cupped his stubbly cheek. "You're not finished yet, are you?" she asked after a long silence.

His eyes opened, and there was something hard and resolute in them now. "No," he said. "We still don't know who really killed Junior Obregon. I think Sleepy killed Lottie, but I can't even prove that, now that he's dead. We're going to go out to Joe Dante's roadhouse in a minute, and see what we can squeeze out of him. Maybe it's all been for nothing."

"No," she said, shaking her head on the pillow. "Not for nothing." She smiled briefly, then said, "How'd you hook up with Dandy?"

Farrell frowned. "Apparently he heard about the fracas at Sass's joint, and tracked us down before we went to Sleepy's house. He's out of his league, but he's so determined to help us that I can't get him out of it."

"He seems pretty knocked around already," Savanna said.

"Probably it's because of Lottie," he said.

"Maybe. Be careful, you hear?" she said.

He reached up to her hand, squeezed it with his own, then put it down on the sheet. They exchanged a lingering look filled with longing before he got up and walked to the living room.

In the living room, Farrell found Daggett at the window. Dandy sat in a chair near the fireplace puffing on a cigarette, his face flat and expressionless. Marcel got up and went to them.

"What happens now?" the youngster asked.

"Daggett and I are going out to a joint Joe Dante owns out on the Old Hammond Highway," Farrell replied. "We might find some of the people we're looking for there, and maybe the answers we need to clear this up. You and Walker can stay here and look after the women."

"You expect any trouble here?" Marcel asked.

"I don't know," Farrell said. "There's been too much lead flying for me to ignore it. Just be ready, and don't let anybody through that door that you don't know."

"I'm goin' with you," Dandy Walker said from his chair.

"Nothing doing," Farrell said. "This isn't for amateurs. Too many people have gotten hurt already."

Walker took a deep drag from his cigarette and stood up. "I got as much right as anybody to come along," he said truculently. "Lottie was my friend, too, and so is Iz. Somebody's got some payin' to do,

I wanna be there when the payin' starts." As frightened as he looked, there was a glint of resolve in his eyes.

Farrell grimaced, looked over at Daggett. Daggett looked at Dandy, then back to Farrell and shrugged.

"All right," Farrell said. "Suit yourself."

Dandy took one more drag from his cigarette, then crushed the butt in a tin ashtray.

Daggett looked at him. "When did you take that up?"

Dandy hitched up his pants and pulled down on the points of his vest. "I just do it sometimes when I'm nervous."

Daggett scratched his head. "Well, in that case, I reckon you got plenty of reason."

As the three men moved to leave the house, Marguerite came forward and took Daggett by the arms. "Do you have to do this? I just couldn't bear it if anything happened to you, too."

Daggett smiled down on her as he put his hat on the back of his head. "No need to worry," he said kindly. "My life's already been ruined once. If I can clean up the mess, it'll be worth the risk." He laid a hand softly on one of hers, and squeezed it gently.

Marguerite stood on tiptoe and kissed him on the corner of his mouth. "Please be careful. Please."

He felt a pleasant tingle as her mouth touched his, and a small, foolish smile spread over his face. "I will. I'll be back soon."

"Let's get this show on the road," Farrell said, and walked out the door. Dandy followed, and after a brief hesitation, Daggett followed, too.

Stella felt tired and alone. She'd spent the night moving around the city, not knowing where she could go that would be safe. She knew that if Joe had put a contract out on her, she wasn't safe anywhere. She'd been by Walt's place, but had found it empty with the front door swinging open. She'd gone inside with her gun drawn, expecting to find Walt dead, too, but no one was there.

Her body felt like a vibrating fiddle string. She remembered something from the time she and Walt had spent a lot of time together, and walked to a closet in the bedroom. As she'd hoped, there was a short-barreled Winchester pump shotgun propped in the corner behind a long overcoat. She picked it up, half opened the breech, and saw that it was fully loaded. She took the gun and went back to her car.

She needed sleep and a chance to pull things together. The best thing might just be to blow town. She had the stash of money that was more than enough to get started somewhere else.

She decided to go to Sleepy's boardinghouse. She knew that there was usually no one there but that halfwit, Huey, but that didn't bother Stella. After last night, a hundred Hueys would never bother her again. The sun was up as she reached Dumaine Street, but when she saw all the foot traffic and general hubbub in the neighborhood, she pulled her car to the curb and watched. Whatever was drawing the people was down near the corner where Sleepy's house was. She got out of the car, and mingled with some of the other people.

"I seen that giant lived in there once," an old man was saying. "It like ta scairt me white, I'll tell ya."

"What happened, Uncle Bud?" a teenage girl asked. "I done slept through the most excitin' thing ever happened in this neighborhood."

"Well," Uncle Bud said, hooking his thumbs sagely in his suspenders. "Near as I can figger, that devil Sleepy Moyer got shot by somebody. I seen them bring his corpse out and the wind blew the sheet off'n him before they could get him in the ambulance. They brung out that giant fella, too. I don't know if they kilt each other'r not."

"Damn," the teenage girl said. The sentiment was echoed all around as the group speculated on how anybody could've killed someone as evil as Sleepy. Several had tales to tell about him, and they quickly became engrossed in trying to top one another.

Stella eased herself out of the crowd as smoothly as she had come in. Walt had done it. That scrawny, shit-scared sonofabitch had killed one of the toughest men in the city, and maybe his cretin in the bargain. That was good news. It meant he was in a groove, and would stay in it until the finish. She wondered if he'd gotten to Joe yet. Probably not. That would take a certain finesse. Joe would be surrounded by bodyguards, so getting to him wouldn't be easy.

A more immediate problem for her was to find a place to hole up. She probably should have stayed at Walt's and waited for him to return, if he did. If he killed Joe, it didn't really matter whether he showed up or not. She felt confident she could run things on her own. She'd never done anything that big before, but this was a case of have to. Besides, Walt would be there to help her. He was plenty savvy.

Her eyes felt like they had sand in them, and she rubbed them with her tiny fist. Damn, it was hard to think right now. She needed a place to sleep as badly as she'd ever needed anything in her life. Worse yet, her mind was filled with the image of Joe's men hunting her, and the pitiless way they'd deal with her if they every caught up to her. Her stomach roiled with the thought of their hands on her body, and on her throat.

Suddenly she swerved the car to the curb, opened the door, and vomited like a sailor in a twenty-five-foot sea with no hope of land. She wondered as she gagged and gagged how one person could make so much vomit.

"*Got*-damn, woman," a country voice said, marveling. "You sho' done got aholt of some bad rotgut."

Stella raised her head with some effort, wiping the vomit from her mouth with the back of her pigskin glove. Her eyes were unfocused for a moment as she fought off the desire to faint, and saw a short, wizened Negro dressed in scuffed brogans, overalls, and a straw hat. He peered at her from beneath the hat brim, his thumbs stuck in the straps of his overalls.

Stella reached behind her on the seat, and found her Colt .32 automatic lying there. She pointed it at him, saying, "Get the hell outa my sight, you fuckin' country yokel."

The straw-hatted Negro's face flattened out with shock, and he backed up, bringing his hands palm up and waving them quickly back and forth. "No offense, sister, no offense. I was just lookin', is all."

"Then look someplace else, you goddamned peckerhead," she said between clenched teeth. She felt like vomiting again, but she was damned if she'd do it in front of him twice.

The man in the straw hat turned and broke into a leg-stretching, shambling run, his arms pumping like pistons. If she hadn't felt so sick, she might've laughed at him.

She sat up behind the wheel again, breathing deeply and trying not to swallow too many times. She found a handkerchief in her bag and used it to wipe her face, checking on her progress in the rearview mirror. When she was certain she'd removed any remaining signs of vomit from around her mouth and chin, she shifted back into first gear, and eased her car back into the early-morning traffic.

She didn't know why she was so upset. All she wanted was a few people dead, and they were conveniently getting that way. All she needed to do was get back her equilibrium, then find a place to hide until all this was over.

She saw a twenty-four-hour Negro pharmacy in the next block, and pulled to the curb. She tucked her automatic into her bag and got out of the car a bit unsteadily. Her head swam a little, but she fought off the nausea and dizziness and managed to walk in and sit down at the lunch counter.

"Yes'm," the young girl behind the counter said. "Can I get you anything?"

"A Coke and a couple asprins," Stella said. Her voice was a little louder than necessary, and the girl stepped back from the counter a bit, her eyes widening. "Sorry," she said in a softer voice. "I'm not feelin' too well right this minute." She offered a sickly smile, and the girl nodded and moved away.

When the girl brought back the cola and asprins, Stella forced herself to sip the drink, letting the syrup and carbonated water drop into her stomach a bit at a time. When the Coke was half gone, she was able to take the asprins without gagging.

She was staring down into her glass, and didn't see the two Negro patrol officers come into the drugstore. They moved very casually, their eyes roving all over everything and everybody in the place. They came in almost every day, so nobody took their entrance as anything unusual.

The first one's hands were empty, and they swung casually at his side, the right one occasionally brushing the butt of his service revolver. The second one had his short daystick in his right hand, the leather strap wrapped around the palm. He twirled it about, first this way then that, a quiet rhythm to the movement.

The first cop spotted Stella. He turned his head and jerked his chin to his partner in Stella's direction. They split up, still very casual, and came to within six feet of her, one on each side. *Goddamn,* she thought. *Everywhere I go, there's some man waitin' to fuck things up for me.*

" 'Scuse me, miss," the first cop said. "That green Buick outside—it yours?"

Stella looked up in the mirror, seeing the cops for the first time. "What about it?" she asked, her slanted eyes flickering and her mouth stretched tight.

"If it is, then you must be Miss Stella Bascomb," the cop with the daystick said. "And in that case, we gotta ask you to come along with us."

"What for?" Stella asked. How could they be looking for her? Nobody had anything on her—or did they?

"Just come along quiet, miss," the first cop said. "Everything'll be explained down to headquarters." He was about forty years old, with a lot of gray strands shot through his sideburns. His eyes were patient and bored, as if this were nothing but more routine in his day. The other cop was younger, cocky. He went on playing with his billy, figuring a little dame like Stella was nothing to worry about.

"Sure, officer," Stella said. "Just let me pay my bill, will you?" She was already opening her purse, rummaging around in the bottom like she was looking for a quarter. They weren't ready when the Colt came up, Stella spinning around, shooting, shooting, and shooting.

The first cop grabbed his guts, then pulled them away, his eyes shocked at the sight of blood on his own hands. The second cop went for his gun, but he was slow. The barrel was just clearing leather when her fourth shot took him just above the bridge of his nose. His eyes had glassed before he hit the floor.

Stella was off the counter stool, the gun pushed out in front of her, moving it around like the needle on a compass, as if searching for the route to another victim. Everybody else in the pharmacy was on the floor, crawling to cover. The counter girl was hunched behind the lunch counter, hugging her knees, whimpering like a lost pup.

Stella grabbed her bag and moved swiftly, holding the gun up and ready. The adrenaline was coursing through her veins now, her nausea forgotten in the rush to escape. She wondered as she broke into the daylight if they'd radioed in when they spotted her car. She had to get out of there and get rid of the car.

She made it to her car without anyone yelling or pointing, got inside, and cranked the motor. She had just enough presence of mind not to gun the engine and squeal out of there, and eased her car out into traffic like a fine Uptown matron. She cast a backward glance at the door to the pharmacy, but nobody had come out.

There was only one thing to do now—get out of New Orleans. She had to ditch the Buick and find another car. Then what? Wait a minute. Joe's roadhouse out in Jeff Parish. She could hide out there, get her bearings, then head north into Arkansas. From there she could get into Oklahoma and really get lost. They'd never look for her there. But another car was the first order of business. Better find one fast.

It was well after sunup when Casey arrived at the Sonnier house. He walked up to the front door and knocked three times. A trim, well-dressed octoroon youngster came to the door, his right hand out of sight behind his back.

"Who is it?" he asked.

Casey fished out his gold shield, and held it up so the boy could see it. "Captain Frank Casey. Let me in, will you?"

The door opened, and Casey went inside. "You're Marcel Aristide, aren't you?" he asked the kid.

"Yes, sir," Marcel replied respectfully. "Mr. Farrell isn't here just now, if you're looking for him."

"Who is here?" Casey asked.

"We here, Cap'n Casey," 'Tee Ruth said as she came into the living room. "Mr. Wes said we should stay home until things settled down a li'l. Is everything all right?"

"I don't know," Casey said. "I was hoping to ask Wes that myself, but since he isn't, they probably aren't. Where is he?"

Marguerite had come in and stood beside her mother. The two men exchanged a glance, then Marguerite said, "We don't want to get anybody in trouble," she said.

"I'm not here to arrest anybody," Casey said. "Do you know where Savanna Beaulieu is?"

The two women exchanged another look. "She's sleepin' in the next room," 'Tee Ruth said. "She been beat and raped by Sleepy Moyer is what she told me. Mr. Wes and Isra'l gone out to someplace on the Hammond Highway lookin' for Walt Daggett and some woman."

Casey shut his eyes and felt his mouth stretch very tightly and thinly. After a moment, he let his breath out slowly and opened his eyes again. "How long ago did they leave?"

"They and Dandy Walker left here about thirty minutes ago," Marguerite said.

Casey looked at her with a peculiar expression on his face. "The three of them went together, eh?"

"Yes, sir," Marguerite said.

Casey went to the telephone, picked it up, and dialed the head-quarters number. When someone answered, he asked for the assistant superintendent's office.

"Captain Casey, sir," he said when the assistant chief came on the line.

"We've been having a minor crime wave for the past thirty-six hours, and Joe Dante seems to be in the middle of it. My information is that he's gone out to a joint he owns on the Old Hammond Highway called the Belle Epoque. Can you call the Jefferson Parish sheriff and ask him to send a couple carloads of deputies to meet me there? Thanks, I'm leaving now."

As he turned, he found Marguerite standing nearby.

"Captain, is Israel going to get into trouble again?" she asked.

"I think I've nearly got what I need to get him cleared of every-thing," Casey said.

"Really?" Marguerite said. She took 'Tee Ruth's hand and squeezed it.

Casey took his pipe out of his pocket and saw the bowl still had remnants of his last smoke in it. He picked up the tin ashtray next to one of the chairs. He knocked the dottle into the ashtray, then moved it around with his finger, seeming to distribute the ashes around the ashes already there. After a moment he put the ashtray down, and filled his pipe with new tobacco.

"Really," Casey said. "But I'd better get going. There's bound to be fireworks out there. Stay here as Wes asked you to, and I'll be back in touch later today." He waved briefly at Marcel and left the house.

The women were silent, but 'Tee Ruth noticed a happy gleam in Marguerite's eye that hadn't been there earlier.

As Casey got back into his car, he heard the police radio issuing his call sign. He picked up the mike and keyed it. The dispatcher said he had flash traffic for him.

"Give it to me," Casey said.

"A woman matching the description of Stella Bascomb just shot two uniformed officers in a pharmacy on St. Bernard Avenue. One officer dead at the scene, the other critical."

"God damn," Casey said, then he keyed the mike. "Throw every car in the vicinity around that area. She'll try to ditch her car if she's got her wits about her at all. Relay her description and automobile license to all cars, and make certain they know she's armed and dangerous. Call me on the radio when you find her."

"Roger," the dispatcher said.

Walt had been to Joe's house on De Saix and his office in the Hibernia Bank Building, and had not found him in either place. He was now headed for the Parish line to try the roadhouse. He had the radio on, listening to a little music to lift his spirits. Cab Calloway was doing "Minnie the Moocher." Walt liked that song, and was beating time on the steering wheel with his fingers. By the time the song ended, he was feeling a little better, and had settled in to enjoy some music when the announcer interrupted the program with a police bulletin.

A Negro woman described as small, attractive, and well dressed had shot two colored officers in a drugstore. A full description of the woman, her automobile, and a fuller exposition of the crime followed.

He had to find Stella, and get her away from here before it was too late. But where would she go? Not home. Stella was too savvy for that. She wouldn't go to his place, either—there was no telling what the cops might know by now.

He was torn by indecision. He needed to take care of Joe, but he wanted to find Stella before it was too late. He had a sudden thought. If she didn't know Joe was at the roadhouse, she might head there to hide out. It was really the only option, since the police knew her name and everything about her. Now his course was clear—he needed to reach the roadhouse and take care of whoever was out there in order to connect with Stella. His back got a little straighter as he urged the car forward.

19

Farrell, Dandy, and Daggett arrived at the driveway to La Belle Epoque sometime before 9:30 A.M., and paused to survey the territory. Two cars, a long black Lincoln and a four-door Ford sedan, were parked near the entrance. In the bright sunlight, without the garish lights and sounds of music, the roadhouse looked forlorn and faded.

"Well, here we are," Daggett said. Dandy leaned forward from the backseat to hear what the other two were saying.

"What next?" Farrell asked. "You're the detective."

"We're past the detecting part, Mr. Farrell," Daggett said. "At this stage, I'll take any advice you've got to give."

"It's a cinch they won't invite us in the front door," Farrell said. "Getting in there without being seen'll be tough. I work better in the dark."

"Let's ditch the car," Daggett said. "We can try to work our way around behind the place."

Farrell let in the clutch and drove the Packard down the road about fifty yards from the roadhouse drive, and pulled into a wayside picnic area. A small grove of trees surrounded a clearing with a half-dozen picnic tables and a brick barbecue pit. Farrell drove behind the pit and cut the engine.

The cold February winds had subsided, and in the bright sunshine it was almost like spring. The threesome left their overcoats in the backseat and walked across the road to enter the trees. Their progress was slow and the ground was marshy and occasionally blocked by patches of briars that caught their clothes and tore into their flesh. The three men bore the discomfort in silence.

Daggett held up a hand after they'd been in the woods about twenty minutes. The three of them were sweating profusely, and their clothing was ripped and spattered with mud. Farrell came up behind Daggett, and saw they'd reached their destination. Between them and the rear of the roadhouse was an old wooden barn that looked to be used for some kind of storage. At Daggett's signal, they all sprinted from cover and gained the back of the barn.

"I'm never gonna leave the city again," Farrell said as he pulled brambles from his jacket and trouser legs.

"We got about twenty yards of open ground between us and the roadhouse," Daggett said as he blotted his sweaty face on the sleeve of his jacket.

"Dante's a city boy," Farrell said. "Just like us. I got a feeling he came here because he felt the rear was safe. I'm betting most or all of his men are watching the front."

Daggett looked at him. "It'll only take one of them to see us, and we're cooked."

"I know that," Farrell said, "but I don't have any other ideas."

"Just then the sound of an approaching automobile reached their ears, and Dandy peeked around the corner of the barn to watch. "It's Walt," he said. "This might give us the openin' we've been waiting for."

Daggett cut around the side of the barn with Farrell and Dandy hard on his heels. They sprinted for the back of the roadhouse, and came to a halt right outside a rear service door. The smell of rotting garbage suggested they might be at the kitchen exit.

Farrell examined the latch of the door and found it pretty rudimentary. He removed a stiff, thick piece of celluloid from over the driver's license in his wallet and pressed it over the latch as he worked the knob. Small grunts escaped his throat as he pushed and strained. Finally, they heard the snap of the catch, and Farrell eased the door open an inch at a time. Satisfied that no one was on the other side, he pulled the door open, and the three of them ducked into the kitchen, pulling the door quietly closed behind them.

The dark kitchen was filled with modern appliances and chrome steel cabinets. A large steel preparation table stood in the center, with pots and implements hanging from a rack directly overhead.

The leavings of sandwiches, glasses of milk, and an open bottle of Canadian Club remained on the table.

A diamond-shaped window in a swinging door gave a view of a large room with a bandstand and tables. A thick-bodied, brown-haired white man sat on the edge of the bandstand, idly leafing through a copy of *Life* magazine while another sat at a table smoking. Neither looked particularly alert. Farrell held one finger to his lips, and opened the door of the kitchen just wide enough to enable them to slip through. The two gunmen, lost in their own thoughts, failed to notice.

Farrell and Daggett split like the skin of a banana, with Farrell heading for the bandstand and Daggett toward the table. Neither had drawn a gun. The man at the table must have caught movement in the corner of his eye, for he straightened suddenly, his hand shooting into the folds of his jacket. Daggett launched himself head-long, and struck the man at chest level. They fell to the floor with a rackety crash of upset furniture.

The man at the bandstand, taken equally unawares, focused first on his partner and Daggett, not even seeing Farrell until Farrell's fist crashed into the hinge of his jaw. Farrell felt the jaw break and the man stiffen as he fell back across the edge of the stage.

Daggett, hindered by his bullet wound, was still locked in a struggle with the other man, thrashing around the floor. Dandy stepped in with his gun and laid it behind the man's right ear with a practiced snap of his wrist. The man went limp instantly, and Daggett pushed the inert body away from him. "Thanks, Dandy," he said in a breath-less whisper.

The three men were tensed to run or fight, knowing their noise could not have gone unnoticed. Daggett drew the .41 from under his arm and followed Farrell toward the front of the club with Dandy close behind. They reached the lobby just as Stella walked in. She held the cut-down Winchester pump at port arms, her left hand on the cocking handle. Dandy leaped forward with his antique pistol raised, shouting an unintelligible cry. With incredible speed, Stella worked the slide and fired the shotgun from her hip. Dandy fell, screaming in pain. Farrell never knew how, but from a distance of only fifty feet she managed to hit only one of them.

He and Daggett threw themselves to opposite sides, each strug-gling to bring a gun to bear on the diminutive woman. She let off a second shot in Farrell's direction, and he felt his new hat disappear.

Damn, there goes another one, he thought. A sharp pain streaked across the side of his head, and he knew a moment's panic when he realized he'd been hit.

Daggett's gun roared twice, and they saw Stella make for the stairs at a dead run. As they barreled after her, they saw she'd abandoned her high-heeled shoes in her flight. They lay carelessly askew on the carpeted stairs.

At the first landing, they paused to look up, and felt the wind of another buckshot charge whistle past them. Farrell tossed Daggett a look, and saw the ex-detective stare back at him with wide, startled eyes. Daggett reached his arm over the banister, and threw two quick, unaimed shots upward. As he did so, Farrell rounded the landing and sprinted up the stairs. His automatic crashed three times, and Stella fell back. "Go," he shouted to Daggett, and fired twice more.

Joe Dante sat back in his desk chair with a look of astonishment on his face while the radio newscaster droned on about the latest in the Crescent City murders. Sleepy Moyer was dead, along with another man at his house, and another report told of a Negro woman killing a couple of cops. The woman sounded a lot like Stella.

Dante leaned back in his chair and began to think. Sleepy's death at the hands of an unknown assailant was happy news. At least he wasn't in the hands of the cops, and he hadn't made any deathbed statement. If Stella shot a couple of cops, she was ancient history. She'd never get out of the city alive after that.

That left Walt and Israel Daggett, and maybe Wes Farrell, if he poked his nose in too far. If things fell the right way, he wouldn't have to relocate to Baton Rouge at all. Walt couldn't hope to keep his head above water alone, so his hours were numbered, too, He even had a couple of people in mind he could give Walt's territory to, and although Sleepy had been an efficient enforcer, Dante knew he could eventually find a suitable replacement for him, as well.

Joe had his feet propped on an open desk drawer, trying to catch up on the sleep he'd lost the night before when a knock sounded at the door. His eyes opened immediately, and he swiveled toward the sound.

"Boss, you awake?" Lars asked.

"I am now," Dante said. "What is it?"

"I got Walt Daggett out here. He is askin' for you."

Dante rubbed his face vigorously with the flats of his hands to get the sleep out of his eyes and straightened his tie. "Send him in."

Lars stood out of the way, his eyes watchful. Walt Daggett, still dressed in his overcoat and hat, walked into the room. His eyes were wary, and his back straight. His hands were empty, but the fingers were slightly curled, as if he meant to fill them with iron at a moment's notice. He seemed not the least intimidated by Lars or Dante. Dante felt a vague feeling of disquiet as he looked at him.

"Well, Walt," Dante said in a mild voice. "This is a pleasant surprise. "What brings you all the way out here at this time of the day?"

"Stella," he said.

Dante's left eyebrow hiked up gently. "I don't know where Stella is, Walt," he said. "I ain't seen her lately."

"That ain't the way she tells it," Walt said. "She said Sleepy's been fillin' you full of bull about her and me. I always played fair and square with you, Mr. Dante. I don't know what Sleepy told you, but you can forget it. He's dead. I killed him early this morning."

"So the radio was right," Dante said, nodding. "I never gave you the credit you deserve, Walt. Anybody who could take Sleepy down is somebody I want for a friend."

"I don't want no friendship," Walt said. "Stella's in trouble with the law. I figure she'll come out here because she'll think the place is deserted so she can hole up. I'm gonna take her out of here, and get out of the state. If you got any objection to that, you better say so now."

Again, Dante's eyebrow rose at Walt Daggett's audacity. He wondered where it came from, and had a hunch that Stella must be behind it. Stella was good at making things stiff, but a backbone was a new accomplishment for her. Dante felt his admiration for her growing. It was really hard luck that she had become such a liability.

"Well, she hasn't gotten here yet, Walt," Dante said smoothly. Dante saw Lars looking over Walt's head into his eyes, and Dante nodded imperceptibly.

Lars shifted his weight forward, and brought his right hand up to the gun butt in his left armpit. Before the hand made contact, Walt made a sudden half turn. The Browning automatic appeared in his fist like a dove in a magician's hand, and Lars let his weight settle back on his heels, his square face settling back into impassivity.

"You'll have to excuse the gun, Mr. Dante," Walt said. "I'm a little jumpy. Kind of ask your goddamn squarehead to stand where I can see him, 'cause it makes me nervous when people get too far behind me these days."

Dante nodded, signaling Lars with his eyes. "Sure, Walt. We're all friends here, so there's no need to get your drawers in a knot. Lars, why don't you get some coffee for Walt. He can wait up here with me."

Lars glanced quickly at Walt, then nodded and left the room. Dante settled back in his chair and regarded Walt for several moments.

"Sleepy was pretty good," Dante said finally. "How was it you were able to take him?"

Walt sat down on the edge of a chair across from Dante. He'd unbuttoned his coat and placed his hat on the floor by his feet. The Browning was still in his hand, but the muzzle was pointed down at the floor. "Sleepy was tied up in a chair bein' roasted over an open fire by my cousin, Iz, and a big white man with pale gray eyes. I walked in while they weren't payin' attention, and shot Sleepy and Iz, then I beat it."

Dante nodded. "Walt, it's too bad you want to leave town. I think you'd make a hellava replacement for Sleepy, now that he's out of the picture. It's really a pity, isn't it. If he hadn't killed the Sonnier woman, probably everything would be as it was."

"Sleepy done a lot of bad things in his life, Mr. Dante, but killin' Lottie Sonnier wasn't one of 'em," Walt said.

Dante sat up a bit straighter in his chair, and looked at Walt a bit more closely. Walt's eyes held no guile, just as they held no fear. "How do you know Sleepy didn't kill her, Walt?"

"Because I know who did," Walt said. "Lottie was askin' too many questions, and she found out some things that'd do us hurt."

"Us?"

"I mean you, and everybody who works for you," Walt said. "Lottie got to helpin' a little chippie named Billie Talmadge. Billie was Junior Obregon's girl, and was with him the night he was shot."

Dante's eyes gleamed, and he leaned forward in rapt attention. "She knows who killed Obregon?"

"She knows because she seen it done," Walt explained. "She was tryin' to get Junior home 'cause he was drunk and near to passin' out. She left him on the sidewalk to go and call for a cab, couldn't find one, and came back to get Junior. She got there just as the shooter was about to drop the hammer. She heard what they said, and saw the gun go off."

"And it wasn't your cousin? Is that what you're saying?" Dante asked, his eyes narrowed to slits.

"Shit," Walt said contemptuously. "You know better than that. Iz Daggett is so square he has five corners. He was makin' trouble for Junior to make him send Billie home to her folks, but he was no murderer. It was just bad luck, though, that the judge downgraded it to a manslaughter beef, instead of murder, or he'd be up at Angola yet."

Walt spoke in a flat monotone, his face wiped clean of emotion. Dante had no doubt he was telling the truth. "Let me ask you something, Walt. Why are you telling me all this? I was glad Junior was killed, and I'm not upset that the Sonnier woman was killed. I might have ordered the hits myself, sooner or later, but I didn't. That means you must have."

Walt sat there watching Dante balefully. "Junior had to be killed because he got fucked up all the time with his own shit," Walt said. "Plus, I wanted his territory, so he had to go. I didn't squeeze the trigger, but you can say I was responsible. In a way, it was the same with Lottie. She'd found out too much about too many things, and too many people. If she'd gone to the cops a week ago, we'd all be coolin' our heels in Parish Prison right now. I didn't order her killed. In a funny way, it was just an accident."

"If you didn't do it, who did?" Dante asked.

Walt emitted a dry croaking laugh. "A man has to have a few secrets, Mr. Dante. I might need to use that information for something one day. You can never tell when I might get to come back here. Me and Stella."

"You and Stella have decided to form a partnership, is that it?" Dante said, surreptitiously pushing a small button set under the edge of his desk.

"The other night, Stella convinced me that together we could cut a bigger swath than if we just kept on workin' for you," Walt said. "I saw the sense in it, but it looks like that's just another pipe dream. Stella and me'll just have to start over somewhere else."

"Seems like I underestimated you," Dante said good-naturedly. "We could have gone a long way with each other if we'd known each other's qualities a little better." As he spoke, he let his left hand fall into his lap, inches from the pearl-handled .38 tucked into his belt.

The door slid open and Lars filled the opening, a .45 automatic dwarfed in the grip of his huge fist. He raised it to fire when Walt dropped to one knee, shifted his weight, and fired once with the silenced Browning. A small dark freckle appeared under Lars's left eye, and he fell over like a chopped tree. Even before Lars fell, Walt whirled on Dante, saw the .38 in Dante's hand, and fired twice more. Dante fell to the floor gasping, his gun clattering away on the floor.

Walt got up, his face dark and twisted with rage as he walked over to Dante. The big, black-haired gangster lay faceup on the floor, his left hand pressed tightly over his smashed collarbone. Blood leaked from between his fingers as he lay there.

"You double-dealin' ofay sonofabitch," Walt said in a dry rasp. "I know you beat Stella. I should kill you for that right here and now."

"No!" Dante gasped. "You got it all wrong, Walt. I didn't . . ."

"Shut up," Walt said from between his teeth. "Act like a man on your way out." He dropped the empty Browning on the floor, and drew the big Astra from under his left arm. He pointed it at Dante's head, his finger tightening on the trigger. Dante was mesmerized by the dark hole at the muzzle of the gun. He wanted to beg for his life, but his brain was so numb that he couldn't make himself talk.

Then came the hard, heavy booms of a shotgun somewhere below. Walt checked his trigger finger, and half turned. He looked down on Dante once more, and said, "Don't go away now, hear? I'll come back to see you in a few minutes." Then he turned on his heel and left, stepping over Lars's prostrate body as he walked.

As he stepped into the hall, Stella came toward him at a run. "Walt," she shouted. "Help me, Walt." She cast her eyes wildly about her, her small, pointed teeth bared. A flush of excitement and fear darkened the satiny smooth skin of her face and neck.

"I'm here, Stella," Walt said as he walked to her.

"Farrell and Daggett are downstairs," she said breathlessly. Her eyes rolled whitely in her head. "We gotta get outa here."

"Gimme that scattergun," Walt said. "I just shot Joe, but he's still alive. Reckon we'll have to let him go this time. I'll take care of Farrell and Iz while you go down the back stairs and get outside. Once you got a car runnin', you honk the horn three times. I'll be comin' out fast."

Stella's eyes stopped rolling and focused on Walt for the first time.

ou on there, too. Go on and leave me and Stella alone. We're leavin'. Y'all don't need us for anything."

"That's not true, Walt!" Farrell yelled. "You know the truth about Junior Obregon's murder. You don't go anywhere until you tell us who killed him."

Walt laughed hysterically. "Y'all are sure stupid. The answer's lookin' you right in the face and has been all along. All you got to do is put two and two together, Cousin." He laughed again, and fired a blast down the staircase.

"You ain't got a chance, man!" Israel yelled. "The cops'll be here any minute. We got you outgunned anyway. There's been too much killin' already. Can you hear me, Walt?"

"I hear you, but I don't hear you, Cousin," Walt said, laughing crazily. He strode down the stairs, firing the shotgun at the banister behind which his cousin crouched. Buckshot pellets rained on the stairs like hailstones.

Israel rolled sideways, shielding his face with his left arm. Walt kept coming, firing and firing as he walked. As he made ready to fire a fourth shot, the hammer clicked dryly on an empty chamber. He dropped the shotgun with a clatter as his right hand brought out the long, black Astra automatic, and began firing it. Israel, his eyes sick, carefully sighted down the barrel of his revolver and fired three times. Two bullets hit within an inch of each other in Walt's side, and the third took him in the thigh. His leg collapsed and he keeled straight over, like a tree falling. His thin body made almost no noise at all on the thickly carpeted floor.

Israel went over to him, and held him in his arms. "Jesus, Walt," he said. "Why'd you do it?"

"Hadda do it. For Stella," Walt said haltingly. "Be all right." His eyes closed and his mouth twisted in pain.

"Why'd you kill Junior and Lottie, Walt? Tell me," Israel said, shaking his cousin.

"Sick of you always bein' the big shot," Walt said. Figgered if you were . . . out of the picture, I'd . . . have chance to take your . . . place. Then you were messin' with Junior. Was 'fraid you'd tumble to . . . drug connection with Dante. But didn't kill Lottie. Junior, neither. Somebody else done it . . . for me. Done both of 'em."

He was in complete control of himself and the situation. I
should stick with him this time. He was more of a man
given him credit for being. She handed him the shotgun.

Walt reached a hand around her waist, dragged her
him and kissed her fiercely. His eyes held a placidity th
never seen in him before, nor in any other human being
remember.

Walt let her go, then turned back to the stairs with a
He racked the slide of the shotgun, charging the breech w
round. He shrugged out of his overcoat, dropping it as h
Stella turned and padded barefoot down the hall from w
had come. Before she left, she had one piece of unfinishe
to take care of. She reached into the top of her stocking an
the spring blade knife she kept there.

She found an open door with a big blond man's body
across the threshold. Lars. Good riddance. She walked into
and saw Joe lying on the floor, trying to drag himself up
walked over and stood over him, her legs spread slightly

"So you sent somebody to take me out, huh, Joe?" sh
voice trilling with some strange pleasure. "Killin' a nigger i
than steppin' on a cockroach to you, is it, honeylamb?
what was on my mind every time you called one of us a nig

Joe looked up at her, his eyes rolling in desperation. Th
his shirt was covered in blood. "Stella. It was a mistake.
and I'll give you anything you want."

"Here's what was on my mind, sugar," she said, slash
with the open spring-blade knife. Joe's mouth opened to sc
as the blade punched into his eye socket and into his b
throat gurgled horribly as blood, yellowish eye fluid, and gr
of brain matter exploded from the socket.

She bent down, wiped the knife and put it away, then
the pearl-handled .38, and moved with resolute dispatch to
stairs.

"Walt!" a voice called from the head of the stairway. "
up there?"

"I'm here, Iz," Walt called back. "You ain't dead, huh?
I'm glad. I got a lot on my conscience, and I'd just as soon

"Who did?" Daggett asked.

Walt's voice seemed to fail him, and he pulled his cousin's head down near his own. He spoke for several minutes, his desperate words punctuated by bloody coughs.

Stella heard the booms of the shotgun echo hollowly throughout the building as she tripped lightly down the stairs in her stocking feet. Good. Walt was keeping them pretty busy. She'd have all the time she needed to get to the car. She wondered if Walt would make it, too.

She reached a dimly lit corridor that led to the kitchen, and headed that way. She'd almost made the swinging door when a voice stopped her.

"Goin' somewhere, Stella?"

She turned and fired twice, then ran for the door.

"You're at the end of the road, honey," the voice said from somewhere behind her. "There's nowhere to go now but down and out."

She flung back two more shots as she entered the kitchen. As the door swung closed, the lights went out with a sudden pop. She caught her breath in fright, and began feeling around with her free hand, trying to find something to orient her to where she was.

"You ought not to've tossed me in the river like that, Stella," Farrell's voice said. "What number was I on your kill list, honey? I must've been pretty high up, no more thought than you gave it."

Stella fired two more reckless shots. The fire leaping from the barrel blinded her, leaving her even more disoriented than she had been.

"Over here, baby," Farrell said. Stella whirled and fired once more, then the gun was empty. Quickly, she dropped the empty gun on the floor, then hiked up her skirt and pulled the spring-blade stiletto from the top of her stocking. She pressed the button and felt the six inches of chrome steel jump open in her hand.

"Tsk, tsk, tsk," Farrell's voice said in the darkness. "The guns were bad enough, but knives, too? That's the trouble with you, Stella. You're too short on talk. If you'd tried talking earlier, this mess would be over by now, with fewer dead bodies. You might even have talked your way out of this, but not now; not when you've got two dead cops, and Lottie, and maybe Junior Obregon, too, on the score card.''

Stella slashed the blade at the darkness, panic rising in her like a sickening miasma. She moved forward and banged into something. Metal clattered around her, and she slashed the air again, the blade making a whispery hiss in the darkened room.

Giving full vent to her fear, she pushed blindly ahead, knocking other things crashing to the floor. She felt a breath of fresh air coming from somewhere ahead, and ran toward it. Her hand met a surface and she felt it give. Her panic gave way to jubilation as light streamed through the half-opened door. But then another hand shot out and grabbed her from behind, checking her progress.

She half turned and flailed out with the knife, feeling it catch in something and tear through it. She bared her teeth and slashed out again, stabbing down over and over. Out of the darkness another blade whispered, and the steel reached out and parried hers. She slashed wildly, her blade clanging as it met and bounced off the one in Farrell's invisible hand.

"You can give it up any time, Stella," Farrell's disembodied voice said. "I invented this game we're playing now, and you can't win it."

She shrilled an unintelligible cry of rage and frustration, whipping the blade back and forth in front of her. Twice it met steel, then something traced a hot, sharp line across the tendons of her right hand, and the knife fell from the nerveless fingers.

A grip like iron shot out of the darkness and grabbed the bleeding wrist, pulling her toward the invisible nemesis. She whimpered and kicked out with her bare feet, but the pressure was unrelenting, and finally the adrenaline in her drained away, taking with it the ruthless bundle of nerves that had made up Stella Bascomb; leaving behind something small and frightened.

A light came on then, and she found herself looking up into Farrell's face. His hat was gone, his hair was wild, and a bloody crease along the side of his head leaked blood down on his shirt collar. It was a face devoid of anything like pity, yet he pulled out a handkerchief and used it to tightly bind the bloody slice in her forearm.

"I got money, lots of money," she said in a hurried, breathy voice. "Leave me go and I'll give it to you. I . . . I'll let you have me. I'll give you such a fling as you never had in your life."

Farrell's mouth softened just enough for an ironic smile to bend it, but his eyes were as cold and empty as a winter night. He pulled her toward him in a fierce embrace, and a dry, hoarse clatter of a laugh escaped his throat, a laugh the like of which she hoped never to hear again.

20

Two days after the shooting at Dante's roadhouse, Frank Casey, Israel Daggett, and Wesley Farrell visited Dandy Walker's hospital room at Charity Hospital. His legs had been shredded by Stella's shotgun blast and he had lost three pints of blood before any help could be gotten for him. It was a miracle he was still alive.

Dandy was at the end of the male Negro ward, and in recognition of the seriousness of his wounds, he had privacy screens around his bed. Daggett stuck his head around the screen, and, upon seeing Dandy's eyes open, walked into the small enclosed area. Daggett was dressed in a new dark-blue wool worsted with a vest, a red-blue-and-yellow striped silk tie, and had a brand-new, pale yellow Stetson cocked at a jaunty angle on his head.

Casey came around next, followed by Farrell. Farrell had a piece of sticking plaster over the buckshot graze on his head, but otherwise he was impeccably dressed in brown barleycorn tweeds, with the creases in his trousers pressed to a knife edge. A pearl-gray, wide-brimmed Borsalino was pulled low over his eyes. The three men's faces were grave.

"What do you say, Dandy?" Daggett asked, taking his hat off and placing it on the end of the bed. There was a sheet-covered platform there to keep pressure off of Dandy's shredded feet and legs.

Dandy moved his eyes over to them a bit slowly. He was heavily drugged with morphine for the pain, but he managed a wan smile. "Hey, Iz," he said in a thick voice.

"They treating you right, Dandy?" Frank Casey asked.

Dandy's face tried to maintain a grin, but the effort was too much. "They say my legs won't be much use to me no more, Captain," he said. "Good thing I give up boxing, ain't it?"

"That was a big risk you took, charging that shotgun," Daggett said. "You didn't need to do that."

"I—I was afraid she'd shoot you if I didn't get her first," Dandy said. "I was just too slow, is all. I guess I ain't got the moves I had when I was fightin'."

"What made you stop fighting, Dandy?" Casey asked softly. "You were a contender until you took that beating against Tod Mulwray in '32. Mulwray was good, but not as good as you. You might've taken him in a rematch, I'd bet my house on it."

Dandy shook his head slowly. "Mulwray was a whole lot better'n he looked. He wiped the floor up with me. I knew I'd never take him if I fought him six times." He shook his head slowly, his eyes a bit mournful as he recollected the end of his ring career. "You think I could have a cigarette?" he asked. "There's some in the drawer here." He waved vaguely at the nightstand beside his bed.

Daggett opened the drawer, found the cigarette pack, and brought it out. He tapped one out for Dandy, and held it so his friend could grip it with his lips. Daggett pulled the pack free, then stood aside while Farrell lit it for the ex-boxer.

"Thanks," Dandy said as he let smoke feather out of his nose.

"You never smoked when we was fighting together, partner," Daggett said.

Dandy puffed a bit more, and reached up to take the cigarette from his lips. He blew out more smoke, and looked at Daggett. "My nerves ain't what they was. Business worries wore me down, and I took up smokin' to take my mind off'n things once in a while. I don't smoke heavy—never did."

Daggett's face had grown cold and sober, and he reached over and picked up the cigarette package and began to turn it over in his hand. "Dandy, we know why you tagged along with us all through yesterday, and why you tried to shoot Stella. We know about you and her and Walt. They both sang like sparrows."

"I don't know what you mean," Dandy said thickly, putting the cigarette back in his mouth for another drag. His face looked placid and a bit stupid from the morphine.

"I've been suspicious of you since the night Skeets Poche tried to kill Daggett in his hotel room," Casey said. "You claimed to have been sapped, but there were no marks, swellings, or anything like a bruise on you. I looked pretty carefully." He took a manila envelope in his hand, tucked it under one arm, and shoved both hands in his trouser pockets. "Daggett remembered that you'd had the idea of going back to his room for a drink, but then you'd tried to beg off. He'd had to insist to get you up there. It's because you knew what was waiting for him, and you didn't want to get caught in the middle of it."

"Then I remembered you and Walt were pretty friendly once upon a time," Daggett said. "Back when you were still a fighter. People remembered it, once we got to asking around. We found a photograph of Stella and Walt at the Brown Fedora. And guess what? You were there with 'em, lookin' to be havin' one hell of a time."

"So what?" Dandy said. "This is a pretty small town. Yeah, we run around together for a while years ago. So what?" His voice was developing an edge that cut through the muzziness of the drug.

"So Walt was a cop then," Casey said. "He got around and knew people who knew things. Like for instance you taking a dive in the Mulwray fight."

The muscles in Dandy's face seemed to ripple slightly, although his eyes remained fixed and dull. "You can't prove that," he said.

"Maybe not," Casey said, "but we can prove something better." He removed the manila envelope from under his arm, and shook out some papers which he held in front of Dandy's face. "I had one of my men do some research down at Notorial Archives and at the Whitney National Bank a couple of days ago. Walt Daggett owned the mortgage on everything—your house, your gymnasium, your fighters, even your car. We found bank records that show all the money you make being funneled into his accounts, with a certain outlay every month to cover your living expenses. He owned you, heart, body, and soul."

Dandy looked at the papers, trying very hard to exhibit no emotion or interest. "So what?" he said again. "Walt was a businessman, and I worked for him. None of that means nothin' at all."

Daggett sighed and scratched his nose idly. "Billie Talmadge saw you the night you shot Junior Obregon, Dandy. She was only fifty feet from you, but you couldn't see her for the fog. Junior was on the ground drunk, and you stood over him and put three .41 caliber bullets into him, just like that," he said, snapping his fingers loudly three times.

Dandy winced, but said nothing. His eyes were fixed on Daggett's, like a rabbit hypnotized by a snake.

"Walt did a little talking before he kicked off," Farrell said. "Walt got the gun for you, wearing his old police uniform. He knew the layout of the locker room, which locker to go to, and how to get it open. Once he had the gun, it was all downhill. All he had to do was put it in your hand, wind you up, and point you at Junior."

Daggett sat down in the only chair. He looked tired and a bit disappointed. "You and me were like brothers, Dandy. When times were hard, whatever I had, you had, too. How could you send me to prison like that? How? I just don't understand it."

A mirthless laugh gurgled in Dandy's throat. "What's to understand, ole buddy? You got out of the fight racket and made a name for yourself as a cop, and a good livin' to go with it. You had Lottie. I was just a busted-up ex-fighter, owned by a crooked cop. I didn't have nothin' that Walt didn't let me have." He puffed desultorily on the cigarette a few times, his glassed eyes locked on Daggett's. "A man can get a little crazy when somebody else owns him—when he don't see no way of gettin' clear of it. After a while, I just didn't care about anything anymore. It was either do what Walt said, or end up on the bricks with nothin' but the clothes on my back."

"There's something you ain't sayin', Dandy," Daggett said. "About Lottie."

A sharp light of pain shone in Dandy's drugged eyes. "I loved her a long time. As long as you, but she didn't have eyes for nobody but you when you were still free. But I wasn't thinkin' of her when Walt sent me to kill Junior. It was only later, when you was in the pen, and I was out here, seein' how lonely she was without you. I was already goin' to hell for murder and for framin' my best friend into jail. I decided to try and get a little happiness before I went to stoke my own furnace." Dandy's eyes had lost their dull look. Now they were quivering and moist looking, and the muscles in his face were doing a jerky rhumba under his dark-brown skin. His voice had become dry and cracked, and his hands quivered as they rested on top of the crisp, white hospital sheet.

"I just wish that was all of it," Farrell said.

"What all do you mean?" Dandy asked. He crushed his cigarette butt in an ashtray on his nightstand, and fumbled with the pack for another. Once he had the fresh cigarette between his dry lips, Farrell flicked his lighter into life and held the flame. Dandy's eyes looked up at Farrell's empty eyes, then he pushed the end of his cigarette into the flame.

"I guess what we're wondering is if you'd talked marriage to her," Casey said from the other side of the bed.

Dandy tried to clear his throat, but seemed unable to do so. His eyes jumped all over the room, and he brushed at his thick, black hair with the fingers of his left hand. "I loved her. I asked her to marry me plenty of times, but she always held back. Because of you. It didn't seem to matter to her that you were nothing but a jailbird. I could've given her anything, anything she wanted."

Casey heard the bitterness in his voice. "But she didn't want anything of yours. She wanted Daggett. Isn't that right?"

Dandy's face looked drawn, as if the pain were coming back. The three men watched him dispassionately, saying nothing. Finally, Dandy turned his eyes from them, and crushed his half-smoked cigarette in the tin ashtray.

Daggett reached for the package and picked it up, then held it up so Dandy could see it. It had a design of a pair of wings on it. "Lottie was trying to help Billie Talmadge get clean, Dandy. But Billie saw a photo of you and Lottie in Lottie's office one day, got scared, and ran out. Lottie found her again, and eventually got Billie to tell her that she'd seen you kill Junior Obregon."

Dandy's face collapsed, and his hands clenched into fists. "I loved her," he said. "I wanted to make it up to her, but . . ."

"But she knew you were a murderer and that you'd framed your best friend into prison. She promised to turn you in unless you went down voluntarily, isn't that right?" Casey said.

"The way Walt told it," Daggett said, "you must have gone crazy and choked Lottie when she threatened to turn you into the police. You called Walt, and he sent Sleepy over in a green La Salle to help you get rid of the body. The two of you took it down to the river, stripped the corpse, and just before you threw it into the river, Sleepy shot the corpse behind the ear with a .32 automatic, to make it look like a gangland hit, just in case the body got found. Except it wasn't supposed to be found. It was just an accident that the body got caught in an eddy, and pushed back to the shore. We found the gun that fired the bullet in Sleepy's boardinghouse, with his fingerprints all over it."

"No, no," Dandy said, waving his hand feebly. "It's a lie, it's all a lie Walt told, tryin' to shift the blame on to me. I loved her—I'd never do nothing to hurt her."

Casey shook his head. "It won't wash, Dandy. We found something near the body that ties you to it."

Walt looked up. "What are you talkin' about?"

Daggett held up the package of cigarettes with the gold wings again. "One of the two people who drove down in the La Salle left the butt from a Wings cigarette near the body. It was wet and shredded at the end by somebody who lips them; somebody who doesn't smoke much and never really got the hang of it." He pointed at the damp, mashed butts in Dandy's ashtray.

"I already had my suspicions before I got to 'Tee Ruth's house yesterday," Casey said. "By then, I had all of the financial ties between you and Walt. And then I saw the tray full of damp, mashed butts in her living room. Marcel Aristide told me later that you were the only one smoking there that day."

Dandy looked from one to the other of the three men, and dropped his head heavily on the pillow. His face crumpled, and hoarse, wracking sobs began to escape his mouth. The depth of pain and misery in them caused the other three men to grit their teeth and turn their faces away from him. After a while, Farrell and Casey left to make arrangements to have Dandy moved to the prison ward.

Daggett stood there for a while with his friend, patting Dandy's shoulder until he became too exhausted to cry anymore. When Daggett finally left, his friend was staring up at the ceiling, more like a dead man than one still among the living.

It was two weeks afterward, and the streets of the French Quarter were filled with the sounds of trumpets as ordinary citizens dressed as cowboys, can-can dancers, pirates, harlequins, and fairy princesses crowded the sidewalks. The weather had changed, as the weather in New Orleans is prone to do. Shifting winds from the South had pushed the wet cold of winter back into the North, and suddenly it was spring. The temperatures on Fat Tuesday were well into the seventies, and there was not an overcoat in sight.

Frank Casey sat on a chair in Wesley Farrell's living room with a rye highball in his hand and a look of contentment on his face. His son sat across from him in his vest and shirtsleeves, and his tie undone at the neck.

"It's good to have a day off," Casey commented.

"Yeah," Farrell said.

"I was able to get a hearing for Daggett in the circuit court, and the district attorney moved that his sentence be reversed, and that he be allowed to come back into the police force with his original rank. He'll get some money from the state to help make up for the time he spent in jail. I tried to get them to agree to give him back pay, but they're just self-righteous enough to figure they've done enough already, so I don't know."

Farrell seemed not to hear, then he said, "How's Dandy? Is he out of the hospital yet?"

"He'll never walk again, so I imagine he'll be in the prison ward for some time. He can only get around in a wheelchair, they tell me. And anyway, he won't run. There's nothing alive left inside of him that I can see." He paused and looked out the window. "Stella's being held on a half-million-dollar bond for about two dozen charges, but the killing of those colored officers is enough. Unless she's got a good lawyer, they'll execute her. They haven't executed many women in this state, but it's been done before. There's nothing to stop it from happening again." He paused and sipped his drink. "When the weather's this good, it makes you feel lucky to be alive," he said in a thoughtful voice.

"I'm sorry I caused you trouble again, Frank," Farrell said. "I should have let you handle it."

"Yep," Casey said. "You should have. But we got lucky again. You managed to knock around all the right people, and they ended up dead, or in jail where they belong. But I've got a few more gray hairs in my head, no thanks to you. When are you gonna stop leading with your chin?"

Farrell shook his head. "Maybe it's the only way I can go through life with a head made out of concrete. Anyway, I'm sorry. Damn sorry. I'll make it up to you somehow."

"Well, things fell about as right as they ever do," Casey replied, chuckling. "I can afford to be forgiving, I reckon."

Farrell got up and walked around, rattling the chips of ice in his drink around in his glass. His mood was dark, and Casey could tell that he was still upset. "How's Savanna doing?" he asked.

"She'll be okay, I guess," Farrell said in a carefully modulated voice. "Moyer gave her a pretty bad time, and she got a terrible scare before we got to her, but she's tough. She'll get past it by and by. I hope."

"You ought to be over there with her," Casey said, trying to match the noncommittal tone in his son's voice. "It's Fat Tuesday, time for a few laughs." He got up, stretched, and put his glass down on the table beside his chair. "Reckon I'll go out and mingle with the merry-makers before the Rex Parade starts. Wanna come along?"

Farrell finished his drink and set the glass down very precisely on a cork coaster sitting on the coffee table. "I'm not much for parades or crowds," he said. "Thanks anyway, Frank. And thanks for all you did. I know it cost you a few favors here and there."

"Favors are made to be traded upon," Casey said. "I'll get some more back later." He picked up his hat and shaped the crease with his fingers before putting it on. "Want to go over to Kolb's and get that sauerbraten we talked about a couple of weeks ago?"

Farrell looked up, nodding. "Sure. Seven o'clock Thursday all right?"

"Swell, I'll meet you there," Casey said. He shook hands with Farrell, and left the apartment.

Farrell paced the apartment after Casey left, feeling anything but in the mood for Mardi Gras. Once again Savanna had been hurt, and all he'd been able to do was sweep up the mess. She still wasn't quite the same, and he didn't know how to fix it.

He went into his office and opened one of the drawers in his desk. The drawer was lined with green felt, and there were retaining pegs set into the bottom that kept the old Colt automatic and the newer one he'd gotten from the merchant in Pilot Town from sliding around the drawer. He picked up the older one and hefted it, but the hard solidity of it failed to comfort him. He put it down, closed the drawer, and locked it. There were fights you couldn't win with guns or knives or fists, 'Tee Ruth had said. He hadn't really understood that until now.

Without really planning it, he found himself out in the street, impeccably dressed, as always, in a pale beige suit, brown oxford cloth shirt, and wine-colored silk tie. His Borsalino was set on his head at just the right angle as he walked through the throngs of costumed celebrants, separating them like the prow of a ship cutting through ocean.

On Rampart Street, he noticed two Negroes standing together across the street. Marguerite Sonnier looked up into Israel Daggett's face with a look of pure adoration. He held her hand, and looked down on her with much the same look on his face. It was plain that in spite of everything, they had forged something in the past few days that might carry them for the rest of their lives.

As he watched them, he was overcome with an envy such as he'd never known. For the first time in many years, he had an inkling of what it was costing him to continue his life as Wesley Farrell.

He found himself at the door to the Club Moulin Rouge, and could hear a drum solo coming from the open door. As he went inside, a man began to pluck a bass fiddle, and then a trumpeter and clarinetist joined in. He recognized the tune, but couldn't remember the name of it. He walked through the crowd without bothering about the music, and continued on until he found the hallway that led to the stairs.

At the top of the stairs, the door to Savanna's apartment was open a crack, as though she were willing to let only a little of the day into her life. He removed the Borsalino and tapped on the doorframe. When he got no response, he pushed the door wider, and stepped quietly into the room.

He found Savanna sitting half turned in an armchair, her forearms resting on the chair back as she stared out the window at the crowd on Rampart Street. She was dressed in a simple print dress with a Peter Pan collar and short sleeves. Her hair was pulled back into a ponytail, and she looked to him more like a thoughtful girl than the worldly woman he knew her to be.

"What are you doing?" he finally asked.

She didn't look up, but smiled slightly. "Making up stories about the people walking down there," she said. "I'm pretty good. Maybe I could be a writer."

He put his hat down on a table, and walked to where she sat. He put his hip on one of the chair arms, and placed a hand on her elbow. After a moment, she took the hand and cupped it around her face.

"I feel lousy," she said when they'd been silent for a while.

"I know," he replied. "Is there anything I can do?"

She pressed the hand against her face a bit more firmly, and said, "Uh-uh, I don't think so."

He didn't know what else to say, and fell into silence. They sat like that for some time before Savanna spoke again.

"I never thanked you for saving me," she said.

"I didn't do much," he answered. "Not nearly enough."

She closed her eyes tightly and pressed her lips together, and he could feel a mild tremor go through her body. A tear leaked from under one of her closed lids, and ran swiftly over the curve of her cheek.

"I should have been there," he said, knowing it was the wrong thing to say, but unable to think of anything else.

"It's not what you didn't do," she said. "Sleepy took something from me, and I didn't have any say in it. For years, I had my self-respect to carry me through almost anything, and in a few minutes he kicked a hole in that. And I—" She paused, swallowed twice, and wiped a hand across her eyes. "I couldn't stop him. *I* couldn't."

He disengaged her hand, got up from the chair arm, and scooped her up in his arms. He walked with her over to the sofa and sat down with her in his lap. Her arms went around his neck, pulling herself into him.

If this was all she wanted, if this was all he could give her now, he would let her take it until he figured out what to do or say. As they sat there, the sound of music and carnival drifted up through the open window, and the room got dim as the winter sun fell slowly toward the horizon.